THE LAST HERO

HILARY GREEN

Independent Publishing, Windy Knowe, Wood Lane,
Parkgate, Wirral, Cheshire CH64 6RA

ISBN No: 978-1-899715-02-2

Printed by Print Domain
107 High Street, Thurnscoe, Rotherham, S Yorks S63 0QZ

Many of the characters in this book actually existed, though little is known about their lives. They were not myths but human beings of flesh and blood, with human desires and fears. I have taken the liberty of trying to imagine what they were like and how they felt at the time of the events described in this story.

Cover design: Samantha Groom

This book is dedicated to my husband David, in gratitude for his unfailing help and patience.

THE HOUSE OF NELEUS

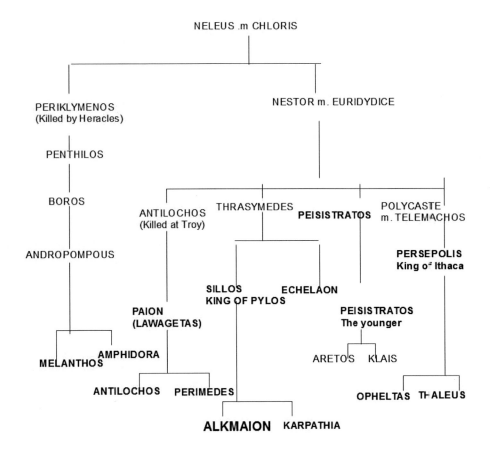

NAMES IN BOLD OCCUR IN THE STORY

Chapter 1.

My name is Alkmaion. My father was Sillos, King of Pylos, but it is my great-grandfather whose name will be known to you, if any fame can reach across the years. He was Nestor, the great charioteer, Nestor the wise, son of Neleus, who fought beside Agamemnon and Achilles before the walls of Troy and returned victorious to claim his throne – the throne which once, in the fullness of time, I expected to be inherit. That was until that fire-riven day when I saw the black ships of the Dorians run ashore on the sandy beaches below the city. Hear me, great Lady of the Mysteries, whose shrine I have established here on these strange shores! Inspire my memory and give me strength to tell my tale, before the black flood of the sons of Heracles extinguishes all those who delight in tales of great deeds long gone by. For now I prophesy that the soaring walls and frescoed terraces even of Mycenae, the golden city, will one day fall; and the spirit of dead Priam, lord of lofty Troy, will rejoice to see the broad streets of Agamemnon's city flooded with the wild-eyed wielders of iron swords; as the long haired Achaeans with their bronze once flooded the streets of Troy.

But now my mind goes back to a day in my fifteenth year, at the beginning of the month which is called Plowistos, 'the time for sailing again'. I remember this day because it seems to me now that it was then that I began to shed my sunlit boyhood and move towards the shadows ahead, although it seemed at the time that I moved only towards a more brilliant noon.

The sacred snake slithered from its hole beneath the altar and coiled itself around my sister's naked arm, winding upwards until it lay around her neck with its head against her bare breast. I shivered in spite of the warmth of the early rays of sun, which struck down to illuminate the altar in the centre of the palace courtyard. It was foolish, I knew. I should have had more reason to shiver if the snake had failed to appear, for that would portend the destruction of the House of Neleus and the throne to which I was heir. I drew myself up and squared my shoulders. It would not do to let my cousins see any sign of weakness. My father, Sillos, the King, offered wine and barley and the snake's tongue flickered as it sipped. I knew that the creature embodied the presence of the Great Goddess herself and watching him perform the ritual I was struck, not for the first time, by a sense of his apartness and the recollection that the King is the earthly consort of the Goddess.

The courtyard was crowded with the men of the royal family. The Neleids had bred prolifically, as became, I suppose, the descendants of the God Poseidon. Standing next to my father was my uncle Paion who bore the title of Lawagetas, commander of the army. Ranged behind him were more uncles and great-uncles, cousins and second cousins; all drawing their heritage from King Nestor and the heroes who had fought at Troy. It was a formidable inheritance to live up to and I was painfully aware that some of them thought themselves more suited to carrying it forward than I was.

Karpathia, my sister, gently detached the snake from round her neck and held it aloft for a moment so all could see it; then laid it down and watched as it slid back into its hole. It was the fifth time I had seen her perform the rite, and I still found it hard to believe that she was now High Priestess in the service of the Great Goddess. She was less than two years older than I and our childhood had been spent constantly in each other's company. Never having known a mother, it was to her that I turned when in need of comfort or reassurance. It was she who cleaned my grazes when I fell, wiped away my tears and defended me against the bullying of older boys. Then, just over a year ago, she had reached her eighteenth birthday and the time had come for her to take up the office, which was hers by right of birth. Two priestesses had taken her away to the sanctuary among the groves on the Holy Mountain, which it is death for any man to penetrate except during the great Festivals. There she had remained for a whole year and was now but newly returned to us. And returned how changed! So quiet, withdrawn into herself as into a citadel. Her eyes, which had once sparkled with mischief, now gazed through me with a power that chilled the blood. When I went gladly to embrace her on her return she checked me with such a look and gave me a cold cheek to kiss, and I noticed for the first time how full her breasts were above the tight laced bodice of her ceremonial gown.

The ceremony completed, the men began to disperse. My father

2

turned towards the porch in front of the Megaron, great hall of the palace; Uncle Paion and the others who made up the Royal Council went to join him. It was their custom to sit in judgement or discuss affairs of state there every morning. I turned towards the gateway that led out of the palace, intending to join the other young men in our daily routine of exercise, but at that moment my father called my name.

'Alkmaion! Come here.'

I went to him with a quiver of anxiety at the pit of my stomach. Where had I fallen short this time? What duty had I scanted or neglected? I could think of none but I had good reason to know that my uncle would be delighted to find something. But my father smiled as I approached and put his hand on my shoulder.

'Come with us. It is time you began to learn something of matters of state.'

My heart leaped and I smiled back at him. 'Thank you, sir. I shall be glad to learn whatever you can teach me.'

To my surprise, he led me, with the rest of the council following, into the megaron itself. It was always his custom to hold council in the open air, under the porch, where all could see, rather than in the lofty but dim confines of the hall. I saw the older men look at each other as I followed my father into the Hall but no one dared challenge my presence.

As we walked my father said, 'I had word today that Kerkios has returned from his first voyage of the season.'

'So soon?' I queried.

My father nodded. 'It is typical of him to be at sea before the rest have finished caulking their vessels for the season, but he has returned sooner than he planned. He sent me a message that he has information that the Council should hear urgently. I think you should hear it too.'

When we were all seated Kerkios was summoned. He was a small, dark man, swift and neat in his movements. I knew that of all his sea-captains there was no one my father trusted more, whether for a raid on an alien town or for a trading voyage.

My father spoke. 'Now Kerkios, you have news for us?'

Kerkios glanced around the assembled company and began his tale.

'My voyage, sirs, as you must know, took me northwards to those mountainous and thickly forested shores where the tribe of the Dorians lives. They are a rough and uncultivated people, living in crude huts without any of the refinements of civilised life, although they speak our language – or a version of it. They have few craftsmen and therefore make an excellent market for our goods. In exchange we bring back amber and tin, which they in turn obtain from tribes further north. I have been there many times and, in spite of their rough ways, I have always found them friendly enough but this time … this time there seemed to be a different spirit abroad amongst them.'

The captain hesitated and my uncle Paion growled, 'How d'you mean, different spirit?' He was not a subtle man and had no liking for abstractions.

Kerkios said, 'It is hard to explain, my lord, but for a start I was received with much less friendliness than hitherto. There was no trouble, but I had the impression I was being watched – as a man sizes up a possible enemy. And also, they showed much greater curiosity about our country. I was questioned closely about the wealth of our cities and the power of the King.'

'Surely it is natural for a backward people to be curious about such things,' my father commented.

Kerkios bowed his head in assent. 'True, my lord, but why have they never shown such interest before? And to add to this, for the first time in my experience, the Dorians are showing an interest in sea-faring. They are building ships – clumsy ones, I admit – and wanted my advice on many matters connected with their fitting out. And then …' He paused again.

'Well?' The Lawagetas fidgeted in his chair.

Kerkios fixed his eyes on my father. 'This is the strangest part, and the hardest to describe. I felt all the time that there was some secret that was being kept from me. I sensed an excitement, a kind of triumph, in the leaders of the tribe, but when I tried to discover its cause they grew silent and hostile. I noticed that there was a great deal of coming and going along a path that lead into the forest. One evening I decided to see where it went, but I had hardly set foot upon it when three or four warriors burst from the undergrowth and ordered me back in a way

4

that brooked no argument.'

'Perhaps you were about to intrude on some religious mystery,' suggested my father. 'We also have our Festivals at which we would not care for foreigners to be present.'

'True again, sir,' Kerkios conceded. 'But why this year? It has never happened before.'

My uncle snorted. 'Is this all your information amounts to? Dreams and imaginings! Take a little more water with your wine, Kerkios, and don't disturb us again with your wanderings. What is all this supposed to lead to anyway? You don't imagine these barbarians are proposing to attack us, do you?'

My father smiled and said soothingly, 'I hardly think Kerkios was suggesting that.'

'I should think not!' Reasonable words were not going to improve my uncle's temper that morning. 'Let one Dorian ship show itself on the horizon and we could be on them with a dozen war galleys before they got to land. And if they did get ashore, d'you imagine that barbarian rabble would stand up to a single chariot charge? The whole thing's nonsense!'

'I do not doubt our army's superiority, cousin,' my father said quietly. 'And I agree with you that we need not worry ourselves about an invasion. Nevertheless, we trade a good deal in that region so it behoves us to know what is going on. So I am grateful to Kerkios for what he has told us. Is that all, Kerkios?'

'Yes, my lord.' Kerkios hesitated and then added, 'Except for something which was said to me – a curious remark. It may mean nothing.'

'Let us hear it.'

'It was spoken by the brother of their King, one Cresphontes. He sent for me and questioned me closely about our country and how to reach it, saying he would greatly like to see such a fine, rich city. Then, when I rose to leave, he said, "Bear my greetings to your King – and tell him that the third seed has grown".'

'The third seed?' my father queried.

'Those were his words. I have no idea what he meant by them.'

'Nor I neither!' My uncle got to his feet. 'I told you, Kerkios, you've been drinking too much.'

'I think not,' my father said sharply. 'I know him better than that. But I am at a loss to interpret Cresphontes's words. Perhaps they will be clearer in time – or perhaps they mean nothing. Have you anything further to report?'

'Nothing unusual.' Kerkios offered my father a rolled skin, tied and sealed. 'Here is the record of goods traded and the materials purchased in return.'

My father took the roll and dismissed him and Paion, who looked as if he was bursting to relieve himself, begged leave to retire as well. The rest of the council dispersed soon after but as I moved to follow them the King said, 'Tell me, Alkmaion, what did you make of Kerkios' report?'

I would have said I thought it valuable, merely for the pleasure of contradicting my uncle: but it had genuinely piqued my curiosity.

'I found it very … interesting, sir.'

He nodded slowly. 'So did I. Kerkios is not a man to see imaginary dangers, whatever the Lawagetas may think.' He caught my eye and a quick masking of his gaze warned me, a second too late, that this was not to be taken as an invitation to join him in a joke against my uncle. 'We must give it some thought.'

He was silent for a moment. I waited. Presently he looked up and said absently, 'Go along now.'

I went out into the porch. In the courtyard the sunlight was blinding after the dimness of the megaron. From the paved court in front of the palace I looked out over the rooftops of the city towards the sea, blue and purple under the brilliant sky. Before me the land sloped away in fertile ridges and deep, shady valleys to the narrow coastal plain. At this season of the year it was still green and patched with bright blossom and the grass was thick with wild flowers. Beyond I could see the bay, almost encircled by a long promontory which ended in a rocky crag - Pakijanes, the Holy Mountain. Here was the most sacred site of all, the cave where the secret mysteries of the Goddess were performed. I had never yet set foot there but I knew that the time was close when I should be initiated. The prospect sent a chill tremor of fear through my flesh.

A voice hailed me and I turned to see three of my cousins approaching; Melanthos, the eldest and enviably risen above the mists of boyhood, and Antilochos and Perimedes, Paion's sons.

'We are going to look at the bull your father's herdsmen brought in yesterday,' Melanthos said. 'Come with us?'

There was no love lost between Antilochos and myself, but I got on well enough with the other two and I was at a loose end, so I nodded. 'Yes, if you like.'

The bull stood with his great head lowered, grazing. He seemed to have forgotten the long rope knotted around one hind leg tethering him to the oak tree. It gave him liberty to graze the rich pasture and probably, after the previous day, he was tired.

'The herdsman say he fought like one of the Titans,' Melanthos said.

'He gored one man,' said Antilochos, with his typical sardonic grin. 'The physicians say he will live – with luck.'

Perimedes said, 'I feel sorrier for the bull than the man. The man lost only blood. The bull has lost his pride.'

Melanthos laughed. 'If you were to go down there now you'd soon find out that he has plenty of spirit left.'

Perimedes shook his head. 'No thanks! That rope is quite long enough to allow him to charge someone.'

'You wouldn't have fancied being a bull-leaper then,' Melanthos said. 'How would you like to try the 'jump of death', like the pictures in the frescoes – where the man turns a hand-spring over the bull's horns?'

'Not me,' returned my youngest cousin. 'That may be the Cretans' idea of sport. I'll stick to running and wrestling.'

Antilochos murmured, 'It seems to me a truly princely sport.'

I looked at him out of the corner of my eye. I knew that tone of voice, that faint, sarcastic emphasis on the word 'princely'. He had never been able to forgive me for the fact that it was my father, and not his, who reigned in Messenia.

'Really?' I said casually. 'The princes of Crete soon tired of it – or found it too dangerous. After that they had slaves trained in the sport to do it for them, like Theseus in the stories.'

7

'Ah,' said Antilochos, 'perhaps that is why the Cretans are no longer the power they once were and Achaeans rule now in Knossos. When princes lose their courage, no people can stand against attack.'

'Meaning …?' I could feel my temper rising and I knew that, in spite of myself, I was being lured into one of the traps that my cousin was so adept at setting for me.

'Why not prove to us, Alkmaion, *son of the King,* that the princes of Pylos still preserve the courage of their ancestors?'

I felt my blood begin to quicken. 'Do you doubt it? Remember that you, too, are a prince of the House of Neleus.'

'Oh, I do not forget,' he replied. 'But not the son of the King. Though you might do well to remember that, had not my grandfather been killed at Troy, the throne would not have passed to your grandfather, Thrasymedes. We are the senior branch of the family.'

'Nevertheless,' I answered sharply, 'my father is considered by all men to be rightfully king. And, remember, Thrasymedes also fought at Troy.'

'Oh,' Antilochos laughed negligently, 'no-one doubts the courage of your *ancestors,* Alkmaion.'

'What do you want me to do?' I demanded, my muscles tightening.

He looked across towards the bull. 'Nothing a captive slave could not perform.'

Melanthos said quickly, 'Don't be a fool, Antilochos. A man has to be trained for months to perform that feat.'

Antilochos shrugged. 'Alkmaion is renowned for his prowess as an athlete, isn't he? I should have thought that, given a certain amount of courage ….'

'Why don't you try it yourself, then?' retorted Melanthos.

Antilochos plucked a grass stem to put between his teeth and replied casually, 'That would hardly prove anything for Alkmaion.'

I looked at the bull. He was bigger and more powerful than any in my father's herd. Beneath the sleek hide I could see the huge muscles moving and above the lowered head the great horns spread upwards in a deadly curve.

Perimedes said nervously, 'Anyway, it's impossible. He's tethered.'

8

Antilochos turned on his younger brother. 'You said yourself the rope was long enough to let him charge.' And then, looking at me, 'One would have to go near enough, that's all.'

In the silence that followed we heard the rumble of chariot wheels and the beat of hooves. The road ran behind us along the top of the slope and then curved down to circle the edge of the pasture before climbing the opposite hill towards the city. As soon as the chariot came in sight I recognised the occupant. It was one of my father's Companions, the Count Alectryon, son of Eteocles. He was at that time about twenty-two years old, in the prime of his strength and beauty, and one of the most admired and envied men at my father's court.

When he saw us he signalled his charioteer to stop and saluted us courteously. It was for me, as became my rank, to be the first to respond but somehow with Alectryon I always found it hard to strike the right note. In his presence I felt tongue-tied and awkward.

I answered, 'Good day to you, Count,' and knew at once, from some subtle change in his expression, that there had been a little too much of the prince in my tone. However, when the others had greeted him, he said smiling, 'I see you are inspecting the latest addition to the King's herds. You are wise to keep at a safe distance.'

Antilochos said, 'As a matter of fact we were just suggesting to Alkmaion that he might try the so-called 'jump of death'.'

Alectryon looked at me and laughed, shaking back the long ringlets of fire-coloured hair from the golden skin of his shoulders.

'I don't think the Prince is fool enough for that!'

He saluted us again and ordered his charioteer to drive on. Before the chariot had turned the corner to begin the descent I was scrambling down the slope towards the bull.

Behind me Perimedes cried, 'Alkmaion, you're mad! Come back!' and Melanthos invoked Poseidon, master of bulls. I reached the flat pasture and began to walk towards the bull. The ground between the blades of grass was already drying out, beginning to parch and crumble under the fierce sun. I could feel the hard earth under my sandals and the sun beating down on my bare shoulders. Out of the corner of my eye I saw Alectryon's chariot come out of the bend onto the level road beyond the pasture, but I could not take my attention from the bull long enough to look at him.

The bull had seen me now. He lifted his head and stared towards me, motionless. I calculated the distances with my eye. He was about half the length of his rope from the tree; I must be more than that distance from him. If he charged now the rope would pull him up short before he reached me. He stirred, shifting his feet and swaying his great head from side to side. My body felt heavy and limp, shaken by the pounding of my heart. My hard-trained muscles seemed to have no more strength in them than those of a child. I could see the bull's body beginning to bunch, contracting itself into a single hard mass of energy. In a minute he would charge. I realised that I was still beyond the stretch of his rope and heard in my head Antilochos's mocking laughter – 'Of course, he was careful not to go near enough for the bull to reach him!'

I forced myself into a run and felt that I moved like an exhausted man at the end of a long race. A sudden wave of despair swept over me. What was the use of a body trained and practised to be the ready instrument of my will, when the touch of fear could turn it into this useless, shambling thing?

As I began to run I was aware, dimly, of a rumbling that quivered through the ground beneath my feet. I thought the bull had begun his charge, but my eyes told me it was not so. I ran on, straight towards him. He snorted, pawed the ground, and then began to come forward. I could see the whole great weight of him gathering speed towards me and suddenly I felt my body lighten and my muscles regain their strength. At that instant Alectryon's chariot swept between me and the bull, the horses legs bunching under them as they were hauled to a momentary halt right before me. An iron hand grabbed me by the arm and dragged me into the chariot and we surged forward as the bull, fighting now to check his speed, thundered past behind us.

I had been flung into the chariot with such violence that we had covered almost half the distance back to the road before I recovered my balance and turned on Alectryon. He had left his charioteer behind and taken the reins himself and now his face was set as he guided the racing pair over the uneven ground; but as I looked at him he glanced over his shoulder, saw that the bull was still tethered and eased back his panting horses. Then he turned to look at me and suddenly burst into laughter. I stared at him, speechless with fury.

After a moment he controlled himself and said, 'Forgive me, Prince, but I really could not stand by and watch the King's son make an entirely unnecessary sacrifice of himself.'

'There was no question of sacrifice,' I snapped, ' and anyway it was none of your business!'

He gave me a quiet, inscrutable look and said in a different tone, 'Perhaps. However, I fear you will have to explain your actions to someone who can call them his business. It was unfortunate that your uncle happened to be passing.'

He pointed with his whip and I saw that there was now a second chariot on the road, followed by a small retinue of slaves. It was my uncle Paion. I raged dumbly at fate for adding this to crown my humiliation.

Alectryon drove the chariot back onto the road a few yards from my uncle's. I dismounted and walked over to him, trying to look unconcerned and conscious of the indifferent stares of the slaves. Alectryon, instead of remaining as tact might have suggested out of earshot in his chariot, followed me, in spite of the burning look I intended as a dismissal.

Uncle Paion leaned his heavy body on the rail of his chariot and greeted me with the voice of ironic respect that he reserved for those moments when he felt he had me at a disadvantage.

'Good day, Prince.'

I returned the greeting and stood silent.

'May I ask whether you were intending to perform some act of sacrifice – a blood offering for the good of the people, perhaps? If so, would it not have been more appropriate to do it at some sanctuary – or at least in the presence of a priest?'

I replied, 'If such a sacrifice was required of me, Uncle, I hope I would not hesitate to perform it, but I am unaware of any such need at the moment.'

'Then may I ask what you were intending?'

'A feat not scorned by the princes of Crete, nor even by the great Theseus. That which men call "the jump of death".'

'Jump of death indeed it would have been! May I remind you

that you are not the great Theseus, Prince? '

I bit my lips in silent fury and stared at the heavy gold necklace swinging from my uncle's neck.

'May I also remind you that you are the only son of the King, and as such you have a duty to your father, and to the rest of us, to stay alive?'

Alectryon said, 'Under your pardon, Prince Paion, I believe it was your son Antilochos who challenged the Prince to make the leap.'

I gave him a furious look. Now Antilochos could claim that I had betrayed him to save myself. However, I did have the passing comfort of seeing my uncle look momentarily disconcerted. He straightened up in the chariot and said, 'You will understand, of course, that your father must know of this. Meanwhile you obviously owe a great debt to Count Alectryon. I trust you will express your gratitude suitably.'

He gave the order to drive on and the chariot rattled away down the road, the slaves trotting stolidly in the dust raised by its wheels. I turned to Alectryon. He was looking at me and I read sympathy in his face. I drew myself up and said, with totally intentional haughtiness, 'Although I was not in need of your help, Count, it is true of course that I owe you a debt. If you will take the trouble to speak to my father's Chief Steward I will see to it that he has orders to reward you suitably.'

I saw from his face that the insult had struck home but instead of replying he gave me another long, quiet look. I would dearly have loved to end the interview by a suitably dignified departure, but since we had come on foot to see the bull the only way to do so would be to turn and begin the long, dusty walk back to the palace. So I stood my ground and returned his gaze unflinchingly.

After the space of a heartbeat or two he bowed his head and said, 'Very well, Prince. I will claim my reward as you suggest – though perhaps not from your father's steward. And now, if you will permit me …'

'You are excused, Count.'

He mounted his chariot and drove off. I watched the bright gleam of his hair until it was blotted out by the dust and then turned to see my cousins panting up to the roadway, having made a wide circuit from their position on the slope in order to avoid the bull. I turned my shoulder on them, and set off towards the town.

It was shortly before supper time that I received the summons to my father's presence. I had spent what remained of the day kicking my heels around the palace and exercising my ill-temper on the slaves. Then I had bathed and dressed with more than usual care, but there had been very little comfort in the hands of my old nurse, Mukala, as she massaged the perfumed oil into my body.

He was in his private apartments near the Great Hall - pleasant rooms opening off a porch that led to a small courtyard with a little stream of running water and green things growing. He sat in a tall-backed chair of ebony inlaid with plaques of carved ivory, his feet on a matching footstool and a small circular table bearing a golden goblet and wine jug at his elbow. I greeted him and stood waiting.

He said, 'I have been speaking to your uncle, Alkmaion.'

'Yes?' I answered.

His eyes brooded on me thoughtfully. He did not seem *very* angry, I thought.

'Will you tell me what, exactly, you were intending to do, before the Count Alectryon snatched you up in his chariot?'

'I was going to try the 'jump of death', sir.'

'You know why it is called 'the jump of death'?'

'Yes, sir.'

'Have you some wish to die?'

'No, sir.'

'Then why perform so hazardous a feat?'

I gazed at the painted octopus on the plaster floor between us.

'Because it seemed to me that the son of Sillos, with the blood of Nestor in his veins, should give some proof that the courage of his ancestors still lives in him.'

'I see.' I stole a glance at my father. It seemed to me that there was a hint of a smile above the mingled black and silver of his beard. 'Do you feel some reason to doubt that?'

'No man can be sure of himself, I think, until he has proved his

13

courage.'

'To himself — or to others?' I looked at him. How much had my uncle told him? I said slowly, 'A man should not need the opinion of others in order to know himself.'

'Exactly,' said my father. He allowed that to sink in for a moment and then continued, 'You are aware, as you should be, that the blood of Nestor runs in your veins. Tell me, when your great-grandfather fought at Troy, was it for deeds of rash daring that he earned his fame?'

'No, sir.'

'For what then?'

I consulted the octopus on the floor again.

'For his wisdom in council.'

'Precisely. Nevertheless, his courage was never doubted.'

'No, sir.'

'Tell me, Alkmaion, if a man was faced with an attack by several opponents, and if there was nothing to be gained by standing his ground, except perhaps a reputation for unprofitable courage: and if, on the other hand, he could quite easily retreat and later meet his opponents one by one on more favourable terms, what would you advise him to do?

I traced a tentacle of the octopus with my sandal.

'To retreat, sir.'

'Thereby setting wisdom above daring?'

'I suppose so.'

'And again, suppose we were facing an attack by a vastly superior army — let us suppose for a moment' - (I could see the smile quite distinctly for a second in his eyes) 'that such a thing is possible. If I were to propose to lead the first chariot charge, do you imagine my advisers would allow it?'

'No, sir.'

'Why?'

'Because an army cannot risk losing its King in the first charge. The effect would be too demoralising.'

'You would therefore advise me to put prudence before valour?'

I contemplated for an instant how neatly and unavoidably the snares were laid for me.

'Yes, sir.'

'Then perhaps I might suggest that the only son of a King must do the same.'

'Yes, sir.'

'In short, Alkmaion, a man may win renown by wisdom as well as courage, but either without the other may bring him into disgrace. And for the son of a king it is even more important that the two should go hand in hand. Do you understand me?'

'Yes, sir.'

We looked at each other for a moment and I reflected, not for the first time, that I understood very little of what passed behind those deep-set eyes, like as they were to my own. Then my father said, 'Your uncle Paion thinks I should have you whipped. Do you think that you would learn wisdom from that?'

From my childhood my uncle had undertaken to discipline me. I could see his face vividly in my mind as he drew the whip between his fingers. I had good cause to understand why he was known as having the strongest right arm in the whole army. But, to do him justice, I should add that he punished his own sons just as severely.

I answered, 'No, sir.'

'Why not?'

'Because I think I am too old to be whipped. Because …' I floundered for words,

'because I do not think it is possible to make someone learn by beating him … and because I think it is against your honour for the son of the King to be whipped.'

My father nodded. 'It is well spoken. And because of this – and also because your actions, though they showed rashness and some lack of thought for me, showed also some courage – I have told him that I will not have it so. Nevertheless, it is necessary that you should receive some punishment, if only to fix the lesson in your mind – and to pacify your uncle.' (Was there a faint hint of laughter in the dark eyes? If so, it was gone at once.) 'Therefore I forbid you tomorrow's hunting. You will remain behind in the palace.'

Chapter 2.

I stood on the gallery above the central courtyard, well back in the early morning shadows, and watched the bustle below me. The Royal Companions were assembling for the hunt. The sun flared back from the bronze points of long hunting spears and struck fire from the jewelled hilts of daggers. Bare arms and torsos gleamed bronze and gold, with the brighter flash of metal from bracelets and necklaces. The long hair of the young men and the beards of their elders shone silver or red or blue-black in the clear, bright air. There was talk and laughter and a sense of heady excitement. Beyond, through the open gateway, I could glimpse the painted chariots and the tossing manes of restless horses.

Alectryon had arrived and stood with a little group of friends at the far end of the courtyard. I could see him laughing but he seemed restless, like the horses. Antilochos and Perimedes came into the courtyard. Antilochos saw me and nudged his brother, laughing: but Perimedes shook his head and said something that made him shrug and turn away.

A stir below me told me that my father had come out into the porch. As he crossed the courtyard the crowd parted but as he neared the gateway I saw Alectryon step forward and drop to one knee before him. So this was what he had meant by claiming his reward, but not from the Chief Steward! I reflected bitterly that he could have chosen a less public moment.

I watched him looking up at my father, smiling, speaking persuasively. Then he rose, apparently satisfied, and with a gesture directed the King's attention towards me. I found myself the object of the concentrated stares of the entire company and stepped back quickly towards the door leading to the stairs. As I did so my father's voice rang across the courtyard.

'Alkmaion!' I turned back, unwillingly. 'Come here!'

Heavy-footed, I descended the stairs and made my way through the crowd to stand before my father. He seemed, as far as I could tell, to be amused about something.

'Alkmaion, it appears you have a good friend in Count

Alectryon. Yesterday he risked his horses and chariot, and possibly himself, to snatch you from danger. Now he claims his reward – which is no less than my indulgence to you, to allow you to hunt with us today.'

My gaze shot past my father to Alectryon's face. He lifted an eyebrow, quizzically.

My father went on, 'I can hardly refuse him in the circumstances, so I have agreed, on one condition - that he takes charge of you. He has therefore agreed to take you as his charioteer.' He paused and I stood staring at the ground to hide the fury in my eyes. He added, 'I hope you will know how to thank the Count for pleading on your behalf.' Then, raising his voice, 'Come, gentlemen, let us not waste any more of the morning.'

He moved away, the others closing in behind him. I followed Alectryon, wordlessly, biting on the bitter taste of my humiliation. His charioteer, a boy only a year or two older than myself, stood holding the fretting horses. Alectryon said briefly, 'The prince does me the honour of becoming my charioteer for today, Dexeus. I shall not require you. Be here again at sunset for my return.'

I saw Dexeus's face fall and realised that he, too, had been looking forward to the hunt, but he merely saluted me respectfully and stood aside. I mounted the chariot and took the reins and Alectryon got in beside me.

He said quietly, 'I agreed to let you become my charioteer, Prince, to meet your father's condition – and indeed I am well satisfied with the bargain. But if you prefer, I will take the reins and give you my spear.'

I answered bitterly, 'Indeed, no, Count. I owe you so much already, you must allow me to pay you the service my father has decreed.'

The procession of chariots had begun to move off. I gave the horses a quite unnecessary cut with the whip and they plunged forward into the crowd. Chariots on all sides were hastily reined in and I could see the angry words quickly checked as the drivers saw who the inept charioteer was. Fighting to control the animals I cursed the unlucky fate that seemed to have sealed that day. Although our violent start had almost jerked him off his feet Alectryon said nothing, but when he had regained his balance I could feel his eyes upon me and saw myself momentarily as he must see me, as a proud and petulant boy.

I had the horses under control by now but they still needed all my attention. After the rude start I had given them and feeling an unfamiliar hand upon the reins, they were disposed to show their mettle by overtaking every other chariot in the party. I was grateful to Alectryon, in spite of myself, for saying nothing until I had them quieted.

At length he said, 'I think you are angry with me.'

I had my tongue under better control now, as well as the horses, and answered, 'Why should I be angry?'

'I don't know,' he said. 'Tell me.'

I made no answer. Such a confusion of emotions boiled within me that I could not explain them to myself, let alone to him. And it was a turbulence that was only compounded by my acute physical sense of his presence close beside me. I was well accustomed to the attentions of the men about my father's court. It had been a fact of life since before my twelfth birthday. But from the beginning I had been aware that the flattery, the gifts, the meaningful glances had more to do with gaining the King's ear than with my personal charms. Besides, I had seen too many sudden love affairs flare up only to die down as quickly when the boy grew up, leaving one party or the other to nurse a broken heart. Alectryon had always treated me with perfect courtesy, but there had been times when I had caught his eyes and read in them an invitation to a more intimate relationship. It was an invitation I had studiously ignored. And yet, no one at court had the power to disturb me as he did.

At length he said, 'I am afraid perhaps you took my laughter yesterday for mockery. Believe me, it wasn't. It was laughter born of relief … and something else … excitement – admiration. What you did was foolish but nevertheless … magnificent.'

'My father didn't think so,' I remarked grimly.

'That is understandable. You are his only son and he fears to lose you.'

'He need not fear for heirs to the throne. The sons of Paion would gladly take my place.'

'The Lord Poseidon preserve us from that!' he commented

piously and I shot him a glance to see if he was mocking me again. It was hard to tell. He added, 'I promise you, if I had known before I turned the horses that the Lawagetas was on the road I would have driven you back to the palace by another route.'

This time I caught his eye and suddenly we both laughed. I said, 'You didn't know he was there?'

'Not until it was too late to go the other way!'

We drove in silence for a little. The horses had settled into a steady canter and I felt my hair streaming back in the cool wind of our speed.

Alectryon said, 'Why did you attempt that leap? Was it just because Antilochos taunted you?'

'Partly,' I answered, and then, softly so the words were almost lost in the noise of the wheels, 'and because I thought you didn't believe I would.'

Ahead of us my father's chariot halted at a fork in the road, while he consulted his huntsmen as to where the best hope of game lay. As the movement around us ceased a sudden quiet fell which hushed men's voices as well. The sun beat down hot on my shoulders now that we were still and I could smell dust and the sweat of the horses. I took a deep breath and turned to Alectryon,

'Count, I'm sorry. You probably saved my life and I've been behaving like a spoilt child.'

He smiled. 'It's over – and I have my reward. Let's forget it.'

The column of chariots moved on and I urged the horses forward. The day had suddenly regained its promise.

The road climbed along a deep valley, the sides of which rose steep and rocky on either side. The horses slowed and in the shadow it was suddenly chill. I looked about me and shivered a little. It was one of those wild and secret places that belong only to the Mistress. The rest of the party felt it too, for the talk and laughter died around us.

As we climbed the trees grew thicker and at length we came out of the narrow defile into a broader valley with a level, grassy bottom and thickly wooded flanks. Towards the head of it the huntsmen had pegged out their nets so that they cut off a wide half-circle of open grass, backed by the forest. The chariots arrayed themselves in an arc, my father in the centre and one of my uncles on each wing. I took up a position half way between them and we waited tensely for the huntsmen to drive whatever game lay hidden among the trees into our nets. There had been talk for months of a large boar in this section of the hills.

I ran the reins through my fingers, testing my grip, and wiped damp palms on the linen of my kilt. Alectryon shifted his feet, balancing himself for a sudden start, and took a firmer hold on the smooth ash shaft of his spear. There was a long silence. Then we began to hear the shouts of the beaters and the baying of the hounds. A crashing and scuffling came from the thick undergrowth. I poised myself. It would be some honour still to position the chariot swiftly and precisely for Alectryon to make a kill.

A few small animals hurled themselves across the open space and tangled themselves in the nets. We left them for the dogs or the huntsmen to finish off later. Then came a heavy crashing from amongst the trees and I felt my stomach contract. A heartbeat later a huge boar burst into the open. He charged the nets and broke through as though he scarcely felt them, heading straight for the line of chariots. My father's horses leapt forward but the boar veered away and came towards us. I gave a cry and whipped the horses forward, sending them full speed towards the beast. Then, when it seemed his tusks must rip their sweat-streaked chests, I swung them to the left so that the boar's speed carried him along the right side of the chariot. Alectryon needed no better opportunity and the bronze point of his spear went in deep in front of the animal's shoulder. Our combined speeds and the force of the heavy body snatched the spear from his hands, but when I wheeled the horses we saw that it had done its work and the boar had sunk to the ground a few yards in front of the remaining chariots.

I could not have wished for a greater triumph. Though most of the credit was due to Alectryon, since he had made the kill, he generously turned it all to me, saying with a laugh, 'How could anyone fail, when his charioteer gives him such a perfect opportunity?'

As the sun began to curve towards the sea we turned our horses heads towards the city. Tired now, they kept a steady pace, the yoke rocking smoothly up and down on their necks.

Alectryon said, 'Prince, are you at liberty tomorrow?'

I glanced at him, hesitating. 'So far as I know.'

'I ask because I know that you love horses and take an interest in their breeding. Last night I had a message from my brother Nequeus, who manages the estate. Do you recall that my father, before he died, brought from Thessaly a fine white stallion to improve his herd? He never saw the results, sadly, but yesterday they brought in the first yearlings to be broken. Nequeus tells me that some of them show great promise. I plan to go out to the farm tomorrow to see them. Would you do me the honour of accompanying me?'

He could have offered me no more tempting bait. Almost before I had time to think I heard myself saying, 'I should enjoy that very much. Thank you.'

He nodded, not attempting conceal his satisfaction. 'I shall wait on you in the morning, then.'

The chariot clattered onto the stones of the paved road that led through the town and up the hill to the palace. At the gates the slaves ran forward to unyoke our horses and manhandle the chariots into the sheds. I said goodbye to Alectryon, saluted my father and headed towards my own rooms in search of a much-needed bath.

There was great feasting in the Hall that night and when everyone had stuffed himself with as much roast boar as he could eat, and the bard Sirios's voice had begun to grow hoarse, the lyre was passed from hand to hand. It was no surprise when the first name to be called on was Alectryon's, for he was as well known for his skill as a musician as he was for his prowess as an athlete. What did surprise me was the sudden surge of pride I felt when he stepped forward and bowed to my father before taking the lyre.

I had only just risen the next morning when an attendant came to tell me that Alectryon was waiting for me in the courtyard. I dressed hastily and fidgeted under Mukala's hands until she said with a sniff, 'If he were the prince instead of you, you might have some reason to hasten and harass me so!'

After that I kept myself quiet and even decided I had time to eat the honey cakes she brought me, but when I came into the courtyard and saw him kicking his heels like a servant I was ashamed of myself and apologised for keeping him waiting. He replied courteously that it was of no importance but as we walked to his chariot he glanced sideways at me and said, 'I cannot help wondering what – or who – it is that keeps the Prince awake so late that he lies so long in the morning.'

I felt myself blush and could think of no quick reply. We mounted the chariot and Alectryon laughed as he took the reins.

'It seems I have spoken truer than I guessed. Will you tell me the girl's name?'

I managed to get out, 'You are mistaken, Count. There was no girl.'

'What? Such a blush, and no girl?'

'No! I swear it!'

There was a moment's silence and then he said in a different tone, 'Forgive me. I apologise for my curiosity.'

I burst out, 'There was no-one! Please believe me. I lay alone last night.'

He looked at me, his blue-green eyes, which were as changeable as the sea, glinting with amusement. 'So it was for your solitude that you blushed?'

'I had things on my mind last night – and no desire for company.' I spoke stiffly, but I was determined that he should not know that I had never yet had company in my bed.

'I see.' He gave me another sideways look and I found my irritation dissolving into laughter.

Alectryon's estate lay some half hour's drive from the palace. We were met by his younger brother, Nequeus, and after we had taken wine and water in the shady colonnade which surrounded the house he led us to the paddock where the young horses were corralled. There were six of them and Alectryon's report had been correct. They were superb.

'What do you think of them?' he asked.

'Magnificent!' I exclaimed. 'Especially that one. He's almost pure white – and what a head!'

Alectryon called to some of his men, 'Catch the grey colt and bring him here.'

The men expertly cornered the colt and slipped a rope around his neck. He reared up and then, feeling the rope tighten, stood still, rolling his eyes and snorting. Nequeus walked slowly up to him, speaking softly, and the colt lowered his head and flicked his ears towards him. Nequeus scratched him behind the ears and blew into his nostrils and after a moment the horse allowed himself to be led towards us.

'Nequeus must have some horse magic!' I exclaimed and Alectryon chuckled.

'It's true, I think Poseidon the horse tamer has given him some special powers.'

We approached carefully and the colt snorted and eyed us warily. Close to he was even more impressive than I had thought, with strong legs, a deep chest and a beautiful, intelligent head.

'He's going to be too big for chariot work,' I commented. 'He will be big enough to ride.'

'Give him a name,' Alectryon said unexpectedly.

I thought quickly. 'How about Pedasos, after Achilles' horse who was good enough to keep up with the immortal pair that drew his chariot?'

'Pedasos it shall be,' Alectryon agreed. He took the halter rope from Nequeus and put it into my hand. 'He's yours.'

I felt my jaw drop. A gift of any horse was a magnificent gesture, but such an animal as this … Beside me I could sense that Nequeus was as amazed as I was. Abruptly I realised that my response must be as magnanimous as the gift.

'It is a truly noble gift, Count, as befits the giver. It would be churlish of me to refuse.'

He smiled and nodded. 'Good. But may I make a suggestion? Leave the colt here until he is old enough to ride. When he is ready Nequeus will break him in for you. You have already seen his talent with horses.'

I turned to Nequeus. 'I think that is an excellent arrangement. I shall be grateful to you, Nequeus. But there is one condition. You must let me come and visit him often.'

Alectryon laughed and said easily, 'As often as you like. I shall keep him as a hostage to ensure your company.'

We set the colt free and Alectryon showed me the rest of the farm. We ate our midday meal on the shady terrace and when we had finished Nequeus pleaded pressure of work and excused himself. Alone with Alectryon I was suddenly uncomfortably aware of his eyes on me. I got up and moved to the edge of the terrace, where I could look out over the meadow where the colts were grazing.

'You shouldn't have given Pedasos to me. Nequeus wanted you to keep him for yourself.'

He rose and joined me. 'He'll get used to the idea. I wanted to find a special gift for you. It's almost your naming day, isn't it?'

I glanced at him in surprise. 'It must be. I'd forgotten. How did you know?'

He lifted his eyebrows. 'Oh, I knew. You will be sixteen, yes? It's an important time. Think of the horse as a birthday present.'

Again I felt the colour rising in my face. 'Thank you.'

He put up his hand and touched my cheek with his fingertips. Taken by surprise I instinctively flinched and turned my head away and felt, rather than saw, his hand drop to his side. Immediately I was suffused with embarrassment at my own ineptitude. He turned away and when he spoke again it was as lightly and casually as if nothing of importance had passed between us, but I knew intuitively that he would never reach out to me again unless I first signalled my acceptance. And that was something I could find no way of doing.

His behaviour as we drove back to the palace was unchanged but I was burdened with the sense of my ingratitude. The reason was not clear to me, but I felt that I had missed a chance that might not come again.

As soon as I reached my own rooms I sent Mukala for the chest that contained my jewellery and other treasures and tried her patience by refusing to get into my bath until I had selected a bronze dagger. It was an antique piece, of a craftsmanship unequalled before or since, the blade inlaid with running leopards in gold and niello and the pommel covered with gold leaf embossed with rosettes. It had belonged to my grandfather Thrasymedes, who had in return received it as a gift from the great Achilles when they fought together against Troy. It was one of my most treasured possessions and I hoped Alectryon would understand that it meant more than just a ritual exchange of gifts. I called an officer of the royal guard and sent him to deliver it.

Next morning after exercise I felt restless and uneasy. Alectryon was occupied elsewhere, and I did not feel confident enough to seek him out. To distract my thoughts I concentrated on the long beach that followed the curve of the bay. I could just make out the hulls of ships ready to be launched, and I felt a sudden stab of envy. How often had I dreamed of setting off on such a voyage? I turned away to meet Melanthos coming out of the palace.

'Where are you going?' he asked.

'Nowhere,' I replied, and then, 'Actually, I thought I might drive down to the beach to watch the ships being launched. Will you come?'

'Why not?' he agreed.

I called a slave to yoke up a pair of horses and we rattled off towards the sea. Melanthos was four or five years my senior but I had always preferred him to the rest of my cousins and I was glad of his company.

As we drove he said, 'I owe you an apology.'

'What for?'

'That business with the bull. I should have seen what Antilochos was up to and put a stop to it.'

I shrugged. 'It wasn't your responsibility. I shouldn't let him get under my skin, I suppose – but it's difficult sometimes.'

'I know,' he laughed briefly, and then added in a different tone, 'Don't under-estimate Antilochos. He could be very dangerous.'

'What do you mean, dangerous?'

'He is jealous of you, and he has a wicked tongue.'

'Because I am heir to the throne?'

'That – and because Alectryon prefers you to him.'

I felt myself blush and, to cover my embarrassment, I muttered, 'Sometimes I think he would be welcome to take my place. Being heir to the throne has its drawbacks, you know.'

'The gods forbid!' Melanthos exclaimed. 'He's bad enough now. I can't bear to think what he would be like in your position. But I understand what you mean. I'm thankful that the succession passed out of my branch of the family generations ago.'

I glanced at him. 'You would make a good ruler.'

He laughed. 'No thanks. No kingdoms for me!' But I had meant what I said.

We spent some time watching the sailors prepare their ships and as we drove home we both suddenly realised that it was past midday and we were hungry. I drew rein outside the door of a peasant's cottage and at my request the woman of the house brought us bread and goat's milk and a little cheese. She offered them with nervous respect but as we ate I was aware of her dark eyes, hooded like a bird's, watching us, and the expression in them disturbed me.

As we drove away Melanthos said, 'These people still hate us.'

'Why should they? The land is peaceful and taxes are not too heavy.'

'Because we are Achaeans and they are Leleges, who were here before we came.'

'But the Achaeans have been their lords for generations.'

'Nevertheless, to them we are still the conquerors.'

'I think you're exaggerating, Melanthos. The woman was probably angry because we were taking food from her family. When we get back to the palace I shall see she is sent some extra wheat, or perhaps a female kid. She will think less unkindly of us then.'

Melanthos looked at me and smiled. 'Well, do it if you like. You may win one family that way. But the gulf is too great to be bridged by gifts.'

I shook my head obstinately. 'I won't believe that.'

'Well,' he remarked quietly, 'perhaps that's for the best. After all, you have to be their king one day.'

Back at the palace I took leave of him and wandered away, seeking somewhere to be alone with my thoughts. At the side of a small stream that curled around the foot of the hill I came upon Sirios, sitting on a flat- topped rock with his lyre on the ground at his side. He would have risen to greet me but I waved him back and dropped onto the grass at his feet.

He said, 'If the Prince is seeking solitude I can take my lyre elsewhere.'

'On the contrary,' I returned, 'it is I who am intruding on you. I should be glad of your company – but perhaps you are composing a new song and I am interrupting.'

He smiled and sighed. 'I did sit down here with that intention – but I find the noise of the cicadas and the sound of running water make me drowsy.'

I stretched myself full length and closed my eyes. 'Yes, it is peaceful … hard not to fall asleep …' I yawned and let my mind drift. Hovering on the brink of a dream the words of Kerkios suddenly came back to me. I opened my eyes.

'Sirios, if you heard a Dorian say that the third seed was grown – what would you think?'

He turned his head quickly and fixed his eyes on me.

'I should think it was time to look to my defences. But where have you heard this?'

'What does it mean? Do you know?' I sat up and leaned towards him.

'Have you not heard the tale of Heracles?'

'Who has not? But which tale? There are so many I find it hard to believe that one man could have accomplished so much.'

'Nor did one man,' the bard replied. 'There have been many princes of that name, and who is to say of which of them the tales are told? But this is sure. The last prince of that name ruled Tyrins of the mighty walls when Nestor, your great-grandfather, was young. But when he died and his sons laid claim to the kingdom they were driven out.'

'Well?'

'Do you not know that the Dorians call themselves the sons of Heracles?'

'No. Why should they? Are they indeed his descendants?'

'Their princes claim it. Perhaps his sons went north and settled amongst the barbarians. If so, it is likely that they mingled their blood with that of the chieftains of the tribe.'

'But what has this to do with 'the third seed'?'

'When the sons of Heracles consulted the oracle at Delphi it was prophesied that they should return with victory 'at the third seed'. So, when the harvest came round for the third time, they made the attempt and were met by the armies of Atreus, High King of Mycenae, at the isthmus of Corinth. There Hyllus, their leader, challenged any champion in the opposing army to single combat. Echemus, King of Tegea, accepted and Hyllus was killed, so the Heraclids withdrew defeated.'

'Then the prophecy was false?'

'Perhaps. Or perhaps the third seed referred not to wheat or barley but to the seed of man.'

'The third generation? And that would be ...?'

'You are the third descendant of Nestor.'

We gazed at each other for a moment in silence. Then Sirios said, 'But tell me where you heard the phrase.'

I repeated Kerkios's story and added, 'But I cannot understand why Cresphontes should send such a message to my father. If the prophecy really refers to him and his brother it is surely to Tyrins that they must return – or perhaps to Mycenae, since Heracles also claimed the High Kingship. What has it to do with Pylos?'

'You are right,' returned Sirios, 'but there could be a reason. Neleus once did battle with the great Heracles and was defeated. Perhaps Cresphontes believes that this gives him some claim over Messenia, too.'

'But it's laughable!' I exclaimed. 'They are barbarians, who scarcely know how to construct a ship. How can they imagine they could match themselves against our army?'

Sirios lifted his shoulders. 'It seems far-fetched, I know. But then, they have never encountered our soldiers. Or perhaps it is only bravado. Who can say? I have told you the old stories, that is all.'

I rose abruptly, all thoughts of sleep forgotten. 'My father must hear this. Come with me, Sirios.'

I began to hasten up the hill and then realised that he had dropped behind. When I turned to wait he said, smiling, 'My dear Prince, I do not think that the danger is so imminent that an old man needs to strain his heart panting up hills.'

I took his lyre and gave him my shoulder to lean on and forced myself to match my pace to his until we reached my father's apartments. He was sitting in his private courtyard, studying some documents.

I said, 'Forgive me for intruding, father, but I must speak to you. It has to do with what Kerkios told us the other day.'

He gestured to both of us to be seated. 'Well?'

I turned to Sirios. 'Repeat what you have just told me.'

My father listened to the old man in silence and when he had finished said, 'You have done well, Alkmaion. I should have thought myself to consult Sirios. He knows more of what has passed in years gone by than any of us.'

I said, 'What do you think, sir? Is there any danger of an attack?'

He shook his head. 'I cannot believe so. The Dorians have little bronze and little skill in forging it. The gods have not seen fit to impart to them the sacred mysteries of the smith's art. I judge it this way. The old King, Aristomachos, is dead. His sons are young and hot headed. They are planning, perhaps, a few raids on neighbouring territories. But Cresphontes, having heard the prophecy, cannot resist hinting at it to Kerkios. It is bravado, merely. What do you think, Sirios?'

'Perhaps so, my King. As you say, they cannot hope to match us.'

'Nevertheless, it is well to be forewarned and I am grateful to you. I shall give it some thought. Meanwhile, let the knowledge remain between us three. You understand me?'

When Sirios had gone I said, 'Then you believe there is no danger, sir?'

He turned his brooding eyes upon me. 'I believe it is best that we should appear to think so.'

'Then you believe there is?'

'Cresphontes is a man of ambition. Perhaps he plans a little piracy, an attack on one of our merchant ships – maybe even a raid on one of our villages. If he really thinks he can do more then he is a fool. Your uncle was right this morning when he said the Dorians would not withstand a single chariot charge. But we shall do well to be on our guard. I shall send another ship north to see if we can pick up any further information.'

As I left my father's apartments I saw Karpathia crossing the courtyard. Normally she was attended by two hand maidens but for once she was alone and on an impulse I called out to her. She stopped and turned and for a moment her face lit up as it used to when we found ourselves together. The next instant, the smile was gone, leaving the cold mask I had come to expect.

I put my hand out to her. 'Karpathia, why do you have to be so distant? We never talk now. We used to be such good friends.'

She looked at me and for a moment I thought I saw the glint of tears in her eyes. 'Dear brother! I wish we could be as we once were. I miss it, too. But you have to understand, things are different now. I am different. Now that I am dedicated to the Great Goddess I have to put aside all other loves, all other friends.'

'Isn't it lonely?' I asked.

Her lips quivered and then she pressed them hard together. 'No. I have companions. The other priestesses ...' her voice tailed away.

'But that isn't the same,' I protested. 'They don't love you like I do. You can't laugh and joke with them, can you? And what about the future? Don't you want a husband, children?'

She shook her head suddenly, almost angrily. 'Alkmaion, you don't understand. You can't ... yet. But you will soon. Once the Goddess has taken you to herself, you don't need mortal friends. We can't go back to how things were – even if we wanted to. I have always known that this was my destiny. It is the greatest honour a woman can have. Beside that, nothing else matters.'

She turned quickly and walked away, but not before I had seen a single tear escape and glisten on her cheek.

31

Chapter 3.

Before bedtime that evening I had something more immediate to occupy my thoughts. I had just finished my bath and was scarcely dressed when I was summoned to my father's presence. To my surprise I found my sister Karpathia and the Chief Priest already there. The Priest was a tall, thin-faced man with dark, hooded eyes whose gaze I found it hard to sustain. As a child I had been terrified of him. Now I knew him for a man second only in power to my father, the guardian of the mysteries of the Great Goddess. I saluted them and turned enquiringly to my father.

He said, 'Alkmaion, in a few days you will enter your seventeenth year. Also, it is not long now until the Great Spring Festival. I have been thinking that it is time for you to begin to play a full part in that Mystery, but before you can do so you must be initiated.'

The Chief Priest said, 'We have consulted the omens, Prince. The Goddess is willing to receive you.'

My throat had gone dry. I had never found anyone who would speak of what happened during those rites. I said huskily, 'When?'

It was Karpathia who spoke. 'Tomorrow. Your period of initiation will last twelve days and will end three days before the night of the full moon. That will be at the start of the New Year Festival. Come to the sanctuary at sunrise. You must be fasting, and alone.'

I slept little that night and rose while it was still dark. I had given orders for a chariot to be prepared for me and as I left the palace I could see it waiting. In the grey dawn light it took me a moment or two to recognise that the charioteer was Alectryon.

'You knew!' I said.

'I guessed,' he replied.

I hesitated. 'I am to go alone.'

'I know. But I will drive you to the foot of the Holy Mountain.'

I mounted the chariot in silence, unable to trust my voice. A cold fear clasped my belly and I could have wept with gratitude for his company.

He said softly, 'Don't be afraid. We have all been through it – and survived.'

I swallowed and forced myself to speak casually. 'Well, at least I shall know the answers to all the questions I've wanted to ask all these years.'

'No-one is permitted to know all the answers,' he replied soberly. 'There are some questions it is best not to ask.'

After that we drove in silence. I huddled into my cloak and watched the sky over the mountains flush pink and then become streaked with crimson and gold. We skirted the wide curve of the bay until we came to the cluster of buildings that housed the slaves who tended the sanctuary. At the bridge crossing the channel that divides the Holy Island from the mainland Alectryon drew rein and laid a hand briefly on my shoulder.

'Be of good courage. My thoughts go with you, even if I cannot. We shall meet again in twelve days.'

I muttered my thanks and set off along the broad ceremonial way that led towards the Sacred Cave and whatever awaited me there.

Of what happened during the days that followed it is forbidden to speak. Yet I am afraid that those who come after me may be unacquainted with the Sacred Mysteries and I wish them to understand why it was that the young man who presented himself for the final ceremonies in the grove of sacred oaks was not the same as he who climbed the path to the sanctuary in that chilly dawn.

Those who have watched and fasted for many days and nights will know something of what I experienced. Deep in the caves there is no dawn and no sunset, only the endless chanting of the priests and the inexorable chill that gnaws its way into the very bones. Initiates will remember the desperate struggle to remain awake and upright and the cruel pricks of the goads that brought us back to our senses each time sleep tried to claim us. Only they will know how it feels to be bound to the pillar that is the holiest dwelling place of the Mistress and scourged until your seed spews out upon the altar stone. Only they will remember the power of the smoke from the sacred fire, which robs a man of mastery over his thoughts and brings the terrible messengers of Her power. I fled Her as a stag, with Her hounds snapping at my heels. They ringed me with fire and my spirit soared up as a bird to float above the mountains and the sea, but She pursued me as an eagle and stooping bore me down, down into the depths of the ocean, choking and struggling for breath; until at last I was reborn on her altar, helpless and slippery as a new born infant.

They permitted me to sleep then and when I woke one of the Priestesses was kneeling by my bedside. Her name was Eritha and from my first arrival I had been aware of her. She was not beautiful as most people would use the term but there was something compelling about her face that constantly drew my eyes. She was very dark, with high cheekbones and huge, luminous eyes above a wide, curving mouth. The ritual garments of a priestess, a long flounced skirt and a small, tight-waisted bodice, left her full breasts bare and her thick, dark hair hung in heavy ringlets over her honey coloured shoulders. She touched my hand and held out a goblet.

'Drink. It is warm wine. It will soothe you.'

I sipped the hot, spicy potion and almost at once felt a delicious languor spreading through my body. Eritha reached out and caressed my face and hair. As I drew back from the touch she whispered, 'Be at ease, Prince of the Achaeans. I am here to bring you comfort.'

Her hand moved down over my chest and rested on my belly. Whether I willed it or not I could not have prevented my body's instinctive response. She lowered her head and I gasped as I felt her lips upon me. Desire surged through me in great waves but when I was almost at the peak of excitement she drew back. I reached for her, groaning with frustration, and she slipped off her garments and straddled my body. I took the heavy breasts in my hands and cried aloud as her soft flesh encompassed me.

I understand now that she was a courtesan, trained in the arts of the Great Goddess, but at the time she played upon my senses as a musician plays upon his instrument. She came to me several times after that and the lightest brush of her finger could raise me to new heights of ecstasy and yet, even at the time, I felt my craving for her as a kind of sickness.

Once I asked her for how many others she had performed similar services but she only smiled and stroked my thigh and murmured,

'Not all who come here are Princes of the Blood. Besides, you chose me with your eyes the day you arrived.'

I returned home on the evening before the beginning of the Festival. Since my childhood I had been accustomed to the processions and offerings that accompanied the season but I had never understood their meaning. Why, for example, was it called the festival of the New King? Why did my father disappear for three days, during which time the Household went into mourning? Once I had asked Mukala to explain it to me but she had so terrified me with her warnings against inquiring into the Mysteries that I had never dared ask again. Now all would be revealed to me, but I felt only a heavy dread mingled with a sickening excitement.

The following day the mysteries began.

In preparation the casks of new wine had been brought out of the palace storerooms. As the sun neared its zenith the people began to gather on the hilltop and the casks were broached. Glad to dull my senses, I drank greedily until, with whoops and yells, the whole assembly moved off towards the Holy Mountain. I may not speak of what followed, and even if it were permitted I should find it hard to do so, for after the first few cups of wine my brain was clouded. I recall the frenzy that gripped us all and the ecstatic rhythms of the dance. At one point my hands and lips were red, not with wine, but with the warm blood of some still-quivering animal. And then, as the moon rose, Eritha's arms drew me down into oblivion.

I woke in the chill of early dawn. My body felt sore and stiff, my head pounded and my stomach crawled. Eritha lay beside me, her lips parted and still smeared with blood. About me I could dimly make out other bodies, sprawled together like corpses on a battlefield. The air of the cave was stale and foetid.

I dragged myself painfully to my feet and staggered towards the pale light at the entrance. The air struck cold on my body. I flung myself down across a rock and was miserably sick. Then, like a wounded animal, I crept from bush to bush until I felt I had reached a place where no one was likely to stumble across me. There I dropped to the grass, trembling as if in the grip of fever. A twig cracked behind me and I started up, as a hunted stag that has taken refuge in a thicket gathers itself at the approach of hounds for a last, desperate flight. But it was Alectryon who had followed me. We looked at each other in silence for a moment and then I let my head drop back onto my arms. He sat down beside and laid a hand briefly on my tangled hair.

After a moment he said, 'You are shivering and the ground here is still wet with dew. On the other flank of the mountain the sun will be shining. Let us go and find a warmer place to sit.'

I forced myself to sit up, though my head swam. He helped me to my feet and wrapped his cloak about me, then led the way along a faint path that led around the shoulder of the hill. As he had predicted the sun here was already warm. We found a flat-topped rock from which the morning damp had dried and sat down. I hugged the cloak about me and felt the fits of convulsive shivering become less frequent.

At length Alectryon said, 'I wish I could have warned you, but it is forbidden.'

I nodded, averting my face. After a moment I said, 'Why must it be like this? I thought I understood, during the initiation, but now ...'

He replied gravely, 'The Goddess must be served.'

'But why like this?'

'Because She is the Mistress of Birth and Death, the fount of regeneration for man and beast and the fruitful earth. If we wish to partake of her bounty we must accomplish her rites.'

'And so the King must seem to die every year, and on the third day be re-born.'

'Even so. He dies, as the fruits of the earth die, and is conceived as a child in the womb or a seed in the earth, and is re-born; and the Goddess is at once his Mother and his Wife.'

'But sometimes we worship Her as the Virgin Queen,' I said.

'She is all three – virgin, wife and mother, changing as the moon changes.'

I shivered. 'Is it true that at one time the old king was really torn to pieces by his followers and eaten, and a new king took his place?'

He looked out gravely across the shadowy bay. 'I believe it must have been so, once – perhaps among the Old People, before we Achaeans came here.'

'And the Sacred Marriage,' I persisted. 'That was spoken of –

but what happens?'

He hesitated, then said, 'At one time the King himself performed the rite. Then it must have come about that the king grew too old or too infirm and so a younger man was permitted to take his place. No one knows who he is or how he is chosen, except the Priestesses.'

I stared at him. 'But how can a mere human mate with the Goddess?'

He turned away abruptly, 'It is best not to speak of these things. Ask me no more.'

I was silent for a while and then I said, 'I do not understand it, Alectryon. Amongst us the man is master, and the Kings of Pylos draw their descent from the god Poseidon. And yet the King must submit to the Goddess even unto death!'

He said sharply, 'Alkmaion, be careful what you say! This land has always belonged to Her. The king rules only as Her earthly husband. It is a fearful thing to rebel against Her, here on Her Holy Mountain and on this day of all days. If you are wise you will make Her some special sacrifice, to appease Her wrath.'

As I gazed at him, trembling, a sound behind us at the entrance of the cave ripped the still air. It was the cry of a woman in desperate sorrow. At once it was taken up by other voices until the valleys about us re-echoed with the sound of mourning. I leapt up, wild with terror, but Alectryon gripped my arm and brought me to myself.

'It is the Lamentation for the Dead King. Come, we must join them.'

And so, with weeping and cries of desolation, the procession returned from the mountain to the city and everywhere we passed the lament was taken up.

And now I must speak of forbidden things. The next night was the night of the full moon. At sunset another procession formed outside the palace gates and made its way once again to the mouth of the Sacred Cave. Here the priests brought forth to us, from the deepest recesses where only those in Her service are permitted to penetrate, my father, newborn of the Goddess. With him at its head the procession moved on towards the top of the mountain, where the sacred pillar carved with the symbol of the double axe declared Her presence. I was about to follow when a hand touched my arm and I turned to find Eritha at my side. She laid her finger to her lips and pulled me towards the entrance to the cave. When I protested she moved close to me, rubbing herself against me until my desire became unconquerable. Breathlessly, I followed her into the darkness as behind us on the mountain top a faint, mysterious hymn began.

Inside the cave I reached for Eritha but she laid her fingers on my mouth and breathed, 'Not now. Not here. Come — you are the Chosen One.'

Then I realised that the other priestesses were waiting in the shadows. As if in a dream I allowed myself to be led deeper into the dark recesses where, in the flickering torch light, huge shapes loomed above me. I held back,

'No. It is forbidden! I am not consecrated...'

But Eritha repeated, 'You are the Chosen One. The Goddess awaits Her bridegroom.'

They brought me to the beginning of a narrow stair cut steeply into the rock and Eritha thrust me forward.

'Go, blessed among men!'

As I began to climb I could hear the hymn echoing louder above me. Suddenly I was in the open air and I could see the moon through a screen of leafy branches. Before me I could make out a couch spread with silken draperies and on it the body of a woman. I could see her slender, naked limbs and her full breasts but her face was covered by a golden mask. The hymn swelled to a climax and my mind reeled with terror and desire. I loosed my belt and let my garment fall and a hand reached out, warm and faintly trembling, and drew me forward. I stretched myself upon her, feeling the cool, firm flesh, the soft roundness of her breasts, the legs parting to receive me. Then the woman in my arms gave a low cry and the blood seemed to stand still in my veins. I jerked my head back and stared down at her. Familiar eyes looked back at me through the slits in the mask, wide with horror. All desire drained from my body as I recognised my sister, Karpathia.

I flung myself back and in that instant the hymn came to an end with a triumphal shout and the light of a hundred torches blazed into life around the sanctuary. Blindly I sprang back to the narrow staircase and hurled myself down it. Hands caught at me as I fled, women's hands. I broke free and reached the cave, stumbling and battering against the rocky walls. Behind me I could hear them, the Priestesses, wild with fury at the insult to their Mistress. They were upon me, panting and breathing curses, their hands tearing at my body. Again I flung them off and ran on, sobbing with terror.

They were close behind me as I burst into the moonlight but here, on the open hillside, I could outstrip them. It was a long time, however, before their cries faded behind me and I dared to sink down against the bole of an oak tree. Even then I paused only long enough for my agonized breathing to slow a little. Then, as a wounded animal makes for its lair, I stumbled back towards the city.

It was only when the outline of the sentry on the palace roof showed clear against the sky that I realised I could not go home. For the first time the true horror of what I had done broke upon me. I had, all unwittingly, profaned and disrupted the most sacred rite of the Goddess. The Holy Marriage remained unconsummated. I wondered why it was that the whole gathering was not combing the hillsides for the offender. What my punishment would be I could not guess, any more than I could comprehend why I had been chosen as the Bridegroom. I only knew that whatever ill might now befall my people must be laid upon my head.

I was shivering now, and my wounds throbbed in the cold air. I turned away from the palace and slunk like a wolf towards the town. Only the animal instinct to find refuge kept my limbs from folding under me. I remembered that Alectryon had a house on the edge of the city. Some remnant of honour warned me that I did him an ill service to involve him in my downfall, but my need was imperative. The main entrance was locked and barred, the servants asleep and everyone else away on the Holy Mountain. I circled round to the olive groves behind the house and scaled the low garden wall. Like most houses, all the windows at ground floor level looked into the central courtyard but above my head there was one balcony, built to catch the breeze from the hills, and near it a pleached fig tree grew against the wall. With my last strength I scrambled up the branches and fell into the room.

The light of the moon showed me a large chamber and, on the opposite wall, a bed spread with richly woven covers. As I had guessed, this was Alectryon's bedroom. I dragged myself across the floor and crept under the blanket. At once my nose was filled with the faint, unmistakable perfume of the oil that he habitually used after the bath. A wave of yearning swept me and helpless tears soaked his pillow. Then unconsciousness claimed me.

A very short time later, it seemed, I was woken by the light of a lamp being shone on my face. I started up with a cry but Alectryon's hand went firmly across my mouth to silence me. He put down the lamp and laid me back on the pillow.

'Thanks be to the lord Poseidon. I prayed you would have the sense to come here, but I was afraid they would catch you in the cave.'

I seized his arm and clung to it.

'What is happening?'

'Nothing. You are safe for the moment.'

'But the others … my father …?'

'He is still at the banquet. I slipped away as soon as I could without being noticed.'

I gazed up at him dazedly. 'The banquet? But… how can they hold the banquet? The … the holy rite … was never performed.

He laid a hand on my shoulder and said, 'Hush. Only a few know that… your father and the priests who stood near him. When the torches were lit your father had the presence of mind to raise the cry of rejoicing. Karpathia said nothing and if the rest thought it strange that the Bridegroom should have disappeared so quickly, they did not doubt that the marriage had been consummated. I should have guessed nothing, except that I saw who it was that fled.'

'But don't people think it strange that I am not at the feast?' I asked.

'Your father told everyone that the oracle had bidden you to spend the night in prayer and fasting. He made it seem a special sign of favour from the Goddess.'

Relief drained the last resistance out of me and my tears flowed again. Alectryon stroked the hair back from my face and spoke soothingly, like a nurse to a frightened child. Then he fetched water and

40

carefully washed my wounds. Finally he covered me warmly and said, 'Try to sleep. You are quite safe and there is no more to be done until morning.'

I reached for his hand and gripped it.

'How could I have done it, Alectryon? No-one told me that my sister has to represent the Goddess.'

He sighed and said quietly, 'I do not understand how you came to be chosen. There is something amiss here. But we will speak of it in the morning. Try to sleep now.'

I closed my eyes and drifted into an uneasy doze that deepened slowly into a profound sleep. He told me later it was almost dawn before I loosed my hold on him.

Chapter 4.

The sun was high when I woke and I was alone. Every movement seemed to set up a jab of pain somewhere in my body. I lay still, trying to order my thoughts: but my only consciousness seemed to be in my senses, where two memories burned like a brand – Karpathia's body in my arms, and the hands tearing my flesh.

A step outside the door brought me to my elbow ready for flight, but it was Alectryon who entered. He came swiftly to the bed and sat down beside me. 'Good morning, prince. I am sorry you woke alone, but I had to see your father to tell him you were safe.'

'What did he say?'

'He is thankful for your safety but profoundly disturbed by what has happened. He thinks it best you should remain hidden today. Meanwhile, he will consult with the Chief Priest and your sister as to how the Goddess may be placated. Also, he bade me ask you how you came to be the Chosen One. Was it by some Divine prompting, or was some more earthly agency responsible?'

I looked away, not knowing how to speak of what had happened. Seeing my distress he added, 'First you must eat something. Then we will talk.''

He went to the door and I heard him speak to someone outside. When he returned I said, 'Your servants know that I am here?'

'No, only Dexeus, and he is completely faithful.'

Dexeus came in, carrying a tray, which he put down on a low table by the bed. Then he knelt and kissed my hand, saying, 'I beg the Prince to believe that he may depend on me entirely.'

Alectryon smiled at him. 'It is well said, Dexeus, and the Prince will remember it. Go now, and make sure no-one else comes in here.'

The tray held a cup of goat's milk, bread and figs and a small cup of wine. The thought of food repelled me but Alectryon made me taste it and when I did so I realised I had not eaten properly for three days. I managed to swallow a good deal more than I had thought possible to begin with.

When I had eaten he said, 'Now, I must ask you again how it was that you were led to that couch last night.'

I caught his eye and saw that he guessed, at least in part, what had happened. This made it easier to speak and I told him the whole story. He listened in silence and then said with a sigh, 'It is very strange and I am at a loss to understand it. The woman must have known what might occur if you recognised your sister. How could she have dared to risk profaning the sacred rite – unless it was by express order of the Goddess?' I shook my head miserably and he went on, 'It is useless to trouble our brains. These questions are not for us to answer. If it was the will of the Lady we must seek to know how we may avert Her anger. If not, the punishment will surely fall upon the handmaiden who betrayed Her rites. Either way, we must wait to hear what your father decides when he knows your story. For today, you must rest.'

So I spent the day lying on his bed, sometimes sleeping, sometimes gazing blankly at the ceiling while the shadows of the fig tree outside the window moved across it as the hours dragged past. Alectryon came and went, spending as much time with me as his duties would permit. Then, towards evening, he returned after a longer absence.

'I have been with your father. The Chief Priest has consulted the Goddess by all the rites of divination. You must present yourself before Her at dawn tomorrow.'

'To what end?' I could feel myself beginning to tremble.

'I do not know. I am bidden to take you, at first light, to the Holy Mountain. Then you must go alone to the Sacred Cave. Your father will be there to meet you and the Goddess will make known Her will concerning you.'

I gazed past him, my mind full of a blank, cold terror, and whispered, 'I fear Her curse is already upon me.'

He gripped my shoulder and said, 'No, Alkmaion! Your intentions were innocent. You must not give way to despair.'

I looked at him. 'I spoke against Her the other morning on the Mountain. You warned me, remember? But I forgot to send the sacrifice.'

His eyes held mine for a long moment. Then he said gently, 'Nevertheless, Her anger may yet be appeased. Take courage. Let us eat and then sleep, and forget tomorrow until it comes.'

He called Dexeus and ordered food to be brought for both of

us, then instructed him to take his lyre and play while we ate.

After the meal I stirred myself from my despair enough to say, 'I have already kept you from your bed for one night. It would be ungrateful of me to do so again.'

He gave me one of his long, quiet looks and then said, 'As to that, you are welcome to my bed. Besides, I cannot let you sleep elsewhere without the risk of the servants finding out that you are here. And for the same reason I cannot sleep elsewhere myself. I will have Dexeus make up a bed for me on the floor in here, if you will permit it.'

I blushed, for I knew what was in both our minds. 'Let me sleep on the floor.'

He smiled. 'It is generous of you, but I think my limbs are in better condition to sleep hard than yours tonight.'

Dexeus laid a fleece and some blankets on the floor beside me and then withdrew. In spite of a day of complete idleness I found myself already drowsy again. Half asleep, I watched Alectryon prepare for bed. At length he came and stood over me, the light from the lamp in his hand turning the ringlets on his shoulder to amber.

'Goodnight, prince, sleep well.'

I put out my hand to him. It occurred to me that there was one simple way to pay my debts. 'We could share the bed …'

He shook his head. 'Not tonight. Believe me, the offer is tempting – but I do not expect you to pay for your lodging.'

I began to protest, but he shook his head again and lay down on his makeshift couch.

Alectryon roused me while it was still dark. Outside, Dexeus had already unbarred the gate and yoked the horses to the chariot. I had trembled when Alectryon drove me to Pakijanes for my initiation, but my fear then was as nothing compared with the chill terror that now possessed me and no words of comfort from him could touch me. We parted almost without speaking, save that when I was a few paces from the chariot I turned back to him.

'Prince?'

'I am thinking that this may be the last time we see each other.'

I turned away before he could answer and went hastily across the bridge.

My father was waiting outside the Sacred Cave. I knelt before him in silence and he laid his hand upon my bowed head.

'This is a grave misfortune to have fallen upon our House, Alkmaion. We must try now to discover whether it has been brought upon us by human or Divine will. Come!'

He led me into the cave and the smell turned me sick with recollected panic. We penetrated deeper into its recesses than I had ever done before, until we reached a heavy screen of hides that hid the innermost chamber, the abode of the Goddess Herself. The walls here were smeared with red paint, the colour of blood in the torchlight. Before the screen sat Karpathia, statue-still in her ceremonial robes, and at her side stood the Chief Priest.

My father turned to me. 'Alkmaion, we have heard from Alectryon what passed between you and the woman Eritha. Let me hear it again from your own lips.'

My voice came faint and hoarse but I told the story, holding nothing back. When I had finished my father said, 'We have heard Alkmaion's story. Now let the woman speak.'

Karpathia appeared to rouse herself from some profound depths. 'Let her be brought before us.'

Her voice must have carried to those waiting in the shadowy recesses of the cave for a moment later Eritha was brought forward between two of her attendants. In the light of the torches her eyes gleamed like a wild thing's. Karpathia signed to the attendants and they left us.

My father said, 'You have heard what the prince has said. Do you deny any part of it?'

'Why should I?'

'Then tell us, was it at the order of the Goddess that you led him to the sacred couch, or was it for some reason of your own?'

'I serve the Goddess.'

'But did you do this on Her express command? Did She appear to you in a vision, or did some oracle bid you take the Prince for the Chosen One?'

'I am the handmaid of the Goddess. I serve Her with my whole

45

being. You Achaeans have never served Her with more than your lips. She was our Goddess, long before you came and pretended to worship Her, and put your ancestors in the place of Her earthly husband in order to take our land away from us.'

'But was it the Goddess Herself who chose the Prince?'

'I chose him, to try his faithfulness – and yours, daughter of the King. Had you been truly Her priestess the Chosen One would not have rejected you. Had he been utterly Hers he would have forgotten that you were his sister and remembered only that he was Her chosen Bridegroom. Now the Holy Marriage has not been consummated and the proof is clear that She has rejected the House of Neleus.'

Karpathia suddenly rose to her feet. 'It is you whom the Goddess rejects! I am still Her priestess and I speak with Her voice. You betrayed your trust and used the Chosen One for your spite. It is upon you that Her anger falls!'

My sister was not tall, yet now she seemed to tower over the other woman. Her body was like a flame in the shadowy cave. I saw Eritha's wild triumph waver.

Karpathia's voice went on, 'You thought to speak for the Goddess, but it was your own will that spoke. Now Her anger upon you is terrible and you cannot hide from it. Already you feel Her curse eating at your heart. Already Her power is drawing the life from you. She took you to Herself and you were born again in Her, but now She will cast you away and for you there will be no rebirth.'

As she spoke I saw Eritha begin to tremble so violently that the flounces on her dress shook like leaves in the wind. Then her legs folded under her and she sank to her knees. Karpathia ceased and we all stood silent, watching the crouching figure. A low, keening wail broke from her and her hands began to claw her hair. She lifted a distorted face and cried, 'She is our Queen and my people have always been her priestesses. You came and took our land and made us slaves, and I have been a servant in the sanctuary where I should have been supreme. It should have been to me that the Goddess spoke, and into my body that She entered. Now Her anger is upon me and my life is leaving me: but She will punish you also and he who rejected Her will never sit upon the throne of Pylos!'

Her voice rose to a scream on the last words and then broke into frenzied sobs, while her nails ripped at the pale skin of her breasts, leaving long red weals. My father called out and several attendants came running and dragged her to her feet. Her cries echoed about the cave and died away.

My father turned to the Chief Priest. 'So, it is clear that the woman devised this terrible affair out of her own madness. Can the Goddess's anger against us be placated?'

The priest looked slowly from one of us to the other. 'I cannot tell. No matter how, the Prince was the Chosen One, and his rejection was an insult to the Lady. Some atonement must be made.'

'And my daughter?'

Karpathia lifted her head and looked first at the priest and then at our father. 'When I spoke just now the power of the Goddess was upon me, but it was for the last time. One thing is clear. I can no longer be the instrument of the Goddess. This I understand. What Her will is concerning Alkmaion I do not know.'

My father turned to the priest again. 'How may we find out what the Mistress demands?'

'I have prepared all that is needful within, in the Holiest place. Let the Prince come before Her.'

'I must go into the very presence of the Goddess? It is death to do so!'

'Go you must, and abide Her will.'

I stared from Karpathia to my father. Her face was white as marble, and as dead. His was wrought with anguish. The priest drew aside the curtain and beckoned me. I went, with the blood singing in my ears, towards the darkness.

The heat on the mountainside was like a physical blow, yet it seemed powerless to touch the cold within me. I stood alone outside the Sacred Cave, with no sense of the world around me.

Then I looked down and saw Alectryon waiting a little below me. The slope between us was steep but I took it at a run and he had to catch hold of me to prevent me from falling.

He said, 'You are shivering again.'

47

I answered, 'It was cold in the cave.'

'But here it is warm. You can feel how hot the sun is and smell the thyme. The air is as sweet as honey.'

Slowly, with his words, the real world gathered again around me. I loosed my grip on him and he set me on my proper balance and looked into my face.

'You see. We meet again.'

'Yes.'

'May I know what is the Goddess's will?'

I stared back at him, so dazed that my mind could not frame an answer.

'Perhaps you have been forbidden to speak of it?'

'No ... no, it was not forbidden.'

'Then?'

'The Goddess has been merciful – beyond all that I could expect.'

I heard him release his breath in a low cry of relief. 'I was sure it would be so!' Then he added more gravely, 'But there is a penance?'

'Yes. I am to leave Her land and not return until I have achieved purification.'

'And where may that be obtained?'

'To the west there is an island whose people are closer to Her than any on this earth. It is to them that I must go.'

'Is it specified that you must go alone?'

'No.' I looked at him, still trying to gather my thoughts and understand what had happened to me.

'Then when do we leave?'

In my dazed state it was a moment before I took in the meaning of his words. Then I asked, 'You would undertake a hazardous voyage with one on whom the displeasure of the Goddess rests?'

'To the ends of the earth, if necessary. But I do not believe that She intends you harm. It is Her mercy that sends you to this place, where you may rid yourself of this accidental defilement.'

I nodded slowly, my eyes on his face. 'I believe it may be so. And if it is, surely I should rejoice, rather than despair?'

'So you should. So let us be grateful and look forward to the

48

adventure ahead of us.'

Suddenly I remembered how I had envied my ancestor Periklymenos who had sailed in the Argo with Jason. Was not the Goddess offering me an adventure that would give just as good an opportunity for glory? On the way to the sacred island and back again who could tell what might happen? I lifted my head and began to laugh, and the laughter became mingled with tears and only ended when Alectryon gripped me hard by the shoulders and sternly bade me stop. Then he made me sit down with him on the warm grass and tell him what had passed in the cave. I told him everything, up to the point where I entered the innermost sanctuary and there I stopped.

'Then?' he prompted me.

I shook my head. 'I cannot speak of that, save that it was there that I learned the will of the Goddess.'

'And your sister?'

'She will no longer be a priestess, but she has no other punishment.'

'And Eritha?'

'I do not know. Karpathia says she will die – that the Goddess will take her life without human intervention. Do you think it is possible?'

He nodded gravely. 'I have heard of it. Well, the punishment is deserved.'

I shuddered, remembering the passionate body I had held in my arms.

Alectryon said, 'Where are the King and your sister now?'

'Within, performing the last sacrifice. I may not take part until I am purified. They told me to wait for them.'

My father and Karpathia came out of the cave at that moment and we rose to greet them. My father's face was like that of one who has just recovered from a painful illness. He took me by the shoulders.

'The Goddess is merciful.'

'Yes, sir. I thank Her for it with all my heart.'

'Later we must make arrangements for your journey. Kerkios's ship is ready for another voyage. I shall entrust you to him.'

I lifted my head and looked him in the eyes. 'Sir, Sirios was making a new song the other day. It concerned your voyage to Asia when you were not much older than I am now. Did your father send you in the care of the captain? Or were you commander of the expedition?'

I saw that I had struck home. He answered slowly, 'It was my first command.'

I dropped to my knee. 'Then I beg you, father, have as much trust in me as your father had in you. I must go a long journey. Who knows if I shall return? Let me, at least, go as a Prince. Then, whatever the end of the voyage may be, I may have a chance to make you proud of me. I have caused you trouble and anxiety, I know. But the Goddess permits me to attempt to regain Her favour. Will not you do likewise?'

My father bent and raised me. 'This trouble was not of your making, Alkmaion, so I will grant your request. You have long been fretting for a chance to prove yourself, I know.'

I embraced him and then Alectryon came forward and knelt in his turn.

'My lord, once before I knelt to beg the Prince's company. Will you now grant me that favour again?'

'You would go with him?'

'I would, my lord, and he has given his assent.'

My father smiled for the first time that day as he raised Alectryon, saying, 'Count, I shall part with my son with far less anxiety, knowing that you are with him. Come now, both of you. Let us return to the palace. We must make plans for your journey.'

We turned to go down the hill, Alectryon and I laughing together with excitement and relief. Then we saw Karpathia, seated silent on a rock, her head hanging in utter dejection. My father went to her and drew her gently to her feet and we passed in silence from the Holy Mountain.

I see in memory a bright morning on the beach below Pylos. The sacrificial fires burnt clear and pale in the sunshine and the smell of the roasting flesh of the bull that my father had just sacrificed to Poseidon drifted to my nostrils and set a keen edge to my appetite. The Prince of Pylos was being despatched on his first voyage in truly royal style!

My father had given out, truly enough, that I was undertaking the journey at the express command of the Goddess, but he had let it be understood that this was a mark of Her special favour. After a few days of rest the shadows were beginning to fade from my mind and I was looking forward eagerly to the adventure ahead. At the water's edge our ship was ready, her black hull trim and shining with pitch, her crew waiting nearby. Only Kerkios knew the real reason for the expedition. He had served my father too well to be sent on a voyage under the command of one who, as well as being inexperienced, was also defiled in the sight of the gods, without fully understanding what was required of him. He had taken the news philosophically, commenting, 'Since the Lady wills it the Prince must go. I shall not fear to assist him in obeying Her commands.'

The voyage had been planned like an ordinary trading venture. We were to sail north along the coast and hope to make Ithaca by evening on the second day. Here we were sure of a welcome, since the Royal House was related to our own through the marriage of Odysseus's son Telemachos to Nestor's youngest daughter, Polycaste. From there we would continue north to Corcyra, whence we could cross the narrow strait and follow the opposite coast line southwards until we came to the great island of Sicania. From here, Kerkios told us, it was only a day's sail to the Holy Isles.

The sacrifice over and the ceremonial meal eaten there remained only the final libations. The wine cups were filled, libations poured on the altars, and my father offered a prayer to Poseidon to grant us a prosperous journey. Over the edge of the goblet my gaze met Alectryon's. His eyes were sparkling and I could see that he was as eager to be away as I was.

My father handed his cup to an attendant and turned to me.

'The time has come, Alkmaion. Your ship awaits you. Remember to greet Persepolis of Ithaca from me. And keep well to the fore-front of your mind all that I have said to you.'

All that he had said to me! There had, indeed, been a good deal, all of it wise and no doubt necessary advice to a rash young man eager for glory. Yet, even as I promised him that I would remember it all, my mind leapt ahead to a plan I knew full well he would have forbidden. He embraced me and kissed me on both cheeks and I returned the

51

salutation warmly. After all, it might be for the last time – but I could not bring myself to believe that.

'Farewell, my son. The Gods go with you and may the Lady of the Mysteries grant you a happy return.'

Suddenly I saw that there were tears in his eyes and instantly my youthful confidence humbled itself. I was his only son. All his hopes rested on me and I knew he would rather have me back alive, with no glorious deeds to boast of, than dead, no matter how honourably, in some unnecessary raid.

I kissed him again and then made the round of all my relatives. Uncle Paion touched my brow with formal, fleshy lips. Antilochos's cheek touched mine, hard and smooth as stone. He was consumed with jealousy, and I delighted in it. But Perimedes' eyes looked honestly into mine as he wished me good fortune and Melanthos hugged me hard and bade me hasten my return.

I looked round and saw that Alectryon was waiting for me under the stern of the ship. I joined him and we climbed the ladder to the after-deck. The ship was already half afloat, only her stern still on the beach. Most of the crew of thirty were already on the benches, the rest waiting to shove us off. There was a pause. I looked around and realised, with sudden exultation, that Kerkios was waiting for me to give the order to cast off. To savour the moment, and to cover my hesitation, I took a last look round, at the beach with the crowds of people, at the rooftops of the palace shining on the low hill beyond, at my father standing among his Companions a few yards away.

Then I turned and said, 'Cast off, Kerkios.'

Orders were issued, the hawsers thrown aboard, the crew who were still ashore put their shoulders to the hull and the ship slid gently into the water. On shore a hymn began to Poseidon. A last member of the crew hauled himself over the side and took his place and the oars began to strike. I raised my arm in salute and was suddenly glad of an excuse to keep my face turned away from those in the ship.

I stood in the stern and watched the shore recede until we cleared the straits guarded by the Holy Mountain and gained the open sea. Everyone else on board had the tact not to speak to me until I turned. Then I found that an awning had been rigged over part of the after-deck and Dexeus was spreading fleeces for us to lie on.

Alectryon smiled at me. 'Shall we sit down? We have a long day ahead of us.'

A long day it proved to be. After the excitement of our departure the long pull up the coast seemed flat and dull. The wind, as we had expected, was northwesterly so it was useless to put up the sail. I watched the steady, rhythmic swaying of the rowers' bodies and wondered how long I could have kept it up. The shore slid past almost imperceptibly. Up to Phea it was familiar. This was the most northerly town of the kingdom and I had made the journey before with my father. After that there was a little more to interest me, as unknown country came into view but it was much like Messenia and I was quickly bored again.

That night we camped at the mouth of the river Peneus and the next day we resumed our slow progress northwards until, in the late afternoon, the helmsman called to Kerkios and pointed ahead. The captain turned to me.

'We've sighted Ithaca, Prince.'

I jumped up and stared towards the horizon. I could just make out the dark outline of an island. Ithaca, the realm of Odysseus! A hundred stories crowded into my mind and, as if in response to my new mood, I felt a breath of wind stir my hair. In a few minutes, as the sun dipped to touch the horizon, the breeze from the mountains on the mainland was strong enough to make it worth stepping the tall fir mast and hoisting the big square sail. The men shipped their oars thankfully and we began to hear the water hissing under the keel. The difference in the sensation, after our laboured progress under oars, lifted all our spirits. I looked at Alectryon. His hair was blowing across his face and he laughed with pleasure through it and said, 'This is better!'

The island ahead drew closer with a speed that had seemed impossible an hour ago. We could see it now as a rocky, mountainous place.

Alectryon said, 'Odysseus must have been glad to see this sight!'

'Do you think that all the things that are supposed to have happened to him are true?'

He shrugged. 'Who can say? He certainly had some remarkable adventures. But no bard was ever satisfied with simple reality! No matter how exciting a story, they must still embroider it. You know that. But I've no doubt Odysseus had had enough excitement by the time he got home, without the bard's additions!' Then he added, 'I daresay you're regretting that we have no such tales to tell, but remember it took him ten long years to get home from Troy, and I've no desire to wait that long before I sample King Persepolis's hospitality. So kindly don't tempt some god who happens to be listening to grant your wishes!'

'Very well,' I agreed with a grin. 'I'll wait until tomorrow.'

We slid along the coast of the island until we came to the sandy haven with the town running down to the beach and the palace above it. It was not a big place and the palace was not much larger than the house of a nobleman in Pylos, but it had an air of prosperity and peace. The sail was lowered and the men took the oars and drove the ship through the quiet waters until she grounded, and then leapt overboard and dragged her up the beach.

Our approach had obviously been noted while we were still some way off and a small crowd had gathered. Among them was a young man who, by his dress and bearing, appeared to be in some authority. I threw my cloak across my shoulder and disembarked, with Alectryon following. The young man came forward and said courteously, 'My greetings to you, friends. I am Opheltas, son of Persepolis, the King of this island. May I know your names and parentage, and for what reason you have made the journey to our island?'

I answered him, 'I am Alkmaion, son of Sillos, King of Pylos. And this is the Count Alectryon, son of Eteocles, a Companion to the King.'

I saw from his eyes that he was surprised and impressed. He said quickly, 'My dear Prince Alkmaion – I may say cousin, may I not? – my father and I are most honoured. He had already bidden me offer you our hospitality but now I know he will be doubly anxious to make you welcome. Let us go up to the palace at once. Some of these men will bring your belongings.'

He turned to lead the way but I stopped him with a gesture. I would gladly have avoided what was to follow but I knew I could not.

54

'Prince Opheltas, before I accept your father's hospitality there is something he should know. Will you allow me a few words in private?'

He looked puzzled but replied, 'Certainly' and we went a little way along the beach until we were out of earshot. Then I said, 'I must tell you, Prince, the reason for my journey. When you have heard it you may feel it is better if I remain and sleep by my ship rather than coming up to the palace. If so, I shall quite understand.'

Frowning he replied, 'Say on, son of Sillos.'

'I travel on the orders of the Great Goddess. At home in Pylos I was unfortunate enough to commit an act of sacrilege during the great Spring Festival. It was quite unintentional, I beg you to believe that, but in order to escape the anger of the Goddess I must go to the Holy Islands to the south west where, She has told me, I shall receive purification. I believe Her favour will rest upon anyone who helps me in my voyage, but if you prefer not to take under your roof one who is defiled I shall understand.'

He hesitated for a moment, biting his lips in indecision. Then he said, 'It was an accident in some part of the ritual only? There is no blood guilt on your head?'

'No, none.'

He nodded, as if satisfied. 'Then, as you say, I can only think the Goddess will look with favour on those who help you. I thank you for taking me into your confidence, but I feel sure that my father would still wish me to bid you welcome.'

I thanked him with relief and we set off for the palace, Opheltas having given orders that Kerkios and his men should be well cared for and the chests containing our personal belongings brought up after us. In the palace courtyard the King was waiting for us, his second son Thaleus, a boy a little younger than myself, at his side. I saluted them respectfully.

'Greetings, King Persepolis, son of the wise Telemachos and grandson of far-famed Odysseus. My father, Sillos, greets you though me.'

He came forward and took me by the hand. 'My dear Prince Alkmaion, this is a delightful and unexpected honour. The houses of Nestor and Odysseus have ever been friends, since our forefathers fought together at Troy, but it is years now since I saw any member of my dear wife's family. You are most welcome.'

After we had bathed and put on fresh clothing we joined the king and his family in the megaron where we were entertained to a royal feast. When we had eaten I called for my sea chest and presented the gifts which my father and other members of my kindred had entrusted to me – bracelets of gold, a bronze mixing bowl and, most precious of all, a golden drinking cup whose rim was ornamented with helmeted heads in black enamel. This last was reputed to have been among the treasures looted from Troy and must once have graced the table of King Priam himself. In return Alectryon and I both received gifts from Persepolis – necklaces of precious amber from the far north and lengths of scented woollen cloth woven from the fleece of the hardy sheep of Ithaca and, for my personal use, a gold cup which had once belonged to the gallant Odysseus himself. After that Persepolis ordered the bard to sing but my eyelids were already drooping and I was glad when Opheltas led us out into the porch where beds had been prepared for us in the cool air.

Next morning Persepolis would have detained us, suggesting a hunt to be followed by games and other entertainments, but I pleaded the urgency of my mission and by midday we were at sea again. The breeze had fallen light but it was sufficient to make it worthwhile putting up the sail and under it the ship slid along all day until we came in the evening to the island of Corcyra, where we made camp.

During a good part of the day I had been turning over in my mind the plan that had come to me before we left home. If it was to be put into practice, this was the time. So, when the evening meal was over and we were lying around the fire, I looked across the straits towards the mountains of the mainland and said, 'That's where the Dorians live, isn't it Kerkios?'

He followed my gaze and nodded. 'That's right, sir. Their nearest settlement, Cresphontes's village, is only an hour or two's sailing time from here.'

'Good,' I said. 'Then we shall be there before the sun gets too hot tomorrow.'

His head snapped round towards me. On my other side I was aware of Alectryon's being raised more slowly, as if he was not altogether surprised by what he had heard.

Kerkios said, 'My instructions were to take you to the Holy Islands, Prince Alkmaion. There was no mention of visiting the Dorians.'

'Your instructions,' I returned sharply, 'were to place yourself under my command. In matters concerning the ship I respect your authority, but you steer the course I choose. Our ultimate destination is the Holy Islands, but that does not stop us visiting the Dorians on the way.'

I had an uncomfortable feeling that Alectryon was mildly amused to hear me asserting my authority, but he spoke up in my support.

'The Prince is right, of course. Besides, what harm can it do to pay Cresphontes a visit? I understood that his people have never been hostile – although I gather that you have detected a change in them.'

(I had long ago told him of Kerkios' report and my subsequent conversation with the bard Sirios.)

Kerkios said reluctantly, 'I will do whatever the Prince commands, of course. But I beg you to believe,' he looked me in the eyes, 'that what I told the King was not mere fancy – whatever the Lawagetas may have thought. Is it wise, do you think, to place the person of the Crown Prince in the hands of these people?'

I answered, 'Kerkios, I believe all you said. That is why I wish to see for myself what is going on. But as far as placing my person in their hands is concerned, whatever do you imagine they are going to do with me? If they thought of holding me to ransom, or some such thing, surely they would realise that they would gain nothing in the long run but my father's enmity. They do far better out of trade with us than anything they could hope for from that.'

Alectryon put in, 'It is true Kerkios. What possible advantage could there be to them in an act of hostility? I cannot see that there is any danger.'

Kerkios shrugged. 'It is for the Prince to command.' He got up and walked away down the beach, obviously put out at being over-ruled.

Alectryon said, 'Why did you not mention this plan to me before?'

I dropped my eyes. 'I suppose because I thought you might try to stop me.'

'Then you think yourself that it is dangerous?'

'No. Not necessarily.'

'Why else should I try to prevent you?'

'Oh, I don't know. A sense of duty – something boring like that.'

He grinned. 'You do me an injustice. I am as keen for adventure as you, and I must admit I'm curious to find out what has disturbed old Kerkios. Besides, if there is something going on, your uncle Paion is more likely to pay attention to us than to him.'

I caught his eye. 'I'm sorry. I should have trusted you.'

He lifted an eyebrow ironically. 'Yes. I thought you might, by now.'

The next morning we set course for the Dorian village. We found it at the mouth of a fast-flowing river, on the narrow strip of land between the mountains and the sea; a collection of rough huts around a single stone-built dwelling which I guessed to be the house of the ruler. Around the village were a few plots of cultivated land but behind it the foothills rose steeply, clothed in heavy forest. As the sailors rowed the ship into the mouth of the river, straining against the current to beach her on the sweep of sand below the houses, people began to gather on the beach. Mostly they were poorly dressed in tunics of rough wool but as we drew nearer I could see a group of older men whose garments proclaimed them to be somewhat higher in rank.

As the keel jarred on the sand Kerkios said, 'Let me go ashore first, Prince. They know me well.'

I assented and he went forward and jumped down onto the beach. I waited, glancing at Alectryon. We had both armed ourselves as a precaution and hung our long bronze swords from our shoulders. I found myself thinking that he looked his best in armour, the bronze plates of his corselet echoing the red-gold of his hair.

He caught my eye and said, 'Well, Kerkios seems to be getting a friendly enough welcome. But where are all the young men, I wonder? All those I can see are obviously peasants. Where are their warriors?'

'Good question,' I agreed. 'Let's go ashore. Kerkios has had time enough to explain who we are.'

When we reached the beach the man to whom Kerkios had been talking came forward to greet us. He was an elderly man with grizzled hair but still upright and dignified in his bearing. He spoke our language but with a strange guttural accent that made it difficult to understand at first. He introduced himself as Lampadon, uncle to Cresphontes, and explained that the prince and the other young men were away on a hunting expedition but were expected back the next day. Then he led us to the stone house in the centre of the village. It was a simple dwelling, consisting solely of a porch, an ante-room and a large hall with a rounded end opposite the door across which hung a curtain of hides. This, presumably, was the prince's sleeping quarters.

We were offered chairs of plain rough wood and presently a shy, down-trodden looking girl with dark hair hanging in tangles about her face brought a bowl and a jug of cold water and washed our hands and feet. We were not offered a bath and my nose told me that the Dorians were not much given to bathing. After we had eaten the simple food we were offered and exchanged a few commonplace remarks conversation dwindled. Then Alectryon suggested that we might look round the village and instantly I sensed a stiffening in their manner. I had begun to think that we were wasting our time but now my suspicions were revived.

They took us out into the midday heat and patiently conducted us around the little huts and the fields of poor crops. No wonder they found our curiosity suspicious, I reflected. There was nothing to see. The only point of interest was down by the shore, where a ship was being built. I saw Kerkios purse his lips with contempt at her clumsy construction but he caught my eye and gave me a meaningful nod. I noticed that a little group had gathered around our own trim vessel and were studying her curiously.

Kerkios muttered in my ear, 'The question is, will any of them know how to sail that tub when she's finished.'

As we returned to the village Alectryon touched my arm. Ahead of us a path led round the shoulder of a hill and disappeared into a valley on the far side. A woman was walking up it carrying a basket.

'That's the third,' he murmured. 'I wonder where they're going.'

'Taking food to a shepherd or a herdsman up in the hills?' I suggested.

'Maybe,' he replied, 'but I was just remembering what Kerkios said.' He turned to our hosts. 'Your flocks and herds are up in the hills, I suppose?'

'Naturally,' came the reply.

'And that path leads up to the pastures?'

It was an innocent enough question but I saw their faces stiffen. Then Lampadon said, 'No, it leads to the sanctuary of a god. It may be visited only by one of our tribe — and then only by those who are initiates.'

Later that evening, after a meal of rather tasteless stew and black bread, our hosts caused couches to be spread for us in the hall. Left to ourselves, we talked for a long time, but in the end had to admit that we had learned nothing and might as well be on our way as soon as we had paid our respects to Cresphontes.

At length we fell silent and I could soon tell from their breathing that Kerkios and Dexeus were fast asleep. Alectryon, I had learned, was a quiet sleeper. It was hard to tell whether he was awake or not. It was hot in the hall and stuffy from the smoke of the fire. I tossed about and threw off my coverings. By craning my neck I could look up through the hole in the roof above the central hearth and see the stars. The night sky looked cool and clear.

I got up quietly and reached for my kilt. Alectryon did not speak so I concluded he was asleep too. I picked my way to the door and slipped out into the ante-room. At the open doorway that led out to the porch I stopped abruptly. A few yards away a man sat on the bare ground, facing the entrance. In the moonlight I could see the gleam of a sword laid across his knees. He was gazing up at the stars and did not see me and I drew back quickly and sat down to consider the implications.

Clearly, the guard was not there for our safety, for then he would have been looking outwards. So obviously he was there to see that we remained in the building. A moment's panic seized me. Had we let ourselves be taken prisoner, without the least resistance? Then common sense reasserted itself. It would be too easy for the four of us to over-power one guard and the commotion would have brought our crew running to our assistance. I reckoned they would have been a match for any of those we had seen about the village that day. In which case, the man was simply there to see that we did not go wandering about unsupervised. There was something we were not supposed to see – and I immediately determined to find out what it was.

I crept to the doorway again and squatted on the floor to peer out. The guard was still watching the sky but he was too close for me to slip out without attracting his attention. Then a movement to one side caught my eye. A second man crossed the space in front of the building and the first rose to meet him. The guard was changing. The two stood together, speaking in low tones, and the first pointed to the sky. While they were both looking up I slipped round the doorpost and scuttled round the corner of the building. Then I stood under a tree and made water so that if I had been seen I could show a reason for leaving the hall. My heart was thumping, but there was no sound of alarm or pursuit. After a moment I peered round the corner again. The new guard had taken the sword and was walking up and down. The other man had disappeared, presumably gone home to bed.

So far so good, but I had no plans for my next step. I sat down with my back to the still warm stones to think it out. The only place we had not seen was the valley beyond the ridge so if there was a secret it must be there. I was tempted to set out directly up the path but I remembered how Kerkios had been waylaid and cast round for an alternative route. It struck me that, if I could slip out of the village unseen, I could follow the river inland and then climb the ridge nearer to the point where it joined the main mass of the mountain range. This should bring me to the head of the forbidden valley and it was unlikely that they would expect anyone to approach from that direction.

I got to my feet and moved stealthily along the wall to the back of the building. From here I slipped silently through the cluster of huts, keeping carefully to the shadows. Once a dog growled from a doorway, sending my heart thudding in my ears, but otherwise no one stirred and I reached the riverbank safely. There was a path here, quite broad and well used, and I set off up it at a good pace, aware that to complete my exploration and return before dawn I should have to hurry. There was still the little matter of getting back into the hall without being seen but I put that to the back of my mind. My blood was running fast and I was light footed and perhaps a little light headed with excitement.

The moon was in her first quarter so there was not a great deal of light, but on the open ground by the river I could see my way quite well. It was when the valley narrowed and the trees closed in around me that I began to find myself stumbling more and more often on rocks and roots. My elation began to fade. The night breeze rustled in the trees, merging with the hiss and splash of the river. Other than that there was no sound, but I found myself remembering that there must be wolves in these hills. I laid my hand on the dagger at my belt and wished I had brought my sword with me.

At length I came to a standstill. From the village it had seemed an easy thing to judge where to leave the river and start my climb up the ridge but here, close under the flank of the hill, it was not so simple. I hesitated for a few moments longer and then took a deep breath and struck off the path, climbing at an angle up the hillside.

At once I began to realise how foolhardy my enterprise was. Under the trees the darkness was almost impenetrable and the ground was rocky and treacherous. I struggled on, trying to keep always uphill but sometimes forced out of my way by old watercourses and gullies full of thorny undergrowth. It seemed hours before I finally scrambled clear of the trees and out onto the open hillside. A glance at the sky told me that the night was well advanced, but now I was out in the open I was able to make better progress. I continued to climb, trying to ignore my growing weariness, and reached the crest of the ridge at last. Here I paused to get my breath and consider the situation. From the position of the stars I knew that there were not many hours of darkness left. If I turned back now I might just make it back to the village before dawn, but it seemed unlikely, and the whole wretched effort of the night would have been wasted. On the other hand, if I went on I might get a look at whatever was in the valley at first light. The problem was to explain my absence when I got back. I decided to say that I had woken early and gone to bathe in the river. A quick dip on the way back would lend colour to my story. It crossed my mind to consider Alectryon's anxiety when he awoke to find me gone and my stomach clenched. I wished, most profoundly, that I had woken him to come with me.

Having re-planned my actions, I set off again, this time down hill towards the trees that clothed the sides of the forbidden valley. By the time I reached them the first faint light of dawn was showing in the sky beyond the mountains. Aided by this thinning of the darkness I made my way through the trees and came at last to a point where I could look down upon the valley floor.

Below me was an almost circular green depression protected on all sides by the steeply rising hillside, except where a narrow defile brought the path from the village into it. In this hollow stood a cluster of huts. I counted ten of them. They were arranged in a circle and in front of each was a raised, circular hearth, from some of which still rose faint wisps of smoke. Before each of these stood a large, flat block of stone topped by a strange, dark object that I could not properly discern in the half light. Altars, I wondered? And the ashes on the hearths the remains of sacrificial flames? It occurred to me, like a cold hand closing round my bowels, that I might really be intruding on the mysteries of a God. Yet, in spite of my fear, I had a strong sense that there was something about the place that spoke of human activity, not divine.

I crouched under the shelter of the bushes for a while longer but there was no sign of life from any of the huts. Then somewhere a cock crew and a dog began to bark and I realised that I could not afford to wait any longer. I crawled back among the trees and got to my feet. I was chilled and stiff and wished I had brought my cloak with me. The thought of the long climb back over the ridge and down to the river filled me with gloom. I looked towards the path leading from the village. That way must be less than half the distance I had come. I noticed that the flanks of the narrow defile were clothed with trees and scrub. Surely it must be possible to make my way through them without being seen. Any guards would be watching for people coming from the village, not from the opposite direction. I decided it was a risk worth taking.

I worked my way through the forest until I found myself at the top of the sharp slope that led down to the path, which twisted and turned as it climbed through a rocky valley. I kept along the side of the cliff, following a narrow ledge that clung to the scarp, the drop into the valley on my right and the steep slope of the hill on my left, often forced to cling to the branches of trees for support. I was so absorbed in the problems of finding a route that I had almost forgotten about the guards, when I heard their voices.

I froze, clinging to the trunk of a twisted oak, and looked about me. At length I spotted them, sitting together on a flat topped rock above the path. I guessed that one of them was meant to be on the other side, but even so anyone coming up the path would not have stood much chance if they had not given themselves away by talking. As it was, it was not too difficult to slip past high above them, though my heart was in my mouth at every stone that slipped away from under my feet and rattled down the slope.

Beyond the guards the valley took a sharp turn to the left and once I had rounded it I saw that I was at the end of the narrow cleft to whose sides I had been clinging. Ahead of me it joined another, broader valley with a second path along its bottom and from where the two merged a broad track led towards the village. I scrambled down the rocky slope and dropped onto the track. The guards were behind me now and a short walk would bring me to the village. When I came in sight of it I would rely on the inspiration of the moment to account for where I had been.

The two men who jumped on me must also have been crouching on a rock above the path, but, unlike the other pair, they were silent. My first warning of their presence was when one dropped onto my back, sending me crashing forward onto the stony ground. Half-stunned and sick with pain I tried to gather myself to fight, my body cringing at the anticipation of their daggers in my flesh. There were shouts and the sound of running feet and I was aware of others gathering around us. Then I was dragged to my feet, my arms twisted behind me and a dagger at my throat.

Chapter 5.

As soon as I had shaken the hair out of my eyes I knew whom I was facing. He was tall and strongly built, in his mid-twenties I guessed. He wore his dark hair short and roughly cut, as did the rest of them, and his leather kilt and woollen cloak were simple and unadorned, but there was that in his eyes, which were of a brilliant light brown the colour of amber, which proclaimed him a prince.

Cresphontes put his hands on his hips and looked me up and down for a moment, then jerked his head at my captors, who loosed their hold on me. One of them said, 'We heard him coming down the path behind us, so we dropped back and he walked right into us.'

Cresphontes nodded, his eyes on my face. I stared back at him, my mind racing. Still without speaking he reached an arm sideways and snapped his fingers. A boy came forward from the group of young men behind him and stood at his side. Cresphontes laid a hand on his shoulder and said, in slow, mocking tones, 'What is it, little wolf? Man or woman? Or something in between, perhaps?'

The boy grinned and left his side to walk slowly around me, making a parody of inspecting me closely. Then he reported, 'It's a sort of man – I think. It has no tits.' He grinned again, baring sharp white teeth in a manner that made it obvious how he had earned his nickname. Then he reached for my belt. 'Shall we see if it's got a cock?'

I struck his hand away and met his eyes defiantly. In spite of its wolvish expression his face had a strange, wild beauty, lean and high cheek-boned and dominated by a pair of huge eyes whose colour came nearer to perfect green than any I had seen.

Cresphontes said, 'No, leave him be.' He came closer and picked up a lock of my hair, examining curiously. I realised that our aristocratic manner of wearing our hair in long ringlets was foreign to him. 'Tell me,' he went on, 'what is such a beautiful young gentleman doing wandering alone in this valley?'

I drew breath to answer but a shout from one of those further back interrupted me. Cresphontes called 'Let them pass' and a moment later Alectryon rounded the bend in the path and came into the centre of the group, closely followed by Dexeus and Kerkios. I gritted my

65

teeth. Now we were all prisoners!

Alectryon looked around him and then said, as if we stood in the courtyard of my father's palace, 'You are too fleet of foot, Prince. We thought to have caught you up before this, since you left the village so little ahead of us.' And he stared hard into my eyes.

I replied, trying to emulate his casual tone, 'Forgive me, Count, but I felt so full of energy after such a good night's sleep — and you take so long to dress! I have had a very pleasant walk while you three were still struggling out of bed.'

Cresphontes was looking from one to another of us. 'So,' he said. 'Two more beautiful gentlemen — and Kerkios, whom we know. May I ask the names of my guests?'

Alectryon looked at him haughtily. 'Cresphontes?'

'Yes.'

'You ask our names. It is a pity you did not observe the normal rules of courtesy and do so before you allowed your followers to manhandle this gentleman. He is Alkmaion, Crown Prince of Pylos, son of Sillos and great-grandson of the renowned Nestor.'

Cresphontes regarded me for a moment. If he was surprised by the disclosure of my identity he did not show it. Rather he seemed to be comparing my person with the dignity of my titles. I drew myself up, conscious of a trickle of blood from my nose, and wished that at that moment I felt more worthy of them.

He said, 'And I am Cresphontes, Prince of the Dorians, son of Aristomachos and great grand-son of the even more renowned Heracles.'

'Tributary prince to your elder brother Temenos, I believe,' Alectryon remarked smoothly and I saw Cresphontes' eyes flash anger.

'And you are?'

'The Count Alectryon, son of Eteocles, hereditary Companion to the King of Pylos.'

'And the Prince's friend?'

'I believe I have that honour.'

Cresphontes grinned suddenly. 'How do you value friendship in Pylos, Count? Will you challenge me to personal combat for the life of your Prince? If you win you shall take him and go free. If I win I shall

…' his eyes roved over me for a moment, 'I shall make a present of him to Xouthos here, who is *my* friend. What will you do with him, little wolf?'

I stared in desperation from him to the boy and then to Alectryon, who replied without the slightest sign of disturbance, 'I shall do nothing of the sort. I had no idea the Dorians were such barbarians. The prince has come here on a visit of courtesy, with nothing but peaceful intentions, only to be met with this completely unprovoked hostility. If you do not at once release him and allow us to return to our ship you will very rapidly find your village laid waste by Pylian warriors.'

Cresphontes' grin hardened. 'You must think me very ill-informed, Count. A runner reached me last evening with the report of your arrival. I knew very well with whom I had to deal. And I know too that you came with only one ship. There are no warriors.'

'Indeed?' returned Alectryon. 'But your runner could scarcely bring you report of Pylian warships lying in harbour over in Corcyra, could he? Do you imagine the Prince of Pylos travels with so small an escort? We are expected back before dark.'

If I had admired Alectryon before, it was nothing to my feelings now. I watched Cresphontes, willing him to believe the story. He was looking at Alectryon, sizing him up as a wrestler sizes up an opponent. Then he smiled slowly.

'You've a cool head, Count. I admire a man who doesn't get flustered when he's in a tight spot. I think we should be friends. But if you're in charge of the Prince's safety you shouldn't let him go prying into secret places that don't concern him.'

I found my voice at last. 'I cannot think what you mean, Prince Cresphontes. As you heard me say to the Count, I woke early and came for a walk to get some exercise after several days on shipboard. I have pried into no secrets.'

He looked at me narrowly. 'How far up the valley have you been?'

'I came to a point where the paths divide. I went a short distance up the narrower path. You and your party must have passed on the other track during those few minutes.'

The man who had jumped on me said, 'He was coming down

the valley when we caught him.'

'Naturally,' I returned. 'The path I had chosen seemed to be leading nowhere and I was hungry. I decided to turn back.'

There was a moment's silence. We waited tensely. I do not think Cresphontes was convinced by what I had said but he dare not risk calling Alectryon's bluff about the warships. I guessed he was looking for a way to save face.

At length he said, 'Very well then. Let us speak no more of it. I am sorry you have been roughly handled, Prince Alkmaion, but we do not like strangers to wander too close to the sanctuaries of our gods. However, since you apparently intended no offence, please accept my apologies. You must allow us to try and make up for our lack of hospitality. Shall we go on together?'

So the whole party turned and began once again to descend the path towards the village. My legs were trembling under me with weariness and shock but I caught Alectryon's eye and managed a smile. There was no answering smile in his eyes and I realised dismally that for the first time he was really angry with me.

Having chosen his course of action Cresphontes obviously intended to carry it through with style. He began to play the part of the courteous host with considerably more polish than the rest of his people had shown. Within minutes of our return we were sitting down to a simple but plentiful breakfast, while his young men set to to flay and prepare the two young bucks which they had brought back from the hunt. I noticed that the boy Xouthos remained close to his prince, saying little but watching us intently with those huge green eyes.

After my night's exertions I was not hungry but longed only to lie down and sleep. The strain of appearing wide-awake under Cresphontes hawk-like gaze and the unwavering stare of Xouthos was almost unbearable.

At length Cresphontes said, 'You say you have to rejoin your other ships before nightfall?'

Alectryon was alert at once. 'That is the arrangement.'

'It's a pity. As you see, our hunting has been good. Tonight there will be feasting. Let me persuade you to stay a little longer. We rarely have the pleasure of such noble visitors.'

Alectryon began to say 'I fear it is not possible …' but I cut him short. In part it was because the thought occurred to me that there might still be information to be gleaned, but in part it was sheer perversity. Once again he had rescued me from a tight spot and the sensation of being at a disadvantage rankled.

'Thank you, Prince Cresphontes,' I put in quickly. 'We shall be pleased to accept your hospitality. There is no reason, Count, why we should not send a message to the rest of the fleet. They are in a safe anchorage and well provisioned. They can wait for us for a day or two.' Ignoring Alectryon's hastily masked glare of surprise I turned to Kerkios. 'Kerkios, take the ship over to the anchorage and deliver that message. Then return here.'

Whatever the old seafarer thought of me for sending him and his crew on a completely objectless voyage, he did not show it. He took his leave and gathered his crew together and presently we saw them launch the ship and row out across the straits.

Cresphontes, meanwhile, rose to his feet, saying, 'Please excuse me, Prince. There are matters that need my attention. I hope you can find some entertainment for an hour or two.'

I assured him that we should be quite happy left to our own devices and he went off, with Xouthos at his heels.

Alectryon looked at me. 'Well, now we are completely at the mercy of these people. Just the three of us – and no ship!'

'Kerkios will be back,' I said, trying to sound unconcerned. 'Anyway,' I went on, trying to stifle a yawn, 'I don't think Cresphontes intends us any harm.'

'Let us hope not,' he remarked grimly. Then, looking at me, 'Let's walk down to the beach, before you fall asleep where you sit.'

We walked along the edge of the sea until a group of pines offered us some shelter from prying eyes. Alectryon turned to Dexeus, who as a good squire was never far from his shoulder.

'Stay here and keep watch. If anyone approaches from the village, whistle.'

A little further on he said, 'When we set out on this expedition I thought I enjoyed your confidence. I was obviously mistaken.'

I looked at him and saw the hurt in his eyes. 'That's not true.

You know I trust you absolutely.'

He lifted an eyebrow. 'Really? You didn't choose to confide in me last night. Which is just as well, since I should certainly have forbidden such a mad enterprise.'

'You have no authority to forbid me anything!' I flashed back, and could have bitten my tongue off an instant later. 'Anyway,' I mumbled, 'it would have worked if I hadn't had the bad luck to run into Cresphontes and his hunting party.'

'And what were you going to say when you walked back into the village?'

'I was going to have a quick dip in the river and say I'd been down to wash.'

'Is that the story you were going to tell me, too?'

'No, of course not.'

'You were very careful to wait until you thought I was asleep before you set off.'

'If you were awake, why didn't you say something?'

'I thought you were just going out for a pee.'

I flung myself down on the sand in the shade of a pine tree. I felt sick and thick-headed and miserable. 'Anyway, I didn't know I was going anywhere, except out on the porch for some fresh air, until I saw the guard.'

He turned from looking out to sea and frowned down at me. 'Guard? What guard?'

'Didn't you see him?'

'No.' He sat down on the sand beside me.

In as few words as possible I told him how my suspicions had been aroused and what I had seen, adding, 'It all happened so quickly I didn't have a chance to wake you.'

As I spoke I saw curiosity replace the anger in his face. When I finished he said, 'All right. So there is a settlement of some sort that they don't want us to know about. But beyond that I can't see that what you saw helps us very much.'

I sighed. 'No, you're right. But that's why I wanted to stay. They might let something drop, after a few cups of wine.'

'Maybe,' he said grudgingly. 'But promise me, no more midnight expeditions.'

'I promise,' I agreed, yawning.

He looked down at me. 'You'd better get some sleep. If you keep nodding off this evening Cresphontes is going to get suspicious.'

I settled myself as comfortably as I could and he folded his cloak and put it under my head. Drifting into sleep I remembered that there was something I had not said.

'You were magnificent, the way you bluffed Cresphontes. He still doesn't know whether to believe in those other ships or not.'

He slanted me a sideways glance and grinned. 'Hush!'

When I awoke the sun was already dipping towards the sea and Alectryon and Dexeus were playing draughts a short way off. After a dip in the sea to clear my head I was none the worse for my night's adventures by the time we returned to the village. Cresphontes was waiting for us, but if he was surprised at our long absence he gave no sign of it – except that he looked from my face to Alectryon's and then exchanged glances with Xouthos as if some guess he had made had been confirmed. For the rest of the afternoon we lounged on the porch, chatting, and to my surprise I found him an entertaining companion. He asked many questions about Messenia, but none that any interested stranger might not have asked. I return I questioned him about his people and their customs. In particular I had been struck by the crude simplicity of the houses but when I asked him why he did not see to it that his subjects built him a more fitting dwelling he laughed and said, 'What would be the point? In a year or two, or maybe a little longer, we may wish to move on. We shall need new land, better pasture for our flocks.' Then, his face darkening, he added, 'There are many peoples to the north of us. Every year we have to fight harder to keep them out of our territory. One day, perhaps, it will be easier just to move. There is good land to the south, I hear.'

I looked across and caught Alectryon's eye. A tightening of his lips told me that the significance of the remark had not passed him by.

Kerkios had returned with the ship by this time and I asked him to have my sea-chest brought up so I could change my clothes. Cresphontes, rather to my surprise, had put on a tunic of fine cloth and

71

a necklace of amber beads and I fancied he had even bathed. Guessing that this would be a suitable moment I opened my chest and presented him with a good bronze dagger, the handle covered in gold foil and decorated with lion's heads. Among the treasures of my father's palace it would scarcely have warranted a second glance, but he was clearly delighted with it.

I saw that Xouthos was watching me with hungry eyes and presented him with a gold ring. He took it greedily and I saw him examining the stone in it with great curiosity.

'It is iron,' I told him. 'It is found in the thunderbolts flung by the gods, so it is very rare and has magical powers.'

Xouthos looked at me for a moment and then turned to Cresphontes and laughed. I began to wonder if he was as intelligent as his looks suggested.

As I fastened my chest again he leaned over to his prince and said something in a low tone. Cresphontes chuckled and said, 'Xouthos is disappointed that the fight I proposed this morning between Count Alectryon and myself did not take place. He suggests instead a friendly contest between us and he, if it is not too presumptuous, would like to challenge you, Prince Alkmaion. What do you say?'

I glanced at Alectryon, who said quietly, 'What sort of contest?'

'Three rounds. A footrace, a wrestling match and a bout of swordplay – first man to draw blood to be the winner. How does that suit you? I'll offer two good prizes. If the Prince can win two out of his three contests against Xouthos I'll give him the fine pelt of a bear I killed last spring. It'll keep you warm on the chilliest night, I can promise you. And if Count Alectryon can beat me in more than one bout I'll give him a young bull from my own herd, which will make a feast for all your men and leave you with some valuable leather afterwards. What do you say? Is it agreed?'

I looked at Xouthos. He was a little younger than I was, I guessed, but in build we were much alike and he was clearly in hard training. We would be evenly matched. It would be hard to refuse without appearing cowardly. Once again I consulted Alectryon with a look and, rather to my surprise, he nodded.

I said, 'It is agreed. And for my part I will offer a bronze cauldron if you can get the better of Alectryon and a dagger for Xouthos if he can beat me.'

'Excellent!' exclaimed Cresphontes. 'The men will be delighted to have some sport to watch and I shall be glad of the chance to try myself against such a distinguished gentleman. When shall it be, then? Tomorrow, when the hottest part of the day is over?'

It was agreed and Alectryon remarked, 'Have you among your warriors a man of good breeding who is a good marksman with a bow and arrow?'

'I know of such a one,' Cresphontes responded. 'Why do you ask?'

'Because Dexeus, my squire, is one of the best archers in Pylos. I should be interested to see if any of your men can beat him and I will offer a prize of half a talent of unworked bronze for the winner.'

Dexeus's eyes sparkled. Alectryon had not over praised him. Young as he was, his skill with the bow was well known at home and he was delighted with the opportunity to display it here.

So the contest was decided and we suddenly began to feel like old friends and in this happy frame of mind we went out to join the feasting. Seated around a fire in the open space before the megaron we ate roast venison washed down with draughts of rough red wine. It seemed that the Dorians had no bards and knew nothing of the art of song but when the meal was over some of the young men got up to dance to the music of flute and drum. Their bodies moved supply in the firelight, stamping and turning. Soon Cresphontes and Xouthos rose to join them. Xouthos was a natural dancer, his movements strong and graceful, his eyes flashing with pleasure. We Messenians applauded warmly when the dance ended, and then, of course, they insisted that we show them a dance from our own country. Alectryon and I rose to dance the Heron Dance, and I do not think we did Messenia less than credit.

As Cresphontes led the way back into the hall he said, 'I have had your squire's couch and the captain's moved out into the porch.'

Alectryon replied, 'Then I think we will join them. It is very warm in here.'

Cresphontes looked at him in surprise. 'As you wish. I thought

73

you would prefer a little more privacy.'

I felt the dark blood rising in my face. Alectryon said stiffly, 'There is no need.'

Cresphontes stared from his face to mine and a slow grin of disbelief spread across his face. 'Do you mean you don't … you're not …?' He let the words hang in the air, unfinished. I gazed into the embers on the hearth, unable to met Alectryon's eyes.

'Well, you Messenians are cold fish, I must say!' Cresphontes commented at length. 'It's your choice of course. But, if the Prince will permit me the liberty,' his eyes roved over me for a moment, 'I do think it's a terrible waste!'

Then he laughed and threw his arm about Xouthos's shoulders and they both disappeared behind the curtains at the end of the room. I could feel Alectryon looking at me and occupied myself with slowly removing the bracelets and necklace I had put on for the feast. Ever since the night I had offered to share his bed I had been expecting some sign from him, but he had made no move.

After a pause he said, 'Well, shall we take our couches out into the open?'

Before he had finished the question I was already dragging my bedding towards the door.

The next morning we retired once again to our secluded spot on the seashore to prepare for the coming contests, working off idle days on board ship, and too much food and wine the night before.

Alectryon said, 'Watch out for Xouthos He's the sort that gets carried away by his temper. It can be a serious weakness, but it could also make him very dangerous.'

By the time the sun had begun to slip towards the horizon the men of the village had assembled in the open space before the megaron. With them were the crew of our ship, who were just as eager for the sport. An open, flat stretch of ground ran between the huts towards the sea and a turning post had been set up at the far end for the footrace. The prizes which had been promised were set out on the porch and a fine young bull was tethered near-by.

The proceedings began, as was fitting, with offerings to the gods. Alectryon and I sacrificed to Poseidon, god of the sea and of bulls and fast horses, most powerful of the gods after the Great Mother Herself. I was surprised to see that Cresphontes and Xouthos sent up their prayers to Zeus and wondered why they gave allegiance to such a comparatively minor deity.

When the ceremonies were completed Cresphontes beckoned forward a man who carried a curious article of bronze, shaped somewhat like the horn of a bull. This he put to his lips and blew and a noise split the air that made all us Messenians jump almost out of our seats. It was clear and harsh like the wind from the mountains in winter, and rang about the village like the voice of a god.

Alectryon said, 'Poseidon! What a terrifying sound!'

It was not until much later that we were to know the full terror of the trumpets of the Dorians.

When the noise had died away Cresphontes announced the order of the contests. My trial against Xouthos was to come first, then Dexeus would challenge the best archer in the village, and finally we would have the battle between himself and Alectryon. Meanwhile, I was loosening my muscles for the footrace and watching Xouthos. We were both stripped and I could see better how well muscled he was, but somehow he didn't look like a runner. I wished there was someone else in the race to make the pace, since I knew nothing of his ability, but I resolved to let him lead on the outward leg.

We took our places on the starting line and I saw his green eyes flicker towards me. Lampadon and Kerkios, who had been chosen to act as umpires, took their places on either side of us and Lampadon gave the signal to start.

Xouthos went away fairly fast, which was just what I wanted, and I settled down on his heels. He flung a look over his shoulder and grinned. Did he think he had me beaten already? The pace slackened slightly, but I kept just behind, letting him make the running. Then coming towards the turning post he sprinted, hoping to get there well ahead of me and not be crowded on the turn. I kept exactly the same station as before and this time the look he threw me was puzzled, almost angry. I wondered how fast he was when he really stretched himself. We came round the post together and headed back towards the village. He glanced at me again and increased the pace. I did the same and drew level, telling myself the race was mine unless he could call upon an unexpected turn of speed. Seeing us coming in without a stride between us the spectators were on their feet, yelling with excitement. I decided the time had come to make my bid and went ahead. For a few paces he kept up with me, then I put on an extra spurt and he was gone. As I raced over the finishing line with the cheers of the ship's crew in my ears I could not even hear his footsteps. He came in several yards behind and looking spent and I realised that he had run completely without tactics and had simply gone all out most of the way.

Alectryon ran up and congratulated me, while Dexeus brought a sponge full of water to wipe my face. Then they led me to a spot in the shade of the megaron to prepare for the next event. As Alectryon rubbed oil into my shoulders he said,

'Right. You've beaten him in the running and he's angry. He'll be out to get his own back, and he won't mind too much how he does it, so be careful. He's at least up to your weight, and he's a born fighter.'

I promised to take care but it was not until the wrestling match started that I really understood what he meant. The moment the signal was given to start Xouthos closed with me with a ferocity that took me off my guard and we both went down in the dust. This was something utterly different from the wrestling bouts I was used to at home. There the object was to display skill and polish. There was none of that here, only the intention to hurt as often and as much as possible. This reminded me less of a wrestling competition than of those silent and bloody scuffles I used to have with Antilochos when we were children.

Pain and humiliation roused the fighting spirit in me and I forgot the skills I had learned and fought him back in his own way. But by then it was too late, he had the advantage and in a few minutes I was pinned to the ground, my face in the dust and one arm twisted agonisingly into the small of my back. I was not sorry to hear Lampadon declare the contest over.

Alectryon greeted me with a wry smile. 'You understand now what I meant?'

I nodded, angry and ashamed. He handed me a cup of water to rinse the dust out of my mouth and said kindly, 'Don't fret. It was a victory won without skill. At home he would have been howled out of the ring. And there is still the sword fight to come. The honours are even at the moment.'

I brightened at this. I was on my mettle now and Xouthos would not take me unawares this time. Dexeus brought my armour and Alectryon was about to help me into it when Cresphontes came over.

'We fight without armour here, Prince,' he said with a grin. 'Put this on instead.'

'This' was a tunic of linen reinforced with panels of leather. It would be some protection against a glancing blow, but nothing more. I felt my stomach contract as I put aside my good bronze corselet. All that was required to win was to be the first to draw blood, but I remembered the blind ferocity with which Xouthos fought.

Alectryon clapped me on the shoulder and said, 'Cheer up! You are an excellent swordsman. This will simply mean that you have to be doubly on your guard, that's all.' But his set face belied his confident words.

I took my long sword and gripped my round shield with its pointed boss and went out to meet Xouthos. He was looking triumphant and very full of himself. As soon as the signal to start was given he came at me, his sword flailing. This time I was ready for him and as I parried the blows I realised that he had no more finesse with the sword than he had at wrestling. I let him weary himself with vain attempts to get through my guard and suddenly found myself laughing at his efforts. This made him more furious than ever and I saw that in his frantic attempts to reach me he was forgetting to guard himself. I could hit him whenever I liked. I controlled the urge to lash out. His movements were so erratic that it would be easy to misjudge my thrust and I reckoned that it would not be politic to kill Cresphontes's favourite. However, I decided that the time had come to abandon my defensive attitude. I saw Xouthos's expression change as I came onto the attack, driving him back and back across the open space. From anger it turned to surprise and then to fear. He knew I could hit him wherever I wanted to and remembered, I fancy, how hard he had used me in the wrestling match. I spent a little time giving him a lesson in the finer points of swordsmanship, watching him get more and more desperate and waiting for my chance. He gave it to me perfectly in the end, with a wild slash that left his right arm extended and his shield in no position to cover it. My sword flashed in and laid open a long shallow cut on his upper arm. Anyone could see that I could have completely disabled him if I had wanted to. The blood began to run and Cresphontes leapt in at once and stopped the fight. I could see he had been worried too.

However, he presented me with the bearskin very graciously and congratulated me on my skill while Xouthos went off into a corner to staunch his wound and sulk. Then it was Dexeus's turn to show his prowess.

Two staffs had been set up some distance down the running track and a captured wood pigeon was tied to each one by a foot so that it fluttered in the air in a vain attempt to get away. Dexeus took his bow and quiver and went to the centre of the ring, where he was joined by his opponent, a man perhaps twice his age who walked with a pronounced limp.

Each man was allowed three arrows. Dexeus's first hit the staff, while his opponent's passed so near the bird that it seemed he must have winged it; but it continued to flutter, unharmed. Then Dexeus's second arrow struck his bird fairly so that it dropped and hung from the tether stone dead, while the other man's last two shots were further from the mark than his first. So Dexeus walked off, highly delighted, with the prize.

The time had come for Alectryon to try his strength and skill against our host. As I helped him prepare Cresphontes came over and said,

'Count, would you be agreeable to a slight change in our events? It has occurred to me that an exact repetition of those we have already seen may be boring for the spectators.'

Alectryon looked at him warily. 'What do you have in mind?'

'The foot race to begin, as we planned. Then, instead of simple wrestling, all-in fighting, no holds or punches barred, and the sword-fight to finish.'

It was easy to see what was in his mind. He hoped that the all-in fight would give him the opportunity of so disabling Alectryon that he would not be able to show himself at his best with the sword. I opened my mouth to bid Alectryon refuse but he silenced me with a touch and said, 'Agreed, Prince, but with one further alteration. It seems to me that neither of us is likely to be at our best after the fight, so let us begin with the foot race, as planned, and then have the swordplay before the fight. Will that suit you?'

Clearly it did not suit Cresphontes at all but there was no way he could refuse, so he agreed with apparent indifference.

'I don't like it, Alectryon,' I said, as soon as he was out of earshot. 'You've seen the way they fight. You could be badly hurt.'

'Don't worry,' he returned, with a grim smile. 'I think I can give him as good as I get – particularly if I can wing him in the sword fight.'

So the contest began. There was never much doubt about the footrace. Cresphontes was heavier than Alectryon and nothing like so fleet of foot. He contented himself with not allowing Alectryon to get too far ahead and saved his strength for the other events.

Then came the sword fight. It did not look as though there was going to be much doubt about that either for it was clear that, although he was much more skilful than Xouthos, Cresphontes was no match for one of the best swordsmen in Pylos. However, he put up a good defence and Alectryon had to wait for his opportunity. I noticed that, more by sheer weight than skill, Cresphontes was forcing him back across the arena towards the megaron. Then I saw the reason. The bull that was tethered there had deposited a pile of dung. I cried out to Alectryon but it was too late. His foot slipped on the filthy stuff and while he was off balance Cresphontes's sword caught him on the side of the neck. It was only a small cut, but Lampadon was quick to cry first blood to his prince.

My heart sank. I could not see Alectryon winning the next bout. Indeed, I was afraid for his safety, though I tried not to show it as I staunched the blood from the cut on his neck. He was angry at his bad luck, but amused as well at Cresphontes's cunning. It was on the tip of my tongue to order him to call the whole thing off but I had a feeling that he would not obey me.

As they went out to meet for the final bout I noticed that Xouthos had stopped sulking and was lying on a sheepskin nearby, watching his lover with burning eyes. He looked up and for a moment understanding flashed between us. Then the fight began. To start with the spectators roared as they had done for all the other events. Then a silence settled over the whole crowd, for we were watching a battle of giants, a battle in which no mercy was asked or given. My heart seemed to be trying to tear itself free from my body as I watched them, now writhing in the dust, a tangle of twisted limbs and groping hands, now standing chest to chest while blows rained on heads and faces. Soon Alectryon's face was streaked with blood and I could see one eye was half closed. Cresphontes was in no better shape. Blood trickled from his nose and every now and then he shook his head to get rid of it and bright drops flashed through the air and splashed heavily onto the ground. Both men's backs bore long, red weals where the other's fingers had sought for a hold. And still neither could get the better of the other and neither would give in.

As the fight went on I glanced wildly around me. Would no one step in and stop it? I saw that neither would stop of his own free will until a broken limb or some other severe injury forced him to. But Lampadon sat impassive and Kerkios, though officially one of the umpires, had no real authority. The fighters were on the ground again now, the only sound their hard drawn breath and the occasional harsh grunt of pain. I saw Cresphontes trying to twist Alectryon's leg and it seemed to me that at any moment his hip joint must give way, but with a huge effort he brought his other foot up under his opponent's stomach and flung him off. Cresphontes flew backwards and his head hit the ground with an audible thud.

As they both staggered to their feet and closed again I leapt up, unable to sit passive any longer. As I did so Xouthos also jumped to his feet and seized my arm. I thought he meant to stop me and turned on him, but he cried out, 'Stop them, Prince Alkmaion! They will listen to you!'

This was sufficient. I rushed into the centre of the ring and shouted, 'Stop, both of you! Enough! You have done enough!'

They did not appear to hear me and continued grappling. I flung myself between them, catching a blow from Alectryon that made my ears sing, braced a hand on the chest of each and forced them apart, shouting, 'Enough, I say! Will you stop? The honours are equal. You have both acquitted yourselves well. Let you, Cresphontes, give Alectryon the bull you promised and I will give you the bowl I offered as a prize. But let there be no more fighting.'

Alectryon's eyes were glazed and I was not sure he had heard me even then but after a moment he nodded and said thickly, 'It is well spoken. I agree.'

Cresphontes simply nodded and turned away. He would have fallen had not Xouthos been there to catch his arm and help him to the side of the arena. Dexeus rushed up to support Alectryon and I said, 'Get him into the shade and make him lie down. Then get some water and bathe his face.'

As Dexeus helped his master away I looked round the assembly. I had taken it upon myself to stop the fight, over the heads of the umpires, and I could tell from the murmur of the crowd that some were not best pleased at my intervention. I raised my voice and shouted, 'My friends, Prince Cresphontes and Count Alectryon have given us a wonderful show. Now they have both agreed to call it quits and each will take a prize. We have had a good afternoon's sport and the honours are even.' A Messenian voice shouted 'Not quite!' but I ignored it and went on, 'Now, I will take it upon myself to promise you, on Count Alectryon's behalf, that the bull he has won shall be slaughtered at once to provide a feast for all of us this evening. And I will provide the wine, so that we can drink to the friendship of our two peoples.'

The Messenians led the cheers, which warmed my heart, but the Dorians were not slow to follow. While they were still applauding I left the ring and hurried over to where Alectryon was lying in the shade of the building. Dexeus was bathing his face and Kerkios, whose years at sea had given him plenty of experience as a physician, was kneeling over him, carefully feeling his limbs. He opened his eyes as I came up and said, between swollen lips, 'Well spoken, my prince.'

'How is he, Kerkios?' I asked and the captain looked up and gave me a reassuring smile.

'Not as bad as he looks, praise be to Poseidon. There are no bones broken and when Dexeus gets all the blood washed off I don't think there will be too much damage. But he won't be much to look at for the next few days!'

Alectryon opened one eye again and looked at me. 'Damn!' he muttered thickly.

I put my hand on his shoulder. 'Be quiet. You fought like a god. You don't need to look like one. What can we do for him, Kerkios?'

'Put a cold compress on that eye. Then make him as comfortable as possible and let him rest. He'll do well enough in a little while.'

I looked across to the other side of the porch where Xouthos was kneeling by Cresphontes. No one else seemed to be taking much notice. I said, 'Go and see how Cresphontes is, Kerkios. I don't think they have a physician in the village and he may be in a worse state than Alectryon.'

Kerkios nodded and went over. Dexeus finished washing the blood off Alectryon's face. As Kerkios had suggested, the damage was less than I had feared, though he had a split lip and one eye was almost closed. He had bound up his hair for the fight but it had come loose and I saw that the wisps of hair sticking to his neck and forehead were annoying him and sent Dexeus for a comb. Then I carefully unbound the thick braid, its brightness dulled with dust and oil and dried blood, and gently combed it into some sort of order.

When we had made him comfortable I went over to where Cresphontes lay. Kerkios met me on the way.

'How is he?'

'Not too bad. I think that last fall did him more harm than anything, when he cracked his head on the ground. It's lucky for him you stopped them when you did. He's been sick but he's conscious. He'll be all right.'

I went across and stooped over Cresphontes. He was pale and his eyes were closed. The sharp smell of vomit hung in the air and Xouthos was busy cleaning up. He looked at me and his eyes, instead of being hostile, were sad and frightened. I smiled and said, 'Don't worry. He will be all right. Kerkios says there is nothing seriously wrong.'

Xouthos said, 'I have seen men die like this. My father fell from his horse when I was a child. He lay for a day and a night like this and then he died.'

I was about to reply when Cresphontes opened his eyes and

82

muttered, 'Quiet, little wolf. No one is going to die.' I caught Xouthos's eye and smiled again and then left them to themselves.

Alectryon seemed to be asleep so I left Dexeus to watch over him and went down to the river the wash the sweat and dust off my body. The water was cold and marvellously refreshing. I sluiced myself all over and then sat on a rock and began to scrape the oily dirt from my limbs with a bone strigil. I managed it quite well except for a patch in the middle of my back, which try as I might, I could not reach. A low giggle interrupted my efforts. I looked round and saw the girl who had waited on us the first night. She stood with her hand clapped over her mouth, obviously terrified at having drawn my attention.

It struck me that my contortions must have looked extremely funny, so I laughed and called out to her, 'Well don't stand there giggling. Come and scrape my back for me.'

She hesitated a moment, then hitched up her gown and waded out to me. I handed her the scraper and she took it with her eyes modestly cast down and scraped my back with great care.

I said, 'What's your name?'

'Purwa, my lord.'

'And you are a servant to Prince Cresphontes?'

She raised her eyes questioningly. 'Servant?'

'You work for him?'

'Oh, yes.'

'Who are your parents? Do they live in the village?'

'My father is Lampadon.'

'Lampadon! Then you are – cousin to the Prince!'

"Yes, I suppose so.'

'Then why are you so poorly dressed and treated like a slave?'

She looked at me again. 'I do not understand. I am a woman. I do as a woman must. We must serve our men.'

It was on the tip of my tongue to tell her of the state kept by the ladies of my father's court, but I kept it back. She splashed my back with water and said timidly, 'I have finished. Is there anything else you require?'

I looked at her again and saw that under the lank hair and the coarse dress there was a kind of beauty. Her eyes, when they met mine, were large and soft. Something stirred in me that had been quiescent since the night of the Spring Festival. I had thought that I could never desire a woman again but, after all, I was young and had no other outlet for my feelings. I kissed her before I thought of the implications of the act.

To my surprise she did not resist and her compliance gave an edge to my desire. But at that moment we heard the sound of woman's voices approaching from the village. Purwa pulled away from me and whispered, 'I must not be seen with you. But I will wait for tonight on the bank just here – at moonrise.'

Before I could reply she slipped from my arms and splashed hastily back to the bank where the water pot she had come to fill stood waiting. A moment later three other girls came down the path and stopped, stifling their giggles at the sight of me, naked on my rock. With as much dignity as possible, under the circumstances, I waded down stream to where I had left my clothes, dressed, and returned to the village.

I found Alectryon sitting up and drinking wine mingled with water. I told him where I had been, but did not mention my encounter with Purwa. When I asked after Cresphontes I was told that he too was much recovered. Already preparations were under weigh for the feast and I sent some of the crew to bring up a couple of jars of wine from the ship. The men were ready for another night of drinking and dancing, but it was obvious that neither Alectryon nor Cresphontes were up to it. I was weary too and made no objection when Cresphontes suggested that we should dine quietly on our own in the megaron.

Rugs and sheepskins were spread around the hearth so that we could sprawl at our ease. The servants brought us bread and meat and I opened a flask of my father's best wine. Dexeus filled our cups and went out to join the others, leaving the four of us to ourselves. Cresphontes lifted his cup and looked across the fire at Alectryon.

'Count, you're the best fighter I've met in my life. No one else has ever stood up to me like that. I admired you when we first met and I do so even more now. No hard feelings, I hope?'

Alectryon smiled, 'None at all.'

'Then,' Cresphontes went on, 'let us drink to noble adversaries and good friends. We have been the first, now let us be the second. I'm sure Xouthos will join me. Will you drink, Prince Alkmaion?'

'Most willingly,' I returned and the toast was duly drunk.

When we were toying with the last morsels Cresphontes said, 'May I ask you one question?' When we nodded he went on, 'I am certain that the Prince of Pylos has not made this long voyage – together with his escorting ships – merely to pay a visit of courtesy to us. Is there some purpose in your visit that you have not yet disclosed? Or are you perhaps on your way to some other city with some embassy from the King your father? It must be a matter of some importance that sends the Prince himself voyaging over inhospitable seas.'

I answered, 'Your second guess is the right one. We are indeed on a voyage to another land, and the matter is of importance. We go to the Holy Islands, where I must seek purification from the priestesses of the Great Queen.'

'The Great Queen?' he queried.

'The Supreme Goddess. Surely you too worship Her?'

He shrugged. 'She has Her altars here, but it would go hard with the temper of my people to worship a goddess above all other deities. Our God is Zeus the Thunderer, mighty lord of heaven.'

Alectryon said, 'And ours is Poseidon, master of land and sea. But the Goddess is Mistress of birth and death. She holds all living things in Her hand and it is at his peril that any man slights Her.'

Cresphontes said, 'And these Holy Islands, where are they?'

'Across the sea, beyond the island of Corcyra, is another land whose shore runs south for three day's sail. At its foot is another great island we call Sicania. It is rich in crops and flocks and men of my race have built cities there. The Holy Islands lie a little west from there.'

I saw Cresphontes's amber eyes narrow with interest. 'And when you have visited these islands, do you return to Pylos?'

'If the Gods so will.'

'Empty handed? Or are there settlements of people other than your own on that island so rich in crops and flocks you spoke of?'

I glanced at Alectryon. He said, 'That remains to be seen. I trust we shall not return to Pylos with nothing to show for our exertions.'

My pulse skipped with excitement. I had hardly hoped to find him so ready for such an enterprise. Cresphontes teeth gleamed in the firelight as he said, 'Bravely spoken, Count. Now, what do you say to this? Will you take Xouthos and me with you? Two more swords will not come amiss and you can rely on us to use them with a will. And as for booty, since you provide the ships and the men, we'll be content to take a third of all we win. How about it?'

I looked at Alectryon again. It would be hard to refuse without offence and, to tell the truth, I was beginning to enjoy the company of this strange pair. Also, they would undoubtedly be useful when it came to a fight.

Alectryon nodded slightly and I said, 'Very well, Cresphontes, it is agreed.'

'Not quite,' Alectryon put in. 'Since, as you say, we provide the ship – ships – and the crew, you must be content with one quarter of the booty.'

I thought for a moment Cresphontes was going to argue but he appeared to think better of it and said, 'Very well. It is settled then.' He looked down at Xouthos and pulled his ear. 'What do you say, little wolf? Does it please you?'

Xouthos's grin and his gleaming eyes showed that it pleased him very well.

'When do we sail?' Cresphontes asked.

'Tomorrow,' Alectryon said. 'Already we have delayed longer than we intended. Can you be ready by then?'

'Certainly. By the time you have provisioned your ship we shall be ready.'

Xouthos yawned suddenly and Alectryon laughed and said, 'I think we could all do with an early night.'

When Cresphontes and Xouthos had retired to their sleeping quarters there was an uncomfortable silence. I looked at Alectryon but he was gazing into the embers of the fire.

I said, 'Shall we take our bedding outside?'

He looked up and answered quietly, 'Do, if you prefer it. I'll stay where I am. I've stiffened up, lying here, and to be honest I'm not sure I can raise the energy to move.'

I went over and knelt beside him. 'Are you in pain? Can I do anything?'

His eyes met mine and he shook his head slowly. 'I'll be asleep in a moment.'

His eyelids were already drooping and I guessed he had drunk more wine than usual to dull the aches in his limbs. I laid his cloak over him to keep off the chill that would come later in the night and murmured 'Sleep well, then.' Then I retired to my own couch.

Outside the sounds of revelry slowly died away. Soon it would be moonrise. I thought of Purwa, waiting on the riverbank. My conscience told me I should not leave Alectryon tonight but then, I reassured myself, I should be back long before dawn. There was a knot in my belly that needed to be untied, and Purwa had the means to loosen it.

I waited until there had been no sound from outside for some time and then rose and reached for my clothes. At once Alectryon's voice said drowsily, 'Where are you off to this time?'

I stopped, for a moment angry and embarrassed. Then in spite of myself I laughed. I went over and crouched beside him.

'Don't you ever sleep? You're like the watch dog in the stories – Argus of the hundred eyes.'

'Need to be, with you to look after,' he muttered.

'Well, there's no need to worry,' I said firmly. 'I'm not going exploring tonight – and there's no guard on the door. There just happens to be a rather nice girl waiting for me on the riverbank.'

He lifted his head and gave me one of his long, inscrutable stares. Then he dropped back on his pillow with a grunt. I waited a moment, then got up and started for the door, saying, 'I shan't be long. Go to sleep.'

I was almost out of the room before he said, 'Alkmaion! Be careful.'

Purwa was waiting as she had promised. As before, she accepted my caresses without resistance but she had none of the arts I had learned to expect with Eritha and after the first moment or two I found her passivity unexciting. I satisfied myself quickly and she made no attempt to cling to me when I wished her goodnight.

When I returned to the megaron Alectryon was asleep – or if he was not, he did not speak.

Chapter 6.

Morning came too soon for me, but not apparently for Xouthos who roused us soon after first light. Cresphontes too seemed to have made an astoundingly rapid recovery and immediately set about preparing for the journey. It amazed me to see that one in his position could leave on such an expedition with no more formality than a brief conference with the village elders, which he conducted while we supervised the preparations for sailing.

Alectryon, on the other hand, had woken much the worse for wear. His face was swollen and discoloured and it was clear that movement pained him. He was unusually taciturn all morning, but I put that down to the fact that he was suffering.

Xouthos was like a young hound at the beginning of his first hunt, questing hither and thither, watching everything and getting under the sailors' feet, but always returning after a few minutes to Cresphontes's side. At length he came to a standstill by me and said abruptly, 'What is beyond the island?'

I looked at him. 'You have never been?'

He shook his head. 'We are not seafarers. What is out there?'

'Sea – and then more land.'

'What land?'

'I don't know much about it myself, except what I have heard from men like Kerkios. It is rich land, they say.'

'Are there men there?'

'Yes.'

'Men like us, or the strange creatures the stories speak of?'

'Men like us, I suppose, although most of them speak strange languages. There are one or two cities of Achaeans. One was founded by men from my own city of Pylos, on their return from Troy. We shall call there.'

'But are there monsters and giants, like in the stories?'

I laughed. 'I don't know, Xouthos. There may be, but you had better ask Kerkios when he's not so busy. Although I've never heard him speak of monsters.'

Alectryon came up. 'The ship is ready to sail and we should be on our way. Is Cresphontes ready to leave?'

'I will fetch him.' Xouthos was off again at a run.

Alectryon said casually, 'I hope you enjoyed yourself last night.'

I told him I had, but I was glad to see Cresphontes approaching with most of the village at his heels to put an end to the conversation.

Shortly we were all embarked, and, suitable sacrifices having been performed, the ship slid into the water and the sailors took their places at the oars. I looked back to salute the men on the shore but I noticed that Cresphontes did not turn his head. He seemed fascinated by everything that went on and as soon as we were safely into deep water and Kerkios had set the course he called him over and said, 'Kerkios, I am no seaman, so I hope you will forgive my curiosity and let me ask you a few questions.'

There was no subject Kerkios was more ready to talk about and soon he and Cresphontes were deep in conversation.

The last few days had been eventful enough even for me and for once I was glad to stretch out under the awning on the after-deck and drowsily listen to the rhythmic creak and splash of the oars as the mountains of the Dorians home-land fell behind us and we rounded the coast of Corcyra and headed for the open sea.

Abruptly Cresphontes looked up. 'What about those warships of your escort?'

Alectryon looked across and raised an eyebrow quizzically. 'What warships?'

For a moment Cresphontes stared at him, unable to speak for the conflicting emotions that chased each other across his face. Then he lifted his head and shouted with laughter, and we all joined in

The gods favoured us and we had calm weather for the crossing. Thereafter we sailed south, passing the first night at the Pylian settlement of which I had spoken to Xouthos, where we were received with great hospitality, and on the second camping by the ship. The days of enforced idleness benefited all of us, but particularly Alectryon. Both he and Cresphontes developed rainbow-hued bruises, but with time I saw that movement caused him less pain. I was relieved, too, to see him recover his spirits and return to his usual even-tempered self.

One evening we found ourselves skirting the coast of Sicania. It was clear that we could not reach any Achaean town before dark, so we were watching the shore for a suitable place to beach the ship when we rounded a promontory and came in sight of a deep bay with a shelving beach and above it, on a little hill, a small town. The houses looked well built and the land about them was cultivated and gave promise of good crops. I could see a flock of heavy-coated sheep being driven towards the town, while down by the water's edge a group of men had just beached three or four little fishing boats and were unloading their catch.

I looked at Kerkios. 'That looks a good anchorage. Do you know the place?'

He shook his head. 'It's a Sicel town, I should guess, my lord.'

Cresphontes said, 'They look as if they should have enough to spare for a few hungry travellers.'

'I agree,' I returned. 'Kerkios, let us put in there and ask for their hospitality.'

This being agreed upon the steersman turned the ship's prow towards the shore. I saw one of the fishermen run up the hill towards the town and guessed he was going to inform someone in authority of our arrival. I grinned at Alectryon. 'I hope he's gone to tell them to slaughter one of those fat sheep and start cooking it. I could eat one all to myself!'

He was watching the shore with narrowed eyes. I followed his gaze. The men were standing in a little group, staring towards us, and I noticed that they had short spears in their hands, probably, I thought, used for spearing fish. The messenger, meanwhile, had disappeared among the first houses.

Alectryon said, 'Kerkios, I don't like it. Be ready to put about in a hurry.'

I began to say, 'But surely they wouldn't ...' when I saw the men on the beach raise their spears. Alectryon shouted a warning and sprang for his bow and quiver. Kerkios gave a sharp order and the rowers backed water vigorously as a shower of spears and stones fell around the bow. The lookout tumbled back into the bottom of the ship, struck on the head by a flying rock, but no one else was hurt. Without Alectryon's warning and Kerkios's quick response we should have sailed

91

straight into a rain of missiles.

The crew flung themselves into action to take the ship out of range, while the five of us on the after-deck returned a shower of arrows at our attackers. A few more weapons were thrown, until Dexeus hit the man who appeared to be the leader in the shoulder and the rest scattered behind the shelter of their boats. Meanwhile, a crowd of men had issued from the town, some armed with spears and swords and others with a variety of agricultural implements, and the whole lot swarmed down towards the beach.

When we were out of range Alectryon cupped his hand to his mouth and yelled, 'You monsters! Have you never heard of the laws of hospitality? May the punishment of the gods who protect travellers fall upon you!'

Kerkios said, 'It is useless to strain your voice, Count. These men do not speak our language. Clearly they are so used to pirates in this area that they assume every vessel must have come to attack them.'

'Well,' said Alectryon warmly, 'if they cannot tell the difference between a pirate and a peaceful traveller, and will not wait to find out, they deserve no better.'

'I quite agree,' put in Cresphontes. 'They should be taught a lesson. Besides, it is obviously a town of some wealth. Since they will not spend some of it by way of hospitality I think they should be forced to share it. What do you say?'

We looked at each other and fire glanced from eye to eye. Alectryon opened his mouth to speak, then stopped and turned to me.

I said, 'Very well. We will talk of it and if it seems possible we will undertake it. But not now. Tonight they will be on the watch, knowing we cannot be far away. We will complete our journey to the Holy Islands and on the way back we will attempt to show these barbarians the foolishness of receiving their guests in such a hostile fashion.'

It was agreed and we found a place to camp some distance further along the coast and spent the evening discussing the best method of attack.

The following day we sighted the Holy Islands. They rose steeply from the sea and as we sailed under the coast of the larger one I saw on the high plateau above the cliffs what I took at first to be two huge mounds of earth. As we drew closer I realised that they were in fact vast buildings, whose mighty walls were half hidden by the earth which had been heaped against them, so that they appeared to be a part of the land upon which they stood.

'Is that the dwelling of the ruler?' I asked Kerkios.

He shook his head, his eyes grave. 'No. The people of the islands build no great houses for their rulers or for themselves. Many live in caves in the hills, the rest in rude huts. What you see there are two of the great sanctuaries of the Goddess. There are many others in the islands. No one knows who built them, or how long ago. The men and the rulers who were responsible have vanished from memory. But these people carry on Her worship. They have no other purpose in life than to serve Her.'

We sailed into a deep inlet, where the land rose in steep cliffs on either side and found a safe anchorage. As we beached our ship we were met by a little group of men, simply and poorly dressed by our standards but with an air of grave dignity that impressed us all.

Strangely enough I had given little thought to what awaited me at the end of the voyage. There had been enough distractions to allow me to push it to the back of my mind. Now that it was upon me I was possessed again by a faint, sick fear. Purification had seemed a simple thing at home in Pylos, after the terror of penetrating into the very presence of the Goddess. But now that I was here, among these strangers whose very language was unknown to me, I found myself wondering what painful rites I might have to undergo and how long a period of penance I might be expected to undertake.

Kerkios was known in the island, though he had only been there once or twice, and he had a little knowledge of the language, while one of the men who had come to meet us spoke a few words of ours. When my request was explained to him he did not seem unduly surprised, but conveyed to me that I should be conducted to one of their temples that evening. They led us to one of a cluster of huts that stood at the top of the cliffs and took care courteously of our needs, but I paid little attention to my surroundings. In the evening the men returned and led me to one of the great temples I had seen as we approached. The great curved facade was built of blocks of stone that it must have needed a hundred men to move. My guides placed me in the care of two priests, who led me through a succession of great oval chambers until we reached a central court. At the entrance I checked my steps, possessed by the same fear that had gripped me when I entered the holy place in the Sacred Cave at home. Painted on the doorposts were spiral designs like eyes that seemed to warn me to keep back, but the priests indicated that I should go on and I stepped forward into the echoing, shadowy space. As my eyes adjusted to the dim light I became aware of a sight that made me weak with terror. I stood before a huge female figure, seated on a stool with one hand raised to her breast, so vast that the men and women sheltering under her skirts appeared like toys. After the first shock it took me a moment or two to realise that the figure was carved in stone but I knew nonetheless that I stood once again before the Goddess.

The only light came from a small fire burning in the middle of the floor in front of the image. As I watched, a priestess came forward leading a white kid, while another stood waiting with an ancient flint knife. When the sacrifice had been performed and the appropriate parts burnt in the altar flames the priests and priestesses withdrew and I found myself alone.

What followed was so fearful that my knees buckled under me and I fell to the ground before the Goddess. A voice, speaking from nowhere and seeming to belong to neither man nor woman, boomed around the chamber. It was a few minutes before the sense of the words penetrated my mind and I realised that they were in my own language and were demanding of me the reason for my visit. Falteringly I explained what had happened at the Festival, concealing nothing. Then the voice spoke again.

'Tomorrow morning be ready. Men will come at dawn to conduct you to the place of your purification. Place yourself in their hands, do as they bid you, and the Goddess will be gracious to you.'

Summoning all my courage I asked, 'How long shall I be away? I must tell my friends how long they will have to wait for me.'

The voice answered, 'If your friends are loyal they will wait.

Those who journey into the realms of the Goddess must abide Her time.'

Then the priests returned and led me back to the temple entrance, where my guides were waiting. I reached the hut cast down and full of fear and asked Alectryon to come and walk with me. We found a spot away from habitations, over-looking the sea and watched the moon come up.

He said gently, 'Courage! It is almost over now.
I shook my head. 'No. It is only just beginning.'
'The Goddess intends you no harm. Surely that is clear?'
I looked at him. 'But how long will she keep me, Alectryon? I cannot help remembering that there was no word of my returning to Pylos in the order I received from Her.'

He reached out and put his arm round my shoulders. 'Of course you will return.' Then he added softly, 'I do not believe She will keep you long, but no matter how long it may be you will find me waiting here for you. You can be certain of that, if it is any comfort to you.'

The following day I descended into the realm of the dead.

At the core of my being is the memory, powerful yet confused, of the three days I spent among the rock cut chambers beneath the hillside of the Holy Island. Here the dead lie in tombs leading off vaulted halls whose walls and roof are smooth and curved and painted womb-red. Here, in the innermost, enfolding chamber I fasted and slept while the voice of the Goddess spoke to me in strange dreams. Yet in the heart of this darkness I found kindness. On the third day I was summoned into the presence of an ancient priestess who sat upon a stool before the sacred fire. Her face was as shrivelled as a raisin and her hands were curled into claws but her voice was gentle as she bade me welcome.

'Approach, Prince of the Achaeans. Let me see your face.'
I went forward and knelt before her and she took my face between her hands. Looking deep into my eyes she murmured, 'Yes. You have suffered much. The Goddess understands this.'

Emboldened I asked, 'What further penance does the Mistress demand of me?'

The old eyes glazed and for a moment she rocked to and fro as if in pain. Then her eyes cleared again. 'It is the journey that matters, not the arrival. You have travelled far, and will travel farther. For now the Lady permits you to return to your own land in peace. But She has not done with you yet. She has marked you for Her own and will not be satisfied until you have planted Her altars among people who know her not.'

'When must I do this?' I asked.

'She will show you the time and the manner. You must wait for Her. For now, go in peace, son of Sillos. Your penance is completed.'

The next day we sailed and all morning I lay under the awning as the ship glided along under the big white sail, aware that voices around me were subdued and that every now and then Alectryon cast me an anxious, sorrowful look. At length I fell asleep and dreamed that I was chained to a rock but a god came down in the shape of an eagle and set me free. When I woke we were slipping along the shores of Sicania. I sat up and looked around me. Alectryon sat nearby, staring morosely at the horizon, and Cresphontes and Xouthos were a little way off. Something in their faces told me that there had been an argument while I was asleep. I felt a sudden upsurge of energy.

'Well, what is wrong with all of you? You look as if you had been quarrelling.'

My words took them by surprise. They all turned sharply and the look of guilt on all their faces made me laugh.

Xouthos jumped up and came over to me. 'You see. He is himself again.'

Alectryon, more cautious, said, 'How do you feel? Your sleep seems to have done you good.'

'You all speak as if I had been ill!' I exclaimed. 'I am in perfect health.'

'Perhaps,' he returned, 'but we have been anxious for you nonetheless. It seemed almost that you had left your spirit on the Holy Island and that your body alone travelled with us.'

I smiled at him. 'I understand what you mean. But now, at last, I feel that all my troubles are behind me. In fact, I feel ready for anything.

Is there anything to eat? Now, what are the plans for tonight?' They glanced at each other uneasily and I added, 'Is that what you have been arguing about?'

Cresphontes said, 'The Count thought you would not be fit enough for any fighting.'

'I felt that, under the circumstances, our aim should be to get home as quickly as possible,' Alectryon replied. 'I still think so.'

'May I remind you that we accompanied you on the understanding that there would be an opportunity for booty?' Cresphontes exclaimed. 'If you break that understanding now you break friendship between us for ever!'

Alectryon was about to reply when I laid a hand on his arm and said, 'There is no need for an argument. The bargain stands. None of us are going home empty handed if we can help it.' Alectryon still looked as if he was disposed to disagree, so I added, 'I'm perfectly all right, Alectryon.'

He still hesitated, saying, 'I am responsible to your father for your safety.'

'Nonsense!' I returned crisply. 'No one is responsible for that except myself. I am tired of being watched over like a child. Cresphontes, we attack the town at the first good opportunity. It is agreed.' Then, seeing Alectryon's face, I grinned at him, 'Come on, you know you are as eager as the rest of us for some excitement.'

He looked into my face for a moment, torn between his inclinations and his sense of duty, and then shrugged and said, 'Oh, very well. I am at your orders.'

Though it was only mid afternoon we were near the place and decided to make camp. We found a safe anchorage on the near side of the rocky promontory guarding the bay where the town was situated and when we had disembarked I turned to Kerkios and said, 'I will speak to the men and tell them what we plan.'

He called the men together and I faced them, feeling my heartbeat quicken. This was my first chance to see if I could win men to follow me willingly into battle. 'Men,' I said, 'you have served me well until now and I am sure no prince ever had a better crew. Now I am going to ask you to do something which requires more courage and spirit than your normal duties, and I am sure I am not asking the wrong men. You remember how badly we were treated by the people of that town over the hill and I doubt if there is one among you who didn't say to himself or to his friend "those people should be taught a lesson".' There was a murmur that told me I had struck the right note and I saw eyes beginning to gleam with anticipation. 'Well, we are going to teach them that lesson - and at the same time we are going to relieve them of a little of that wealth they obviously don't know what to do with. And if we are lucky there will be a share for every man in the value of the booty when we get home. What do you say?'

The cheer that went up left no doubt about their feelings. I congratulated them on their spirit and ordered a jar of wine to be opened. While its contents were being passed round and preparations made for a meal we sat down to make our plans.

It was obvious that a straightforward frontal assault on the town was doomed to failure, since the inhabitants outnumbered us by at least ten to one and had shown themselves disposed to defend their property. After some thought I suggested a feigned attack from the inland side, which would, if their former behaviour was anything to go by, draw the entire male population out to repel it. Meanwhile, the ship could slip unobserved into the bay and those on board could grab what booty they could find before the defenders came back. The plan was approved and Cresphontes immediately volunteered to lead the decoy force, taking with him half a dozen good men including Dexeus, whose skill with the bow would prove invaluable.

Alectryon said, 'I see one problem. With the ship round the other side of the headland, and half the town at your heels, how are you going to get back?'

At that moment the lookout whom we had posted in the stern of the ship gave a low call. We ran down to the water's edge to see a small boat heading towards us. It was a fishing boat from the town, by the look of it, and there were four men in it. They were well out in the bay at the moment and as we were drawn up in the shelter of a jutting shoulder of rock they had not yet seen us.

Alectryon said, 'If they spot us and take the news back to the town we might as well not bother with any further plans. Kerkios, get the men into the ship and be ready to put out.'

Kerkios did as he ordered and the men embarked rapidly and silently. From the after-deck we watched the little boat. It was obviously on its way back to the town, cutting slantwise across the bay. It was possible that they might not notice us. Then I saw a man rise to his feet and point and the boat rocked wildly.

'Put off,' Kerkios,' Alectryon said crisply. 'Dexeus, I want the two men rowing disabled as soon as we're within bowshot.'

The rowers in the little boat were already making frantic efforts to round the promontory before we could catch up with them, but the crew of our ship bent to their oars with a will and we rapidly over-hauled them. Kneeling in the bows Dexeus drew his bowstring to his chin and the arrow found its mark in the neck of one of the rowers. He fell backwards out of the boat and the other three immediately gave up the struggle and fell to their knees, raising their hands in supplication. We took them on board and towed the little boat back to our anchorage.

The three men could speak nothing but their own language so it was useless to question them and we simply tied their hands and feet and left them under guard by the ship.

Cresphontes said, 'Well, that solves the problem of getting back after the attack.'

'Maybe,' I said doubtfully. 'It's a very small boat.'

'It will take six or seven men at a pinch. When we have drawn off the men from the town and laid a false trail for them to follow we will come back here, get into the boat and row out to sea. You can pick us up off the end of the promontory.'

'Will six or seven of you be enough?' I asked.

Cresphontes grinned. 'From the noise we shall make the town will think a whole army is upon them, never fear.'

For the next hours we attempted to rest but I do not think any of us slept. Cresphontes roused us in the chill darkness and we prepared for the coming fight, for none of us was so foolish as to think that we should get away without striking a blow, in spite of our planning. I shivered as Dexeus helped me to buckle on my corselet. I had dreamed so often of my first battle, seeing it always as a great triumph, but now I was finding it hard to stop my teeth from chattering. I looked at

Xouthos, sharpening his dagger on a stone a few feet away, and reflected that I had never seen him look happier.

Alectryon came up from the ship, already in full armour. 'I have given orders for the chests containing the weapons to be broken open and the contents distributed.'

I nodded and said, 'Good,' between clenched teeth. He gave me a sharp look and said, 'It might be a good idea to open another jar and give the men a drink to warm them.'

I nodded again and gave the order. After a mouthful or two of wine my teeth stopped chattering. I put on my bronze helmet and Dexeus fastened my greaves and hung my sword over my shoulder. My shield and spear lay ready to hand.

Cresphontes gathered his party together and gave them a few words of encouragement. We wished them all luck and watched them disappear into the darkness under the trees that clothed the side of the ridge.

Our three prisoners were pushed into the bottom of the ship and the crew shoved off and dipped their oars into the dark water. The first faint grey light of dawn was breaking. We reached the end of the promontory and lay close under the cliff, the men backing water gently to keep us from drifting aground, watching the light strengthen and waiting for Cresphontes to attack. He had said, 'You will know my signal when you hear it.'

I glanced at Alectryon. His face was set and calm. He caught my eye and smiled encouragingly. The wait seemed endless and I began to wonder if Cresphontes had let us down.

'He's had plenty of time to reach the outskirts of the town by now,' I whispered to Alectryon. 'What's he playing at?'

'That's what I'm wondering, too,' he answered.

At that moment, clear across the water, came the noise we had first heard in Cresphontes's village. Again and again the sound split the air. Alectryon laughed softly, 'Of course, the trumpet! That ought to rouse the town!'

I said, 'Ready, Kerkios?' and he answered, 'Ready, sir.'

From the town we could hear a confused murmur of sound, then men began to appear beyond the houses, running to and fro apparently without direction: and then, as bees will suddenly leave the hive in a great swarm, they set off along the ridge.

'Now, Kerkios!' I said.

At his order the men bent to their oars and sent the ship scudding across the open water of the bay. Still men were pouring out of the town in the opposite direction, brandishing their weapons.

Suddenly I was aware of the same sensation that had swept over me just before Alectryon had snatched me from the path of the bull. My limbs seemed to lighten and I felt a surge of elation. I knew that he was watching me, waiting to see how I would bear myself, and as the keel grounded on the sand I leapt from the after-deck and ran forward, waving my spear and calling the men to follow me.

As we raced up the slope towards the town I could hear shouts and the screams of women and somebody began to bang some metal object so that its clangour resounded around the valley. The men who had gone after Cresphontes would soon be back now. As we ran between the first houses an arrow sang past my ear and I heard a cry from behind me, but no one came out to oppose our advance. We charged straight up to the main building and as we reached it two men, servants I guessed, were attempting to close the heavy wooden gate across the entrance to the courtyard. One seized up a baulk of wood and swung it at me. I rushed in under his guard and thrust at him with my spear. It went in deep and was almost wrenched out of my hand as I flung him off, but it was not until I saw his body lying there on the way out that I realised I had killed my first man.

Alectryon was at my side now, and together we raced into the main room of the house. Three women, two young and one older, and an elderly man were cowering in a corner. Alectryon drew his sword and said to the men behind him, 'Take the two young ones down to the ship.'

He swung round to the old man and demanded, 'You rule this god-forsaken hole?'

To my surprise the old man stammered an assent in our own language. Alectryon ground out, 'Tell your people that we came in peace the first time but they drove us off with spears and stones. Now see what comes of treating guests in that barbarous manner!'

I tugged his arm. 'We don't have time!'

We set a guard over the old couple while we ransacked the house for valuables. We made a good haul, for the place was obviously prosperous and traded extensively. We found vessels of bronze and items of gold jewellery, curiously worked, besides several bales of woollen cloth of excellent quality. I despatched three of our men to carry the booty back to the ship. They had just left when a voice from outside shouted, 'They're on us!'

We ran out into the open again to see the men who had been lured away pouring back into the streets. Alectryon yelled, 'Keep close to me. We are going to have to fight our way back to the ship.'

The remainder of the crew rallied to his call and we formed a tight group and headed for the sea. Six or seven men sprang at us, but they were armed only with hoes and shovels and we cut them down and went on. Then some more appeared from behind a building and blocked our way. They were well armed and in the centre was a tall, powerfully built man who shouted something at us in his own language. For a second the men around us wavered but I shouted 'Charge!' and we closed with a clash of metal. I found myself face to face with the leader and for a second his eyes glared into mine. I thrust at him with my sword and felt a blow ring off my armour with a force that almost drove the breath from my body. But my thrust had gone home too and I saw him double over with pain. I struck him on the side of the neck and blood splashed over my arm. He went down and I stooped to seize the good bronze sword he carried. This might have been my last action, for the rest of the party had already broken through and were heading for the ship and as I straightened up another enemy leapt forward. I saw his spear drawn back to stab. He could not have missed me had not Alectryon swung round and flung his shield before me. The spear glanced off it and Alectryon made short work of the owner. Then we dashed onwards towards the beach.

Here Kerkios and a handful of men were fighting off another group of attackers, while the rest were on board and ready to shove off. Caught between our two forces the enemy broke and fled and we flung ourselves over the side with the last of the crew. As the ship cleared the shore missiles began to rain about us but Alectryon and I seized our bows and poured arrows into the crowd until the straining oarsmen took us out of range.

Alectryon turned to me. 'Are you all right?'

'Yes,' I said, panting. 'Thanks to you, as usual. And you?'

'A scratch here and there. No harm done.'

I looked round. 'I wonder where Cresphontes and his men are.'

We rowed until we came to the point off the promontory where we had arranged to pick up the raiding party and waited, the tired men resting on their oars. For a moment I was afraid that something had gone wrong, but then the boat put out from the shelter of some rocks and made towards us. It was very low in the water and as it came closer I saw that there were eight people in it instead of seven.

'They've got a woman with them,' Alectryon said. 'I wonder where she came from.'

'Someone is wounded,' Kerkios said, his sharp, seaman's eyes on the boat. 'See. He is leaning on Cresphontes's shoulder in the stern.'

'It's Xouthos!' I said.

The boat came alongside and we hastened to help our friends aboard. Xouthos was only half conscious, the haft of an arrow protruding from his shoulder. We laid him on a fleece on the after deck and knelt around him.

'How did it happen?' I asked.

'The arrow was meant for me,' Cresphontes replied briefly. 'He threw himself in front of me.'

'I killed the man who shot it,' Dexeus added grimly. Alectryon looked across and grasped his wrist briefly in greeting.

Cresphontes said, 'Kerkios, can you get the arrow out?'

Kerkios had been examining the wound. 'I think so. It will be a painful business. But we should be wise to put a little more distance between ourselves and the town before we attend to such matters.'

The ship got under weigh again and soon the little town on its hill slipped out of sight. Kerkios staunched the blood from Xouthos's wound as best he could and the rest of us took stock of our situation. One man had been lost, killed, I learned, by the arrow that had so narrowly missed me. Apart from that no one had been seriously hurt, though most of us had wounds of some sort. On the other hand, it seemed no one had come away empty handed. Apart from the booty that we had removed from the chief's house there were four fat ewes and the captives: the three men we had taken prisoner the night before, the two servant girls and the woman Cresphontes had brought with him. Altogether the raid had been a success. I wondered why I felt a heavy sense of disappointment. It had been just what I had expected: but not what I had dreamed of. However, one thing was settled, and my heart lifted at the thought. My courage had not failed me and I could lead men into battle if the need arose. I thought, 'Antilochos won't be able to taunt me with that any more!'

As the ship drove along the coast, taking us steadily further out of range of the people in the town, we stripped off our armour and tended each other's wounds. As he cleaned a cut from a flying stone on Dexeus's forehead Alectryon asked, 'Who is the woman, Cresphontes?'

Cresphontes, who was leaning over Xouthos, looked up and grinned briefly. 'The chief's daughter, I fancy.'

'What? How did you come across her?'

'It seemed to me that once the people in the town discovered that we were not attacking but running away they wouldn't follow us far unless we had something that was important to them. So, when we got to the town we crept right up to the chief's house. It was simple, no guard, no watchdog, nothing to give the alarm at all. It wasn't difficult to figure out where the women's quarters were. Xouthos and I climbed up on the roof and made a hole big enough to get through - it was only made of branches with clay smeared over the top. I let myself down and found myself in the girl's room. She was still fast asleep. I guessed who she must be, seeing as she had a room of her own. She woke up a few seconds later, so I gave her a quick tap on the head to keep her quiet and pushed her up to Xouthos on the roof. Then we all crept out of town as quickly as we could, carrying the girl. When we got to the first bit of cover I told Xouthos to blow his trumpet. That woke up the town all right. The girl had come round by this time so I took my hand off her mouth and let her scream a couple of times, which brought them all running. I imagine they thought we were the tail end of a much larger force. It would have worked out perfectly except for two youngsters who were very quick off the mark and managed to cut us off somehow.

They suddenly appeared on a rock above us. I didn't even know they were there until Xouthos threw himself in front of me.'

When we had gone a safe distance we put into the land again and carried Xouthos ashore. He had been very quiet ever since we took him aboard and I though he was unconscious until I saw his face twist with pain as we moved him. Kerkios ordered his men to get a fire going and then came and knelt by him, his knife in his hand. Cresphontes lifted the boy gently and took his head on his knees, then drew his dagger and put the hilt of it between his teeth.

I had never seen an arrow removed before. I saw Xouthos shuddering with pain, but Cresphontes held him tightly and he did not struggle and the only sound he made was the hiss of hard-drawn breath. By the time Kerkios had finished my own body was clammy with sweat. When Kerkios had cleaned the wound Cresphontes asked, 'Is it finished?'

Kerkios shook his head. 'It must be cauterised. Nothing else will stop the bleeding.'

He turned to the fire, which the men had blown to a fierce heat, and drew out a knife, the blade glowing dully. I caught my breath and gripped my hands tightly together between my knees, looking at Xouthos. He raised his hand feebly towards Cresphontes and I thought the gesture was an appeal for mercy, but Cresphontes clearly understood him better. He nodded and took the knife from Kerkios's hand.

Xouthos made no sound as the hot metal seared his flesh, but his body arched in Cresphontes's grip as if it would thrust itself into the ground. After that I was sure he had fainted but when Kerkios had finished bandaging the wound with a poultice of herbs from a leather pouch at his belt he opened his eyes and whispered, 'Thank you.'

Kerkios said, 'I'm sorry I had to hurt you so much, lad. But you're lucky to be alive at all. A little further down and that arrow would have been in your heart.'

Xouthos smiled. 'Then I should have died for Cresphontes. What better death could I have?'

Cresphontes stooped over him and whispered something and the boy's eyes flickered and closed. I looked at Alectryon and we rose and left them together.

There was obviously no prospect of continuing our journey that day. Everyone was exhausted and Xouthos could not be moved. For the first time I looked at the captives, huddled miserably by the ship. The two servant girls were snivelling but the chief's daughter sat erect and silent, staring before her with an expression of despair that touched me more than the others' tears. I sent Dexeus to them with bread and wine, but they ignored it.

Cresphontes sat with Xouthos cradled in his lap for most of the day. Towards evening the boy grew feverish and began to moan and stir restlessly. Cresphontes bathed his face and gave him sips of water and turned a face of blank hostility to anyone who offered help, so we left them alone.

I ended the day feeling heavy and dispirited. The great event was over and the glory I had imagined was not there. The sight of the miserable captives and the sound of Xouthos's moans depressed me and when bedtime came I found I could not sleep. I tossed about on the hard ground until Alectryon said, 'Can't you sleep either?'

I shook my head. He rose and threw his cloak across one shoulder.

'Let's walk a little.'

I scrambled to my feet and followed him down to the edge of the water. The night was warm and still, the waves breaking with scarcely a sigh around our ankles. I waded out a little further and splashed my face and shoulders with cold water. The faint night breeze from the hills felt cool on my naked body. I had not bothered to bring my cloak.

He said, 'You did well today. You can be sure of yourself now.'

I glanced at him. 'You knew I wasn't sure?'

'I guessed. It's the same for everyone. How can a man be sure until he proves himself?'

I kicked a stone into the water. 'But what was the point, Alectryon? We lost a man's life today, and Xouthos has suffered horribly. We brought misery to the people in that town and now they will be even less likely to receive strangers kindly. Was it worth it for a few trinkets we don't even need?'

It was a moment before he answered. 'We are warriors. That is

106

our purpose. Some men are born to till the land or to be priests or craftsmen. Our job is to defend our people.'

'To defend them, yes!' I said. 'But those men were no danger to us.'

He said quietly, 'True. But you answered the question yourself just now. We need to be sure that we can fight if we have to. You have learned lessons today that may serve you well in the future.'

I looked out to sea. 'I hope I never need them.'

'So do I,' he answered. 'But try to put all this out of your mind now. When you have rested you will feel better about everything.'

We strolled along the beach towards a low headland crowned with a small group of pines. We walked in silence, but we no longer needed speech to feel at ease together. When we reached the hilltop Alectryon spread his cloak on the soft mat of pine needles beneath the trees. There was no moon but the summer sky was hung with stars and the breeze was spiced with the resinous scent of the trees. I stood looking out over the ocean, trying to shut my mind to the images that the day had imprinted on it.

He spoke from close behind me. 'I keep thinking it could be you, lying down there like Xouthos. What we did today was stupid. I should never have permitted it.'

I looked at him. 'It was my fault. And it could have been you - or worse, one of us could be dead.'

The breeze had blown a lock of hair across my face. He put up his hand and pushed it back over my shoulder, and suddenly I knew that we had come to a defining moment. If I made a mistake now things would change forever between us. He would never abandon me, I knew that, but something in him would die, a flame that could never be re-kindled.

I found myself staring at the sand between his feet. I forced myself to look up and meet his eyes and felt his hand slide round the back of my neck. I leaned towards him and his lips brushed mine in a touch as subtle and as brief as a whispered question. My searching mouth left him in no doubt about my answer.

At the end of that first, long kiss he held me close and groaned softly into my ear,

"Oh, my dear, I've waited so long for this! I had almost convinced myself that it would never happen."

"I'm sorry," I whispered in return. "That day at the farm, you took me by surprise. Since then I've never known how to show you how I felt."

"If only I'd known," he murmured, his lips against my neck. "If anything had happened to you today..."

"But it didn't. We're both safe, and we have the rest of our lives in front of us. Let's not waste any more time.'

He kissed me again and then drew me down onto his outspread cloak and folded me into his arms. For the first time in my experience passion and tenderness went hand in hand. He was a skilful lover, though it was not until sometime later that I asked him where he learned the art. The past was irrelevant and the future hardly more real, only the present mattered, poised upon the needle point of desire.

Our lovemaking was not prolonged that first time. We were both too tired. When it was over he wrapped his cloak about both of us and drew me against his shoulder. Drowsily I asked, as I suppose all new lovers do, 'How long? When did you first...?

He hugged me closer. 'Longer than you would ever imagine. Since you were twelve years old.'

I drew back to look at him. 'So long? But you never gave any hint - until the day we went hunting.'

'I never intended to,' he replied. 'I daresay if I had spoken at the start you would have done whatever I asked. But I swore to myself I would say nothing until you were old enough to make your own decisions. And then, well, it never seemed the right time. I didn't want you to come to me out of gratitude, or because you were afraid.'

'And I had almost decided it wasn't what you wanted after all.'

He groaned and gave a wry smile. 'I know. I was beginning to think I had made a terrible mistake.'

'No,' I said softly, settling once more against his shoulder. 'I was the one who almost did that.'

'Sleep, my prince,' he murmured. 'It is almost dawn.'

I mumbled into his neck, 'You can't go on calling me prince. Not after what we've just done.'

108

I felt him laugh softly. 'Oh yes, I can. More than ever now, you are my prince, the ruler of my heart.'

'I'll remember that,' I murmured drowsily, 'next time I want to do something you disapprove of.'

He said nothing but tightened his arms around me, and in a moment more I was asleep.

When we walked back to the ship, our shadows long in the first rays of the sun, we found Xouthos sleeping quietly. Cresphontes was still sitting by him, his head hanging in exhaustion. As we approached he looked up and a shadow of his familiar ironic grin crossed his haggard face.

'So, you finally came to your senses! About time, too!'

Chapter 7.

All that long, golden day we coasted northwards under oars. The sailors pulled with a will, content I suppose with the thought of the extra reward they had won themselves: but it seemed to me that my own happiness had infected the whole ship. Certainly I was incapable of concealing it. Now I could look back on yesterday's raid and count it a triumph and it seemed that my ordeals were over and I was returning home in glory.

Xouthos lay quiet under the awning, making no complaint although he must have been in pain. The fever had left him and Kerkios had brewed a foul smelling infusion of herbs for him to drink that seemed to have dulled his senses. Cresphontes, convinced at last that the boy was going to live, slept most of the day.

As we made camp at nightfall I saw Kerkios surveying the sky with narrowed eyes. A small number of clouds had drifted up from the west.

'What's the matter, Kerkios?'

'Nothing, maybe, sir. But I think we may have a storm tomorrow.'

'A bad one?'

'Probably not, but it may be enough to keep us ashore.'

'I hope not,' I said. I was eager now to be home.

After supper Cresphontes remarked, 'Forgive me for raising the matter, but I think it's time we divided the spoils among us.'

'Certainly,' I responded. 'How shall we go about it?'

'Well,' he said, 'since a third is to come to me and Xouthos …'

Alectryon, who had seemed to be dreaming of something else, looked up quickly and said, 'A quarter. That was the agreement.'

'A quarter then,' said Cresphontes grinning, quite undisturbed. 'On one condition. The woman I took from the chief's house is mine by right. She is not part of the deal.'

The girl had sat silent all day in the bottom of the boat and met the casual insolence of the sailors with stubborn pride. I thought of the timid, downcast eyes of Purwa and reflected that this girl would find it hard to bend herself to the Dorian idea of a woman's life. I felt sorry for her and was on the point of protesting but Alectryon had already said, 'Naturally, that goes without saying. She is yours.'

When the booty had been divided and we had each presented a suitable gift to Kerkios and Dexeus for their part in the enterprise, we strolled down to the ship to examine the captives. Seeing us approach the servant girls clung to each other and began to weep, but the other merely lifted her head and gazed at us with a look that was at once defiance and acceptance of her fate. Cresphontes took her by the wrist and pulled her to her feet, saying with a cruel grin, 'You are mine, so you might as well come to understand it now.'

The words, of course, meant nothing to her but the gesture and the look in Cresphontes's eyes must have been unmistakable. She bent her head and her hair fell about her face.

Cresphontes was about to lead her away when I said abruptly, 'Cresphontes! Let me buy the woman from you. I'll give you more than her value.'

He checked and looked back at me, surprised. I was aware, also, of Alectryon's eyes on my face. Cresphontes came back a pace or two.

'You surprise me, prince. I thought your desires were elsewhere.'

'It's not a question of desire,' I returned stiffly. 'She appeals to me. Her bearing would fit her to attend upon me at my father's palace.'

He laughed and made a coarse joke, then looked at the girl and considered. Finally he said, 'What will you give for her?'

I thought of the contents of my treasure chest and made him an offer.

He grinned, 'It's a generous price, but it won't meet my needs tonight. I'll tell you what. I'm not so particular about this girl. She looks a sullen bitch to me. Give me one of the others in her place – the little plump one who is crying. I'll soon cheer her up! And then throw in those other things you mentioned and it's a deal.'

I bargained over the additional articles but finally let him have more than the woman was worth. He shoved her over to me so that she fell at my feet and seized the other girl. Her howls faded into the forest behind the beach. I stooped and took the chief's daughter by the arm to raise her and she looked up at me with wide, hopeless eyes. I looked at Alectryon.

'I wish I could speak to her.'

'Are words necessary?' he answered shortly.

I lead the girl back to her companion and sat her down. The food we had sent them from our evening meal stood nearby, untouched. I put a piece of bread into her hands and nodded encouragingly.

'Eat.'

Slowly, without taking her eyes off me, she raised it to her mouth. I pointed to my own chest and said, 'Alkmaion.'

She gazed at me. I pointed to her and, after I had repeated the two gestures and my own name once or twice she whispered, 'Andria.'

'Good,' I said. 'Now don't be afraid, Andria. No one is going to hurt you.'

She seemed to understand my tone, if not the words, and some of the fear went out of her eyes. I rose and rejoined Alectryon, who had moved away up the beach.

'I just wanted to reassure her,' I said curtly, and walked on past him.

He came after me and caught my arm. 'I'm sorry.'

I met his eyes and found myself smiling. My anger had never been more than pretence. We walked on along the beach together. He said, 'You gave Cresphontes too much for her.'

'I know.'

'Why do you want her so much?'

'I couldn't bear to think of her in Cresphontes's hands. At home she will be treated more in the manner she has been accustomed to.'

He smiled. 'Lucky girl! Trust you to be more concerned about the happiness of a slave then her value. What will you do with her?'

'She can attend on me.'

'Mukala will be jealous.'

I shrugged and sat down in the shelter of a rock, looking up at him. 'So what? Let them fight it out between them. It doesn't concern me at the moment.'

We woke next morning to an overcast sky and a brisk wind from the south west. Kerkios was doubtful about putting to sea but I persuaded him that it would be foolish not to make use of the wind to help us on our way. So we launched the ship and for a while she sped along under the straining sail, the keel slicing through the water. The cool breeze was refreshing after days of heat and voices rang cheerily. Even the captives looked a little more reconciled. In fact, the girl whom Cresphontes had taken the night before giggled every time he looked in her direction, until her one-time mistress spoke sharply to her.

The sky, instead of brightening, grew darker and the wind freshened. The ship began to pitch and Xouthos let out a little moan and went very pale. Cresphontes propped him across his knees to steady him against the movement of the ship and I noticed that he, too, had changed colour.

Then the steersman called to Kerkios, 'The wind's veered round. We're being blown out to sea.'

Kerkios nodded briefly and shouted to the sailors to lower the sail. They leapt to his command, battling with the canvas as if with a living creature, and as they did so the wind freshened still further.

'Get to your oars,' Kerkios shouted. 'We must try to make the shore.'

I got up and braced myself against the wind. We were further from the coast than I had realised and the wind was blowing directly from it. There were white crests on the waves now. Alectryon rose also and I shouted, 'Do you think we shall reach it?'

He shrugged, pushing back the hair from his face. 'I can't tell. Kerkios knows what he's doing.'

The crew took their oars and strained against the force of the wind. The waves began to break white over the figurehead in the prow and flying spray whipped our faces. Then a sudden squall struck us and the ship yawed and began to roll broadside on to the waves. Kerkios shouted to his men. I saw that the helmsman was struggling with the great steering oar and leapt to help him. Somehow we got the ship round into the wind again. Kerkios was down among the crew, shouting above the noise of the storm, giving them the stroke. Alectryon called to Dexeus and they jumped down to help pull an oar apiece, but after a few minutes of such effort it was apparent that we were making no headway.

Kerkios came back onto the deck and shouted, 'It's no use! There's only one thing we can do and that's run before the wind.'

He gave orders and we let the ship fall off until she was broadside on again and then, with a struggle, brought her round with her stern to the wind. At once we seemed to rush forward as though hurled from the hand of a god. Each wave lifted us and swept us onwards into the wild grey waste of the open sea. Alectryon and Dexeus struggled back on deck and we huddled together, clutching our cloaks around us and gripping on to anything that gave a firm hold.

'What are our chances, Kerkios?' Alectryon asked.

The captain was watching the scudding clouds above us. 'Who can say? We are in the hands of Poseidon now and we must pray that he will save us. But if he lets us live we may be home sooner than you expect, Prince Alkmaion.'

'Home?'

'The wind is now almost due north-west. South-east of here, if I am right, lies the coast of your own country.'

'But that is wonderful!'

He gave a small, ironic smile. 'Perhaps. But there is a great distance of wild and hostile sea between us yet, with who knows what rocks or craggy islands. And if the wind is more northerly than I think we may be blown past the south cape and on towards Crete.'

'Then let us invoke the Lord Poseidon,' I said, 'and beg his favour.'

This we did, and I prayed, 'Father Poseidon, great ancestor of my family, I have already promised you the sacrifice of a black bull when we reach the long beaches of sandy Pylos again. I beg of you, do not let the great line of Neleus, your son, perish but bring me home safely with my friends. And I will offer a still richer sacrifice to show my gratitude.'

Then we sang a hymn and settled down with as much cheerfulness as we could muster to endure the violence of the storm. During the struggle to reach land and the offering of the prayers I had been too occupied to notice our Dorian companions. Now I saw to my surprise that Xouthos's face was streaked with tears. I remembered his earlier courage and thought it strange that he should cry now, until I realised that he was weeping with sheer terror. Cresphontes was in little better case, his face strained and white. As I watched he clapped his hand to his mouth and I was just in time to catch Xouthos out of his arms before he dived for the side of the ship.

I propped Xouthos against me and held him tightly, trying to cushion his shoulder, and said in his ear, 'Don't be afraid. Poseidon is the forefather of my family and has ever favoured us. We shall survive.'

He shook his head and cried wildly, 'Nothing can live in this!'

Kerkios heard him and gave a short, grim laugh. 'Come, there's worse than this, you know. I've lived through far greater storms and come safe home to tell the tale.'

'And I,' shouted Alectryon, who had once, to my great envy, travelled as far as Egypt. 'This is nothing to the one that drove us onto the coast of Crete that time.'

In this way we tried to reassure ourselves, and particularly our two friends, but they were not to be comforted. Cresphontes hung over the side, moaning as loudly as the wind, and Alectryon had to take a firm hold of his belt to prevent him from falling overboard, while Xouthos clung to me, shivering with terror. And so we drove across the wind-whipped sea all day and into the night.

At nightfall we shared what cold provisions we had and I gave orders for one of the remaining jars of wine to be broached. I also had the prisoners untied so that they could eat, and so that if some disaster struck us during the night they might have at least a chance of survival.

Cresphontes was laying on the deck now, his eyes closed. When we tried to cheer him his only comment was that he wished the ship would sink quickly and bring an end to his misery. Night closed round us and still we fled before the wind. Each wave flung the stern of the ship up into the turbulent darkness until it seemed we must drive prow first into the depths, and then let us fall sickeningly back while the lookout in the bows hung above us. We were silent now, watching the dark sea ahead for rocks or the cliffs of some unknown island. Alectryon moved over to me and took Xouthos from my numbed arms and the three of us huddled close to each other.

Then, sometime in the middle of the night, the wind abated as suddenly as it had arisen. For a while no one spoke, for fear that it might be only a temporary lull. Then the first stars appeared through a rift in the clouds and Kerkios said, 'The storm is over.'

Everyone stirred and breathed a prayer of relief, but he added warningly, 'The sea is still running. We are not safe yet.'

Then he called to the lookout to keep a closer watch, now that the star-light enabled us to see a little further ahead, and told the men to be ready to take the oars. But Poseidon was not unmindful of my promised sacrifice and all night the ship sped onwards without harm.

At dawn the sky was clear and delicate as the petal of a flower and the air was still. When the sun rose the sea stretched around us, brilliant blue and sparkling with crests of white foam. For a few minutes our view was bounded by mist and then, as it cleared, the lookout gave a shout.

'Land!'

Kerkios leapt to his feet. I disentangled myself from Alectryon and Xouthos and jumped up also, stiff from bracing myself against the movement of the ship. Ahead of us a long, mountainous coast stretched from north to south. I stared, afraid to voice my hopes, until Kerkios said, 'Well, Prince Alkmaion, don't you recognise the mountains of your own country?'

I stared a moment longer and then whispered, 'Truly, the Lord Poseidon has taken us in his hand and brought us home.'

Like an echo the grateful prayers of the whole crew rose into the still air. Then the sailors took their oars and began to row for the distant land as if they had spent the night in refreshing sleep rather than crouched on their thwarts amid the flying spray. The sun's warmth began to make itself felt and we spread ourselves gratefully before it. Soon everything on board was steaming. Alectryon laid Xouthos down and turned to Cresphontes, who had fallen into an exhausted sleep. He shook him gently, saying, 'Wake up, Cresphontes. The storm is over and the coast of Messenia is before us. We shall soon be ashore.'

He woke and staggered to his feet, grey-faced, to stare out across the sea. Then he looked at me and said, with a faint echo of his usual grin, 'Pylos?'

'Yes,' I said. 'You and Xouthos must be our guests for a day or two, since the God has brought us to my home first. Then we will sail on and see you safely back to your own village.'

He nodded slowly. 'Your guests? Yes, that is good.' And again he smiled to himself.

There were crowds on the beach already when we reached the shore. Someone with sharp eyes must have seen whose ship it was approaching. I stood on the after deck and pointed out places of interest to Cresphontes and Xouthos as we sailed in. We had tidied ourselves us as best we could and Alectryon had combed my tangled hair into some sort of order and clasped around my neck a golden necklace I had taken from the house of the chief. I was determined that, weary and salt splashed as we were, it should be obvious at once that we were returning in triumph.

As the ship grounded men leapt forward from the crowd to pull her up the beach. I could see people pointing curiously at Cresphontes and Xouthos and at the captives. I was the first to disembark, amid the salutations of the crowd, and knelt to lay my hand on the soil of my own land with a prayer of gratitude to the Mistress and to Poseidon. Then I turned to Cresphontes, who had followed me ashore, raising my voice so that those around me could hear and know that he came as my guest.

'Welcome, Prince Cresphontes, to the land of Messenia. As heir to the throne of the Neleids, I bid you welcome to my father's fair city of Pylos.'

As he thanked me the crowd parted and Damocles, the Governor of the Province, strode towards us. His greetings were scarcely delivered before a horse came at the canter into the crowd and Perimedes threw himself from its back and ran up to embrace me, crying, 'Welcome home, Alkmaion! We have been watching for you, but we hardly expected you home today. How have you managed it? There was a terrible storm here last night, and yet …'

I cut him short, laughing. 'The whole story later, Perimedes. Does my father know I am back?'

'Yes. I was with him when the message came. He will be waiting for you.'

'Good. Then ride back to him quickly, bear my greetings and tell him that I bring two guests with me. Hurry, we shall be hard on your heels!'

Perimedes leapt to his horse again and rode off. I turned to Kerkios and bade him see that the chests and the spoils from the raid were sent up to the palace and that he should then let his men go to their homes, adding that if they came to the palace next day I would see that they received the rewards I had promised. I also sent for a litter to carry Xouthos, who was still too weak to stand. Chariots were ready for the rest of us and we mounted into them and set off across the fertile plain towards the town.

In the courtyard of the palace the whole household was assembled. My father stood under the porch of the megaron with my uncles around him. To one side I could see Karpathia with the other ladies of the palace, but there was no time to look at her yet. I went up to my father and knelt before him. He raised me to my feet and kissed me and then held me by the shoulders and looked into my eyes. For once I was certain that he was pleased with me.

'So, you are back safely. The Great Goddess and the Lord Poseidon have answered my prayers. And you do not come empty handed, or alone.'

'Neither,' I agreed, smiling. 'Father, may I present Cresphontes, the son of Aristomachos and Prince of the Dorians?'

An audible gasp went up from those standing nearby. My Uncle Paion stifled an exclamation and I saw my other uncles, Echelaon and the younger Peisistratos exchange glances. My father's eyes widened and then his face became the inscrutable mask I knew so well. The brightness went out of the day.

However, my father greeted Cresphontes courteously and immediately gave orders for a bed to be prepared for Xouthos and for his own physician to attend him. Meanwhile, I greeted my uncles with varying degrees of affection and embraced Melanthos and my other cousins. There was no sign of Antilochos, I noticed.

Finally I was free to greet Karpathia. I was saddened to see how the shadows that had been lifted from my spirit seemed still to hang over her. She was pale and thin and scarcely raised her eyes to mine. I took her hand and kissed her cheek, saying, 'You see, my dear sister, the Goddess is no longer angry. Her commands are accomplished and She has sent me home with honour.'

She answered in a flat little voice, 'I thank Her for it. Welcome home, Alkmaion.'

Cresphontes, meanwhile, was gazing about him wide-eyed, though I noticed that whenever he saw anyone watching him he assumed a casual air, as if such wonders as the palace with its colonnaded courtyard and frescoed walls were nothing strange to him. My father gave him into Melanthos's charge, with instructions to see that he had everything he needed, and when he had gone bade us follow him into the megaron.

When he was seated and my uncles had ranged themselves around him he said, 'Alkmaion, have you done wisely in bringing these Dorians here?'

I answered, 'I think so, sir, although I will admit it was not originally my intention.' I looked around the room and determined to give a good account of myself. 'My voyage, as you know, took me to within a few hours sail of the land of the Dorians. So, remembering the report which Kerkios brought back from his last voyage, I decided to visit them myself and find out if there was any reason for anxiety.' I hesitated a moment, wondering whether to embark on an account of my expedition to the Forbidden Valley, and then decided to keep it for my father's ears alone. 'Prince Cresphontes received us courteously and entertained us for two days with games and feasting. Then, learning the purpose of our voyage, he asked me to permit him and his young friend Xouthos to accompany us. It seemed to me good that there should be friendship between us, so I agreed. They proved noble companions and readily assisted us in the attack which won the spoils you have seen being brought up from the ship. It was in that fight that Xouthos was wounded. Even then, it was not my intention to bring them here but to leave them at their own village as we returned. However, yesterday we were caught by the storm, which I believe you also suffered, and by the mercy of Poseidon were blown to within sight of the city. It is thus that we returned with our companions still aboard.' I had kept my eyes away from my father until now, but now I turned to him and his look

119

emboldened me. 'It still seems to me good that we should win their friendship and I therefore beg your majesty to give them hospitality.'

I ended and there was a silence. Then Melanthos's father, Andropompous spoke.

'It seems to me that Alkmaion speaks wisely. This may lead to an alliance with the Dorians that could one day be useful. I think he is to be congratulated.'

I think my father was waiting for someone else to speak before he showed his feelings, for now he smiled and said, 'I think you are right, Andropompous. Let us then endeavour to make Prince Cresphontes and his friend as welcome as possible. Meanwhile, Alkmaion, and you Count Alectryon, accept our thanks for your efforts. And now, since I can see that a day and a night in such weather have left their marks upon you, you have my leave to retire. Wait upon me in my private apartments, both of you, when you have rested. I look forward to hearing an account of all your adventures.'

In my own apartments I found Mukala, my old nurse, torn between delight at my return and tight-lipped resentment of Andria, who sat in a corner of the room, her head drooping with weariness. It took me some minutes of teasing and cajoling to persuade the old woman that this girl presented no threat to her rule over my domestic affairs. I made her send for milk and honey cakes and persuaded Andria to eat, then said, 'When she has eaten you are to show her where to bathe and let her rest. See to it that she has a comfortable bed in the women's quarters and whatever else she needs. I want her to be happy here – and if she is not I shall blame you. Do you understand me?'

She glowered at me under her sparse grey eyebrows. 'I understand, son of the King.'

I gave her a hug and said, 'No, you don't. It's not what you think at all. I just don't want a miserable, sickly woman to attend on me. So you look after her. Promise me?'

She promised, unwillingly, and I let her lead me to my bath and make a fuss of me as she had done since I was a baby. I wallowed in the luxury of hot water and perfumed oil for some time, wolfed the various delicacies Mukala put before me and then dressed and went down to find my father and give a full account of my travels.

That night the megaron was thronged, with every member of the Royal kin and the Companions present. My father had clearly given orders that my return was to be celebrated in proper style and the carcass of a young ox turned slowly on the spit over the great central hearth.

When I entered the hall the first person to greet me was Antilochos, who came up and embraced me smoothly, saying, 'My dear Alkmaion, welcome home. Forgive me for not being here when you arrived. I was up at my father's estate and only heard the news an hour or so ago. I hear your voyage was a great success. My warmest congratulations.'

Melanthos was standing nearby and I saw him frown but there was no time to ask why as others crowded round to greet me. My father entered, bringing Cresphontes with him, and I saw the Dorian's eyes widen at the sight of the Great Hall with its frescoed walls and painted plaster floor. They stretched still further at the tables decorated with precious metals and the plates and cups and mixing bowls of gold and bronze. Indeed, he was so busy devouring these lovely objects with his eyes that the tender slices of meat which the servants laid on his plate and the other tasty morsels he was offered went almost untouched for some time.

When the meal was over I asked my father's leave to send for those things I had brought back from the voyage. This granted, I had the chests brought into the hall and presented to my father and uncles the gifts that had been entrusted to me by Persepolis of Ithaca. Then I displayed the fine bearskin I had won from Cresphontes, together with my share of the spoils from our attack on the Sicel town. All these were duly admired and no one was warmer in his praise than Antilochos, but his eyes burned all the while with envy. My Uncle Paion concealed his feelings better and once or twice I saw him cast warning looks at his son and gained the impression that they were not on the best of terms.

When the feasting was over and my father had retired and everyone was leaving, I found Alectryon at my shoulder. We had had little time to speak to each other since our arrival, though we had exchanged looks across the hall. Now, to my surprise, he knelt to me formally and kissed my hand.

'Goodnight, prince.'

'Where are you going?' I asked, puzzled.

'Home.'

'Then I will come with you.'

He rose and shook his head. 'Better not.'

'Then stay with me here.'

Again he shook his head. 'There are too many jealous looks and sly whispers around the court. I don't want to add to them.'

'But everyone knows – or guesses.'

'Perhaps. But I've no wish to flaunt it in their faces and perhaps give your enemies arrows with which to attack you. Besides,' his serious expression softened into a smile, 'we both need a good night's sleep. I'll wait on you in the morning.' Seeing my downcast looks he added, 'Be patient. We shall soon be at sea again and able to follow our own inclinations.'

'But for how long?' my heavy heart enquired. However, I said nothing further and wished him goodnight with as good grace as I could muster.

I had assumed that we would spend only a day or two in Pylos before resuming our journey north but the surgeons insisted that Xouthos needed a longer period of rest for his wound to heal. In addition to this, my father had obviously decided not to be outdone in hospitality and had ordered a programme of hunts and visits for Cresphontes, to culminate on the seventh day in games which would involve athletes from all over the country. There would also be a mock naval battle between our ships in the bay. I think he wanted to impress on our visitor not only the wealth and culture of our society, but its military might as well.

My first action was to visit the sanctuary of the Mistress and make a thank offering for my safe return and then to fulfil the promise I had made to Poseidon. All the notables of the town assembled at the shrine of the God to see his priest sacrifice a black bull and a white ram, with offerings of oil perfumed with spices, on my behalf.

After this I was free to join Alectryon in showing Cresphontes around the town. We wandered past the magnificent houses of the

Companions, visited the workshops of the weavers and dyers and unguent boilers, the potters and the metal workers, and then drove out through the richly cultivated plain that formed part of the Royal estate. Back at the palace he saw how tithes of wheat and barley and olive oil were collected at the tax office by the gate and rations of seed corn and other necessities distributed, while industrious scribes recorded the dealings on clay tablets. This last activity completely mystified him and I was hard put to it to explain how the intricate characters could be interpreted.

'Can you do this?' he demanded.

I confessed that as a boy I had laboured to learn the art at my father's behest. He had insisted that no ruler could call himself worthy of the name unless he could keep a check on the accounts of his stewards, but I had to admit that I could not recall having written a word since.

One thing weighed on my mind during those days and that was the health of Karpathia. One afternoon we were returning from a visit to one of the Royal farms some distance from the town and I took the reins of my father's chariot in order to speak privately to him.

'Father, I am concerned about Karpathia. I had expected to find that she had recovered from – what happened. But she is so pale and silent that I am afraid for her.'

He sighed and said, 'You are right to be worried. But you should not be surprised to see her like this. For you what happened was almost a disaster, but the Goddess's anger having been averted you may feel yourself free of the consequences. But for Karpathia there is no escape. She was the High Priestess. That was her destiny. Now the Goddess has rejected her what purpose remains for her?'

The words sank heavily into my mind. I realised that I had never paused to consider my sister's future. At length I said, 'It seems hard that she should suffer most, innocent as she is of any intent to dishonour the Goddess.'

'Hard indeed,' he replied. 'But so it is.'

I hesitated and then added, 'Is there no possibility of marriage for her? She is, after all … untouched.'

He looked at me. 'A rejected priestess? What happy outcome

could a man expect from such a marriage?' He paused, deep in thought, and added with a sigh, 'We need not hope that any man of sufficient rank will come asking for her hand.'

'Then what can we do for her?'

'Little, I fear. She will no longer take part in the ordinary pleasures of life. A woman in such a position has little to live for.'

I stared at him, chilled by the flat acceptance in his voice. When we returned to the palace I sent a message to ask Karpathia to meet me in the olive groves surrounding the palace. When she came I began to understand my father's despair. She responded to all my efforts to arouse her interest in the same flat little voice with which she had greeted me. I remembered the joyous, life-loving girl she had once been. There seemed little hope of ever re-awakening that spirit in her. We walked for a while and then I stopped and caught both her hands in mine.

'Karpathia, can you not rouse yourself? Remember how we used to laugh together? Now you have not even a smile for me. What happened was not my fault. The Goddess has forgiven me. Will you not do the same?'

She stared down at the ground, her hands lifeless in my own. 'I have forgiven you, Alkmaion, long ago. But my life belonged to the Goddess. Since she rejects it, of what use can it be to me?'

I left her with a heavy heart and went to seek Alectryon. It disturbed me that he had resolutely refused either to move into my rooms in the palace or to let me spend the nights at his house, but at least it would be some comfort to talk things over with him. I found him waiting for me in the courtyard. He saw immediately that I was distressed and asked the reason.

When I had told him he said, 'Don't give up hope for her. To us it seems a long time since that terrible night, because so much has happened. But really it is little more than a month, you know, and she has had nothing to distract her mind. In time she may recover.'

I sighed. 'I hope so – but I doubt it.'

He said, 'Are you dining with your father tonight?'

'No.' I answered, puzzled by the turn in the conversation. 'He has said that he wants to dine alone with Cresphontes.'

'So we are free to do as we like?'

I nodded, with a jolt at my heart.

'Let's go and see Pedasos.'

I looked at the sky. 'It will be almost sunset by the time we reach the farm.'

He grinned at me. 'You'll just have to stay the night, then, won't you.'

The following evening, back at the palace, I made my way to the field where the young men of the Companionhood were accustomed to assemble for exercise once the sun had lost some of its power. I was uncomfortably aware that after the last weeks my own state of fitness left a lot to be desired and I needed to make up for lost time. It was a pleasant grassy stretch of ground, shaded by a few large trees. There was a track where running feet had worn the ground bare and another patch where the javelins throwers stood, while the wrestlers sought in vain at this time of the year for a place where the grass grew lush enough to cushion their falls.

I was even more out of training than I had realised and by the time I finished I was sweating and panting with fatigue. I threw myself down in the shade and Melanthos came and sat beside me.

'You're out of condition,' he remarked unnecessarily.

'I don't need you to tell me that,' I returned. 'You try lying around on a ship for days on end.'

'Oh, is that what's done it?' he asked, slanting me a sly grin.

Antilochos came over and paused, looking down at me.

'Well, I can see somebody isn't going to be competing in the games tomorrow. But then, I suppose after your recent exploits you don't have to prove anything – to anybody.'

I smiled up at him. After the events of the last weeks I was impervious to his malice. To add to my pleasure, I could see that my serenity annoyed him. He bit into a ripe fig and strolled away.

Melanthos growled in his throat and said, 'There are times when I think the Lawagetas didn't take the whip to him often enough!'

I laughed and said, 'Leave him be. He doesn't worry me any more.'

He gave me a sharp look and said, 'I'm glad. But don't put him too far from your mind, Alkmaion. He thinks like a snake.'

'Why do you say that?'

'Many reasons. Look at yesterday for example. That tale he told you to excuse his absence was a lie.'

'You mean he was not at his father's estate?'

'Oh yes, he was there. But when did he leave the palace? The moment the news arrived that your ship had been sighted he slipped away, had a pair of horses harnessed and drove off before anyone had a chance to notice – or so he thought.'

'Why should he do that?'

'Because he was consumed with envy at the thought of the reception you were going to get and was determined not to be part of it.'

I sighed. 'It's hard to believe he can be so bitter.'

Melanthos sat up. 'Listen, Alkmaion. I warned you once before against him. Now, I've watched him while you have been away. He has done everything he can to win the favour of the Companions, the landholders, the Governor, anyone in a position of importance. I am sure he hoped that you might be lost at sea so that he could take your place as heir to the throne.'

'Well then,' I said lightly, 'he has reason to be disappointed, hasn't he. And after all, if anything happens to me he will be the heir, so it's as well that people should like him.'

'They don't,' said Melanthos curtly. 'And he knows it. But his father has influence, particularly in the army and in the further provinces where the King isn't so well known. And he's very thick with the Chief Priest of Poseidon and you know as well as I do that there are times when signs and omens can be – well, manipulated, if a priest is corrupt. I'm only talking in the air of course but,' he looked me in the face, 'beware, Alkmaion. If he could find a way to do it Antilochos would replace you even while you are still alive.'

I looked back at him. 'That's a very serious accusation, Melanthos.'

'I know it,' he answered. 'Therefore it is for your ears alone – as is what follows. I had not meant to tell, since I thought it could only bring back painful memories, but now I see that I must. You will recall that Antilochos was initiated the year before you.'

'Yes,' I said, my stomach contracting with foreboding.

'Well, I know nothing, of course, of what happened during that time. I only know that on the night of the festival of the New Wine he was with Eritha.'

I turned my head away. 'There must have many others before him.' Then, realising the significance of his words, 'You know about me and Eritha?'

'I saw you together at this year's festival – and I was surprised because I had seen her with Antilochos only a few days before.'

'What?' I stared at him. 'You mean, while I was on the Holy Mountain?'

'Yes.'

'Where? How?'

'I had been to consult the Priest on a small matter for my father and as I returned I noticed a horse tethered just off the road. That drew my attention to the trees beyond. Antilochos was there with Eritha.'

'How?' My question was hoarse and blunt.

'They were having sex.'

I gazed across the valley. Eritha had been Antilochos's mistress even during the first flush of my passion for her. In my surprise I was not sure whether that mattered to me now or not.

Melanthos said gently, 'I would not have spoken of it, but I cannot help wondering if … You see, I saw who it was that fled from the sacred Couch – no, say nothing, the rest is between you and the Goddess and clearly She has favoured you. But answer me this one thing. Was it Eritha who led you there?'

'Yes.'

'Then I cannot get it out of my mind that Antilochos might have prompted her to do it.'

I stared at him. 'You mean to discredit me? Perhaps even to compass my death?'

He nodded gravely. I shook my head, exclaiming, 'I cannot believe it!'

He said, 'We cannot prove it either way. Antilochos will deny it and the woman is - dead.'

'She is dead?'

'Yes, soon after you left. They say it was no human agency and no sickness known to man. The Goddess laid Her hand upon her.'

I swallowed and nodded. 'Karpathia said it would be so.'

We were silent for a moment, then he said, 'Forgive me for distressing you, but I had to warn you. If Antilochos is to blame, his plan has rebounded on him. You are held in greater respect than before. We can do nothing now, but watch him, Alkmaion, and be on your guard. He will do anything to ruin you.'

The games that were to bring Cresphontes's stay to a conclusion where magnificent indeed. Cresphontes was inclined to challenge our wrestlers but I had told my father about his style of fighting and we persuaded him that it was more fitting to his rank merely to watch. Alectryon and I also held back, pleading our enforced lack of exercise, but I found it hard not to be down there among the athletes, particularly when the footraces were on. Cresphontes was full of praise for our runners and javelin throwers, but when the wrestling started I could see him exchanging sideways glances with Xouthos, who was now fit enough to join the spectators. I sat between them, trying to point out the finer points of style, but though they watched and nodded I could see they were not impressed.

When the bouts were over Cresphontes looked across at Xouthos and said, 'You see, little wolf? That is how the fine gentlemen of Messenia fight.' And although his tone was polite the hint of ironic contempt in his eyes was unmistakable.

The chariot race had him standing in his seat and yelling, however. 'Such horses!' he kept exclaiming. 'Such magnificent animals!'

The race was won, as expected, by Telaon, driving my father's superbly matched blacks. But second place went to a complete outsider; a fair-haired lad from the northern Province whom I had never seen before and who had brought a splendid pair of chestnuts all the way from Phea to compete.

Finally we all mounted our chariots and drove down to a small hill above the bay to watch the naval battle. This had our guests totally absorbed, as they watched the ships manoeuvring, the rowers straining at the oars or shipping them in a shower of spray as they attempted to board another vessel. Kerkios and his crew, back in fine fettle after their rest, were adjudged the most successful and received the prize of two fat sheep and a cask of wine.

The farewell feast was almost as magnificent as the one that had been prepared to greet us and closed with an exchange of gifts – Cresphontes, I noticed, handing over some of his booty from the raid – and protestations of gratitude and friendship. I fell into bed feeling well pleased with my first attempt at diplomacy.

The following day we set course for Dorian territory.

Chapter 8.

The winds were more favourable than on our first voyage north and by the end of the first day we had covered almost half the distance to Cresphontes's village. As we made camp I noticed that Xouthos had brought ashore with him the chest my father had given him to keep his valuables in. He was squatting before it, examining the contents. His greedy delight in precious objects amused me and I strolled over to him, my feet silent on the sand.

'Really, Xouthos, you need not have bothered to bring all that ashore. It would have been perfectly safe on the ship.'

At my voice he started and slammed shut the lid of the chest, but he was too late to prevent me seeing the contents. Among the various objects that I recognised as gifts from my father or myself was another, a cup of gold ornamented with a chariot and horses at full gallop, which belonged to a set my father kept for the use of guests. I had seen it in Xouthos's hands in the megaron, but I was certain that it had not been given to him.

'Xouthos!' I said, and stooped to lift the lid of the chest. He flung his arm across it and glared up at me, his teeth bared like those of an animal. For a moment we stared into each other's eyes and then I turned away, profoundly disturbed. I could have called Alectryon and the others and accused Xouthos outright of the theft, but something in me revolted against the idea of charging so mean an act against one whom I had come to regard as a friend.

Xouthos avoided my gaze for the rest of the voyage, although I could feel him watching me out of the corners of his eyes whenever he thought my attention was elsewhere. I decided to say nothing, since to mention the theft would be to start a quarrel which would involve us all, but I could not help wondering what Cresphontes would do if he knew of it. Meanwhile, I reflected on the aptness of Xouthos's nickname and reminded myself that although you might tame a young wolf cub you could never trust it not to turn on you one day.

We reached Cresphontes's village next day and he pressed us to stay with him but I made the excuse that my father wanted me home as soon as possible. However, we agreed for courtesy's sake to stay one day longer – a promise that was more readily given when Cresphontes promised us a day's hunting.

He had boasted many times of the good hunting near his home and we were not disappointed. He himself did not accompany us, excusing himself on the grounds that many things in the village required his attention. But he sent Xouthos and some of his young men with us and we took some of the ship's crew, leaving Kerkios with a handful of men to prepare for an early start next morning. Xouthos, though still unable to use a spear, proved to be an able tracker and found us an abundance of game. We returned to the village in high good humour, ready for another night of feasting.

Cresphontes met us at the entry to the village, grave-faced. Some presentiment told me that he had bad news and that it concerned us.

'What is it, Cresphontes?' I asked.

'My friends,' he said, ' I am sorry to be the bearer of bad tidings but I must tell you that an accident has befallen one of your companions.'

'Who?'

'The excellent Kerkios. Apparently he went swimming near the mouth of the river. The current is very strong just there.'

'Where is he?' I asked hoarsely.

He lifted his shoulders. 'Who can say? His body may be washed up somewhere along the coast. His soul is certainly by now on its way to the abode of the dead.'

I turned and gazed blankly at Alectryon, too shocked to speak. He said quietly, 'Who saw it happen?'

'Several of my people heard his cries. When they reached the riverbank he was already far out and being rapidly swept away. I will call them to speak to you themselves.'

Four of the villagers confirmed the story. Then they took us to the edge of the river, not at the point where I had bathed in the shallows and Purwa had come to fill her water pot, but further down where the swift waters ran into the sea. As Cresphontes had said, the current was strong.

'But why,' I cried, 'did you not summon my crew to put to sea

131

and save him?'

'We did,' Cresphontes responded. 'But of course some of them were with you, and the rest had gone with some of my people to spear fish further up the coast. By the time they returned and launched the ship there was no sign of him.'

The crew were clustered round the stern of the ship, their heads bowed in sorrow. One or two wept openly. All had been with Kerkios on many voyages and loved and honoured him like a father. I said a few words to them, striving to offer some comfort, though my own heart was blank and desolate at the loss of such a brilliant captain and loyal friend. Then I called the helmsman to me and asked if he could sail the ship back to Pylos. He answered that he could, given fair weather and no unexpected hazards, so I gave orders to be ready to sail first thing the next morning.

The game which we had intended for a joyful feast was now put to use as meat for the funeral meal and that night we offered all the sacrifices that must be made to allow a soul to enter the abode of the dead. We were all heavy hearted and Cresphontes again and again bemoaned the fact that the tragedy had occurred while we were his guests.

I brought the solemn feast to an early conclusion and we retired to bed. Just before we slept Alectryon said, 'I don't understand why a man like Kerkios would be fool enough to bathe at a place like that.'

The day's hunting followed by the shock of Cresphontes's news had laid a heavy hand upon my spirits and I fell into a deep sleep without answering him. The next thing I knew was an urgent hand on my shoulder and I opened my eyes to find Dexeus bending over the two of us.

'Be quiet, I beg you!' he whispered. 'Come outside with me. It is Kerkios!'

The urgency of his voice dragged me from my sleep but the words seemed to mean nothing. Alectryon was awake and alert already. We caught our cloaks around us and followed Dexeus out onto the porch. Then my drowsiness fell from me and his words took on meaning, for Kerkios lay propped against the wall. I dropped on my knees beside him and discovered that his hands were clasped tightly to his side and between them the hilt of a dagger stood out, red with the blood that seeped constantly around it. I breathed his name and made to unloose his hands and draw out the blade but he gasped,

'No, leave it! Once it is out my life will go with it, and I must speak first. Listen, Prince, I beg of you!'

He choked and his body doubled around the knife. Alectryon slid an arm behind him to support him.

'Say on, Kerkios. The Prince is listening.'

'Kerkios,' I whispered, 'I don't understand. Cresphontes told us you were drowned.'

'Ah!' he nodded painfully. 'Is that it?' Then he lifted his head and looked at me. 'Beware of him, Prince. He means you harm – and your father. And all of us.'

'How, Kerkios?'

He seemed for a moment unable to speak, then he drew a long, rasping breath, flung his head back against Alectryon's shoulder, and began in a rapid, gasping whisper,

'Today he summoned me. He sent you hunting to have you out of the way. He offered me bribes to stay here and teach his people how to manage ships. They have built more than the one we have seen. Soon, he said, the time foretold by the oracle would come and they would need many ships. When they had conquered, he said, I should have all I asked for in land or treasure.'

'Conquered where?' Alectryon asked urgently, but Kerkios did not seem to hear and went on, 'I refused, of course. Then he had me bound and locked in a hut, saying I should stay as his prisoner. I managed to get free at length ...' his voice was weakening but his will carried him on. 'When darkness came ... I broke through the roof and climbed out. There was a guard ... I crept up behind him but at the last moment he heard me. I had my arm around his throat but he had time to draw his dagger. I finished him and managed ... to reach here.' He groped out and caught my hand. 'The time of the oracle ... what does it mean?'

I caught Alectryon's eye and answered, 'Nothing, Kerkios, nothing. Be at peace.'

He gripped my hand hard. 'Be warned, son of Sillos ... I beg of you!'

I pressed his hand. 'I have heard your warning, Kerkios, and I shall heed it, never fear. I am forever in your debt for bringing it to me. Be assured, Cresphontes will not go unpunished.'

He stared at me, his eyes glazed with pain, then he drew a sudden, harsh breath and slumped against Alectryon. My friend laid him down carefully and stooped to hold his cheek above the blood-flecked lips. 'He is dead.'

I crouched by the body, numbed by what seemed this second death. Alectryon reached out and drew the dagger from the wound. The blood flowed turgidly after it. I discovered that my hand was sticky with blood and wiped it absent-mindedly on my cloak.

Alectryon said, 'Listen. It is dangerous to stay here now. Once Kerkios's escape is discovered none of our lives will be safe. We must try to launch the ship and get away tonight. Dexeus, go to the hut where the men sleep. Wake them and bid them be ready to sail. There must be no sound – you understand?'

Dexeus nodded and slipped away into the darkness. Alectryon gripped my arm and said, 'Come. The time for grief will follow. Now is the time to act.'

We crept back into the megaron and gathered together our belongings, straining our ears for any sound from behind the curtain that covered the sleeping compartment. As we came out onto the porch again I looked at Kerkios's body.

'We can't leave him.'

'We must,' Alectryon returned curtly.

'No,' I said. 'I will not.'

He hesitated a moment and then said, 'Very well.'

A man is heavy to carry at the best of times: the inert weight of a corpse is a far more difficult burden. Somehow we lugged him down to the shore. Under the stern of the ship the crew were gathering, hardly awake, silent and wondering. When they saw whose body we brought I feared their surprise would wake the village but I bade them curtly lift him aboard and keep their questions for later and they obeyed me. We embarked and the men put their shoulders to the hull. Now, I thought, as the keel grated on the shingle, they must wake. But no sound came from the sleeping village. The crew dipped their oars and we slid out across the dark water.

I turned to the helmsman. 'Can you set course for Pylos by the stars?'

He nodded. 'Aye.'

'Very well, then. Let us make as much distance as we can before dawn.'

Alectryon spoke my name. He was examining the dagger that he had drawn from Kerkios's body.

'Look,' he said, putting it into my hand.

I examined the weapon in the moonlight. It was a simple object with a plain wooden handle. Only the colour of the blade struck me as strange. Thinking it was the blood drying on it I rubbed it on the corner of my cloak, but it did not change its appearance. I tilted the blade this way and that in the pale light.

He said, 'What do you see?'

'The blade seems dull. Nothing else.'

'Dull? Look again. It is not the colour of bronze at all.'

'Perhaps it is the light.'

'Look then.' He drew his own dagger and held the two side by side. From his the moonlight struck a familiar gleam. The other was cold and grey. I gazed from the dagger to his face, frowning.

'What can it be?'

He shook his head slowly. 'I don't know. But it's not bronze.'

'Then what? What other metal could be used for making a weapon?'

'I've no idea. But I think we must find out.'

'How?'

He looked at me. 'I may be mistaken, but I think we must pay another visit to that Forbidden Valley.'

'You think perhaps that they have found some new way of working metal – that they are working it in secret in that valley?'

'It is possible, isn't it?'

I remembered the hearths and the stone blocks which I had taken for altars and answered slowly, 'Yes. I think it is.'

As I spoke I took the dagger and tried it against the planking of the deck. Where my own well-tempered bronze would have sprung back to its own shape at once, the tip of this blade remained slightly curved and when I ran my finger over it I could feel that the edge had turned. I handed it back to Alectryon, remarking, 'Whatever it is they have discovered, it won't stand comparison with our bronze.'

'Nevertheless,' he said, 'I think we must try to learn the secret. Let us look for a place to beach the ship, somewhere it will not easily be seen, and return overland to the valley.'

I turned to the helmsman and countermanded my first orders, and we drifted along close inshore until the first light of dawn. It was not long before we came to a sheltered inlet and ran the boat ashore. I called the men around me and related to them as much of Kerkios's story as I thought it was good for them to hear and told them that Alectryon and I intended to return secretly to the village to try to learn more of Cresphontes's plans. I thought it best not to mention the real purpose of our expedition. Finally I instructed them to prepare a grave for their dead captain and await our return. If we were not back by evening they were to bury Kerkios themselves and if by the following night we were still missing they were to sail for Pylos and tell their story to my father. Then I turned to Dexeus and told him to put together provisions for three of us for two days. He had been looking downcast but his face brightened when he understood he was to come with us.

Alectryon, meanwhile, had been examining the dagger in the daylight and now called me to him.

'Look,' he said. 'Doesn't the grey sheen of this blade call to your mind something you have seen before?'

I examined the blade again and said finally, 'The only thing I have ever seen to resemble it are the fragments of iron in jewellery.'

'Exactly,' he agreed.

'But iron!' I exclaimed. 'How could they obtain enough to work it into weapons? It is one of the rarest metals, found only in the thunderbolts that the Gods are supposed to throw. Surely the Dorians cannot have been so showered with such missiles that they have enough iron to work in this way.'

He grinned briefly. 'Remember their God is Zeus, who is usually said to be the wielder of thunderbolts. But there may be a simpler explanation. I have heard it said that there are places where iron is found in ordinary rocks. Perhaps the Dorians have learned how to extract it from the stone.'

The sun was now showing itself above the mountains and it was time to be on our way if we were to have any hope of getting back before dark. During the night we had rounded a rocky headland and now we reckoned that only a range of hills separated us from the river that watered the Dorian settlement. It was a hard, hot climb and I could have wished myself without the weight of my spear and the sword slung from my shoulder, but at length we stood on the shoulder of the hill. Below us the river ran in its deep bed and we could see far to our left the outlying huts of Cresphontes's village.

Keeping to the high ground, we skirted the head of the valley and crossed the river where it was no more than a rocky stream. After a short scramble we came out onto the open pasture above the settlement I had first seen on my lonely night expedition. As we reached the trees that sheltered the village we became aware of a noise I thought at first was the sound of sheep bells. Then I realised it was the clang of metal on metal. I looked at Alectryon and he nodded without speaking. As we descended, slipping cautiously from tree to tree, the noise grew louder until it seemed to fill the air and the tang of smoke came to my nostrils. Then the trees thinned and we had to go on our bellies. I saw Alectryon, who was leading, come to a stop behind some bushes. Then he looked back and beckoned. I crept to his side and he pointed through a screen of leaves, down into the green bowl of the valley.

For a moment I thought that we were indeed spying on some holy sacrifice, for on each one of the hearths a fire blazed, sending up smoke into the still air. But a look at the men around the hearths assured me that it was not so. These were no grave priests, nor were the objects laid before them upon the stones that I had thought were altars sacrificial beasts. The bustling activity reminded me of the workshops of craftsmen at home, though for a while the purpose of the various actions escaped me.

'They are smiths,' Dexeus whispered. 'Like the bronze smiths at home. But what are they working?'

Alectryon drew the dagger from his belt and showed it to him.

'It seems they have discovered how to work iron.'

Dexeus felt the edge of the blade and grunted, 'Well, give me my good bronze!'

I pointed. 'Look. That boy is carrying some of the completed work to that hut. They look like sword blades.'

Alectryon nodded. 'That must be the store where they are kept until wanted. I should dearly like to see inside it!'

'It could be done at night,' I said.

He looked at me. 'It would be risky …'

'Not if we are quiet. They are not expecting any kind of trouble, and the only guards last time I was here were far down the valley, watching the path.'

'Will the crew wait for us?'

'I told them to wait until nightfall tomorrow.'

He nodded. 'Very well. We'll try it.'

We made ourselves as comfortable as possible under the sheltering bushes and settled down to wait for darkness. The long afternoon dragged past. We took in turns to doze, or watched the work going on below us. I brooded over the events of the past hours. Since Kerkios's death there had been little time for thought. At length I said, 'It is hard to believe that Cresphontes can be so treacherous. I had come to think of him as a friend.'

Alectryon nodded soberly. 'So had I. Mind you, I always had a feeling that he was only our friend as long as it suited him to be.'

'Apparently our laws of trust and friendship mean little to them anyway,' I remarked, and told them for the first time about Xouthos and the stolen cup.

Dexeus shifted his position and said flatly, 'Well, I never liked either of them.'

Alectryon gave him an affectionate look and said, 'Well, it seems you judged better than either of us on this occasion.'

I loosened my sword in its sheath. 'He will pay for Kerkios's death one day. I swear to that.'

Sunset came and the workers packed up their tools and went to sluice themselves in the nearby stream. Soon the smell of cooking rising from the huts awakened my appetite. The three of us sat sniffing the air until Dexeus's stomach rumbled so loudly that we had to stifle our laughter.

Alectryon said, 'I think we had better eat some of our food, before Dexeus's stomach gives us away!'

So we ate, and wrapped ourselves in our cloaks against the coming of night, and waited.

By the time it was fully dark and the last sounds of activity had died away in the huts below us we were all stiff and cramped from the long wait in our hiding place. Even then Alectryon made us hold back a little longer. I reflected to myself with a brief smile that not long ago I would have bitterly resented his assumption of command. Now I took it as a matter of course. At length he gave the word and we crept out of our concealing bushes and stole down the slope towards the buildings. In spite of the darkness I felt that eyes must be watching me from the huts. At any moment, it seemed, we must hear a cry of alarm. Or perhaps the first warning that our presence was known would be the silent rising of armed men around us, or the fierce bite of a dagger in my flesh.

We skirted the edge of the circle of huts until we came to the one that seemed to be the storeroom. The door was fastened with a wooden bar dropped into slots on either side but there was nothing to prevent us from lifting it. The door creaked on its hinges and we froze, hearts beating wildly, but no one challenged us and we crept inside. The only light came through the open door behind us and for a moment we stood staring blindly about us. Then Dexeus moved and there was a clink of metal as his foot struck something in the darkness. Alectryon gripped his arm and said, 'Wait!'

He turned to the door, paused for a moment looking out and then was gone like a shadow. I almost called after him. We waited breathlessly until he returned, a smouldering brand from one of the hearths in his hand. He blew it into life and held it up. In its dull glow we examined the contents of the hut. Broad, flat iron swords were stacked in piles around the walls. Clay boxes contained arrowheads by the hundred. There were tools and other equipment too but there was no doubt about the main purpose of the work we had seen going on.

For some moments nobody spoke. Then I breathed, 'There

must be as many weapons here as there are in my father's armoury at the palace!'

Alectryon carefully lifted one of the swords from the pile.

'We will take one with us as proof of what we have seen.'

He extinguished the brand and we slipped out of the hut and barred the door behind us. Once we were clear of the buildings we began to run and did not stop until we were safely among the trees again. We did not dare to sleep, and so pressed on through the darkness until we reached the river, where the roughness of the terrain forced us to stop and wait for dawn. The sun was almost at its height before we stumbled wearily down the last slope to where we had beached our ship. The crew welcomed us with relief and told us that they had buried Kerkios as I had instructed when we failed to return the previous evening. They showed us the grave they had dug among the trees just above the tide line. A small cairn of stones had been raised over it and the waves whispered a constant lullaby. I thought Kerkios would have been happy with the choice of such a place. I was weary to my bones but I knew we could not leave until the proper rites had been performed, so at my orders fires were lit and once again we made the ritual offerings for the spirit of our dead friend. Then we embarked, sorrowfully, and I ordered the helmsman to make all speed for Pylos.

We accomplished the journey home in two days, coming to the city just at nightfall. There were fewer people on the beach than at our last arrival, owing to the lateness of the hour, and I was glad to be able to go straight to the palace without any ceremonies of welcome. News of our return had run ahead of us, however, and we found the household in the courtyard to greet us. Our faces must have told them that all was not well for the smiles of welcome faded as we passed. I saluted my father and begged an immediate private audience. He granted it at once, but turned on me as soon as we entered his room.

'Alkmaion, have you not enough sense to hide whatever is troubling you? Soon the whole city will know that the Prince has returned with ill tidings. We shall have rumours of who knows what disasters afoot.'

'I am sorry, sir,' I answered, more curtly than I had ever spoken to him before, for my senses were raw with weariness and anxiety, 'but I have news which will not permit me to dissemble.'

'Well?' he asked shortly, giving me a piercing look.

I floundered for a moment, unable to decide where to begin. Then I said, 'Kerkios is dead.'

'Kerkios? How?'

'Killed by one of Cresphontes's men.'

'An accident?'

'No.'

I told him the facts as briefly as I could. When I finished he turned away and seated himself slowly.

'So. This is the outcome of your "friendship" with the Dorians!'

That struck like a blow and I said sharply, 'I believed they were my friends. I sought only to bring about a useful alliance.'

He gave me a bitter look and remarked, 'When you come to be older perhaps you will realise that a man cannot make friends with wolves.'

The closeness of this to my own thoughts struck me silent for a moment and Alectryon, who had accompanied me, stepped forward.

'This is the dagger that killed Kerkios. I think you should look at it, my lord.'

My father took the dagger from him with a frown, then bent his head to examine it more closely, and finally looked up at us.

'What metal is this?'

'Iron, sir.' I answered, and took the sword from under my cloak, 'as this is.'

He bade us both be seated then and listened in silence while we told him of the metal workers in the Forbidden Valley. Then he said slowly, 'So. Cresphontes is building ships and storing up these new weapons. You say there were as many as my armoury contains?'

'Yes, sir,' I answered and Alectryon added, 'Clearly they have found an abundant source of the metal.'

I went on urgently, 'He also mentioned the prophecy to Kerkios. I am sure he means to attack us. We hastened back here to prepare you.'

My father raised his eyebrows. 'My dear Alkmaion, your news is certainly disturbing, but I fail to understand your haste. One would

141

think the Dorians were at your heels! Cresphontes is building ships. Even so, he is hardly likely to be able to put into service a fleet of sufficient power to dare to attack us. And he has had a chance to see, at first hand, how well equipped and well trained our navy is. I cannot see any particular urgency in the situation.'

'But Kerkios must be revenged!' I exclaimed.

Slowly my father shook his head. 'The days are gone, Alkmaion, when one man's death was sufficient to launch a fleet to avenge him. We have enough to concern us at home, without embarking on a war with the Dorians.'

I opened my mouth to protest but he cut me short, saying, 'You are both tired after your adventures. Go now and rest. Tomorrow, since you have allowed the whole court to see that you bring news of trouble, you had better repeat your story before the rest of the Royal Kin and we will hear their opinions. But an expedition against the Dorians is out of the question at this time.'

I hesitated, still disposed to argue, but Alectryon touched my arm and shook his head. We withdrew and I took him up to my room where I dismissed Mukala with a curtness she did not forgive for some days. When we were alone I paced the room and gave vent to my anger and incredulity.

He gave my temper free rein until I fell silent of my own accord and then said, 'My dear, has it never occurred to you that your father has troubles within the kingdom without courting more outside it?'

I stared at him. 'What do you mean?'

'Do you imagine Antilochos is the only member of the Royal Kin who is jealous, or desirous of power?'

I went and sat down near him, beginning to see more clearly things that I had only dimly perceived before.

'My Uncle Paion is jealous also.'

'And he and Antilochos are the same at heart.'

'And the rest of the Kin? Echelaon?'

'My lord Echelaon will support whichever side seems to offer him the best advantage. Andropompous and Peisistratos are loyal. The rest ... Who can say? Paion and Echelaon have a great deal of influence.'

'But surely they would not scheme to overthrow my father?'

'We have good reason to believe that Antilochos schemed to dishonour you, and has endeavoured to win your place in the esteem of those who have power.'

'But could they succeed? Surely the people would not turn from the King?'

'Not as things are, no. As long as the country is prosperous and at peace. But many would resent being asked to go to war to revenge a man they have hardly heard of.'

'But it is not just that! The Dorians are dangerous.'

'We shall find it hard to persuade them of that. You can be sure that Paion will do his best to make nothing of it, if only to discredit you. If your father forced an expedition Paion would be ready to fan every murmur of discontent.'

'Then send him, too. He is the Commander-in-Chief.'

'And risk allowing him to return with a victory to his credit and the army more under his control than ever? No, my dear. If we wish to help your father we must do it not by demanding a war of revenge but by concentrating on persuading our leaders to prepare for an attack. As your father says, it cannot come this year. It is too late in the summer to start a campaign. We are safe at least until the spring. By then we can be sufficiently prepared to hold them off.' He laid a hand on my shoulder. 'Now, let me call Mukala and tell her to bring some food. You must eat and sleep. We shall need our wits about us in the morning.'

The following morning the Royal Kin were assembled in the megaron. My father took his place and when we were all seated began to speak.

'I have summoned you all here today so that you may hear the news which Prince Alkmaion and the Count Alectryon have brought. It is grave news, indeed sorrowful, but I do not feel that it gives any immediate cause for alarm. However, you shall judge for yourselves. Alkmaion, stand forth and tell your story.'

I did as he bade me, angry that my knees trembled as I took my place. Once again I told of Kerkios's death and of the smiths in the Forbidden Valley and displayed the sword. I ended, 'We saw as many swords like this one as there are in the palace armoury, and the smiths are still working. Cresphontes has betrayed our trust and ignored the laws of friendship and hospitality. I believe he intends to attack us as soon as he has built enough ships to transport his warriors. We must be ready to repel such an attack.'

My father looked round at the others. 'We have heard Alkmaion's story. Does anyone wish to ask him any questions?'

Echelaon, who always spoke coolly and with an appearance of great detachment, said, 'What makes you think that it is against us that these weapons are to be used?'

I hesitated. I knew I must not speak of the prophecy. 'Cresphontes hinted as much to Kerkios.'

'Hints? We need a little more than that, surely?'

Antilochos said suddenly, 'Why did you not confront Cresphontes and demand an explanation for Kerkios's death?'

Alectryon answered him. 'Because I feared that the Prince's life might be in danger when Cresphontes learned we had discovered his deception.'

Antilochos smirked. 'Of course, the Prince must not risk his life!'

My father said sharply, 'You did right, Count. To remain would have been foolhardy.'

Paion shifted impatiently in his chair. 'I fail to understand what all this is about. Are you seriously suggesting, Prince, that those barbarians are going to attack us?'

'I think it is very likely.'

He leaned forward and favoured me with the stare that used to intimidate me not so long ago. 'Then they must be mad – and so must you to raise such an alarm. Has the Prince never heard of the prowess of his ancestors? Does he imagine that the seed of Nestor can be conquered by a handful of barbarians?'

'They will not be a handful!' I cried. 'Already they have enough swords in one village to arm every man in it.'

'Ha!' My uncle threw back his head and the thick flesh of his neck shook. 'Arm every man in the village! Do you think giving a man a sword makes a warrior of him? Oh no, my boy, you've got a lot to learn if you think that!' He laughed loudly and Antilochos joined in.

Alectryon sprang to his feet and came to where I stood, my cheeks burning with humiliation. It was the first time I had seen him roused but now his eyes flashed with anger.

'I support the Prince and urge you all to take steps now to prepare for an attack. The Prince risked his life twice to penetrate the secrets of the Forbidden Valley – and I hope you, my lords, will take due account of that fact.'

'Let me have a look at that sword.' Paion rose and came towards us. I handed it to him. He peered at it and weighed it in his hand, then ran his thumb along the edge and gave a little laugh. Then he took the blade in both hands and bent it. The soft metal gave in his hands and remained in its curve. Paion threw back his head and shook with laughter, holding the drooping sword at arm's length for all to see. 'There's your new weapon for you! A hundred or two untrained men with these in their hands! That is what worries the Prince so much! Let them come, I say. Let them build their ships. Half of them will probably drown on the way. The rest will be seasick like their precious prince. I've never seen a man look so pale and wet as he did when he arrived! And those that don't run away the moment they see a squadron of our chariotry with their good bronze armour will have to stop and bend their swords back into shape after a few hacks at us!'

His laughter seemed to rock the room and Antilochos joined in wildly. Even Echelaon permitted himself an amused smile. I felt a sudden impulse to seize the sword from my uncle's hand and drive it into his quaking belly.

As soon as he could make himself heard Alectryon shouted, 'But don't you see? They can arm the whole people. Our warriors are trained men, yes, with the best armour. But they cannot stand against odds of ten to one!'

My father raised his hand for silence and when Paion had rumbled and guffawed his way back to his seat said, 'I think you exaggerate, Count. The whole population of Cresphontes's village could scarcely provide those odds.'

Andropompous, who had sat silent until now, put in, 'May I ask what defence measures the Prince and the Count have in mind?'

'We should set the smiths to work increasing the stock of

weapons immediately,' I said at once.

My father replied, 'That is difficult, as you well know. Our stores of copper and tin are small. All we can obtain is already in heavy demand.'

'Then we should try to obtain more,' said Alectryon.

My father gave a grim smile. 'Every civilised country in the world is already trying to do that. Competition is very great.'

'We should build defensive walls,' I put in, 'as they have at Mycenae and Tyrins.'

'Since when have the seed of Nestor cowered behind walls?' growled Paion. 'Our forefathers needed none. Are we grown so puny in comparison with them?'

'Mycenae and Tyrins were built in very disturbed times,' my father said. 'We have always been more fortunate. I cannot believe that there is sufficient danger to warrant such a tremendous expenditure of effort.'

I gazed round at them and then looked at Alectryon. His eyes told me that he had come to the same conclusion. It was hopeless. They were all so certain of their security nothing we could say would make them change their minds.

In the silence that ensued my father said, 'Listen, now, to what I propose. Cresphontes may indeed have hostile intentions towards us but although he is a prince he is not at liberty to do as he pleases. He owes fealty to his brother, Temenos. I suggest therefore that we send an embassy to Temenos to protest at the murder of Kerkios and demand reparation. This embassy can also hint at Cresphontes's warlike preparations and find out how Temenos is disposed towards them. I think we may find that Cresphontes has over-reached himself. At any rate, let us put aside all questions of preparations for an attack until we know his answer. Is it agreed?'

No one raised any objections. Even Paion, feeling I suppose that he had scored a victory already, seemed content to let the matter rest. As Antilochos passed me on his way out of the hall he handed me the iron sword, which his father had thrown aside, and said with a giggle, 'I suppose you will be using this magnificent weapon from now on. We must have a bout together sometime. But I should wear your bronze armour, if I were you!'

I stood silent as they all passed me, burning with impotent anger. Even my father …!

He called me. 'Alkmaion, I want to speak to you.'

I exchanged glances with Alectryon and he said, 'I will wait for you in the courtyard.'

In his private room my father invited me to sit but I shook my head mutinously and remained standing.

'You are angry,' he said. 'I understand. And you have some reason to be. That is why I want to explain why I acted as I did.'

I looked at him in surprise. I had never heard him speak in this tone before.

He went on, 'You risked your life to bring me news and you have performed exploits well worthy of being celebrated in the songs of a bard. But you have as yet received only humiliation and mockery in return. It is bitterly hard to accept, I know. But you must come to understand that there are many bitter things a king must accept. So sit down, and let me begin to instruct you.'

I sat then and listened silently.

'I do not have to tell you, although we have never mentioned it before, that there has long been bad feeling between the Lawagetas and myself. Until recently he has kept it well hidden but now his son is growing up, and Antilochos has a bitter spirit, as you well know. I believe it is he who has prompted his father into more open hostility. As yet it has not come to much, but they are seeking every opportunity to turn people against me.'

I had been gazing at the floor, at that same octopus on which I had fixed my eyes after the incident with the bull. Was it really only a few short months ago? Now I looked up.

'I understand this now. It was Alectryon who made me see it, last night.'

'That is why you did not press for an immediate attack on the Dorians in council this morning?'

'Yes.'

'Good, you are learning.'

'There is more,' I went on. 'I have good reason to believe

Antilochos played a part in – what happened at the Festival.' I related what Melanthos had told me and saw my father's eyes narrow with anger.

When I had finished he nodded, tight-lipped, and said, 'It would be like him. His mind twists about his jealousy until it loses hold on honour altogether. But this is not the time to accuse him, without better proof. We must wait and watch. I wish at all costs to avoid an open clash with him or his father at present. That is why I am glad you did not ask for an attack on the Dorians.'

'But the rest ...' I burst out. 'It seems to me so vital!'

He smiled for the first time. 'You have been so close to it that it must seem to fill your sight. But what I said in the council is true, Alkmaion. There is no immediate danger. That is the important thing. Just at this time we cannot afford unrest and rumours of war. Dissension feeds upon such things. That is why we must show no anxiety for the future. We have a breathing space now, and in that time we must bind the people to us; the army and the great landholders in particular. That is where our defence lies, first of all. Do you understand me?'

I nodded slowly and then rose and faced him. 'Will you entrust me with the embassy to Temenos?'

He gave me a look that was almost tender, but shook his head. 'No, for two reasons. First, because your discovery of the Forbidden Valley and theft of the sword may be known and that would make it difficult for Temenos to receive you. And secondly, and more important, because I want you here, taking your place as the heir and helping to bind people to the throne. That, I think, is an important enough task.'

I met his eyes. 'Yes, indeed it is.'

He smiled. 'Good. Then we are on friendly terms again. Tonight there will be a feast, to mark your second safe return, and I shall see to it that your deeds are duly celebrated. After that, you will come to see in other ways that I am grateful.'

Over the following days my father's promise was kept more fully than I had ever dreamed. That night there was a feast of even greater magnificence than the one held to celebrate my first homecoming and after we had eaten my father publicly expressed his thanks to myself and Alectryon and presented us with rich gifts from his own treasury. I still have the golden fillet that he gave me. It is one of the few possessions I brought with me when I fled my home and it will be around my brow when they lay my body in its tomb.

That night, however, we banished all thoughts of disaster. My only regret was that Sirios, the bard, and his young apprentice, Philomenos, were not present.

When I asked my father the reason he replied, 'They have gone travelling, as such men will. Sirios came to me the day after you set sail again and begged my leave to undertake one last journey. He wished, he said, to visit golden Mycenae and Tyrins of the great walls once more before he died and also to introduce his young companion to the court of High King Tisamenos. But I believe half his intention was to tell them the story of your voyage. He was always loyal to us, and it will please him to make your name ring about the hall of mighty Mycenae.'

Two days later Andropompous was despatched to carry my father's message to Cresphontes's brother Temenos. It was a good choice, for he was a wise man who listened much and spoke little, and that to the point, and always tending towards reason and peace. Also, he was utterly loyal to my father. Melanthos sued for and won permission to accompany his father and this time it was my turn, as I bade him farewell, to warn him to guard himself.

The pattern of my life was changing. More and more of my time was taken up with assisting my father in his duties, both secular and sacred. The hours that were left I spent with Alectryon but we did not pass them idly. We formed the habit of practising every day with sword and spear, both knowing that before long our lives might depend on such skills, though we passed it off as an amusing pastime. Some of the other younger members of the Companionhood began to join in with us, and we did nothing to discourage them. Only at night did we allow ourselves to forget our forebodings. The court knew well enough by now that we were lovers and I persuaded Alectryon that it was pointless to pretend otherwise. In the palace there were always too many people about me, so when I could I spent the evenings at his house, talking over a simple meal and afterwards taking turns to sing to the accompaniment of the lyre. But I remembered what my father required of me and was careful not to absent myself too often from the evening meal in the megaron, only slipping out of the palace when everyone had retired to bed.

My domestic affairs had taken a turn for the better, too. On the day after my return I had been taken by surprise at the sight of the lovely girl who glided forward, eyes modestly down-cast, to attend upon me. Mukala had kept her promise and seen that Andria was well cared for. Now, rested and apparently reconciled to her fate, she had become a beauty and, amazingly, she and Mukala appeared to be good friends. She had begun to learn our language and told me, brokenly, how much she honoured me for saving her from Cresphontes. Whenever I was in the room her eyes followed me, but I was young and my attentions were elsewhere and it did not occur to me that there might be more in them than simple gratitude.

Andria was not the only addition to my household. The day after the feast to celebrate my return, as I was about to set off for the exercise ground, a page came to tell me that my father wished to see me. I found him, not alone as I expected, but in the company of a young man of about my own age whose face seemed vaguely familiar. He was tall and well built, with fair hair and blue eyes, and his features and bearing proclaimed him to be of good breeding. His good looks, however, were spoilt by an expression of almost sullen reserve.

My father said, 'Alkmaion, do you remember Neritos, the son of Kretheus? His father was Prefect of Phea. He drove the chariot that nearly beat my pair in the games we held for the Dorians.'

I remembered him then and said, 'Of course! I was sorry we did not have a chance to meet then. I'm glad you are still in Pylos.'

He greeted me with formal courtesy but without warmth. My father went on, 'Kretheus died just after the Spring Festival. It was Neritos's mother who sent him here with his horses to compete in the race and asked me to take him under my protection.'

I turned to the stranger with a quick expression of sympathy. The sentiment was genuine for it struck me as hard that he should be sent away from home so soon after such a loss. Phea was at the other end of the country and he was among strangers in Pylos. I learned later that his mother was being courted by two new suitors and that this spectacle had so angered him that she had thought it best to send him away.

My father continued, 'It has been in my mind for some while that it was time you had a young man of good breeding and suitable accomplishments to attend on you as your squire. Neritos comes to us with warm praise for his courage and his prowess as an athlete, and we have seen his skill at handling a chariot. Therefore I have decided to make him your charioteer. Does it please you?'

It pleased me very well, though I gave a passing thought to the fact that a charioteer was of little use to me when I had neither chariot nor horses of my own. I said, 'It does indeed. I hope it will please Neritos as well.'

'Who could fail to be pleased with such an honour?' he returned, but his voice still held the same reserve.

My father said, 'I place him in your care, Alkmaion. See that he is given a room near your own and make sure that he has all he needs.'

'I will, sir,' I promised, and took this as a sign that the interview was over. However, my father rose, saying, 'Come with me. I have something to show you.'

We followed him outside. Neritos would have fallen in behind me but I checked my pace and let him catch me up so that we went on side by side. His expression had not changed but I felt him glancing at me out of the corner of his eye from time to time. My father led the way to the stables. Standing in the yard was a chariot and pair. I recognised the chestnuts at once as the pair Neritos had driven in the race, but the chariot was not the usual light racing rig but something much more elaborate. In fact, it struck me as rather too splendid for someone in his position.

'You have brought your horses with you,' I commented. 'But why have they not been unyoked?'

151

The wind had whipped colour into his cheeks and his eyes were bright.

'They go well!' I said. 'And you handle them well, too.'

He looked away, but I could tell that he was pleased. Ahead of us a cloud of dust marked the approach of another chariot. I pointed. 'That will be Alectryon.'

As we drew closer I could see Alectryon shading his eyes, clearly puzzled by the strange chariot and driver. Then he saw me and raised his arm in salute. The two chariots came to a stop a few paces from each other and Alectryon jumped down, giving the reins to Dexeus. His horses were sweating and I could see he had given them a good gallop.

I went to meet him and he said cheerfully, 'What is this? An important visitor from somewhere?'

I shook my head, laughing. 'No. Guess again.'

'I've no idea. Both the horses and their driver are strangers to me.'

'Well,' I said, 'the horses and the chariot are mine – a gift from my father. The driver is Neritos, son of Kretheus who was Prefect of Phea until his death a few months ago. Now Neritos is to be my charioteer.'

'Indeed!' He looked at the chariot and its driver with closer interest. 'I have been thinking it was time you had your own chariot and charioteer. Your father has certainly provided you with both worthy of your position. Aren't those the chestnuts than ran so well at the games?'

'They are,' I agreed, 'and Neritos drove them. Come and meet him.'

Neritos had been watching us curiously. As I presented him to Alectryon I felt a sudden twinge of anxiety. If they did not like each other it would make life very difficult. However, it was not in Alectryon's nature to be jealous and he set himself at once to break down Neritos's reserve. Few people could resist his charm and my new charioteer was no exception. Then he called Dexeus to come closer and introduced the two of them. Dexeus was habitually taciturn and never one to accept strangers readily, while Neritos was in no mood to take the initiative, so having exchanged formal greetings they eyed each other in silence like two strange dogs. Alectryon, however, was more interested in the horses and neither of us paid much attention to our squires.

'They go like the wind!' I told him. 'How about a race back to the city?'

He laughed. 'As you can see perfectly well, my horses are already spent. Let us go back quietly together and another day I shall be happy to accept your challenge.'

Accordingly we re-mounted our chariots and set off side by side on the broad road leading to the city. The horses went easily and Alectryon and I conversed across the small space between us. We were both so involved in our conversation that it was a little while before we realised that our speed had subtly increased and we were now spinning along briskly. I glanced at Neritos. His jaw was obstinately set and his eyes flickered backwards and forwards from the road to Dexeus. Dexeus's face held the same grim determination. I realised what had happened. One or the other had increased his speed a little and the second, not to be out done, had urged on his horses in his turn and now neither would draw rein. Dexeus was normally steady and utterly obedient to Alectryon, so I guessed Neritos had been the original culprit. I was about to reprimand him and tell him to slow down when we rounded a curve in the road. Ahead of us, about four times the distance of a good javelin throw, the road narrowed to pass an outcrop of rock. Here only one chariot could pass at a time. As I drew breath to speak Neritos threw me a swift, challenging look and laid his whip across the horses' backs. We plunged forward. Dexeus, on his mettle now, touched his pair also and we raced neck and neck towards the rock. I could hear Alectryon shouting at Dexeus, demanding what in the world he thought he was doing. I looked at Neritos and opened my mouth to speak, then closed it again and leaned forward, balancing myself against our speed.

It was true, I suppose, that Alectryon's pair had already been galloped hard, but even so I felt a surge of triumph as we drew ahead. They kept close on our heels but there was no question of who was going to be first through the narrow gap.

On the far side the road widened again and I said, as sternly as I could, 'Stop here, Neritos.'

He drew the horses to a standstill and looked at me under his brows, daring me to rebuke him. I was angry at his disobedience but exhilarated by our success and as I looked at him I remembered his face set in grim determination not to give an inch. So what had begun as a reprimand turned suddenly to a snort of laughter. He looked at me, grinned, put the back of his hand across his mouth to conceal it, and then laughed with me.

Dexeus, meanwhile, had brought his chariot to a standstill nearby and Alectryon was standing with his arms folded, gazing in exasperation from one of us to the others. Dexeus hung his head and scowled. Neritos and I strove to contain our laughter.

Alectryon said, 'Dexeus, that is the first time you have ever disobeyed me. I am very angry with you. As for you, Neritos, if you wish to drive like a maniac don't do it in future when you have the heir to the throne as your passenger. And you …!' His eyes turned to my face. I looked back at him, biting my lip. 'You are as bad as the other two!' But he had dissolved into laughter himself before the words were out of his mouth.

When we had sobered a little he went on, 'Very well, since you two can't be trusted with the Prince you can both return to the city in my chariot and I will drive him.'

Accordingly he got up beside me and Neritos went off with bad grace to join Dexeus.

'What a pity,' I said softly as we started off again. 'They are going to dislike each other.'

Alectryon chuckled. 'Not they! They are two of a kind, however different on the surface. Leave them alone and they'll have come to terms by the time we reach the city. Why do you think I put them together?'

He was right, as usual, and by the time we reached his house they had both ceased to scowl We separated and Neritos and I drove on towards the palace. Alectryon had commented on the way home that I should make it clear to Neritos who was in charge, and now my new charioteer was glancing sideways at me as if expecting a reprimand. I waited until we had almost reached the gates and then said, 'Neritos, I enjoyed our little triumph as much as you did, but in future we race when I say so. You understand me?'

He looked rebellious, caught my eye and changed his expression.

'Very well.' Then, a moment later, as if it had cost him a struggle to speak the words, 'I'm sorry.'

I devoted a good deal of time and attention after that to winning Neritos's confidence. It was some days before his real character became evident, but I had guessed at it and my father gave me a further hint in a few private words a day or two later. He asked how he was settling down and, receiving a favourable report, nodded with satisfaction and added, 'He came, as I told you, highly recommended for many qualities. But there is one thing for which he is criticised which I did not mention in front of him - an excess of youthful daring, a rashness that often leads him into trouble. You must help him outgrow that.'

I looked into those inscrutable eyes and wondered if my father ever did anything without at least a double motive.

At first it seemed strange to have Neritos constantly at my shoulder, then I began to wonder how I had managed without him. He learned his duties quickly and, once he discovered that he was not treated like a servant, performed them willingly. He was also ready to fight my battles for me and took an instant and passionate dislike to Antilochos. I confided to him my fears about the intentions of the Dorians and we spent a good deal of time training the horses for war as well as for racing. We exercised together with the other young men of the court and he soon proved himself as an athlete. He was a great wrestler and I think the discovery that he could throw me three times out of four did more than anything to reconcile him to his position.

Before long my father sent me as his representative to visit Leuktron, the capital of the Further Province. I went with a good deal of inner trembling, knowing that his object was to establish me in the hearts and minds of the great men of the land as the true and only heir, and afraid that I might fall short of their expectations. However, I found myself received with respect and kindness and began, little by little, to grow in confidence in my ability to deal with people. From then on my father began to use me increasingly on official business, sometimes in the city itself, where I found myself not only taking an increasing part in the rituals of the Gods but also hearing disputes and passing judgements: sometimes on missions to other towns up and down the country. When he could Alectryon came with me, but he had his duties too and his own household to administer, so increasingly I travelled with Neritos and a small retinue of the Royal Guard.

Wherever I went I was alert to the faintest rumour of discontent and whenever I detected it I used all my powers to find the cause and remove it. After a little I learned with delight that the word was going about that Prince Alkmaion dealt justly with high and low. On the whole it seemed that most people, particularly the land-holders and the officials appointed by the palace, were content enough so long as they were not required to do more than perform their duties, pay their taxes and enjoy their lands in peace. Time and again I heard the same sentiments expressed: 'The time's gone by for fighting;' 'we're settled now;' 'it's all very well to talk of Troy but the age of heroes is past.' How right my father had been when he said that a war now would create dissension!

Where I could I tried to re-awaken the spirit of our forefathers. Whenever a bard sat by the hearth of a house I was visiting I would call for the old, stirring tales. When there was none I took my lyre and sang them myself. The young men listened readily enough and would join me in dreaming of some great enterprise which would make their names ring like those of Achilles and Agamemnon, but their fathers merely smiled indulgently. At such times a sense of foreboding gripped me at the recollection of the Dorians, with their wolvish faces and their iron swords. But there was too much to think about every day to concentrate on them and I found myself worrying less and less about the possibility of an invasion.

The ship carrying Andropompous and Melanthos returned in due course and my father summoned me to be present when they gave their report. Temenos sent messages of good will. His brother Cresphontes had acted entirely without his knowledge and had been rebuked severely. Kerkios's death had not been intended and the man responsible had been executed. Further, he sent a gift of amber beads and two slave girls in payment for Kerkios's loss. Finally, he insisted that he had no hostile intentions towards us and the ships his brother was building were for raids on the more barbarous tribes to the north. How, he asked, could he hope to defeat the redoubtable descendants of

Nestor?

The news was reassuring, though I had to suffer a very uncomfortable morning when it was repeated to the members of the Kin. However, this was somewhat compensated for by Melanthos, who said to me privately, 'I think you are right, Alkmaion. I wouldn't trust Temenos out of my sight.'

Towards the end of the summer I was returning from an official visit to the Further Province. It was late in the day and Neritos was making the chestnuts step out in order to get us back to the palace before dusk. He touched my arm and pointed with his whip towards a cloud of dust on the road ahead of us.

'Another chariot.'

'Yes,' I said. 'Whose, I wonder. It's going towards the city.'

We soon caught up with the other vehicle and seeing us approach, they stopped and waited As we drew up I saw that the chariot was magnificently ornamented and the occupants richly dressed, though both were strangers to me . I got down and went towards them and the passenger, obviously the higher ranking of the two, came to meet me. He was a tall man in his middle years, with a lean, well-boned face and eyes accustomed to command. From the magnificent necklace and armlets that he wore it was clear that he was of noble birth. I saluted him with fitting courtesy.

'Greetings, friend. I am Alkmaion, son of Sillos the King. May I know whom I have the honour of welcoming to Pylos?'

I saw his eyes widen and his face broke into a warm, humorous smile. 'Why, Prince, this is a most fortunate meeting! I am Penthilos, son of Orestes and half-brother to Tisamenos, High King of Mycenae.'

It was my turn to stretch my eyes in surprise. Here was an important visitor indeed! Half-brother and Lawagetas to the High King himself, to whom even my father owed allegiance.

I answered respectfully, 'We are most honoured, Prince Penthilos. This visit is a pleasure we had not dreamed of. Had we known in advance of your coming I would have met you at the borders of the kingdom. My father will be delighted to welcome you. Your name, if not yourself, is well known in Pylos.'

His smile broadened. 'As is yours in Mycenae, Prince Alkmaion. Your bard Sirios has made us acquainted with your adventures overseas.'

I blushed with pleasure, but replied, 'They are as nothing compared with the mighty deeds of Penthilos of Mycenae.'

He went on, 'I should, I know, have sent a herald ahead of me to announce my coming but my journey was made on an impulse, so I hope your father will forgive the informality. A messenger has gone ahead from the first town we came to so he should by now be informed of my arrival. Tell me, are you travelling far from home, or are we in fact quite close to your father's palace?'

'It is true,' I returned, 'that I have been on a long journey for my father, but we are now almost home. If we make our horses show their best paces we can be there before sunset.'

'Good!' he said. 'Let us do that'.

I said, a trifle hesitantly, 'If it pleases you, let my charioteer ride with yours and I will drive you to the palace. Then we can converse more easily.'

'It pleases me very well,' Penthilos returned with smiling courtesy.

As we drove along I asked him how he had fared on the journey and he enquired after the health of my father and the rest of my family. I longed to ask what had brought him to Pylos but that, I knew, was for my father to do, not me. I found him pleasant company and by the time we were nearing the city we were chatting easily. As we rounded the final bend in the road, with the sun making a path of flame across the sea, I pointed ahead.

'There is the city, and those are the rooftops of my father's palace on the hill.'

Penthilos leaned forward, shading his eyes. Then he turned to me. 'What I have heard is true, then. You have no defending walls.'

I hesitated, slightly taken aback and remembering the argument with my uncles of that very subject. 'When my great-grandfather Nestor rebuilt the palace of his father, Neleus, his power was so absolute he had no need of walls. We have been fortunate in that it has always been so. No foes have come against us and the land is quiet.'

He said, 'Quite, quite. Let us hope it will always be so.' But I could see that he was disturbed.

As we reached the outskirts of the city people came out to watch us pass and many saluted me. Penthilos smiled, 'It is easy to see you are much loved, Prince Alkmaion.'

I kept those words in my heart a long time.

At the palace gates the slaves were waiting to take the horses heads and I led Penthilos into the courtyard. My father was waiting under the porch with the rest of the Royal Kin to greet him with fitting ceremony. There had been no time to prepare a feast of suitable grandeur so we dined simply. I noticed Penthilos making a careful scrutiny of everyone present and reflected that his brother, the High King, would no doubt be interested in his report on the Royal Household of Pylos. Fortunately my Uncle Paion was doing his best to impress and managed to be quite affable, while Antilochos produced that smooth charm which he could affect so easily when he wished.

As the meal drew to a close Penthilos remarked, 'Your bard, Sirios, has praised the beauty of the ladies of the Royal House of Neleus. I hope we shall see them tonight?'

My father smiled at the compliment and replied that they would join us very soon.

'Let me see,' Penthilos pursued. 'You have a daughter, I believe.'

I saw my father's face cloud. 'Yes, I have, Prince. Karpathia. But I fear she has not been well for some time.'

'Indeed? What is wrong with her?'

My father shook his head. 'Who can say? When the Gods lay their hands on a mortal, who can tell what ails them?'

Penthilos frowned and responded, 'Let us hope there is some other cause, for which a cure may be found.'

At that moment the ladies entered the hall. Karpathia was leading them and I guessed that my father had sent her instructions to be present out of courtesy to our guest, for she usually refused to appear. My father rose and led Penthilos forward to introduce him. I saw Karpathia's eyes flicker up to his face and then drop to the ground again. She was paler and thinner than ever now, but once or twice during the evening I noticed Penthilos looking in her direction. Indeed, even in her sickness, there was something about her face to draw the eye. Her eyes had always been large, and dark like my own. Now they dominated her face, and her skin was white as ivory against the black of her hair.

The next days were given up to entertaining Penthilos and the duty of looking after him largely devolved upon me. I had no objection, since I found him good company. There was hunting and feasting, music, dancing and games and he was lavish in his appreciation of everything.

On the second day, as we drove home from the hunt, he said to me, 'It is a pity your sister does not join us. Is she really so ill?'

I hesitated, not knowing what to say. 'It seems so. She cannot be persuaded to take any interest in life.'

He sighed. 'It is sad. She is very beautiful. Everything your bard, Sirios, has told us is true, then.'

'What has Sirios told you?' I asked, aghast.

'That she accidentally offended the Goddess and has since lived almost completely in retirement.'

I swallowed and nodded. 'Yes, that is so.'

He frowned. 'Has anything been done to ascertain the Goddess's will? Since the offence was accidental it seems hard the poor girl should suffer like this. Or did some oracle tell her of the Goddess's doom?'

I shook my head. 'There has been no need of that. We have watched her wither and no physician can find the cause for it.'

'But is it not possible that she herself has mistaken the Goddess's intentions? If she could be persuaded to take part in the pleasures of life at court again perhaps she would begin to recover.'

I gave a short, sorrowful laugh. 'Then you must try to persuade her yourself, Prince. I have tried again and again without success.'

'Perhaps I will,' he returned lightly. I looked at him quickly, trying to read his intentions, but he turned away and shortly changed the subject.

That night after supper we retired to my father's apartments to talk privately. For some time I listened while he and Penthilos discussed affairs of state. At length Penthilos brought up the question of defensive walls but my father put aside all suggestion of danger with a smooth show of confidence that made it seem as if he had never heard of the Dorians.

Penthilos, however, was not to be so easily put off. 'You are fortunate in the situation of your kingdom, my lord. In this quiet corner the whole world seems peaceful. But I assure you it is not so. Every merchant captain and every foreign ambassador who comes to my brother's Court brings the same story. Every civilised nation reports the movement of barbarian peoples on their borders. Many have already had to fight them off, and their numbers are growing. Our traders in Ugarit and Alalakh speak of mounting unease among the rulers. Even Egypt is worried. If this movement continues to spread westwards, as it appears to be doing, who is to say that we shall not one day find the barbarians pressing on our northern frontiers?'

My father replied, 'I have heard similar rumours from my own merchants, Prince, but I cannot see these rude hordes as a real threat to cities like ours. Anyway, here in Pylos we have always preferred to rely on good men and good equipment rather than on walls – not that I wish by that, you understand, to infer any slight on the army of Mycenae. Everyone knows that that is second to none.'

Penthilos was too tactful to press the argument further and after a pause he changed the subject. 'I was glad to see your daughter Karpathia among the other ladies this morning. I find it hard to believe nothing can be done to help her.'

My father returned gravely, 'I fear she has little to hope for, Prince, and that, no doubt, weighs as heavily upon her as the anger of the Goddess.'

'Surely,' Penthilos said, 'it is possible for her to marry?' He paused a moment and added, 'Of course, I have no experience of these matters myself. I am not married, though my brother Tisamenos often tells me that I should look for a lady of suitable birth to be my wife.' Then he rose and, making the excuse that the day's festivities had tired him, retired to his room.

When he had gone I turned to my father. 'Does he mean what I take him to mean?'

My father nodded slowly, a smile beginning somewhere in the depths of his beard. 'At all events, I think we have discovered the purpose of Prince Penthilos's visit.'

'To woo Karpathia?'

163

'Shall we say, to see if Sirios's praises were justified, and if the marriage was possible.'

'Can he really intend to marry her?' I asked.

My father raised his hand warningly. 'We must not come to hasty conclusions. All we can say at this moment is that he wished to sound my feelings in the matter.'

'But why should Penthilos come seeking a woman   ... in Karpathia's position?'

'Remember,' my father said, ' he is not the legitimate son of Orestes. Though his reputation is good and his brother obviously reposes complete trust in him, that could be a bar to his forming an alliance suitable to his position. Then again, Messenia is the second most powerful kingdom in the Peloponnese. Tisamenos would look far for a better alliance. Had Karpathia not been destined for the service of the Goddess many princes would have been here seeking her hand while she was still a girl.'

'Will you consent if he asks for her hand?'

'It would be very foolish to refuse. But then, there is the question of Karpathia herself.'

'She must do as you bid her.'

He looked at me. 'Alkmaion, the girl is dying. If nothing can be found to lift her out of her despair she will not outlast the winter. Would it be of any use to betroth her to Penthilos if she dies before the marriage ceremony?'

'But perhaps this might be just what she needs. You said yourself that she had nothing to hope for.'

'That is what I am thinking. So we must do our best to see that she is in Penthilos's company as much as possible. If he can rouse her liking and still wishes to make the match then I believe we may save her.'

'But what of the Goddess?'

'If matters proceed as I hope, we will consult the oracles and seek to discover Her will. It may be that Penthilos's arrival is a sign that She has already relented.'

The next day, when the sun began to sink and the air grew cooler, I sent Andria to my sister to ask her to walk with me in the olive grove. When she came it seemed to me that her eyes held something more than the blank despair I had almost come to expect. It was a hint only, a trace of interest or curiosity, but at least I felt that she wished to hear what I had to say.

I took her hand, which lay cold and small in mine, and we wandered down the slope towards the stream.

'How are you?'

Her only response was a little movement of her shoulders. She no longer wore the ritual dress of a priestess with its tight bodice that left the breasts bare, but the simpler robe of a court lady. It made her look younger and more fragile. I remembered her terrifying dignity in the days of her priesthood and saw how it had become frozen into this obstinate despair.

I said, 'It's curious, but even though you have grown so thin lately you have grown more beautiful than ever. Prince Penthilos has praised your beauty to me more than once.'

Her eyes flickered up to me and then away again.

'I must say,' I went on, 'I find him a very pleasant companion. Also, of course, he has a reputation for courage and wisdom that I should say is well deserved – and he's a splendid athlete. It is strange, is it not, that a man in his position, with his looks and accomplishments, is not married?'

For a moment she looked me full in the eyes. I had guessed, rightly it seemed, that she had not permitted herself to ask that question, even of her handmaids.

'Tomorrow,' I went on, 'I am taking him to see the royal herd of horses up on their summer pastures. You should come, Karpathia. The air is pleasant in the mountains and you have scarcely left the palace for months now. Will you?'

She began to shake her head but I clasped her hand tightly and said, 'Don't refuse, my dear, please! If you will not do it to please yourself, at least give us the pleasure of your company. Do not turn yourself away from us so completely.'

She looked up at me, her eyes searching my face. Then she nodded and said huskily, 'Very well, I will come.'

I took both her hands and said, 'Karpathia, believe me. I am sure the Goddess is no longer angry. Try to escape from the shadows you have hidden among and perhaps She will show you favour.'

She bent her head and warm tears fell on my hand. I put my arm round her and held her against my shoulder and for a moment we stood quietly together. Then she drew back, brushing away the tears with the back of her hand, and said, 'Dear Alkmaion, I will try. But I do not think there can be any escape for me.'

'There can!' I cried. 'I am sure of it. Only try to live again!'

She reached up and kissed my cheek with a faint, wistful smile. 'Very well. I will try.'

She kept her promise to join us the following morning. Several other ladies were to accompany us also, together with a party of my father's Companions. I noticed that Karpathia was looking even more striking than usual but it was a moment before I realised that she had painted her eyes and lips like the other ladies, something she had not troubled to do for some time. However, her general demeanour had not changed and she remained quietly on the fringe of the crowd, her eyes gazing ahead of her without expression.

The procession of chariots wound up into the mountains. After we had inspected the horses, stools were set and rugs spread in the shade of some trees and refreshments were served. I noticed that Penthilos had contrived to find a seat near the ladies and went over to join him. He was at his most charming and the other ladies vied for his attention. Karpathia sat silent, but from time to time she raised her eyes for a second or two to look at him and I thought a faint flush of colour tinged her cheeks.

That evening Penthilos requested a private audience with my father. I lurked in the courtyard outside the royal apartments until my father came to his door and called me in. He was smiling.

'Prince Penthilos has just asked for your sister's hand. I have told him that nothing would please me better, but that the will of the Goddess must be ascertained before I give my consent. Also, he understands Karpathia's position and is willing to listen to her wishes in the matter. I have sent for her so that we may discover them.'

Karpathia appeared a few moments later. I think she had expected our father to be alone but she responded to Penthilos's presence by no more than a stiffening of her body and a lowering of her eyes.

My father went to her and took her hand, saying gently, 'Karpathia, Prince Penthilos does us the honour of asking for your hand in marriage. You have been much distressed of late and he knows the reason for this. Therefore, he is prepared to abide by your answer. I need not describe to you the honour of the position he is offering you, for as his wife you would be second only to the Queen in Mycenae. We all desire your happiness and long for you to cast off the shadows that lie upon you, and the love of a noble gentleman like Prince Penthilos should make that possible for you. What answer can you give him?'

Karpathia did not raise her eyes. 'How can the Prince desire to marry one whom the Goddess has rejected?'

Penthilos came forward. 'I do not believe it is so, lady. On the night after your bard Sirios first told me about you I had a dream, and I believe it was sent by the Goddess. I was in a vineyard and the harvest was in progress. All around me men were picking the grapes. In the centre of the vineyard was a vine more beautiful and more fruitful than the rest but no one was picking the grapes from it. When I asked why they told me that it was accursed and would poison anyone who touched it, but then a voice spoke to me, saying, 'Pluck this fruit, Penthilos, for it is yours and yours alone.' So I plucked the grapes and pressed the juice and immediately it became the sweetest wine I had ever tasted. I believe that you are that vine, lady. The next morning I determined to set forth as soon as possible to see you, and now I am more than ever convinced that my dream was a message from the Mistress Herself. But I have agreed with your father that we should again consult Her will, provided that you will it also.'

Slowly Karpathia lifted her eyes to his. 'If the Goddess will permit it, I shall be willing also.'

Penthilos thanked her formally and kissed her hand, after which she begged leave to retire. When she had gone I congratulated him warmly and he said, laughing, 'The ties between our houses cannot be too strong. We must see if we can find a princess of Mycenae to suit your tastes, Alkmaion.'

I hesitated, for nothing was further from my mind than marriage, but my father put in smoothly, 'Alkmaion is a trifle young for marriage yet. When the time comes our eyes may well turn to Mycenae.'

'Of course,' said Penthilos. 'I understand. Besides,' he grinned and clapped me on the shoulder, 'I know the Prince's affections are elsewhere at the moment. The Count Alectryon is an excellent gentleman and a fitting companion for a prince. But that will pass in a year or two.'

The words were lightly spoken but they echoed in my heart for a long time. That night in bed Alectryon and I discussed the events of the day, as was our habit. He was delighted by the news of Penthilos's proposal but as always was sensitive to my mood.

'You are sad, my dear. What is it?'

I told him what Penthilos had said. He sighed and commented, 'It's true, you will have to marry – and sooner rather than later. In fact, I am surprised that we have not already had embassies from Mycenae or Athens or Crete offering you the hand of some princess or other.'

I groaned. 'I don't want to think about it!'

'Oh come!' he tugged my hair playfully. 'Is it such a terrible prospect? After all, as I remember it, you are not entirely averse to feminine company.'

'But to be tied to someone you have never met and may not even like …!' I protested.

He dropped his teasing manner. 'Your father is a good man. I cannot believe he would force you into a marriage that was not to your taste.' Then, as if the idea had only just occurred to him, 'You're not harbouring a secret passion for some other lady, are you?'

I looked him in the eyes. 'Have you ever seen me look at a woman since that night in Cresphontes's village?'

'No,' he said gently. 'I was joking.'

We were silent for a minute. Then I said, 'You will have to marry too. You must produce an heir.'

He yawned and rolled onto his back. 'There's no hurry for me. No kingdoms depend upon a suitable alliance cemented by my marriage. It can wait until I'm thirty – longer perhaps. If anything happens to me in the meantime the land will go to Nequeus. He cares more for it than I do.'

'He wouldn't make such a good member of the

Companionhood, though,' I commented.

'No,' he agreed. 'Perhaps not.' He turned towards me again and grinned. 'I'll tell you what. You and I will go on our travels again until we find two beautiful foreign princesses to bring back as our brides. How's that?'

I knew he was trying to tease me out of my melancholy but Penthilos's words had struck too deep for that. I tried to smile in return.

'As long as it's a very long voyage before we find them.'

He put his arm round me. 'Don't look so tragic. The time will come, but the next few years are ours.'

'But when one of us does marry,' I said, 'everything will have to change.'

'Perhaps. But things are always changing. Life doesn't stand still. You know that. Change doesn't have to be a bad thing.'

I moved closer to him, feeling tears sting the back of my eyes. 'I don't want to lose you!'

He sighed. 'I wish I could promise you that that would never happen, that I shall always be here. But if I did some listening God might decide to punish me for my presumption. No one can tell what may happen. But I will swear this to you. As long as I live you will always have my love. No one on earth, man or woman, can alter that.'

He kissed me then, and I forgot my fears in his embrace.

The following day Penthilos took me aside to make a request.

'Beg your sister to give us a few minutes of her company. I have seen her only in the midst of crowds of people. By all means remain at hand yourself, but let me speak to her privately for a moment.'

I assented willingly and told him to wait for me in my favourite spot by the stream. Then I sent Andria to find Karpathia and when she came asked her to walk with me. When we were beyond the palace I said tenderly, 'I am happy to see life beginning again for you, Karpathia.'

She answered softly, 'We cannot tell yet. The Mistress must be consulted.'

'The answer will be favourable. I am sure of it. And you? You are glad?'

She looked at me, then away. 'I do not know.'

'But do you like Penthilos?'

'He is courteous … and gentle … I cannot tell whether I shall like him.'

I took her hand. 'He is waiting for you by the stream and begs a few words in private. Will you let me take you to him? I shall wait nearby.'

I felt her tremble and she cast about her as if for a way of escape. 'Karpathia,' I said, 'he is a man of honour. You have nothing to fear.'

She looked at me and I saw her pride reassert itself. 'Very well. Let us go to him.'

I led her down to the grassy bank where Penthilos waited and seated her upon the rock where I had once found Sirios. Then I retired out of earshot and settled myself self-consciously under an olive tree with my back to them. It was a long wait.

At length Penthilos called my name and I rose to see them coming up the slope towards me. Karpathia's eyes were modestly downcast but her hand rested in his and her face no longer appeared to be carved out of ivory.

The following day my father and I, Penthilos and Karpathia, with a few attendants, made our way to the Holy Mountain. Once again I entered the Great Cave of the Mysteries, but this time only Karpathia passed into the sacred inner recesses. I followed her in my mind and trembled. While she was gone we made fitting sacrifices to the Thrice-Queen.

At length she returned with the Chief Priest. She was pale and swaying with exhaustion but as she stood before us she drew herself up and I saw once again the power of the Goddess in her. 'The words of the Goddess are 'Marry, and bear my worship to your new home, for the days are coming when I shall seek a new abode."

Penthilos started. 'But the Lady is already worshipped in Mycenae, as She is here.'

My father said, 'Let us not seek too deeply into the meaning of the oracle. It is sufficient that the anger of the Goddess is ended and She gives Her blessing to your marriage.'

The following day Karpathia's betrothal to Penthilos was

formally celebrated and two days after that he took his departure, promising to return again in the spring for the marriage itself. I escorted him to the borders of my father's land and there parted from him with many expressions of friendship and goodwill.

Chapter 10.

The time of the vintage came and with it the celebrations that always accompany the harvest. Before the great religious festival that marks the end of summer and the waning power of the sun each village held its own feast when the first grapes were pressed. Alectryon suggested that we should join the celebrations at his estate and I was happy to agree, since I always felt more at my ease there than anywhere else. Yet when the day came I found myself possessed by an unaccustomed melancholy. There was something about the shortening days and the softer light which always laid a subduing hand on my spirit. As we strolled up to the little village where the workers lived the full moon hung low and swollen over the sea and the air was heavy with the scent of herbs.

Alectryon rested an arm on my shoulders. 'Something is troubling you.'

I sighed and shook my head. 'No, nothing important. I am often sad at this time of year. It makes me feel as if I had lived a thousand years and could remember them all.'

He laughed softly. 'But aren't they happy memories?'

'Some of them.' I looked at him. 'This summer will be a happy memory.'

'For me, too,' he agreed. 'But why be sad? The summer ends but we have many more ahead of us.'

'I know,' I said, forcing a smile. 'Ignore me. It's nothing.'

We reached the village and the people greeted us respectfully. They all knew and loved Alectryon, but I could see that they were a little over-awed by my presence. I hoped I was not going to dampen their enjoyment. The festivities began, as was proper, with due rites and sacrifices, but then the casks of wine from the previous vintage were opened and the night's revelry began. I was tempted to withdraw quietly after a cup or two, but the village was famous for the quality and potency of its vintage and before long the faces around me looked more relaxed, the fires seemed to burn brighter and the music of the pipe sounded sweeter. Then Neritos ran up to me with his arms around the waists of two pretty girls, both of whom were carrying full wineskins. It would have been churlish to refuse when they offered to refill my cup.

Soon the young men rose to dance and Alectryon dragged me into the circle. I had always loved to dance. Any kind of movement where I felt my body supple and obedient, whether running or riding or in the graceful figures of the dance, gave me pleasure. The dances grew wilder and in between we refreshed ourselves with further draughts of wine, until, quite suddenly it seemed, most of the dancers had disappeared. I leaned against a tree trunk and peered round me. Neritos had gone and I had not seen Alectryon for some time. Then my eyes found him, standing alone on the other side of the fire. I waved, but I was beyond the firelight and he did not see me, so I started towards him. Then a girl ran up and caught his hand. From the way he turned and drew her to him I knew he had been waiting for her. I watched them walk away from the firelight and disappear among the trees.

Unsteadily I began to make my way down the path away from the village. There was a scuffle and a giggle behind me. I looked round. A pair of dark eyes in the pale oval of a face gleamed at me from the trees beside the path. I took a step towards them. They vanished with another giggle, to reappear a few yards further away. I plunged into the bushes in pursuit.

When we arrived back at the palace the following day I found that Sirios and his young apprentice had returned as unexpectedly as they had departed. Sirios was full of news and gossip from the courts of Mycenae and Tyrins and new songs learned from other bards, but when I tried to question him about his part in Penthilos's visit he pretended not to understand me.

The great festival of the autumn equinox passed and I was relieved to find it quite different from the New Year Festival. Once it was over life began to fold in upon itself in preparation for winter.

One more event occurred, however, before the rains of winter came. With the fading of the year came the death of my great-uncle, old Peisistratos, the last remaining son of Nestor. I believe every member of the Royal Kin felt the breaking of this last link with the heroic past. Now Nestor and Odysseus, Helen and Menelaus lived in stories only. There was no one left who could remember them.

We buried him in the great domed tomb a little distance from the palace, where his brothers had been buried before him – except for the first Antilochos, who had left his ashes before the walls of Troy. His corpse was decked with rich grave ornaments and a mask of beaten gold covered his face. Round his body we set those objects he had treasured most during his life and sacred vessels of bronze and silver. We held a solemn feast and drank a toast to the spirit now beginning its long journey to the abode of the dead, and smashed our cups against the pillars that upheld the mighty lintel of the doorway. Then we returned to the city to prepare for the funeral games my father had ordered in his honour.

These games were on a far more magnificent scale than those held for Cresphontes and people thronged into the city from all over the country to take part in them. My father had provided an impressive array of prizes and every athlete in Messenia was eager to compete for them. Alectryon and I, and our two squires, were no exception and we had no reason to be disappointed in the results. Dexeus as usual won the archery contest and Neritos beat all comers in the wrestling, while Alectryon carried off the prize in the men's footrace and the javelin. I won the footrace in my own age group but the event my heart was really set on was the chariot race.

Six chariots were entered. My father's, driven as always by Telaon, my own and Alectryon's made up three. The fourth was driven by Antilochos, who had acquired his own pair very soon after I received mine, and the last two belonged to other members of the Companionhood. I mounted the chariot and took the reins from Neritos. It seemed hard that this time he would not be driving. We had talked it over and I had offered to let him drive but he had shaken his head and said with his usual generosity, 'It would not be right. They are your horses now. Besides, I had my chance. Now you must see if you can win for both of us.'

From the moment of the starting signal Antilochos went ahead, laying the whip hard across his horses' backs and setting a cracking pace. 'Fool!' I thought. 'They'll never be able to keep this up.' The course consisted of two laps, with a turning post at each end of an oval track. By the end of the first lap the two chariots belonging to the

Companions were virtually out of the race. Antilochos still led, with myself and Telaon neck and neck behind him and Alectryon's pair thundering hard on our heels. As we headed out away from the Royal Pavilion for the second time I could see Antilochos's horses were flagging, although he plied the whip more vigorously than ever. 'Now,' I said to myself, 'if I can overtake him and get to the turn first I shall win.' I had deliberately kept on the outside of the leading chariot, forcing Telaon even further out and preventing him from boxing me in behind Antilochos. Now I called to my horses and touched them with the whip. They surged ahead and began to overtake Antilochos. I saw him turn and cast a furious glare behind him. Then he jerked the reins and his horses swung across, right into my path. If we had been any closer nothing could have prevented a collision. As it was I hauled on the reins and swung my chestnuts behind him as his animals careered, out of control, across the track. I had to bring my pair almost to a standstill and as I fought to get them under control another chariot thundered past on the inside. It was Alectryon's. On my other side I was dimly aware of my father's horses plunging off the track to avoid Antilochos, and then the way ahead was clear and I sent my pair flying after Alectryon's. As we rounded the turning post, with only the length of a chariot pole between us, I heard the crowd shouting, but it was not a shout of encouragement for either of us. Glancing over at the opposite side of the track, where the mêlée had occurred, I saw my father's horses running wild towards the sea and between them and the track the broken remains of the chariot, among which lay the still figure of Telaon. The picture was still in my mind as I thundered over the finishing line just behind Alectryon.

Neritos ran up and caught the horses' heads. 'That was deliberate! Antilochos fouled you!'

I jumped down and went to caress the sweating horses. 'Yes, but it's Telaon who suffered. Is he badly hurt?'

'They are bringing him in now.'

He was alive, though at first sight it seemed impossible that such a battered and bleeding body could still hold life. My father stooped over the litter and spoke gently to him and then ordered his attendants to carry him to the palace and to place him in the care of the King's physician. Then he turned with a face of stone and told the herald to proclaim the winners.

Alectryon took the first prize of a sword and shield while I received a gold cup and a sturdy little mare, which I gave to Neritos. But none of us had any pleasure in our victory. Alectryon, trying to cheer me, said, 'Don't let Antilochos's dishonourable behaviour rob you of your triumph. You deserve the prize. If he had not fouled you, you would have won the race. I was badly placed and I doubt if I could have done better than third.'

I said. 'It's the thought of Telaon that grieves me. He is the innocent victim of Antilocos's terrible jealousy.'

'Well,' Alectryon said grimly, 'this time he has gone too far. His father will not be able to protect him from the King's anger.'

When we returned to the palace my father sent for us and questioned us closely about what had happened. When he had assured himself that there was no doubt about Antilochos's intentions he dismissed us and I hear him order one of the guards to tell the Lawagetas to attend on him. I never knew what passed between them, but that night Antilochos was missing from the feast and Paion's face was black with anger.

The next day Perimedes sought me out and begged a few words in private. I led him to my own apartments and he said, blushing, 'I want to beg your forgiveness for what Antilochos did yesterday.'

'Did he send you?'

'No.' He met my eyes proudly. 'But I ask on behalf of – of all my family.'

I said awkwardly, 'Perimedes, I have no quarrel with you. What Antilochos does is his own responsibility. You have no need to be ashamed.'

He turned away and said darkly, 'He shames us all.'

I laid my hand on his arm. 'Don't think that. Everyone knows you are not like him.'

He flung my hand off and glared back at me. 'He is my brother.'

I hesitated, uncertain how to reach him. Eventually I said, 'Where is he now? I haven't seen him since yesterday.'

'He has been sent out to the family estate. He is not to return until the King your father gives his permission.'

I paused again and then said, 'Perimedes, I hope this will not cause bad feeling between us. I should be very sorry if it did, truly.'

He dropped his fierce pride. 'Yes. So should I.'

'Then let us agree that what Antilochos does makes no difference to us.'

He hesitated, then nodded and we embraced to seal the contract.

Winter came. I was more than ever employed in state business, although the condition of the roads made it impossible to travel as much as I had done. This gave me more time to consider my position among my contemporaries at court. We had grown up together and I had been a boy among boys. Now I needed to establish myself as their leader. I studied their characters and tried to find the right approach to each. I invited them to hunt or exercise with me, and dined in their houses. By mid winter I had gathered about me a close, loyal group of some of the most vigorous spirits, all equally filled with the desire for some honourable exploit. I did not mention the possibility of invasion to them, but I kept them busy practising swordplay and chariot manoeuvres even in weather that would have seen most people indoors by the fire. It was not long before people began to call this distinct little band ' the Prince's Companions'.

Antilochos returned to court after the mid-winter festival. He made me a public apology in front of the whole Royal Kin and presented generous gifts to Telaon, who had survived to the amazement of all of us, though he would walk with a limp for the rest of his life. Antilochos himself seemed subdued and genuinely contrite, but I noticed before long that he had begun to gather around him all the misfits and malcontents of the court, in a kind of mirror image of my 'Companions'.

My preoccupation with all this left me less time than before for Alectryon. One evening, a chill night in the coldest part of the year, we were dining together, sitting close to a fire of charcoal burning in a three-legged brazier in the centre of his room. He seemed more taciturn than usual and after a while I asked, 'Are you not well? You're very quiet tonight.'

He shook his head. 'No, it's not that. I was thinking, that's all.'

'Thinking of what?'

He looked at me with one of his wry smiles. 'You. You have grown up so quickly over this winter.'

'Is that a bad thing?'

'No, of course not. It's as I said to you when Penthilos was here. Things have to change.'

I felt a sudden sense of shock. 'Change, yes. But this has nothing to do with us.'

'Doesn't it?'

For the first time I saw the sadness in his eyes which he had tried to keep hidden from me. I left my chair and went to kneel beside him.

'No, it doesn't. Nothing has changed between us. Can you really believe I am so fickle?'

'I never accused you of that. You have other things to occupy your mind, that's all.'

'Don't you understand?' I said. 'It's you who have given me the confidence to do what I am doing. Without you I should be lost. But I have been thoughtless and stupid. I never meant to hurt you.'

He looked down into my face and pushed my hair back with a familiar gesture.

'I'm not trying to hold you back. You know you are free to do as you wish.'

'Idiot!' I groaned, reaching up to him. 'I don't want to be free!'

After that night he was his old self again and I made sure that my companions recognised him as their leader, on an equal footing to myself.

With the first days of spring came a messenger from Mycenae to say that Penthilos would come to claim his bride as soon as the New Year Festival was over. All through the winter I had watched Karpathia. It was like watching a seed hidden in the dark earth and waiting for spring. Since Penthilos's proposal she had ceased to fade and wither and her body had filled out, but she was still withdrawn, closed in on herself, her whole being arrested in the one state of passive waiting.

I was with my father when he sent for her to tell her the news. She received it without apparent emotion and we were both saddened by her lack of response, but from that day on we began to see a change in her. At first she was too proud and self-contained to let her joy and eagerness be seen by any but those closest to her but as she grew more absorbed in the preparations for her wedding a radiance began to shine from her that nobody could have mistaken. I realised that all this time she had been in love, and growing more so every day.

Plowistos, the month for sailing again, came round. The days were bright and clear and the sun regained its strength. Out on Alectryon's estate Nequeus started breaking in my white colt. Alectryon and I celebrated the first anniversary of the beginning of our friendship with offerings to the gods and a small dinner party for our closest friends. The only shadow on my happiness was the thought of the imminent New Year Festival. The memory of last year still filled me with terror and as the time approached I began to fear that I should not be able to force myself to go through the ritual again, even though the priestess who represented the Goddess and Her chosen consort would be as unknown to me as to the rest of the assembly. I performed my part in the ceremonies of purification on the day before in a dreamlike state. Then came the day of the New Wine. It was Alectryon who filled and refilled my cup until the divine ecstasy of the Goddess overtook me. From then on I closed my mind to memory until the third night, when I stood once more upon the mountaintop before the leafy bower that enclosed the Sacred Couch, and heard in the darkness the faint hymn beginning. I stood still, listening, sensing the breathing of the waiting throng about me. Last year the rite had meant only horror for me. Now, for the first time, I sensed its power. With the lighting of the torches and the cry of rejoicing my spirit flew free like a bird from a snare and the world for me, as for everyone about me, was regenerate. I felt the hot tears on my cheeks, and brushed them away to take my place at the banquet of rejoicing.

The next day my father despatched a ship under Skamon, his best captain since the loss of Kerkios, to visit the Dorians and bring back news of any further developments. And I increased the frequency of our exercises in chariot fighting.

179

This was soon put out of our minds, however, by the arrival of Penthilos. He came as fits a prince going to his bridal, attended by a train of young noblemen and bearing rich gifts. I looked at him when we met and thought that Karpathia would not be disappointed. Penthilos, however, cannot have been prepared for the change in her, for when my father led her forward to greet him I saw his lips part in wonder and he became quite speechless and confused. From that moment they had eyes only for each other.

Alectryon, watching them together, remarked, 'Penthilos is a lucky man. He came seeking a suitable alliance, and found the love of his life.'

The marriage celebrations lasted several days and the palace of Nestor can never have seen greater feasting or more lavish gifts. The megaron and the courtyard were filled every day with a throng of people dressed in the richest and most colourful fabrics and bright with jewels, for the men of my father's court were not going to be outshone by those from Mycenae and there was much comparing of the latest fashions in both cities.

When the time came for them to leave we renewed our pledges of friendship and I repeated my promise to visit Mycenae in the summer. Karpathia and I parted with tears and kisses. For a short time we had regained the closeness of our childhood but now, I knew, we would inevitably grow apart again. Still, I could only rejoice to see her go, radiant with such happiness, and comforted myself with the thought of frequent visits.

After their departure the court relapsed into a kind of exhausted lethargy, like a man sleeping off the effects of too much feasting. There was a lull even in state business and my father expressed a desire to see Pedasos, the colt whom he had heard me praise so often. Alectryon and I escorted him out to the farm and Nequeus led us out to the paddock behind the house. The colt lifted his head and whinnied when he saw us. He had grown into a magnificent animal. His coat was almost pure white and his flowing mane and tail shone almost silver in the sunlight. He approached us, lifting his feet delicately, ears pricked, his dark, intelligent eyes flickering from one face to another. Over the year since Alectryon gave him to me I had contrived, in the middle of all my other duties, to visit him regularly and he knew me and came to nuzzle my hand in search of titbits. I had picked up a handful of wheat and he took it with soft lips, blowing warm breath over my wrist. I stroked his sleek neck and rubbed him behind the ears, looking across him to my father.

'Well, what do you think of him?'

'He is a horse worthy of a prince,' was his answer. 'And a gift worthy of the giver,' he added smiling at Alectryon. 'Is he broken in yet?' This last to Nequeus.

'I have accustomed him to the bridle and he is used to me leaning over his back and resting my weight on him, but I have not mounted him,' Nequeus replied. 'I thought the first man to do that should be the prince.'

I caught my breath with excitement. 'Shall I try … now?'

'He's ready,' Nequeus said. 'This is as good a time as any.'

He fetched the bridle and Pedasos allowed him to slip the bit into his mouth without protest. It was easy to see that he had always been so kindly handled that he had no fear. I ran my hand along his neck and then over his spine, then leaned my body across his back. He shifted his feet but made no other movement.

Alectryon stepped closed. 'Let me give you a leg-up. Better not to leap onto him the first time.'

I bent my knee and he grasped my leg and lifted me so that I could swing my other leg over and settle gently onto the horse's back. He jerked his head up and his ears flicked back towards me but he stood still. I picked up the reins and said softly, 'Walk on, Pedasos.' I accompanied the words with the lightest pressure of my calves against his side and to my delight he walked forward, tossing his head but making no attempt to unseat me.

I walked him once round the paddock and was tempted to push him into a trot, but I knew it was wise not to ask too much of him at one time. There would be plenty of other opportunities to ride him. I slipped off and handed the reins to Nequeus.

'You have done a wonderful job with him, Nequeus. I'll leave him here with you for a few months longer, but I'll come more often now and we can school him together.'

My father added his compliments and then we let the colt go free and returned to the house for refreshments. Towards evening we set off back to the palace and, as we came in sight of the sea, we saw a ship heading in towards the haven. She was under sail, but the rowers were pulling at the oars as if they wished to make all possible speed.

My father turned in his chariot and called, 'That is Skamon's ship. Let us drive straight down to the shore and see why he is in such a hurry.'

I looked at Alectryon and caught his eye. His face was grave and I felt fear stir in my belly. Our charioteers urged on the horses and we sped down to the seashore, arriving just as the crew were beginning to disembark. Skamon saw us and came hurrying forward but before he could reach us another figure leapt down from the ship, ran forward and flung himself down to clasp my father's knees in the attitude of a suppliant. He was a boy whose garments, dishevelled as they were, proclaimed him of good birth and as he lifted his face to my father I realised with a shock that I knew him.

'Noble Sillos,' he cried, 'I beg your protection! For the sake of the friendship between our houses receive me as a suppliant.'

My father stooped to raise him, his lips beginning to frame a question. I stepped in and answered it for him.

'This is Thaleus, sir. The second son of King Persepolis of Ithaca.'

'Thaleus?' My father drew the boy to his feet and looked into his face. He nodded dumbly. 'What sends the son of Persepolis to me as a suppliant?'

Thaleus swallowed and turned away his face, which was already streaked with tears. Skamon said, 'The Dorians, my lord. They attacked his people and drove them out of the city. The prince here and one or two companions escaped to the other end of the island. When they saw us coming they rowed out in a small boat and intercepted us. Otherwise we should have sailed straight into a Dorian trap.'

My father turned his head and looked at me. I stared back into his eyes. Then he turned to Thaleus and said gently, 'Your father?'

The boy gulped. 'Dead. He fell in front of the gates of the palace.' He paused and added, 'They wouldn't let me fight.'

I laid my hand on his shoulder. 'And your brother Opheltas? Dead also?'

He nodded and a tear splashed on my wrist. I looked up at my father. 'This is Cresphontes's doing.'

Thaleus lifted his head and sniffed. 'No. The leader was a man called Temenos. He sent a message to my father telling him to surrender.'

My father gripped him by the shoulders and said, 'How many Dorians, Thaleus?'

The boy shook his head helplessly. 'I cannot tell. There were hundreds of them. Ship after ship, each one filled with armed men. They seemed to cover the beach. Our men were only a handful beside them. It was hopeless. Then there were crowds of them, storming up the streets. Their swords are made of iron, and they killed everyone they met. Sir, I beseech you – revenge my father!'

'Ithaca, the realm of Odysseus, is in the hands of the Dorians. His last descendant is here among us, begging our help against the men who killed his father. And he has good cause to turn to us. His grandmother was a daughter of Nestor, and the houses of Neleus and Odysseus are sworn to amity and mutual assistance. Already the Dorians have killed one of our men and we have let the deed go unavenged. Let us now arm ourselves and go out to show them that they cannot lightly attack those who have the friendship of the descendants of Neleus!'

It was my voice, ringing out in the torch-lit megaron. Around me the men of the Royal Kin sat grave faced. I went on, 'We have let these Dorians think that our courage had left us. Let us show them that it is not so, before we find their black ships running ashore on our own beaches. I have sworn friendship with the sons of Persepolis and the blood of Opheltas cries out to me for revenge.'

Antilochos was on his feet now. 'Are we to shed our blood to redeem your pledges? I prefer to consider the good of our own people.'

'Then consider it, Antilochos!' I cried. 'We must show these Dorians that we are not going to sit idle and wait to be attacked. Do you want Pylos to suffer the same fate as Ithaca?'

'What?' Paion rumbled. 'Does the Prince still suggest that we might be overcome by a rabble of barbarians? The line of Odysseus is noble indeed but the people of Ithaca are a mere handful compared to ourselves. I have maintained from the first that the Dorians will not dare to attack us, or if they are so foolhardy we shall drive them into the sea at the first charge. I still maintain it. The Pylian army under my command is a match for any in the world.'

'Then let them prove it!' Melanthos was on his feet now. 'Let us drive the Dorians out of Ithaca.'

'Once again I ask why we should shed our blood for the men of Ithaca,' Antilochos shouted.

Echelaon raised his hand for silence and said, 'On this point I am inclined to agree with Antilochos. Persepolis is dead, and so is his eldest son. Thaleus is too young to rule and the handful of boys who escaped with him is all that is left of the nobility of Ithaca. I can see little to be gained by driving out the Dorians.'

'Only honour,' I cried. 'Does that mean nothing today?'

'Prince Alkmaion, you have always placed honour before prudence,' said Paion. 'You must not now place it before the good of your country.'

I turned in despair towards my father, who said, 'Alkmaion, the Lawagetas and your uncle Echelaon are right. We must think first of what is best for Pylos. Let us therefore concentrate our minds on preparing for an invasion, should it come.'

'But sir,' I exclaimed, 'may not our best defence lie in a sudden and swift attack? The Dorians must have suffered some losses and they have not had time yet to reorganise. We might cripple them now with an unexpected blow.'

My father said, 'We do not know what the Dorians' position is, nor exactly where their main force is to be found. We must have more information.'

Andropompous put in mildly, 'After all, we have no proof that they have any hostile intention towards us. It may well be that they will be content with Ithaca. It is a fair prize.'

Peisistratos the Younger rose abruptly. 'There are many in Pylos who would prefer to think so, rather than risk their lives for the sake of honour.'

184

He was normally a quiet man, never quick to anger or apt to speak without considering his words and this sudden outburst surprised us all. He went on, 'My father was the devoted friend of Telemachos, the son of Odysseus. Now his grandson cries to us for help and I am amazed to find my own kin too occupied with anxiety for their own skins and their own lands to heed that cry.'

Andropompous had recovered from his amazement and burst out, 'Do you suggest, Peisistratos, that those are my motives? I am willing to sail tomorrow, if need be, but I am attempting to give the wisest council in my power. I do not need to remind you that I have spoken face to face with Temenos and he has assured me that he has no hostile intentions towards us. My lord Echelaon has rightly pointed out that there is little to be regained by a reconquest of Ithaca. What purpose is there, then, in shedding Messenian blood?'

I cried out, 'Do not be led astray by Temenos's lies, Andropompous. The Dorians mean to attack us all. They are calling themselves the Sons of Heracles.'

There was a dead silence in the megaron and I saw my father gazing at me, tight lipped. I set my jaw obstinately. It was time their eyes were opened.

Paion said heavily, 'May I ask the Prince to explain that last remark?'

My father said curtly, 'Alkmaion is referring to an old prophecy that the sons of Heracles would return in the third generation to conquer the lands that were once his. Temenos and his brothers are calling themselves the sons of Heracles, but since Messenia never belonged to him I cannot see that the prophecy has any relevance to us.'

The silence continued while each man present weighed the implications of this revelation.

I said, 'I do not believe in the prophecy, but I believe the Dorians will make it an excuse for attacking us.'

'Let us therefore,' my father said, 'take steps to find out how serious a threat this is.' Paion began to rumble a protest but my father cut him short. 'You will forgive me, my lord the Lawagetas, but I think we must consider that there is a threat. I will consult with all of you in due course about the measures to be taken, but for now I propose to send a ship to our allies in Pleuron. They lie to the north of the gulf and their lands are close to those of the Dorians. If there has been any large-scale movement of people they will know of it. Until then I beg you all to say nothing that might alarm the general populace.'

When the council broke up I went straight to the room that had been given to Thaleus. I hoped to find him sleeping but he was still awake and came anxiously towards me.

'What is the news? When will your father send an army to revenge my father?'

I laid my hand on his arm. 'I am sorry, Thaleus, deeply sorry. There will be no army. I fought for it with all my power but my father and my uncles have decided against it. They cannot see what would be gained by reconquering the island when there are so few of you left to rule it.'

He jerked his arm free and turned away. 'So this is the worth of the friendship of the sons of Nestor!'

I tried to reason with him but he would not speak to me again and I saw that I was only succeeding in driving him nearer to the end of his overstretched endurance, so I left him to himself. Bitterly, I left the palace and headed for Alectryon's house. He was waiting for me at the gate.

'What news?'

I shook my head. 'None. My uncles will not fight and my father dare not force them.'

The following morning I found my father giving his orders to Alxoitas, the Chief Steward, in the privacy of his own apartments, as he always did when there were matters to be discussed which he did not wish to become part of general palace gossip. His face was strained and his eyes more deeply sunk than ever. I guessed he had slept little. My eyes were heavy also, for Alectryon and I had lain awake most of the night going over and over every aspect of the situation.

My father greeted me and said, 'You have come at the right moment. I am about to deal with matters arising from yesterday's news. Alxoitas, I want a ship made ready for a voyage to Pleuron. Not a merchant ship, the fastest we have. One of the thirty-oared war galleys.'

186

Alxoitas would have considered it a failure in his duty to express either surprise or curiosity. 'Very good, my lord. A crew will have to be levied.'

'Naturally. Call in thirty of the best men and tell them they will be well rewarded if they make good speed. Ask the Counts Hoplomenos and Dikonaros to attend me. I am sending them to Pleuron. Also I want a full list of all warships and the men available to man them and I want an inspection carried out to see that they are all sea-worthy. I want the inventory checked of all the chariots in the kingdom. I want to know how many, what condition they are in and whom they belong to. I also want a complete check made of all the armour and weapons in the palace armoury. Have you understood all that?'

Alxoitas's eyes were fastened on my father's face. He nodded slowly. 'I understand, my lord.'

'And, Alxoitas – there is no need for word of this to go all round the palace. Your scribes need know no more than their own individual tasks.'

'I understand, my lord. You may rely on me.'

My father smiled briefly. 'You are one of the few men on whom I do rely, absolutely. That is all now.'

The steward withdrew and my father turned to me. 'You see, I do not intend to sit idle and allow the Dorians to have it all their own way.'

'I never imagined you would, sir,' I returned.

'Yesterday I had the impression that you thought me too slow to respond to the danger.'

'Sir,' I replied, 'I do not presume to criticise you. It is just that I feel certain that our best form of defence lies in attack.'

He gave me a grim little smile. 'Perhaps it does, Alkmaion, but not until we have the leaders of the people behind us. If the danger is as great as you imagine perhaps the news from Pleuron will shake them out of their complacency. Meanwhile, there is enough to be done here. No attack can be mounted until we have checked that every ship is sea-worthy and every man can be armed.'

A guard came to the door to announce the Chief Priests of the

Great Goddess and of Poseidon. My father greeted them and said, 'It is possible that a grave danger threatens our people. I would have you consult the omens to ascertain if the Gods are angry with us, and if so by what sacrifices they may be placated. I would also know if it is Their will that we go out to attack our enemies or whether it is better for us to wait and meet them here.'

As the priests took their leave I watched their faces and suddenly recalled what Melanthos had said about the close accord between the Chief Priest of Poseidon and the Lawagetas. I put it from me, unable to believe that any priest would dare to anger the God he served by interpreting the omens other than with perfect truth.

Some days later I was at exercise when a message came that the ship had returned from Pleuron. I hurried to my father's room. He was standing with his back to the door, leaning one hand on a table as if recovering from a blow. The Counts Hoplomenos and Dikonaros stood grave faced nearby.

My father turned as I came in. 'Pleuron is under attack.'

Hoplomenos said, 'We slipped out of the harbour during the night. Next day we could see smoke going up. I think the city has fallen.'

'The Dorians?' I said.

Hoplomenos nodded and Dikonaros took up the tale. 'We arrived just as they were about to send a ship to Pylos to ask for aid. The Dorians burst over the borders a few days before and began to ravage the countryside. The people withdrew into the city, hoping it was only a raid. Then they realised that a huge army was gathering outside the walls. We were sent off with urgent pleas for assistance, but it must be too late by now.'

My father had recovered himself by now and took his seat. 'Who leads the Dorians, Temenos or Cresphontes?'

'Neither, my lord,' responded Hoplomenos. 'The army before Pleuron is led by Deiphontes.'

My father drew a long breath. 'Then all three branches of the family of Aristomachos are involved. The whole tribe must be on the move.'

'It is so, my lord,' Hoplomenos said. 'Thrasyanor, the ruler of Pleuron, told us that reports of similar attacks were coming in from all around him. He says that the Dorians are being harassed on their northern borders by strange tribes. Now they are looking for richer lands further south to replace those they have lost.'

My father's fingers tugged at his beard. 'It is the same story as Penthilos told, and as I have heard from the ships returning from Asia. Strange people, pushing down from the north and east, harassing the borders of the settled lands.' He was silent for a moment, deep in thought, then he appeared to recall himself abruptly to the present. 'The danger is greater than we thought. The time has come for strong measures. My thanks to you, gentlemen, for your information. Go now and rest.'

That evening the Royal Kin were again assembled. This time there were no arguments. Even Paion was silenced.

My father outlined his plans. 'The attack will come by sea, there can be no doubt about that. We cannot hope to defend the whole length of our coastline. The Dorians may choose to attack Phea and move southwards overland, or they may sail straight for Pylos. But they might also slip by us, by night perhaps, and round Cape Rhion to attack the Further Province. We must concentrate our forces and be ready to move in any direction. The fleet had better muster in the harbours around Cape Rhion. From there it will be equally well placed to sail for Phea or for the River Nedon. The main land forces will be concentrated here, with forces from the Further Province centred on Apeke. I shall station squadrons of men at intervals along the coast. If the Dorians are sighted they will light beacons to warn us.'

'Father,' I said, 'we know that the Dorians have a very large force and if what I saw in the Forbidden Valley is anything to go by they will all be armed. Can we not increase the number of weapons available to our men?'

'This has already been done to some extent,' my father replied. I knew that all through the winter he had been quietly building up stocks in the palace armoury. 'There is very little bronze available for further working.'

Echelaon said, 'The sanctuaries of the Mistress and of the other Gods are rich in bronze and provided with bronze smiths to work it.'

My father nodded quietly. 'That thought has also crossed my

mind.'

'You mean, take the holy bronze for weapons?' Andropompous looked scandalised.

'I think it would be permitted, in order to defend the sanctuaries themselves.'

'What about fortifications?' I pressed. 'Can nothing be done there?'

'Something must be done,' my father replied grimly. 'Though there is little enough we can do in the time we may have left. I shall order masons to be conscripted and brought here or sent to Leuktron. We will do what we can.'

All through that day I worked with my father and the Lawagetas, together with Alxoitas and his scribes, sending out orders. Messages went out to all those who owed military service to the king to report to the city and Paion drew up lists of officers and men to act as coast watchers and assigned them to their various stations. Demands went out to the villages for extra supplies of wheat and barley, wine and linseed for rations for the troops. For the first time I fully appreciated the value of Alxoitas and the Palace Bureau, whose endless scratching at clay tablets I had formerly despised.

My father summoned the High Priests of all the sanctuaries and won their agreement to the requisitioning of holy bronze. He also requested them to consult the oracles again to discover if there was anything further we could do to ensure the favour of the Gods.

I was sent to Leuktron to discuss the emergency arrangements with Teposeu, the Governor of the Further Province. On my return I found the city thronged with people. Rumours were rife and men and women crowded around my chariot asking for news. I did my best to reassure them and drove on to the palace. Here the warriors from all over the kingdom were assembling, the noblemen with their chariots and bronze armour, their men in jerkins of leather and linen, armed with spears and bows. Already temporary shelters were being thrown up around the hilltop to house those who could not find accommodation either in the palace or the town. Horses grazed under the olive trees and the palace stables and chariot sheds were full. Slaves ran backwards and forwards with rations for the men and fodder for their animals.

A Royal Guard pushed through the crowd and told me that my father was in council and wanted me. I hurried in without waiting even to slake my thirst or wash off the dust of my journey. The rest of the Kin were already there and their faces were grim. I went to my father and saluted him. He said, 'I am glad you have returned, Alkmaion. The news grows graver every day. Now the Chief Priest of Poseidon tells me that we have offended the God in some way and He demands a special sacrifice.'

I looked round and saw the Priest for the first time. He said, 'The omens are bad, Prince Alkmaion. No ordinary sacrifice can please the God now. Something delightful to Him and of great value must be found.'

'What sacrifice might please the God?' I asked.

My father said, 'That is what we are seeking to discover. All through my reign I have paid the God due honour. I have sacrificed many black bulls and snow-white rams upon his altars and given many golden cups to his sanctuaries. What does He ask of me now?'

The priest shook his head. 'This I cannot answer, save that it must be something of great value to you, or one close to you.'

I found myself gazing from him to Paion and Antilochos, suddenly afraid. Into the silence Echelaon spoke.

'When the Achaeans were held up at Aulis on their way to Troy by contrary winds Agamemnon sent for his daughter Iphigenia and sacrificed her. Can the God demand something similar of us?'

I felt my skin turn cold and Peisistratos said, 'Surely not!'

Then Antilochos came forward. 'May I be permitted to speak?' His voice was so full of false humility that I could have struck him.

My father's eyes brooded on him. 'Say on.'

'Our Lord Poseidon is the god of horses, among other things. Might not the sacrifice of a horse be pleasing to him?'

I could see the relief on my father's face as he raised his eyes questioningly to the priest.

'It is possible,' the priest answered. 'Provided that it was a horse of great value to some member of the Royal Family.'

I saw the blow before it fell, and could do nothing to avoid it.

Antilochos said smoothly, 'Prince Alkmaion has a colt which he

191

values highly. If he has described it rightly it is a suitable animal for a sacrifice – pure white and of excellent breeding. Might not that be pleasing to the God?'

'No!' I cried involuntarily. 'Not Pedasos!'

Antilochos looked at me with raised eyebrows. 'Will you put your horse before the good of your country?'

There was nothing further to be done. My father's voice was gentle as he said, 'I will have the colt sent for tomorrow.'

I turned to him, fighting to check my tears. 'No! Let me go for him. He is not used to being handled by strangers.'

As soon as my father had agreed to this I turned and hastily left the hall. I went straight to Alectryon's house. He was there with Nequeus, who had come to take his place with the other warriors. Alectryon took one look at my face and hurried over to grip me by the shoulders.

'What is it? Are the Dorians upon us?' I shook my head, biting my lips. 'Then what has happened?'

I swallowed hard and said in a flat, cracked voice, 'Poseidon has demanded a special sacrifice. They are going to take Pedasos.'

'Pedasos! Whose idea was that?'

'Antilochos, of course. It's just the revenge he's been waiting for.'

Alectryon put his arms round me and held me tightly for a moment. Then he said gently, 'We must hope that he will be pleasing to the God. Certainly there could be no finer offering. If the anger of Poseidon can be averted then Pedasos will have done you a better service by his death than any he could have performed in life.'

I remembered the High Priest's face, his eyes watching Antilochos, but I dared not voice my suspicions. Even to think such things was dangerous and I tried to put them out of my mind, but all that night my heart rebelled against the decree. However, in the morning I went with Alectryon and Nequeus to fetch the colt. As he came eagerly to take the wheat from my hand I wished I had left him to run wild and free like his sire. I thought of trying to ride him back to the city, but I knew that if I once got on his back I would be tempted to gallop away, up into the mountains where he had been born, and only the gods could know the consequences of that. So I tied his halter rope to the rail of my chariot, but as we set off he suddenly splayed all four feet and dragged back and Neritos had to give him a cut with the whip to make him follow.

The ceremony was held at noon on the shore below the town, in the presence of all the troops. I had expected Pedasos to be restive in the hands of strangers but he was very quiet and went almost willingly, it seemed, to the altar. My father performed the sacrifice with a single blow of the sacred double-headed axe and the white mane, which I had dressed with my own hands into three tufts as we always did for special occasions, was instantly soaked in bright blood. The omens, they said, were good.

When it was over I slipped away and walked alone along the edge of the sea. After a while I waded in until I stood shoulder deep and there I lifted my face so that the God might see my tears and prayed him to accept my sacrifice. I did not know then that the Mistress in Her anger had turned away the faces of all the Gods from me.

Chapter 11.

When I returned to the palace I found my father with his Companions in the central courtyard. The Lawagetas was speaking as I arrived, detailing the officers who would take charge of the coast-watching stations. I found my way to Alectryon and stood by his side, needing simply to be near him.

Paion was saying, 'One member of the Royal Companionhood will be stationed with each unit. He will act as representative of the royal power and report back as quickly as possible in the event of an attack or a sighting of enemy forces. The following Companions will be assigned to these duties. With the company of Klymenos near Metapa, Count Alectryon, son of Eteocles. With Kewonos, Count Loukios, son of Krasamenos …'

I turned to Alectryon. Metapa was the most northerly station, the first one likely to be attacked and furthest from the palace. He answered me with a little tightening of his lips and a pressure of his fingers on my arm. I wondered with weary bitterness if there was any end to the jealousy of Paion and his son.

When Paion had finished speaking my father said a few words of encouragement and then the assembly broke up. Alectryon touched my arm. 'I must speak to your father. I shall not be long.'

He moved away and caught my father just as he was about to re-enter the palace. As he knelt I remembered how I had seen him kneel to my father in supplication twice before. I wondered if he was begging to be allowed to remain in the city but I knew it was not in his nature to seek to escape his duty. After a moment my father nodded and went inside and Alectryon returned to me.

'What were you asking?'

He gripped my shoulder. 'Your father's permission to leave my post and return to the city the moment the first Dorian ship passes my station. Have no fear, when the attack comes I shall be here to fight at your side.'

I thought to myself that he might not get the chance, but did not say so. As so often happened, he seemed to read my thoughts.

'Don't worry. I shall not attempt to stem the invasion with

Klymenos and his hundred and ten men. If the Dorians land we shall simply melt into the countryside and head south at top speed.'

I tried to respond to his encouragement with a smile but my spirit was oppressed with sadness.

He said quietly, 'Come, there is no more to be done today and you are tired out. Let us spend the evening quietly at my house.'

I should, I knew, have been with my father, or at any rate about the palace, but my duty had demanded too much of me that day and I went with Alectryon. Neritos sought us out soon after and so, with Dexeus and Nequeus, the party consisted of the five of us who had dined together so often and so happily at Alectryon's estate. It was a gloomy evening, though Alectryon did his best to cheer us. Neritos was silent and downcast. Phea, his home, was the most northerly town in the kingdom and I knew he was desperately anxious for his mother. Alectryon promised to call on her and persuade her to travel to Pylos to be under our protection.

We went to bed early but we were both too tired and tense to think of making love. As we lay waiting for sleep Alectryon tried to comfort me with talk of times to come. After we had beaten off the Dorians, he said, everything would return to normal. I was sure to win distinction in the battle and my prestige in the country would be higher than ever. Then, on another theme, he had another colt by the same sire, almost as beautiful as Pedasos. He would make me a gift of him. After the battle we would drive out and look at him. I pretended to be consoled, but I could not rid myself of the thought that this might well be our last night together.

When I awoke in the morning he was up already, dressing himself in travelling clothes. I went out onto the hilltop to see him off and he held me by the shoulders and looked hard into my eyes. 'I know what you are feeling, but for the sake of the troops you must hide your fears. They must not see the Crown Prince out of spirits at a time like this.'

I knew he was right and made an effort to pull myself together. He smiled. 'We shall meet again before long. The adventure we have dreamed about is before us. And if the worst comes to the worst, perhaps our names will go into the stories alongside Achilles and

Patroclos.'

We embraced and I wished him good fortune. When the chariot had disappeared down the hill I turned to Neritos and said briskly, 'Come along. There is much still to be done.'

In the evening the Council met in the Megaron. Order was beginning to appear. The army was almost assembled, the warships had been manned and were making their way to the mustering points around Cape Rhion under the command of Echelaon. For several days more the feverish activity continued. Then, suddenly, there was nothing to do but wait. Only the masons and the bronze smiths were still working. The troops idled about the city. Alectryon sent a messenger to say that all was quiet in his area and that he had spoken to Neritos's mother but she preferred to remain in her own home. It was hot, and the palace was crowded and the surrounding area dusty and evil smelling. I kept my Companions occupied practising with swords and spears and cheered them with stories of battles long ago, but it was hard to maintain morale.

On the third evening of this apparently endless waiting I went up to my room to bathe as usual and found Andria alone, waiting to attend on me. She was pale and the maidservants who brought the jugs of hot water looked frightened.

I asked, 'Where is Mukala?'

She cast me a swift glance and then dismissed the slave girls. When we were alone she said, 'She has gone, my lord.'

'Gone, where?'

'I do not know, my lord.'

I went closer to her. 'What do you mean, you do not know?'

She kept her eyes lowered. 'She has left the palace, my lord, and taken her belongings with her. I do not think she will return.'

I sat down abruptly on the edge of my bed. 'Why?'

She knelt and began to unlace my sandals. I could feel her hands trembling. 'She is a strange woman. I believe she knows the future. Also, she is born of those people whom your ancestors conquered.'

'What of that? She has always had a good home here.'

'She said … she said …' her voice faltered.

I leaned forward. 'What did she say, Andria?'

196

'That she would not remain in the palace to die for the Achaeans.'

I stared down at her. 'She has left me, at such a moment?'

The girl nodded, her eyes still lowered. I sat silent for a while, trying to come to terms with this betrayal. She took one of my hands and kissed it. 'I am sorry to bring my lord such ill tidings.'

I lifted her chin and said, 'You have not gone, Andria.'

'Where should I go?' she asked. 'Besides, I would not if I could. You are my lord now.'

I caressed her hair, my mind still on Mukala's desertion. 'Who heard Mukala say what you just repeated to me?'

'Only myself, I think.'

'None of the other women?'

'I think not, but we were in the woman's quarters at the time. They could have overheard her. Many of them know that she has gone.'

'Listen Andria.' I took her by the shoulders. 'Mukala is a stupid old woman with a mischievous tongue. Have you heard anyone else, any of the other women who belong to the Old People, say the same sort of thing?'

She hesitated, then murmured unhappily, 'I have heard them say that they do not see why they should shed their blood for the Achaeans.'

I said grimly, 'But they will let us shed ours to protect them.'

I could feel her trembling still and looked down into her eyes. 'Are you afraid, Andria? You mustn't be. I shall not let you fall back into Cresphontes's hands.'

She shivered at the thought, but said softly, 'It is for you I fear, my lord.'

I kissed her tenderly. Since I brought her to the palace I had not laid hands upon her and now I was amazed at her eager, passionate response. I held her tightly and kissed her again. Then I heard Neritos shouting outside the door.

'Sir! It is Alectryon! He is here.'

He burst in before I could disentangle myself from Andria but I did not wait to see what he thought of the situation.

'Alectryon? Where?'

'He has just driven up to the palace.'

197

I leapt up and ran out onto the gallery. Alectryon had just entered the courtyard. I called his name and ran down to meet him. He was hot and dishevelled, his bright hair dull with dust, and his face was grim.

'What news?' I asked.

He looked over my shoulder at Neritos and said, 'I must see your father.'

I could guess then what the news was and felt a stab of mingled fear and anguish. We went in and met my father leaving his room. He led us back inside and asked, 'Bad news?'

'Yes, my lord. Phea has been overrun.'

My father drew a long breath. 'So, they are coming. Tell me what happened.'

'A messenger reached my headquarters about noon. Apparently the Dorians appeared shortly after dawn. They must have spent the night moored just beyond the promontory. There was a very large fleet – at least a hundred ships, he said. The Prefect and the local forces met them on the beach and put up what resistance they could but they were soon beaten down. The boy who brought the news got away as the Dorians entered the city. He says the ordinary people put up no resistance at all.'

My father frowned. 'None at all?'

'So he says.'

He shook his head incredulously. 'The fools! Do they hope to exchange Achaean masters for Dorian ones and not suffer by it?'

I said grimly, 'They will not fight for us. Melanthos told me once that they still hate us, but I did not believe him. Now I have proof.' And I told them about Mukala.

When I had finished my father said angrily, 'Tell the guards to search for her and bring her back. We will make an example of her to any others of her people who think to desert us. But I have no more time for that now. A hundred ships, you say?'

'According to the boy.'

My father chewed his beard. I knew our fleet numbered no more than eighty. 'How can they have built so many, in such a short time?'

Alectryon lifted his shoulders. 'Their land is rich in timber, and we do not know how long they have been at work. They may have had many ships ready and hidden, even when we visited them last year.'

'What was the situation when you left?' the King asked.

'We had seen no ships pass Metapa. My guess is that they will stop in Phea for now – but there is no knowing for how long. The moment the first ship is sighted the beacon will be lit.'

'Very well.' My father had recovered from his shock and his tone was brisk. 'We can only wait until we know what their next action will be. Go and rest. Alkmaion, send the Lawagetas to me – and break the news to Neritos. His mother must be in Dorian hands by now.'

We found Neritos waiting in my father's private courtyard. Alectryon laid a hand on his shoulder. 'Phea has fallen to the Dorians.'

Neritos gazed at him for a moment and then turned away. I went to put my arm round him but he shook me off violently and moved a few paces further off.

'What happened?'

Alectryon told him what he knew. He listened in silence with his back to us. Then he turned, his face expressionless, and said formally, 'Will the Prince excuse me for a little while?'

I said unhappily, 'Of course, Neritos' and he turned and left the courtyard. I looked at Alectryon. 'I feel someone should be with him.'

He shook his head. 'He is one of those who cannot bear to share their grief. You know that. Later he will need you, not now.'

I recalled myself to the present situation and said, 'I have to find my uncle.'

'Yes,' he said. 'And I must have a bath and something to drink.'

I went with him to the gate and said as we parted, 'The Gods have been good to me this far. You are back again.'

He stood still and met my eyes. 'It will take more than Cresphontes and his barbarians to part us. This side of the grave, or the other, we shall be together.'

The evening meal in the megaron was a silent affair and no one called upon Sirios to sing. Neritos was still absent and, though I sent people to search for him, no one seemed to have seen him. Then, as I left the hall, he was waiting for me in the shadow under the porch.

'Here you are at last!' I exclaimed. 'I have been worried about you.'

His face was set and he would not meet my eyes. 'I must leave you,' he said.

'What!'

'I must go to Phea and try to find my mother.'

'Don't be a fool! Phea is overrun. You wouldn't stand a chance.'

'One man could slip into the city without being noticed. I shall dress like a peasant.'

I took a deep breath. Somehow I had to find the words to convince him, but to do so I had to be brutal.

'Neritos, think. You know what happens to the population of a conquered city. If your mother is still alive, she will be a prisoner by now. One man alone would have no chance of setting her free.'

His shoulders slumped and he turned away. 'I cannot bear to think of her in the hands of those brutes!'

I said, 'Your mother is a lady of breeding, Neritos. Cresphontes and his like are not so stupid that they cannot tell the difference. There will be enough slave girls and young peasant girls to satisfy their lust. Perhaps they will keep her as a hostage – to be exchanged for any of them who we take prisoner.'

He turned a tear-streaked face towards me. 'I have to do something. I can't just leave her there.'

I gripped his arms. 'Listen to me! Tomorrow, or in the next day or two, they will be here. We both know they will not be satisfied with Phea. They may leave a small garrison there but this is where the main battle will be. If we can defeat them here, then the army will move north to liberate Phea. That is your mother's best hope. *This* is where you are needed, Neritos! I need you. How can I go into battle without a charioteer?'

For a moment I thought he was not listening to me, then he nodded and caught his breath. 'You are right. I'm sorry. But if we are victorious, will you promise to let me go to Phea with the first troops?'

'I'll do more than that!' I said. 'I'll come with you.'

He rubbed his arm across his face and drew a long, shuddering breath. I said, 'Have you eaten since this morning?' He shook his head.

'Go to the kitchen and get something. I shall be outside in the camp. Come and find me when you have eaten.'

I went out onto the open hilltop in front of the palace gates. The moon was up but the city buzzed with restless life. I could see the distant pale crescent of the shore. Tomorrow it might be filled with the dark hulls of ships. About me, on the slopes of the hill, were the huts housing the army. Watch fires burnt at intervals and I could hear voices and the occasional clank of metal. For the first time I faced the possibility that in a day or two all this might be destroyed: the city with its craftsmen and the cottages of the peasants; the palace with its painted walls and graceful columns. I saw in my mind's eye the golden cups and the inlaid furniture, the brazen bowls and dishes and the finely decorated pottery being seized by greedy hands and born away. I heard the screams of the woman as the doors of their apartments were broken open and smelt the reek of smoke. In the warm summer night I shivered.

It was a long night. Alectryon sought me out, with Dexeus at his heels as usual, and tried to persuade me to come home with him to sleep, but I refused.

'I can't leave all this,' I said, indicating with a sweep of my arm the encampment and the city beyond.

'What good can you do here?' he asked reasonably. 'There are watchers set on every vantage point. You need to rest.'

I shook my head obstinately. 'I couldn't sleep, even if I went to bed'

So we spent the next hours wandering the camp, pausing at each camp fire, sharing a draught of wine here, a joke there, answering questions as best we could. At one fire a boy was strumming a lyre and Alectryon took it from him and sat down to sing. I was surprised for a moment at his choice, expecting a stirring tale of battle, but what he chose was a love song. As the men began to join in softly I understood. The time for looking back to old glories was over. Tomorrow, or whenever the battle came, we would fight for all that we held dear in the present, not for the heroes of the past.

Eventually we found a group of my special 'Companions'

clustered round a fire in the lee of the hastily erected wall. Neritos had joined us by then, grim but dry-eyed, and we settled with our backs to the wall and wrapped ourselves in our cloaks. Sometime around the middle of the night I found my eyelids drooping and allowed myself to doze off against Alectryon's shoulder.

When I woke the sky was beginning to pale above the mountains. The others were stirring too and someone passed round a wineskin. We rose, our limbs cold and stiff, stretching and yawning as the light grew slowly towards sunrise. I had started to say 'I am hungry' when I sensed Alectryon stiffen. Then he gripped my arm and pointed. Away on a distant hilltop a point of light gleamed, died, then grew to a steady red glow.

I swallowed, my mouth dry. 'They are coming.'

'So soon!' he said. 'They must have rowed all night.'

'Hoping to take us by surprise. Well, they haven't succeeded.'

He turned towards the city. 'We had better go to your father.'

The news had reached the palace before us and we found the megaron full of men. My father came in hastily and at once silence fell. He said, 'My friends, the attack for which we have been preparing is almost upon us. Each one of you knows his duties. In a moment I shall send you to prepare your men. I ask you only to remember this. The Dorians have come not merely to plunder, but to possess. They are not men like ourselves, who treasure the ways of civilised life, but barbarians. We need expect no mercy from them, and if they are allowed to gain a foothold here you may say goodbye to your homes and your families, your lands and the way of life you love. Let this be in your minds as you face the enemy. Go now to your stations.'

As the men left my father called me to him. Alectryon came with me and my father said, 'I will forestall your request this time, Count. You have my permission to fight at the Prince's side.'

Alectryon thanked him and gave me a quick smile. 'I shall wait for you outside.'

Paion had remained behind also, together with Andropompous and Peisistratos. When we were seated my father said, 'It seems the attack will come from the sea, as we expected. Let us go over our plans once more. Paion will be in charge of the main body of troops.

Andropompous and Peisistratos will command the right and left wings respectively. I shall remain in reserve with the Companions, ready to sally out and attack if there is any sign of a break through. Should our forces be driven off the beaches we will fall back on the city and finally inside the defensive wall, which we shall hold to the death. Is that understood?'

We nodded silently, except for Paion who muttered, 'They will not get beyond the beaches.'

I said, 'What of me, sir?'

'You will be with me.'

I had expected this, but during the night I had been developing a plan and I voiced it now with all the persuasiveness I could muster.

'Father, may I make a suggestion?'

'Well?' The dark eyes searched my face.

'Behind the beach is the flat land where we hold our games – the only good land for chariots to operate on. I know the main chariotry will be occupying that already, but where the promontory curves out towards the Holy Mountain the hills are closer to the coast. A second force could lie hidden there and if the Dorians did break through it could charge out and take them in the rear.'

My father looked at the Lawagetas. 'What do you think?'

For the first time my uncle looked at me with something like approval. 'It is a good plan.'

I turned to my father. 'I have worked hard with those friends whom people call my Companions, practising chariot manoeuvres. Will you give that task to us, and let me lead them?'

My father's eyes brooded on me. I knew he wanted me in his sight and in the safest possible place, but he did not deny me the chance to win myself a greater honour.

'Very well, so be it. Go and inform your friends and arm yourself.'

I saluted him and was about to retire when he said, 'Alkmaion. When you are ready, come to my room.'

On the porch I found Neritos waiting for me, already armed. I clapped him on the shoulder and said, 'Find our friends and tell them to assemble in front of the palace. We have a special commission from my father.'

Suddenly, now that the time for action had come, my depression had lifted. I was excited, as if it was a grand hunt for which I was preparing. Alectryon was talking to some other Companions in the courtyard. I called him over and explained the plan to him.

He looked at me with narrowed eyes. 'I see you're still plotting things behind my back.' Then, as I began to apologise, he grinned. 'Never mind. I like this better than being cooped up with your father's chariotry, waiting for a chance of action.'

I went up to my room to arm myself. Neritos, assisted by Andria, prepared me with deft, practised fingers and when I was ready he took up my shield and held it so that I could see myself hazily reflected in the polished bronze. I was not displeased by what I saw. The bronze plates of my corselet fitted snugly around my body and I had bound up my hair under the pointed helmet. My legs were encased in bronze greaves and my sword, in its enamelled sheath, hung from my shoulder. Neritos handed me the round shield with its pointed central boss and decoration of inlaid metals and I turned to go.

A small sob behind me called me back. I drew Andria to me and said, 'Remember, I paid Cresphontes a good price for you. I'm not going to let him have you back now.' She managed a little smile and I kissed her and added, 'Have my bath water ready at the usual time. I shall be back by then.'

The courtyard was crowded now with armed men and outside I could hear horses and chariot wheels and shouted orders. The main body of the army was moving off towards the seashore. I sent Neritos to prepare my chariot and went to my father's private apartments. It was some time since I had seen him in armour and to my surprise it made him look younger.

He came over and took me by the shoulders. 'Alkmaion, it would be wrong of me, and quite useless I know, to bid you keep yourself out of danger. Only this I would have you remember. It will profit this kingdom little if the throne is left without an heir.'

I said, 'I understand, sir. Believe me, I have no wish to die. But I beg you to remember also that it would be worse still for the country to be left without a king.'

He smiled grimly. 'I am well aware of that, Alkmaion. The days are past when kings could play the hero. Only if all seemed lost should I be justified in risking my life.'

'I pray it will not come to that,' I answered.

'So do I. Now, let us go together. The army will be waiting for me to perform the necessary sacrifices.'

He kissed me on both cheeks and we went out together into the courtyard. Outside the chariots stood ready, each charioteer in his place. I mounted beside Neritos and took the smooth shaft of the spear he held for me in my hand. Nearby, all my friends were waiting and when I raised the spear in greeting they answered me with a cheer. Dexeus brought Alectryon's chariot up alongside mine and the whole procession moved off, following my father towards the sea.

On the shore the priests and priestesses were waiting and the sacrifice was prepared. Offerings to the Mistress had already been made on the Holy Mountain. Now at nine altars nine black bulls were offered to Poseidon. Then my father spoke to the troops, in much the same vein as he had addressed their leaders, exhorting them to fight to the death to preserve their land and their families from the barbarians. When he had finished we were dismissed to take up our various stations. I turned, and with a wave of my spear ordered my companions to follow me. We drove to a position behind a shoulder of rising ground where we would be out of sight of a force attacking the beach. There we tethered the horses and climbed the hill to a point where we could look down on the scene of the coming battle.

The wait that followed seemed endless. The sun was high now and I could feel the sweat trickling down my body under my armour. My excitement failed and I began to feel drowsy and limp, and slightly sick. I remembered that I had not eaten, except for a few snatched mouthfuls while I was getting ready, and sent one of the charioteers to fetch some food. He returned with slaves bearing baskets of bread and figs and flagons of wine mingled with water. We all ate and drank and I felt a little better.

Below us the army sat or lay on the beach, using their shields to keep off the sun. Behind them the main chariot force waited, the horses restless and fretful. Then a point of light winked on a hilltop above us as the sun reflected off a shield. It was the agreed signal.

Alectryon said, 'They are here.'

I sent the charioteers back to untie the horses. The rest of us flattened ourselves on the hilltop. A moment later the first ship came into sight, driving through the narrow straits beyond the Holy Island. She was a heavy, lumbering vessel, far too broad in the beam for speed, but she was crammed with men. A single figure stood on the afterdeck.

'Temenos?' I queried, looking at Alectryon.

He nodded. 'Probably.'

Two more ships followed in the wake of the first. Alectryon said, 'I should guess they belong to the other two leaders, Cresphontes and Deiphontes. The whole tribe is here.'

I said, 'I still find it hard to believe we have got to fight Cresphontes.'

Alectryon said nothing, but his face was grim. Melanthos was counting the ships as they rounded the point. After a little he fell silent and we just watched them coming into the bay, one after another.

Below us the men on the beach were ready for action, a dense line of spears and shields along the water's edge. Behind them the archers stood ready with strung bows. The leading ships took position across the bay, the first opposite the centre of our line, the other two facing the two wings. Behind them the other ships turned clumsily from column into line abreast. I heard an order shouted and saw the rowers bend to their oars and they all came on as fast as they could go towards the beach.

When they were within range the archers opened fire. We could see arrows finding their mark, but still the ships came on. As soon as the keels grounded men swarmed over the sides and up the beaches, to be met by our warriors with sword and spear. Like waves, the lines of attackers rushed up to the solid barrier of our men and fell back again into the sea, many never to rise again. Yet still more and more flung themselves against the defending line.

Alectryon muttered, 'Great Gods! They have courage enough, these Dorians!'

At length the rising tide of armed men began to force our line back. Then there was a sudden wild cheer and I saw that at one point the line had broken and the attackers rushed through the breach and up the shore. A detachment of chariotry was on them immediately and the flood was stemmed, only to break through a moment later at another point. Alectryon gripped my arm and pointed.

'Look. Do you see who is leading the attack on this wing?'

I followed his arm. 'Cresphontes!'

He looked round and said, 'I think our moment has almost come.'

I sent the rest of my followers back to their chariots and Alectryon and I stayed on to watch for the right moment to charge. All along the beach now our line was wavering and falling back. Behind it the chariots dashed to and fro, cutting down those attackers who broke through, but they were becoming more and more numerous and here and there I could see groups of our warriors cut off by the hordes and forced to dismount and fight hand to hand.

Alectryon muttered. 'Our fleet should be here by now! We need them to stop any more disembarking.'

As he spoke a yell went up from just below us and I saw that two ships had grounded beyond the end of our left wing. The crews spilled out into the shallows and charged up the beach to take our men in the flank. The line of defenders wavered, broke and fell back.

'Now!' Alectryon said.

We ran back down the hill. I leapt into my chariot and cried, 'Drive, Neritos!'

We surged forward and the rest of the company closed in behind us. Alectryon took his station on my right, Melanthos on my left. In a tight, compact formation we swept round the shoulder of the hill and up behind the mass of Dorians. As we came in sight of them I raised the war cry and heard it taken up all around me. The Dorians checked and faced about and on the far side our men rallied and returned to the attack. Then we were among them. Faces appeared before me, teeth bared, eyes glittering and I thrust with my spear and dragged it back until my arm ached.

For a few moments it seemed as if we should clear that section of the beach. Then I heard behind me a terrifying, half-forgotten sound – the trumpets of the Dorians. Not one this time but many, braying and shrieking as a fresh wave of men stormed up the beach. The effect was disastrous. Horses reared and plunged and our men everywhere lowered their weapons and cried out with terror.

I tried to shout above the din, 'Don't be afraid! It is only their war horns!'

Then the fight surged around me again. There was no longer room to manoeuvre the chariot. I shouted to Neritos, 'Keep close behind me!' and leapt down to fight on foot.

The time that followed was filled with one grim encounter after another. Some were brief – a new face, a thrust with my sword and the face disappeared. Others were longer – a bitter duel in which the man behind the opposing shield became for a moment a personality. I thrust and cut and parried, my body wet with sweat and my ears deafened with shouts and the clash of metal. I had lost sight of most of my followers. Alectryon had been at my side to begin with, his shield guarding my right flank, but then he had disappeared. At the back of my mind was the terrible suspicion that he had fallen and was lying somewhere in the mêlée, dead or wounded. Only Neritos was still with me, keeping the chariot so near that I could feel the breath of the horses on the back of my neck.

Suddenly, among all the strange faces, I found myself looking into eyes that I knew.

'Xouthos!'

I saw from his wolvish grin that he had recognised me and for an instant I lowered my sword. Only instinct brought my shield up in time to deflect the blow he aimed at me and I felt his blade burn along my jaw. At the same moment I thrust at him and saw the grin vanish suddenly from his face. He fell at my feet. I looked down and saw that my blade had gone in under his ribs and there was no doubt that he was dead.

For an instant no new opponent faced me and I was able to look around me. I realised that my companions and I were a few small islands of resistance in the middle of a great flood of attackers. The main battle line had passed on inland. If we stayed where we were we should undoubtedly perish. I leapt up beside Neritos and yelled to my followers above the din, 'Follow me!' Then, to Neritos, 'Let's get clear of this.

Circle round towards the city, so that we are between them and the palace.'

Neritos touched the chestnuts with the whip and they sprang forward, carrying us clear of the mêlèe. My companions remounted their chariots and followed. On a piece of rising ground, I stopped and the others gathered round me. There was no sign of Alectryon. I questioned them all anxiously but they could only say that, when last seen, he had been on his feet and fighting. In vain I scanned the battlefield. There was only a seething mass of Dorian heads, with not a bronze helmet to be seen among them.

Already the fighting had spread across the flat land and reached the hills and still our men were falling back. Then Melanthos shouted, 'Look!'

He was pointing seawards and I turned to see the first ships of our fleet sailing into the bay. A cheer went up all round the battlefield. I turned to my friends. 'One more charge and we shall sweep them back into the sea, and my lord Echelaon and his men can finish them off for us!'

They gave me a cheer, though it was a weary one now, and we swung about and galloped back onto the plain. Everyone had taken new heart from the arrival of the fleet and for a short time we did begin to drive the invaders back. Then we heard shouts of alarm. Neritos gripped my arm and said, 'Poseidon help us now!'

Out in the bay a second force of Dorian ships, which must have been lying out of sight beyond the point, had closed with our fleet and a fierce sea fight was in progress. Once again our men wavered and the Dorians charged and drove us back. We were fighting on the rising ground now, our forces concentrated on the entrance to the valley where the road led up to the city. The whole of the plain was filled with the enemy. Behind me, and towards the centre of the line, I suddenly heard the war cry raised with fresh power. Looking round, I realised that my father and the Companion chariotry, who had been held in reserve, had charged down from the city. They were the pick of the fighting men and the centre of the Dorian advance was split like a log under the woodman's axe. This much I saw, and then there was no more time to gaze around me.

My memories of the battle after that are fragmentary. For a while we seemed to be winning, but the sheer weight of their numbers drove us back again. We fought on, in the city itself now, giving ground step by step up the steep streets, deserted by those who had lived there. Here, among the houses, it was no longer possible to see the general pattern of the battle.

Neritos and I had just fallen back to the top of a steep and narrow street. The chariot blocked it completely and I had dismounted to face seven or eight Dorians below, who were trying to make up their minds to rush us. Then behind me I heard the rumble of chariot wheels and looked round. It was Alectryon, alone and driving his own chariot. I cried out with relief at the sight of him.

He reined in his horses and called, 'Come! You must come back to the palace at once.'

I stared at him. He had a cut over one eye and his face was streaked with blood.

'Back?'

Below us the Dorians began their charge. Neritos cast his spear at the leader and felled him, which checked the others for a moment. Alectryon dismounted and seized my arm. 'Do as I ask you. You must come!'

Dazed, I let him drag me to his chariot and shouted to Neritos, 'Follow!' As Alectryon wheeled his horses and galloped up through the town I asked, 'What is it? What do you want me to do?'

He did not answer until we reached the hilltop. Then I saw that our forces, or what was left of them, had fallen back inside the wall and fierce fighting was already going on at several points around it. One or two more chariots thundered up behind us. Alectryon jumped down and flung the reins to a waiting soldier. He led me inside the wall and, as soon as we were through, the heavy barricade that had been prepared for the purpose was dragged across the opening.

Alectryon led me across the courtyard, now crowded with weary and wounded men, towards the portico of the palace. As we reached it one of the Royal Companions ran up.

Alectryon said, 'Have you found them?'

'Some,' the other man answered harshly. 'The Lawagetas is dead.'

'Dead!' I exclaimed.

We were in the inner court now. Alectryon took me by the shoulders and looked into my eyes. 'Alkmaion, your father is dead also.' I gazed at him speechlessly. He went on, 'He was killed in that first charge. He insisted on leading it and, of course, every Dorian in the army aimed a spear at him. He fought magnificently and made it possible for the Companions to break through the line, but then there was no way back.'

I stared hard at the baldric from which his sword hung, and murmured, 'Only when all seemed lost, he said.'

Alectryon let me go and went suddenly on his knee. 'You are the King now. You must be crowned at once.'

I stared at him, bewildered. 'Crowned? Now? Don't be a fool! We must fight.'

He rose and said tensely, 'Listen. The men are disheartened. Your father's death seems to them a mark of the disfavour of the Goddess. They must see you, the new King, sanctified by Her blessing. Everything is prepared. We have gathered as many of the Royal Kin as possible. Come!'

Too stunned to argue any further I allowed him to lead me into the megaron. There a handful of men were waiting, and they all fell on their knees as I entered. I looked round. Peisistratos was there, Antilochos and Perimedes, Melanthos, a few of the Companions – and the priests. Peisistratos rose and led me to my father's chair.

The ceremony was hasty and perfunctory and I remember little of it, except that as Antilochos kissed my hand, along with the rest, in sign of allegiance I was struck by the irony of the situation. All the time the noise of battle grew louder and closer.

As soon as the rite was over I leapt up and drew my sword, crying, 'Now! Let us drive this Dorian rabble out of my palace!'

As I did so the door burst open and Neritos flung himself inside.

'It is useless,' he shouted. 'They have broken through the wall. We cannot hold them back.'

I ran to the porch and as I reached it the gates of the palace burst open and the Dorians charged through. At their head was

211

Cresphontes. I would have rushed out to meet him and found my death there and then but Alectryon seized me in a grip of iron and shouted, 'No!'

Someone said, 'This way! The chariots are on the road.'

Perephonios, always one of the bravest of my father's Companions, leapt forward with a shout into the courtyard. Others followed him and for a moment Cresphontes's advance was checked. Alectryon thrust me back towards the ante-room. I protested and Melanthos seized my other arm. I remember that I tried to fight them off, until Alectryon shouted, 'What profits your death now? Pylos needs her King.'

Then I allowed them to hustle me into a corridor that ran towards the storerooms at the back of the palace. Already I could hear the Dorians breaking open the rooms leading off the courtyard. I stopped again, abruptly. 'The women!'

'Safe already,' Alectryon said tersely, urging me forwards. 'They were sent into the hills as soon as the first break through occurred.'

We hurried through the storerooms, between the great jars of oil and sacks of grain, and came to a door leading to the outside. Peisistratos opened it, sword in hand, and looked out. Then he went through and beckoned us after him. As yet none of the invaders had penetrated to the back of the palace. We ran through the olive trees, scaled the wall, which was less than shoulder height at this point, and regained the road above the palace. Here the chariots were waiting and I understood why Alectryon had left them outside the wall.

As soon as we had mounted Alectryon led the way inland at full gallop. As we gained the first rise I looked back. The hilltop swarmed with men. All resistance seemed to be at an end and already I could see bent figures staggering back towards their ships, laden with the spoils of victory. Out in the bay the black hulls or our fleet drifted, waterlogged and burning. The Dorians must have seen us escaping, but no one pursued us. They were too busy carrying off the riches they had once envied from a distance.

Chapter 12

Alectryon led us to a hilltop some distance from the palace where there was a small temple to the Mistress. Already there was a little group of refugees there – my cousins Amphidora and Thalamista; Peisistratos's wife and their little daughter Klais; some of the palace servants – and the boy Thaleus, Persepolis's son. These, together with the survivors of the Royal Kin who had been present in the megaron, seemed to be all that were left of the Royal Household. The two girls fell upon me, sobbing, and I longed to thrust them off, for I was suddenly so weary and sick of heart that I would have welcomed death.

Warm lips were pressed to my hand and I looked down to find Andria kneeling at my feet. I found enough spirit to say,

'You see. You are not going back to Cresphontes.'

Alectryon was beside me and as I looked at him he knelt and bent his head.

'Forgive me, my lord. I used violence towards you which only your own imminent peril could possibly excuse.'

I turned away and sank down on a rock. 'Why didn't you let me stay and die an honourable death?'

'Because we need you alive! You are the last Prince of Pylos – now our King. Who else could rally the men?'

'What hope is there of that now?' I asked dismally.

'Have you forgotten the second army at Apeke? And what of our allies in Mycenae? Penthilos will bring their army to help us. After all, he is your brother-in-law.'

I looked round at him and reached out to press his hand. 'You always see further than I do. I should remember that by now.'

The sun was setting. It was clear that the Dorians were too occupied in ravaging the palace to follow us – or perhaps they had no further interest in us. Wearily we disarmed and the women tended our wounds. When Andria had finished bandaging mine I got up and went to the edge of the rocky platform on which the sanctuary stood, from where I could look down on the city. Alectryon came and stood silently beside me. After a moment I remembered that he had come to find me alone, driving his own chariot. I said, 'Dexeus?'

'Dead,' he said flatly. 'Killed by an arrow in that first charge. I couldn't even go back for his body. That was how I became separated from you. There was no one to keep my chariot near me.'

'Poor Dexeus!' I whispered.

I heard him swallow and then he said, 'He had been with me from his childhood – almost from mine. I shall miss him.'

Neritos, who was standing nearby, turned away and sank down with his head in his arms. In spite of their differences, he had grown fond of Dexeus.

I drew a little closer to Alectryon, beginning to shiver from exhaustion and despair. As usual, he had prudently brought a cloak with him while I had lost mine. He made to drape it round my shoulders and then hesitated and said formally, 'Will you take this, my lord?'

I gazed at him uncomprehendingly for a moment and then shook my head, not in refusal but in mute protest at his tone. He understood and wrapped the cloak round both of us, his arm around my shoulders. I leaned against him, unable as yet to think of the sanctity of the person of the King.

Another memory came back to me. 'I killed Xouthos.'

'Xouthos!'

'We met in the battle. I would have spared him but he struck at me. He gave me this cut on my face. So I struck back and killed him.'

Alectryon was silent for a moment. Then he said grimly, 'Well, at least Cresphontes has paid a price for his victory.'

We stood watching the light fade on the ravaged city. Then I jerked myself upright. On the distant hilltop I saw a flicker of flame. It grew quickly and spread.

Alectryon said, 'Barbarians! They have fired the palace!'

The others joined us and we stood silent, watching the flames leap higher. In their light we could make out small dark figures running from the burning building, still carrying off the last items of booty.

My head swam suddenly. 'Why, Alectryon? Why should they destroy the palace?'

He shook his head. 'It may have been an accident. But I doubt if they would have wanted to preserve it. It would have meant nothing to them.'

Perimedes said, 'Perhaps they are not going to stay after all. Maybe in the morning they will sail away.' But none of us believed that.

One by one the others turned away but I stayed where I was and Alectryon stayed with me. At length I said, 'What is it that is burning down there, Alectryon?' I felt him look at me sharply, afraid I suppose that the shock had unseated my reason. I went on, 'It is not just my father's palace. Not only Nestor's heritage. It is our life. All the things we have cared for – beauty and music and craftsmanship - all the sweet things of life. They will destroy them as they have destroyed the palace.'

He held me tightly. 'For a while perhaps, here in this place. But these things will live on in other cities. Mycenae will not fall. Athens will survive. So long as we live these things will not die and we shall yet return to rebuild the palace and bequeath them to our children.'

I bowed my head and felt the hot tears running down my cheeks. We stayed there until the remains of the palace were just a glowing smudge on the darkness, and then turned back to the rest.

It was a disheartening sight. Amphidora and Thalamista sat clasped in each other's arms, silent and trembling. Perimedes was weeping and Melanthos sat with his arm around him, grim-faced. His father, Andropompous, was missing, killed I presumed. Of all the Companionhood, only three remained. Antilochos sat apart from the others, gazing into the darkness and I wondered with momentary bitterness why he should have survived when so many other, better men had died. I could easily have followed Perimedes's example, but Alectryon pressed my arm and said in my ear, 'You are the King now. You must hearten them and help to plan our next move.'

I took a grip on myself and said aloud, 'My friends, we must not give way to despair. There is still the army from the Further Province. We shall return with reinforcements when our enemies least expect it and drive them back into the sea. For now we must consider where to spend the night, and tomorrow we will head for Apeke.'

They roused themselves at that and gathered round me. Peisistratos said, 'We must find somewhere for the women to shelter, and we all need food.'

Alectryon said. 'Let me make a suggestion. My own estate is about an hour's journey from here, towards the mountains. That should be far enough to put us out of harm's way until tomorrow. Let us make our way there and rest for the night. In the morning as – the King - suggests, we will head for the Further Province.'

No one had any wish to argue with this plan, so we put the women into the chariots and set out. Before the road turned the shoulder of the hill I stopped and looked back at the faint glow that was all that remained of the palace where, for a few brief moments, I had sat upon the throne of my forefathers.

The beat of hooves on the road behind us brought us all to a standstill, swords drawn. A single horse galloped round the bend and the rider flung himself off the nearly foundering beast. As he did so I recognised Hoplomenos, one of my father's Companions. He ran forward and fell on his knees before me, catching my hand.

'My lord, they told me you were safe but I could not believe it until I saw you! Praise be to Enyalios the War-God for preserving you!'

I said, 'And praise be to Him for preserving you, Hoplomenos. I thought all the Royal Companions were dead except these few.'

He kissed my hand and rose. 'I fear most of the rest are dead, my lord, killed in the fighting around your father's body. I survived only because a blow on the head knocked me unconscious. When I came round the fighting was over. One of our men told me that you had been crowned before the palace fell, so I found a horse and set out to seek you. A peasant on the road told me he had seen you pass.'

His words recalled to my mind how grievously I had fallen short of my duty in one respect.

'My father's body, Hoplomenos! It was left on the battlefield.'

Another of the survivors stepped forward. 'No, my lord. We brought him back to the palace and the priests attended to him while we searched for you. There was no time to bury him but the offerings have been made.'

'Then his body is in the hands of the barbarians,' I said.

Alectryon put in quietly, 'It is likely that it was burnt in the fire which destroyed the palace.'

I bit my lip. 'I wish I could believe that!'

We went on along the dark road. A rustle and a cracking of twigs made us suspect an ambush but it was only another small group of fugitives, including two officers from the army, who had heard us coming and hidden among the trees. When we reached the farm at last we found Alectryon's steward and some of the farm workers waiting at the gate. The rest had already fled into the hills.

Alectryon said quietly, 'My brother?'

The steward shook his head. 'We have not seen the lord Nequeus. I hoped he was with you.'

Alectryon shook his head and I said, 'He may yet turn up. We have seen there are survivors.'

He took a deep breath and swallowed, then began to give orders for food to be prepared and beds made up. We sent two of his men to watch the road and then my tattered band of followers collapsed wherever they could find space to sit or lie, either in the main hall of the house or on the porch outside. I sank into a chair and closed my eyes. My head was swimming and images of the battle flickered behind my eyelids. Someone put bread and meat in front of me but I lacked the energy to eat it. Then Andria appeared at my side, a steaming cup in her hand.

'Take some of this, my lord. You must eat.'

It was a posset of milk and eggs, sweetened with honey. She fed it to me sip by sip and I felt a little strength returning.

Alectryon's steward bowed before me. 'There is hot water for my lord to bathe.'

Hardly conscious, I stumbled after him and allowed Andria to strip off my clothes. It was only then that I realised that my whole body was covered in a filthy mixture of sweat and dust and dried blood, though whether this last was my own or that of other men I could no longer tell. I winced as the water found still open wounds or Andria's gently sponging uncovered livid bruises, but it was some comfort to be clean again.

When I was dry she came and knelt beside me with a small bundle of cloth in her hands. I looked at it dully.

'What have you got there?'

She unwrapped it, saying, 'I brought what I thought my lord would most wish to preserve.'

I saw that the bundle held all those things which were most

precious to me:- the circlet my father gave me on my return from Cresphontes's village; the golden cup which had belonged to Odysseus; an inlaid dagger bequeathed to me by old Peisistratos; a ring Alectryon had given me on my name day; and the gold necklace I had taken from her own father. I touched them one by one and then leaned forward and kissed her.

'Thank you, Andria.'

Alectryon came in and I saw that he, too, had bathed and put on a clean woollen robe. I showed him the treasures Andria had managed to preserve and he drew from his finger a ring that I instantly recognised.

'One of the Companions took this from your father's hand and asked me to give it to you.'

I took it and slipped it onto my own finger. For the first time I began to comprehend the fact that I should never see my father again and my throat constricted.

'I never really knew him, Alectryon,' I murmured. 'Was that my fault?'

'No,' he said gently. 'He was the King. That was all any of us could know. But he loved you dearly.'

I nodded speechlessly and he said, 'You must sleep now, if only for a few hours.'

I let him lead me to the bedroom we had shared so often in the past and sank stiffly onto the bed. He drew the coverlet over me and then, through the mists of encroaching sleep, I was aware that he was hesitating. After a brief pause I heard him say, 'Goodnight, my lord.'

I opened my eyes again. He was standing over me with the lamp in his hand, as he had stood a year ago when I took refuge in his bed after my escape from the Holy Mountain. Suddenly I was overwhelmed by an almost unbearable sadness. After one short year, was this to be the end of our relationship as well as everything else? The tears I had been holding back since the burning of the palace welled up into my eyes and I whispered hoarsely, 'In the name of all the Gods, forget all that and come to bed!'

He blew out the lamp then, slipped into bed beside me and took me in his arms. I was asleep almost at once.

Alectryon woke me at dawn, after what felt like no more than a few minutes. The hall, when we descended, was a shambles. Some of those who had fled with us were awake, pale and hollow-eyed. Others slept where they had fallen, still coated in the filth of battle. All were swathed in bloodstained bandages. Amidst the chaos Alectryon's faithful steward and a few servants were passing round bread and milk and mulled wine.

One of the watchers we had posted on the road ran into the hall. 'My lord, a chariot! Coming this way!'

'Only one?' Alectryon asked sharply. When he received an affirmative answer we went out to the gate. As we appeared the driver of the chariot whipped his tired horses into a gallop but it was not until he drew up in the courtyard that we were able to recognise him through the dust and the mask of dirt and blood that concealed his face.

'Aikotas!' Alectryon exclaimed.

He was one of the Royal Companions who had followed Perephonios into the palace courtyard to oppose Cresphontes while I escaped. He almost fell out of the chariot and collapsed at my feet, crying, 'You must fly, my lord! Already they are looking for you. But I beseech you, have someone care for Perephonios.'

It was only then that we realised that there was another man slumped in a pool of blood on the floor of the chariot. I gave orders and two men lifted him out and carried him indoors.

While Andria tended Aikotas's wounds he described, in disjointed phrases, how Perephonios had fallen in the first onslaught and how he had stood over his body until he was himself overpowered and taken prisoner. Later that night, when the Dorians were too drunk and too intent on plunder to notice, he had managed to escape and had made his way back to the courtyard to find his friend.

'But the palace was on fire,' I said.

'The buildings were burning, yes,' he agreed. 'But it was still possible to get into the courtyard. I couldn't leave him to burn!'

I remembered then that they had been lovers at one time.

'Were there other survivors held prisoner?' I asked. 'Any other Companions?'

He shook his head. 'I think no more of the Companionhood

219

survived, my lord. All those who lived to bring your father's body off the battle field perished in the palace, except those few who came to escort you to safety.'

'Any others?' I pressed him.

He dropped his head. 'There were survivors among those who held land from your father. As soon as the palace fell all resistance ceased and then some of those great ones came to Temenos to sue for peace. Temenos greeted them with reassuring words, promising them their lives and their lands. By dawn he was absolute master of Pylos.'

I turned away and ground out, 'They shall see how well it paid them to betray me when I return!' But the words were hollow and fell into a hollow silence.

Aikotas said, 'They are seeing already. Temenos spoke them fair but he has little control over his men. They have plundered and destroyed every great house and every craftsman's workshop. Even the tombs have been broken open and the grave goods carried off.'

I turned with a stifled cry to stare at him. All around me I heard the same sharp sounds of incredulous distress. No one spoke. This was beyond words. I walked away from them to the door, scarcely able to control the flood of anger and despair rising within me.

In the silence that followed Peisistratos, who had gone to help tend Perephonios, came back into the hall.

'He is dead,' he said quietly.

Aikotas gave a sob and buried his head in his hands. 'He lived until this morning!' he cried. 'Why could I not have found him sooner?'

Alectryon laid a hand on his shoulder. 'You did all you could. At least he lived long enough to know that you came back for him.'

One of the servants came in. 'The horses are harnessed, sir.'

Alectryon straightened up. 'We must go. No doubt the peasants who directed our friends here will be equally quick to inform our enemies.'

I said sharply, 'We must bury Perephonios first.'

'Of what use is it to bury him, even if we had time?' Alectryon exclaimed. 'The Dorians have no respect for tombs.'

'We cannot leave him,' I said obstinately. 'If we cannot bury him then we will burn his body, as my father's body was burnt in the ruins of the palace.'

He opened his mouth to argue and I turned on him abruptly and met his eyes.

'It is my command!'

For a moment we looked at each other. Then he bent his head. 'As my lord wishes.'

I knew then that something had changed for good in our relationship, but I told myself that I would make it right with him later – when there was more time.

While the pyre was being prepared we made our final arrangements for the journey. Every farm cart and every horse was brought into service, as well as the chariots. The women and the more severely wounded were to travel in the slower vehicles, escorted by the remnant of our fighting men under the command of Peisistratos, while I went ahead with Neritos and Alectryon and the remaining members of the Royal Companions. As we were making these dispositions I saw the boy Thaleus approach Alectryon and experienced a pang of guilt at the recollection that I had hardly spoken to him since the day he had come to us begging for refuge and revenge.

'Count,' he said, 'may I ask a favour of you?'

Alectryon paused in what he was doing with his unfailing courtesy and replied, 'Of course, Prince Thaleus. I will do whatever is in my power.'

'You have lost your charioteer?'

'Dexeus, yes.' His face shadowed.

'Will you take me in his place?' Then, as Alectryon looked taken aback, 'I can handle a chariot, I promise you. In Ithaca I often won races against older men than myself.'

'I don't doubt your ability, prince,' came the reply. 'But it would not be fitting for me to take as my charioteer the son of Persepolis of Ithaca.'

'Please, Count!' The boy's eyes shone with passionate supplication. 'I was not allowed to fight in the battle for my city, or yesterday for Pylos. I have no chariot or horses of my own, but if there is to be another battle you Messenians will need every man you can get. You must have a charioteer. Let it be me, I beg you!'

221

Alectryon hesitated a moment longer, then he nodded. 'Very well, until this battle is won, you shall have your wish. Then we must find a more fitting solution.'

'You will not regret it, I swear to you!' the boy exclaimed and hurried off to check the harnessing of Alectryon's horses.

When the pyre was ready and the body of Perephonios laid upon it I performed the necessary offerings and cut a lock of my hair to throw upon the flames. Aikotas and the others followed suit, but we could not wait for the body to be consumed. Alectryon had been fretting to be away for some time but as we moved towards the chariots I saw him stop and turn back to look at the house. A lump swelled in my throat at the memory of the happy days and nights we had spent there and I went over and laid a hand on his shoulder.

'We shall return, my dear.'

'But what shall we find?' he asked softly.

'Whatever we find, it can be put right – once we have driven these barbarians out.'

He drew a deep breath and laid his hand briefly over mine. 'Yes, you are right. We must go.'

The horses were still weary from the day before but we made the best speed we could towards Leuktron. Nevertheless, the news of our defeat had got there before us and we began to pass parties of refugees, heading for the mountains. As we swept into the courtyard of the palace the Governor, Teposeu, came running to greet us and fell on his knees to kiss my hand.

'Teposeu?' I exclaimed. 'Why are you not with the army at Apeke?'

He rocked on his knees like a man in pain, his eyes on the ground. 'My lord, my lord – there is no army.'

'What?' I glanced around me. Many of the townspeople had followed and were milling about just inside the gates. I jerked Teposeu to his feet. 'Come inside.'

When the rest of my people had followed us into the megaron and the doors were shut I turned on Teposeu.

'What do you mean, there is no army?'

'My lord, when the news of your defeat and of the King your

father's death arrived this morning, the men mutinied. We gave the order to march for Pylos and they refused. Some of the officers who tried to force them were killed. The rest and a few men who remained loyal returned here with me.'

'A few? How many?'

'A handful, my lord. No more.'

I looked round. Melanthos sagged against the doorpost, his face ashen. Neritos had turned his back. Alectryon sank down on a bench and put his head in his hands. In some strange way their despair gave me strength.

'Very well,' I said. 'Tomorrow we set off for Mycenae. My brother Penthilos will bring the army of Tisamenos to our aid.'

It was a tattered and dispirited caravan that set out from Leuktron: those of us who were left of the Royal Kin – myself and Alectryon, Peisistratos, Melanthos and the sons of Paion; our women-folk; my few remaining Companions and my faithful Neritos; and a motley band of survivors from the army and others who preferred to leave their lands and follow me rather than take their chances under the Dorians. Thaleus begged to continue as Alectryon's charioteer, finding in that role, I suppose, some sense of purpose otherwise lacking in his life.

We followed the steep and difficult road across the inhospitable Taygetos mountains to Sparta, and from there we travelled on towards Mycenae and came one evening to the mouth of the valley commanded by the great citadel. Behind us lay the flat, fertile plain of Argos and beyond it the sea. Ahead the road ran between bare, dun-coloured hills and as we followed it we saw on the ridges the first houses of the town, poor at first but then large and imposing, obviously the homes of men of wealth and importance. As the chariot rumbled up the paved road I began to understand for the first time how much larger and more populous Mycenae was than Pylos. We passed a walled precinct where I could see the headstones raised above many graves and then the huge mound that covers the dome of the tomb of Atreus, the founder of the reigning dynasty, cut deep into the hillside. Then I lifted my eyes and had my first proper view of the citadel.

Now I understood why Penthilos had been amazed at the defencelessness of Pylos. Here was a city built to withstand a hundred attacks. Crowning the hill at the end of the valley, its rear protected by two great mountain peaks separated from it by steep ravines, the palace of the Atreidae stood within mighty walls rising sheer from the sharp flanks of the hill and constructed of huge blocks of stone, each one of which must have taken the strength of many men to lift. Within them, besides the palace itself, crowded many great houses, temples and storerooms, while at their feet huddled the buildings of the lower city.

We swung round a bend and found ourselves facing the great main gate. To our left the wall rose sheer against the side of the hill. To our right a great bastion of stone gave shelter from which those within could threaten the unshielded side of an attacker. Before us was the gate, topped by a mighty lintel, above which stood a triangular block of stone carved with the likenesses of two lions, rearing up to place their forefeet on a column, their heads turned to warn off invaders.

Neritos drew rein and we gazed in silence. How small and puny Pylos seemed now! The captain of the guard came forward and asked our names. His tone was courteous but he frowned as he looked beyond us at the long trail of men and vehicles. Suddenly I did not know how to announce myself.

From his chariot behind me Alectryon shouted, 'You are speaking to the King of Pylos, fellow! Have you no idea how to behave to royalty?'

The captain began to stammer apologies. I cut him short with, 'Send word to King Tisamenos that I have arrived with my family and followers and say that I beg him to receive me.'

There was a stir in the crowd that had begun to gather about the gateway and Penthilos strode through it. He stared at me and then past me to my ragtag following.

'Alkmaion! What has happened? What brings you here like this?'

'The Dorians,' I answered, my voice rasping with exhaustion. 'They attacked in huge numbers. Pylos has fallen.'

'And your father?'

'Killed in the battle.'

I saw him master the shock and take control of the situation. He turned to one of his attendants. 'Run ahead and inform my brother the king of what has happened. Tell him that Alkmaion, son of Sillos and King of Pylos, is here.' Then, to me, 'Come. You can tell us the full story later. My brother will be eager to hear it.'

We passed under the Lion Gate and entered the city. At the top of the slope we got down from our chariots and slaves led the horses away. From here the palace seemed a vast complex of roofs and terraces. Penthilos led us through a long corridor, down some steps and into an open courtyard whose floor was patterned in coloured squares. On two sides the walls rose to the height of two storeys and were decorated with painted plaster. On the third side there was only a low balustrade and from here one could look out down the valley and far beyond to the bay of Argos. Opposite, on the fourth side of the court, was the columned porch of the megaron. We crossed the court and passed under the porch and through the anteroom, into the throne room itself. To my right stood the throne of the descendants of Agamemnon and as I entered Tisamenos rose from it to greet me. I went to him and knelt at his feet, laying my hand upon his knee in the gesture of a suppliant.

'Great King, renowned Tisamenos, son of the valiant Orestes, receive me as a suppliant. I come to beg your aid in revenging the death of my kingly father.'

He bent and raised me, saying, 'Noble Alkmaion, you must not kneel. We are brother monarchs. As your duty is to me as your overlord in time of war, so it is mine to protect the descendants of the might Nestor. Be assured, you shall have my support in driving out your enemies.'

I thanked him and presented my cousins and my Companions. I had just finished doing so when we heard hasty steps at the door and Karpathia's voice cried out 'Father!' She came running in and stopped abruptly, looking round her. Then her eyes rested on me. 'They told me the King was here. I thought perhaps the messenger had been mistaken ….'

I held out my hands to her. 'Our father is dead. I am the King now.'

We embraced, weeping, and then she turned to embrace Amphidora and Thalamista. Penthilos laid a hand on my shoulder.

'Your promised visit to Mycenae is made under sorrowful circumstances, my brother. But be assured, we shall not rest until we have replaced you on the throne of your father.'

Tisamenos raised his voice. 'My friends, you have travelled far. You are weary in body and sick at heart and have many terrible stories to tell us. Let my attendants take you now to where you can bathe and change your clothes. Then we will meet again here and listen to your tale.'

We were led away. I and the members of my family were accommodated within the palace, while the Companions were quartered with the Mycenean nobles who lived close by. When I was bathed and dressed Penthilos came to conduct me back to the megaron, where Tisamenos's people and my own were assembling for the evening meal. Tisamenos presented me to his three eldest sons, Cometes, Daimenes and Sparton and seated me at his side in the place of honour. While we ate he talked of neutral subjects, trying to keep my mind away from my misfortunes, and I found myself warming to him. At that time he was in middle age, lean featured like Penthilos – a characteristic gained from their father Orestes, I presumed - but blue eyed and with hair that must in his youth have been golden, though it had faded somewhat now. I remembered that his mother was Hermione, the daughter of Menelaus and Helen. His colouring, I thought, must be the same as his famous grandmother's.

After the meal the ladies of the court joined us and I saw Hermione for myself. She was still woman of striking beauty and I found myself wondering how much she reflected the looks that had so bewitched the Trojan, Paris. With her came Antigenia, Tisamenos's wife, and Karpathia, of course, with my cousins, and two other women whom I did not recognise. They were obviously mother and daughter and in contrast to Hermione, both were very dark. The older woman had a handsome, imperious face with strong features and commanding eyes under arching brows. The younger was softer looking with delicate skin and a cloud of soft, dark hair. I wondered who they were, but we were not introduced.

When the ladies were seated Tisamenos sent away the servants and asked me to relate the full story of what had happened. The Myceneans listened sympathetically but I could tell that nothing I said made them understand the terrible reality. It was as remote to them as those old battles in the tales of the bards. I was glad when Tisamenos brought the evening to an early end.

As the guests began to leave I was suddenly possessed with a deep desire to be alone with Alectryon, but as I looked across the hall I saw that he was already being conducted out of the door by his host. It occurred to me to send after him but we were too new here for people to understand our relationship and I did not wish to cause any embarrassment, so I went to my room alone and spent a restless night, plagued by recurring nightmares of the battle.

The following morning I was summoned to a meeting with Tisamenos and Penthilos and we talked at great length about plans to defeat the Dorians. They questioned me closely about the strength of the Dorian forces and frowned as I attempted to describe their weapons. I began to wonder if they suspected that Pylian warriors were no longer what they had been in my grandfather's day. Eventually it was agreed that Penthilos would begin to assemble the army and meanwhile he would send out spies to find out how strong the Dorians had made themselves in Pylos. I was impatient for action but I knew from my own experience that it takes time to collect an army together and prepare it for battle, and I was heartened by the firm resolve and the confidence of the King and his Lawagetas.

When the meeting was over I summoned my family and the Companions and told them what had been decided. I concluded, 'We are all that is left of the Royal House of Neleus and the nobility of Messenia. Let us now solemnly bind ourselves to work together and support each other until we can win back our land. Many of you I know as my friends and the others were loyal Companions to my father and I know will now be equally loyal to me.' I turned to Antilochos, who ever since our defeat had been silent and withdrawn. 'Antilochos, there has been some bitterness between us. Let there be an end to it now. We cannot afford to fight amongst ourselves.'

He raised his eyes to my face and then got up and came to me. 'If my lord has felt I have any hostility to him in my heart I beg him to put such thoughts from his mind. I am his loyal servant.'

I embraced him, but it was a formal gesture. I could not like him, nor he me, but I hoped that this reconciliation might serve, at least, to prevent an open breach between us.

As I turned to leave I caught Alectryon's eye and he gave me a grin of approval and opened his mouth to speak. Then I saw him think better of it. It was not his place to judge his King.

From the day we arrived I had few chances to be alone with him. Tisamenos was determined to entertain me in keeping with my position, in spite of the circumstances of my arrival, and kept me occupied from morning until bedtime. I longed for a little peace and quiet, but to say so would have been churlish. Alectryon made no attempt to claim any closer intimacy than the rest of my Companions and when evening came his host whisked him away as soon as dinner was over. On the third evening, unable to bear my loneliness any longer, I sent Neritos to him with a formal message. 'The King requires the attendance of the Count Alectryon.'

He came and greeted me with the same mask of formal courtesy that he always assumed in company. 'You sent for me, my lord?'

I dismissed Neritos with a gesture and replied in the same formal tone, 'I did, Count. There are affairs of state which I wish to discuss with you.'

He looked at me doubtfully under his brows. 'Such as, my lord?'

'Such as, why you and I have not been to bed together for so long,' I replied and met his eyes. Once he would have laughed but now, although a smile hovered on his lips, his eyes were still uncertain..

I went to him and put my hands on his shoulders. 'Alectryon, nothing has changed. I am the same person I was before … before the Dorians came.'

He looked at me and said gravely, 'None of us will ever be quite the same again.' But his hand moved up in the old, familiar gesture to push the hair back from my face and his kiss banished for a moment all recollection of the terrible times we had been through. I held him tightly and whispered, 'We mustn't let this come between us. I can't lose you, as well as everything else!'

'You won't,' he whispered back. 'I have sworn that, for as long as we both live. Remember?'

I drew back. 'Then come to bed – and stop behaving like a stranger.'

The next day I found time at last to talk privately with Karpathia. We sat under the colonnade surrounding the courtyard of Penthilos's apartments and she questioned me at length about the fate of all our friends. It was a sorrowful business as I recited the list of those who had perished and by the end we were both in tears, but eventually I persuaded her to talk of her own life in Mycenae. I noticed that in spite of her grief she looked remarkably well. Her face had filled out and there was colour in her cheeks and when I pressed her she confessed that until I arrived from Pylos she had been entirely happy. Her love for Penthilos had grown with familiarity and now she was expecting his child. I kissed her tenderly and found some comfort in the thought that the blood of Neleus would find its continuation here, if nowhere else.

As we spoke the two ladies whom I had seen in the megaron on the night of our arrival came out of the house and crossed the courtyard to the gate.

'Who are those ladies?' I asked.

Karpathia blushed a little. 'The elder lady is Erigone, my husband's mother. The younger is her daughter, Myrtilis.'

'Penthilos's sister, then?'

'His half sister. Remember, Penthilos is the son of Orestes. Myrtilis is Erigone's child by her lawful husband.'

'Ah!' I began to understand Karpathia's embarrassment. 'But who is Erigone? What is her parentage?'

Karpathia ducked her head. 'She is the daughter of Aegisthos.'

'Aegisthos!' I was stunned. This was a scandal I had heard whispered since my childhood. 'Clytemnestra's lover? The murderer of Agamemnon?'

She laid her hand on mine. 'Hush! I beg you, Alkmaion, think no worse of Penthilos because that blood runs in his veins. No king ever had a more loyal subject than the grandson of Agamemnon has in the grandson of Aegisthos. Were it not so …' She broke off.

'Were it not so …?' I queried.

She flashed me a look. 'There are those who would make use of Penthilos's descent to oust Tisamenos. All is not as smooth and honest in Mycenae as it seems. There are still those who wish to see the true line of Atreus deposed. But Penthilos is so loyal that no one can drive a wedge between him and Tisamenos.'

I frowned. 'I don't understand, Karpathia. Who would wish to depose the King?'

She sighed. 'It is an old story, and you have heard much of it before. The feud goes back for generations. Atreus and Thyestes, the sons of Pelops, were at war. Atreus slew all his brother's children, except Aegisthos. Atreus had two sons, Agamemnon and Menelaus and they married the daughters of the King of Sparta. Agamemnon married Clytemnestra and Menelaus, as you know, married Helen. While Agamemnon was away fighting at Troy Aegisthos saw his chance for revenge. He made love to Clytemnestra and won her heart and when Agamemnon returned, as you said just now, they murdered him. Aegisthos would have slain his little son, Orestes, too but the boy's sister, Electra, smuggled him across the frontier to safety. When Orestes grew up he returned to Mycenae and avenged his father's death by killing both Aegisthos and Clytemnestra.'

'His own mother!' I exclaimed.

Karpathia nodded sombrely. 'It was a terrible deed and for some time afterwards Orestes was so tormented with guilt that he could not take the throne. He wandered the world until the Goddess relented and his sin was forgiven. Then he returned and married Hermione, the daughter of Menelaus and Helen and so united Mycenae and Sparta in one kingdom. Tisamenos is their son.'

'But why …?' I wrestled with the complications of the tale, 'why would Orestes take Erigone to his bed – the daughter of his father's murderer?'

'Who can say?' she asked. 'She is not Clytemnestra's child, of course, but another woman's. And as you have seen she must once have been very beautiful. Also, there is something about her …'

'What do you mean?'

'I can't say. There are rumours – rumours that she has powers that are more than human. Her mother was one of the Old People and they claim to have special gifts from the Mistress, which are denied to others … I don't know. But Orestes could not resist her and Penthilos is the result. Orestes took him into the palace and brought him up as his own son, and Erigone was married off to another man.'

'Myrtilis's father.' I felt a sudden chill. The mention of the Old People had reminded me of Eritha and my initiation. I had no wish to encounter those dark powers again. I turned my mind to a more practical consideration. 'You said there are still those who would like to depose Tisamenos. Is he aware of this?'

She nodded. 'Oh yes, well aware. Thyestes and his descendants have always had their supporters. But I suppose Tisamenos feels secure enough to ignore them.' She turned to me. 'Alkmaion, promise me you will say nothing of this to him – or anyone else. It would only stir up trouble.'

I promised, but found I could not put the two women out of my mind. 'What's the girl like – Myrtilis?'

Karpathia sighed. 'She's a sweet girl. I can't pretend I like Erigone, but Myrtilis and I could be good friends, if only she wasn't so totally dominated by her mother. Erigone hardly ever lets her out of her sight, poor child.'

At that moment Alectryon arrived with two of the other Companions to escort me back to the palace. As we crossed the courtyard Erigone and Myrtilis came through the gate and Karpathia presented them to me. Close to, I found Erigone's aquiline features and strong colouring too overpowering for beauty, but Myrtilis was different. In her all that was striking in her mother's face was present but softer and more delicate and her huge, dark eyes had an innocent, almost childlike gaze.

We exchanged a few words and then, as I turned to leave, I saw with a jolt that Alectryon's eyes were fixed on Myrtilis as if he was bewitched. Later, when we snatched a few moments private conversation, I teased him about it, hoping to discover if it was more than just a passing fascination. He replied with a terseness that bordered on discourtesy that he had other things on his mind than women and I found myself hoping that this was true. I knew from experience that he enjoyed the company of a pretty girl from time to time, but I had never seen him so affected before.

For me the days that followed had a sense of unreality. There was nothing for me to do except wait. I was no longer the carefree prince of a month ago, but as a king I was without power or purpose. All that remained to me was the perpetual ritual that surrounds a king and the struggle to keep up the spirits of my remaining followers. We exercised every day and practised military manoeuvres, so that when the time came to fight we should be ready, and over the days our numbers grew as more refugees arrived from Messenia. From them we learned that the whole country was now in Dorian hands and the stories they had to tell only served to make us hate the invaders more than ever.

One thing that continued to fascinate me was the great citadel of Mycenae itself. Seeing my interest, Tisamenos himself took me on a tour of the palace. He was by nature a builder and showed me with pride the various improvements he had made. His great ambition, however, remained unfulfilled. He wanted to create a Grand Staircase leading up to the palace courtyard in order to provide a more impressive approach. Penthilos, however, had other ideas. He declared that there were far more urgent defence measures, which should take priority.

'Defence measures?' I exclaimed. 'What better defences could Mycenae possibly need?'

He smiled briefly. 'No doubt it looks very impressive to you, as indeed it is. But there are still weaknesses. The northeast corner is one. At that point the wall does not take in the whole of the hilltop, which gives an enemy a chance to muster on level ground before making an assault. If it extended to the edge of the slope it would be much more easily defended. And it would have the added advantage of giving us better access to water. The spring of Perseus is just beyond the wall at that point. We could construct a covered way, part of it underground, to reach the spring, even during a siege.'

'Will it be done, do you think?' I asked.

He looked grim. 'It may have to be. These are unsettled times.'

Another source of disturbance to me during that time was the behaviour of Antilochos. I spent a good deal of my free time in Penthilos's apartments, finding his company more congenial than that of Tisamenos and his sons. When he was busy, as he often was, I would sit and talk with Karpathia and often some of the other ladies would sit with us. I was always attended by some of my Companions and we would while away a pleasant hour or two in idle chatter. To my surprise Antilochos formed the habit of joining us. He had always had a facility for superficial charm when he wanted to employ it and now he seemed determined to make a good impression. His company gave me no pleasure but I knew that it would be a mistake to rebuff him, so I tolerated his presence with the best grace I could muster.

It was not long before I realised that this change in his behaviour had nothing to do with me. Quite often Erigone and Myrtilis were present and Antilochos turned most of his charm on them. It was true that there were few men in the party who could keep their eyes away from Myrtilis, and I was uncomfortably aware that Alectryon was still enthralled by her beauty, but it was Antilochos who claimed most of her attention.

At last the spies whom Penthilos had sent out returned. The Dorians were consolidating their power. The sooner we could move the better. Penthilos announced that the army was ready and sent a small scouting party on ahead. At a solemn sacrifice the omens were taken and an auspicious day chosen for our departure. It was further ahead than my impatience required but the priests were adamant. To move earlier would be to invite disaster. So we waited.

Then, two days before we were due to march, a messenger arrived. The advance party had met up with some of Penthilos's men who had been left to keep an eye on our enemies. The Dorians had embarked their main army and sailed southwards. Only a small force was left to hold Pylos. I was with Tisamenos and his Lawagetas when the news arrived and when I heard it I jumped to my feet, laughing with relief.

'Then we can march into Pylos almost unopposed!'

They looked at me, grim faced. Penthilos said, 'We do not know where the Dorians are heading for. We cannot leave the Argolid undefended.'

Chapter 13

My first impulse was to take my Pylians and march homewards, but Tisamenos dissuaded me. We were not enough to challenge even the small holding force the Dorians had left in Pylos.

It was not long before we knew where their main army was headed. Their ships were sighted sailing up the gulf towards Argos, the port of Mycenae. Immediately orders were given to march and the chariots of the Mycenean war-lords rattled out under the Lion Gate. I had been given my wish in this, at least, and the Pylians marched as a distinct company, under my command. The Myceneans sang and shouted ribald jokes as we marched down the valley, but my men were silent and grim faced. We had met the Dorians before.

On the flat land at the head of the gulf we joined up with a force from Tiryns and awaited the enemy fleet. I looked around at the great army that was gathered and roused the spirits of my men with promises of victory.

I will not dwell on how those promises were broken. The Dorians had been reinforced, for their numbers were greater than ever, and from the moment they stormed from their ships, urged on by the wild braying of their war trumpets, I could see the spirit going out of the Myceneans. They were picked men, highly trained and well armed, but they could not stand against this horde in which every man wielded a sword, albeit an iron one.

The land here was better for chariots than the uneven and sandy country near my home and we made some progress at first with massed chariot charges, but soon the sea of men closed round us and we had to fight on foot. I fought with a black, despairing fury, Alectryon on my right hand and Melanthos on my left, while our charioteers kept our horses just behind us, ready in case of need. From time to time I got a glimpse of Cresphontes and battled to get near him, but he was too well guarded.

At length came the moment when the Mycenean force broke and turned and began to stream away, back towards the citadel. There was nothing to do but regain our chariots and follow them at full speed.

We lost Pleuronios, one of the remaining Companions, in that fight but no others of rank. The Mycenean losses were very heavy.

The Dorians did not pursue us, for we had exacted a price from them also. Halfway across the plain Penthilos succeeded in halting his troops and we sent back a herald to ask for a truce in order to recover the bodies of our dead. They granted it, and when the bodies were brought in, all of them stripped of their armour and other valuables, we made a huge pyre and burnt them. There seemed little point in burying them in ground so soon to be overrun by the enemy. This done, we returned to Mycenae.

It was clear that we could not expect many days' grace before the Dorians followed up their advantage. The interval was spent in preparations for a siege. Then came the message that the enemy were on the march. Penthilos left a force to hold the walls and marched out again to oppose their advance. Archers on the hills harassed the enemy's flanks and for a day of bitter fighting we made them pay for every forward step they took, but at evening we had to fall back and take refuge in the citadel.

Every inch of space within the walls was packed, for all those who lived in the houses clustered below or along the slopes of the hills had crowded in, with their livestock and belongings. I wondered for how long such a multitude could be fed under siege conditions.

I joined the King and his officers in the courtyard of the palace. From here we could look out beyond the walls to where the Dorians were making camp for the night. All round us hundreds of watch fires gleamed in the darkness. We could hear the hubbub of the wakeful city and the restless army. I cradled my left arm, on which a hastily bandaged wound throbbed relentlessly. Suddenly someone gave a cry and pointed. In the town below a spurt of flame licked up and then grew rapidly to a great blaze.

Tisamenos said, 'They have fired the buildings in the Lower City. That must be the unguent-maker's workshop. The oil in the store-rooms would blaze like that.'

The Lower City burned for most of the night. At first light we manned the walls. I took my station with Tisamenos and Penthilos outside the entrance to the palace, where we could overlook a large sweep of the walls, including the main gate. The first attack came soon after sunrise. They began with a frontal assault on the gate and I saw Penthilos smile for the first time in days.

'They clearly haven't got much experience of siege-craft!'

Wave after wave of attackers swept up the narrow defile before the gate, to be mown down by the archers on the bastion that defended it. Finally the Dorians abandoned the attempt and drew off to think again. Then came an attack on the walls, easily beaten off since they had no scaling ladders, nor any other equipment for attacking a walled city. After that they withdrew again and there was no more fighting for that day.

By the following dawn they had constructed a number of ladders and the attack began as soon as there was light enough. This time it went on all day. To begin with it was a time of agonising inactivity for me. My Pylian foot soldiers had been used to help man the walls but there was no employment for those of us trained to chariot fighting. Then came the message that the defenders were in difficulty along the northeast wall. Penthilos rushed off in that direction and I followed, calling my Companions to come with me.

As Penthilos had predicted the attackers had succeeded in massing on the level hilltop beyond the wall and were pressing their advantage vigorously. Every sword was needed here and we flung ourselves into the battle. At some point I heard someone yell 'The palace is burning!' but there was no time to investigate. It seemed for a while as if there would be no end to the faces that glared up at me as they flung themselves at the scaling ladders and then fell back, dead or wounded. Then I noticed a slight wavering and thinning in the crowd of attackers and in the middle of them I caught sight of Cresphontes, urging his men on with shouts and waves of his sword.

I leapt up on the wall and yelled, 'Cresphontes!'

He knew my voice and looked towards me. All round the battle suddenly stilled and men stared up at me. I shouted, 'You and I have a personal score to settle. Call your men off and let us settle that first, man to man.'

He gazed at me for a long moment. Even across the distance I could feel the power of those hawk-like eyes. Then he threw back his head and laughed derisively.

I yelled, 'I killed Xouthos, Cresphontes!'

His laughter stopped and I saw him gesture to a man beside him who held a bow. In that instant Alectryon flung himself upon me and toppled me bodily off the wall, the two of us only being saved from crashing to the ground by falling into the arms of our friends. As we fell an arrow sang over us and embedded itself in the ground beyond. The man with Cresphontes was no mean marksman. The arrow had passed exactly where I had been standing a heartbeat before.

I struggled to my feet, shook off the hands of those who had caught me, and turned to Alectryon. He went on one knee and started apologising for manhandling me. I yanked him to his feet. 'Don't be a fool! You saved my life – again.'

He caught my eye and suddenly the old familiar look of exasperated amusement broke across his face. 'Well, I suppose I'll just have to make sure I'm always around to do it.'

While I stood on the wall I had noticed something and the seed of an idea had taken root in my mind. I turned to Penthilos. 'If you opened the postern I could lead a charge and take them in the flank.'

He considered for a moment, then said, 'Let us see what the situation is.'

The postern gate had proved as impregnable as the main gate and the attackers had abandoned it in favour of the assault on the walls. The ground beyond it was clear. I shouted for volunteers to make a sally with me. Alectryon was at my side at once, Melanthos and Perimedes followed with the rest of my Companions. Antilochos was last to join us and I could not see Neritos. A band of men, Pylians and Myceneans alike, gathered round us.

When I had told them the plan we formed up behind the postern gate. As we waited for it to be opened Alectryon caught my eye again and grinned. Time rolled back a year.

'Satisfied?'

'What?'

'You always wanted to be a hero.'

Then the gate opened and we charged out. We took the Dorians completely by surprise and swept on to clear the hilltop. As we turned to withdraw I missed Melanthos at my left hand and swung about to search for him. Alectryon yelled at me to come but I shouted back 'Melanthos!' and he rejoined me at once. We found Melanthos pinned to the ground by a spear that had passed through the fleshy part of his calf. He was tugging at it desperately and around the edge of the hilltop the Dorians were regrouping for a fresh charge.

Then I heard the war cry of the Neleids behind me and my followers rushed back to surround us, led by Perimedes. They charged the Dorians again to give us time to free Melanthos. Alectryon seized the spear and jerked it out and between us we picked up our comrade and ran for the gate. The rest of the force covered us until we were safely inside, and the defenders greeted us with ringing cheers.

While we were waiting for the surgeon to attend Melanthos we heard a second cheer go up. The Dorians were falling back. Before long all fighting had ceased.

We stood to arms for the rest of the day, uneasily watching the Dorian camp. Towards sunset they sent a herald to ask for a truce so that both sides could collect their dead. Tisamenos granted it and we went to our homes to disarm. To my relief I found Neritos in his room, next to my own, being tended by Karpathia and Andria. He had a nasty head wound and was only half conscious but he tried to mumble apologies for not being at my side during the battle. I brushed them aside and gripped his hand.

He gave me a shadow of his old, cheeky grin and said, 'I wish I had been there, though. I heard about it. You are the hero of the day.'

Later that evening I got a message asking me to go to Melanthos, since he was unable to come to me. I found him in bed, white as his linen but clear-eyed. He began to thank me for saving his life but I put it aside, saying I knew he would have done as much for me.

He answered, 'If I am ever able to offer you help or service beyond the demands of my duty to you as my King I shall do my best to repay you. But since that duty comprehends all service, I can only ask you to accept my gratitude.'

I was to remember those words.

We slept uneasily that night, wondering how long we could hold out against these ferocious attacks, but at dawn a cry went up from the watchmen on the ramparts. I leapt out of bed, seized my sword and ran to the terrace. Below, beyond the burned remains of the Lower City, the Dorian camp was deserted. During the night the enemy had withdrawn.

I dressed and hurried to the main courtyard. It was here that the fire had been started by a fire-arrow the day before. A good deal of damage had been done to the southwestern end, opposite the megaron, but the fire had been contained there. Tisamenos looked at the damage to his palace and gave me a weary smile.

'Well, at least now I shall have to rebuild this section. I may as well have the Grand Staircase added at the same time.'

The Dorians had withdrawn, carrying off with them grain and cattle and anything else of value they could lay their hands on. Sacrifices of thanksgiving were made to the Lady and all the Gods and the people of Mycenae set about rebuilding their city. Some days later we heard that the Dorians were back in Pylos again.

When the news arrived I was summoned to confer with the King and his Lawagetas. Tisamenos was looking uncomfortable and Penthilos's face was grim. When I was seated Tisamenos began, 'Brother Alkmaion, we promised to restore you to your kingdom. It was a promise made in good faith and it may yet be kept. But you have seen that we cannot meet the Dorians in a pitched battle. If we tried now to attack them in Pylos, where they have made themselves strong, all the advantages would be on their side. Our army might well be destroyed and then Mycenae would be at their mercy too.'

He paused and I sat with bowed head. I had known in my heart ever since the battle on the plain that it would be so, but to hear it spoken brought the hot tears to my eyes to shame me.

Tisamenos went on, 'The summer is well advanced and soon it will be harvest time. It is too late in the year to set out on a long campaign and our forces are greatly depleted after the recent battles. Therefore, I beg you, content yourself to be our honoured guest for this winter – you and your family, and all your followers. When the spring comes we will see what can be done. Before the summer ends I will send out my ambassadors to Athens and Crete and all the other cities whose rulers own me as their liege lord. Next spring we will muster a force, greater even than that which went to Troy, and drive the Dorians from our lands. What do you say?'

What could I say? The winter lay before me like a long corridor of darkness, but I knew that Tisamenos had spoken wisely. The idea of the gathering of all the Achaean powers in a great confederation excited me, and gave some comfort. I thanked him humbly for his hospitality and told him that I was entirely in his hands.

When I returned to my own apartments I sent for Alectryon and told him the news. He gave me one of his long, silent looks, reading my thoughts as easily as a scribe reads the scratches on a clay tablet, and then said, 'Why are you down hearted? I believe the Gods heard your prayers when you longed for an opportunity to rank yourself with Achilles and Odysseus. Already you have won yourself an enduring name for courage. Now you will help to lead a great expedition which the bards will mention in the same breath as the war with Troy.'

I forced a smile and said, 'They ask a great price then, if it is indeed their favour which guides my fate – my father's life and my ancestral palace.'

He raised his brows. 'They asked a great price of Achilles, too. First his friend Patroclos. Then his own life.'

I was silent for a moment. Then I said, 'Let them ask my life also, if need be. But I pray them not to require my friend of me.'

I should have been glad of his embrace at that moment, but he touched my arm lightly and looked away.

I said, 'You are troubled about something.'

He shrugged. 'These are not joyful times for any of us.'

'But you have no special sorrow – something I don't know about?'

He turned away. 'None, my lord.'

Tisamenos sent his ambassadors out as he had promised and I waited impatiently for their return. Each one brought the same reply. In every part of the Achaean world, and beyond, there was unrest. Hostile peoples were gathering on the borders, there were rumours of further invasions from the north, trade and communications were being disrupted, hasty fortifications thrown up or existing ones improved.

240

Each ruler promised a contingent for the great army to be assembled in the spring, but with each promise came the same proviso – the size of the contingent would have to depend on conditions around their own borders. 'We dare not leave our cities undefended' was the burden of every answer.

I was always invited to be present when the ambassadors reported to the King and I made my way to the megaron with particularly high hopes when the embassy from Athens arrived. There had always been good relations between ourselves and the Athenians. In fact, my family was connected to the royal house of Athens, since my uncle Andropompous had married an Athenian princess. The ambassador's answer was a sad disappointment. Not only was Athens embroiled in a dispute with the neighbouring Boetians but she was split by internal dissension as well. The King, Thymoetes, was old and had never, the ambassador implied, had a very firm grip on his kingdom. His sons were unruly and ambitious and each was engaged in trying to establish a faction strong enough to drive his father from the throne. To so low a state had the House of Theseus sunk!

The ambassador from Athens asked me for news of Andropompous, who had visited Athens on a number of occasions. When I told him that he had been killed defending Pylos but that his son, Melanthos, was alive and in Mycenae the ambassador begged to be introduced to him. Melanthos had recovered from his wound, except for a slight limp he would never completely lose, and was glad to meet his father's old friend. During the ambassador's stay they spent a good deal of time together.

The Athenian went home, but not long after he returned at the head of a second delegation, all of them men of rank and influence. They came, they said, to assure Tisamenos of their continuing loyalty but their reasons seemed to me hardly strong enough to warrant the trouble of another journey. It was not until later that I realised this was only a pretext. Two days after their arrival Melanthos came to me and begged a private audience. He seemed troubled and clearly did not know how to begin.

At length he said, 'Royal lord, I come to seek your advice.'

Advice was something I scarcely felt qualified to give Melanthos, whose wisdom I had always respected and whose experience was greater than mine by several years. However, I invited him to tell me his problem. He frowned, searching for words.

'You know that I have been a great deal in the company of the Athenian delegation. Are you aware of how things stand in Athens?'

I told him what I knew, or had deduced from the ambassador's words.

He nodded. 'It is so, but there is more. There are a number of powerful men in Athens who have no love for any of the sons of Thymoetes, whom they regard as dissolute, contentious and altogether unfit to rule. Also they can see that if Athens cannot be united under a strong ruler she may fall prey to the Boetians, or if not to them to the Dorians. Therefore they have for some time had it in mind to choose a man who might provide that rule and, by their united power, to drive Thymoetes and his sons from the throne and replace them with their own candidate. However, the plan so far has come to nothing because they cannot agree among themselves who should be king. Now,' he paused awkwardly, 'they have made a certain proposal to me. It seems the House of Neleus commands respect, even in Athens. Also, my mother was of Athenian royal blood and my father was well thought of. They have said that if I will go with them to Athens they will place me upon the throne of the Theseids. The old king has a daughter, Idomeneia, a girl of seventeen who is, they tell me, beautiful and of a modest and gentle nature quite unlike her brothers. They will marry me to her to give the change some colour of legitimacy.'

He fell silent and I strove to order my thoughts.

'What have you told them, Melanthos?'

'I have said that I must first consult you. I am after all your liegeman – at least until such time as I achieve the throne of Athens. Also, I am loath to leave you at such a time. But it seems to me that if I can succeed in uniting the Athenians and defeating the Boetians I shall then be able to bring the full strength of Athens to join with our other allies in driving out the Dorians.'

I nodded slowly, trying to think clearly and not be carried away by a sudden impulse of enthusiasm. 'Very well, then. You have my permission and my good wishes for the attempt, though I shall miss you sorely. But there is a higher permission than mine that you must obtain. Have you yet consulted the wish of the Goddess?'

He shook his head. 'This must be my next task. I have it in mind, if you will permit it, to travel to Delphi and consult the Pythia. It is said that she can most clearly read the will of the Goddess as to the future of a man. I will abide by her decision.'

I agreed that he should do this, giving out that he went on my behalf to ask the favour of the Goddess for our expedition in the spring. As he rose to leave I laughed suddenly and put my hand on his shoulder.

'Do you remember, I said you would make a good king, and you answered 'No kingdoms for me!'? Now we shall be brother monarchs.'

He smiled. 'If the Gods permit, my lord.'

Melanthos set off for Delphi a few days later and returned in due course to tell me that the priestess who served the sacred snake had given him a favourable answer. The Athenian ambassadors returned home to make ready for his arrival and he prepared, with great circumspection, to follow them. We gave out that he had been promised an estate in Attica, through his mother's family. It made him appear less than loyal to me, for which I grieved, but we dared not let his true purpose be known.

One thing disturbed me in connection with his imminent departure. I had noticed that Cometes had been paying a good deal of attention to Melanthos's sister, Amphidora. It seemed to me that Tisamenos would be looking for a better alliance for his eldest son than the daughter of a junior branch of a family which, though illustrious, was now without either lands or power. Yet I could not hint to him of Melanthos's hopes. Accordingly I decided to sound him on the matter. He listened gravely and answered,

'I must thank you, Alkmaion, for bringing this matter before me. I too have noticed my son's interest in your cousin and I have already spoken to him about it. Firstly I have told him that he is too young to think of marriage for a year or two. Secondly, I have suggested that it would be – unwise – to ask Amphidora, or her brother and yourself, to make a decision on such a matter while the fortunes of her family are so much in the balance. He has agreed to let matters stand as they are until next summer, when the outcome of our next attempt against the Dorians will be known.'

I knew well enough that Amphidora herself would find no difficulty in coming to a decision. I could not tell if she loved Cometes but she was certainly enormously flattered by his attentions. She would agree at once. But I understood what Tisamenos was saying. He could not afford to permit the marriage until I was reinstated as King of Pylos. I told him I thought his decision very wise and promised to see that Amphidora knew of it. In the circumstances, it suited us very well.

Melanthos set sail from Argos a few days later, leaving his sister in my care until such time as he felt it was safe to send for her. It grieved me to see him go, for I both loved and trusted him and I knew, as he did, that he was undertaking a very dangerous enterprise. Before he left he promised me once again that if he was successful I should have an Athenian army at my back next spring.

Before winter finally interrupted communications I had a message to say that he had arrived safely but must now wait for his opportunity to move. He added that he had found Messenian refugees in Athens, all of whom were overjoyed to learn that I had survived the battle and sent me their humblest respects.

Autumn came. I began to be almost reconciled to my life in Mycenae. The King's hospitality was generous and, as soon as the city had recovered from the battle, various entertainments were arranged for us. There was hunting and games and feasting and music. My followers, too, began to settle down and I found myself surrounded by a loyal band, not only of Pylians but of young Myceneans who sought my company and acknowledged my leadership. My apartments in the palace became a regular meeting place for all the livelier spirits in the city, but perhaps as a result of this I began to notice a less friendly attitude in Tisamenos's eldest son, Cometes.

There was something more pressing on my mind during those long days of waiting. In spite of his promise, I could feel that Alectryon and I were growing apart. He waited on me daily and was seldom far from my side, but we had no time to be alone together. I could no longer take it into my head to go off hunting or riding with no one but him and our two squires. Nor could I slip out of the palace at night to visit him. My sudden, unannounced arrival at the house of his host would have caused too much confusion. In the same way, he could not come to me without running the gauntlet of sentries and chamberlains. Sometimes I sent for him, but this made our lovemaking seem contrived and unspontaneous. In bed, as always, he was ardent and tender, but I felt a sense of restraint in him, as if he was afraid of overstepping some self-imposed limit. He no longer teased me or tried to make me laugh. What was perhaps more significant, he no longer argued with me. I longed for the old days when we had been so easy together, but somehow I could not find a way of getting back to them. Moreover, his normal light-heartedness seemed to have deserted him. There had always been a deep-seated gravity in his nature, which his humour only overlay, like gold foil on a base of polished stone. Now the bright surface was gone, except for occasional flashes, worn away by the experiences of the past months; by the deaths of his brother and Dexeus, perhaps; and by something else that I could not yet define.

One evening, soon after the celebration of the autumn equinox, Penthilos sought me out and told me that Antilochos had asked for Myrtilis's hand in marriage. I was not altogether surprised, for it had been apparent for some time that he was paying court to her and I had the impression that Erigone, her mother, was encouraging the match. What the girl herself felt there was no way of telling, since she was so shy she hardly ever spoke in company. It was on the tip of my tongue to tell Penthilos that I thought she deserved something better, but Antilochos had done nothing blameworthy since we arrived and I felt it would be unjust to poison Penthilos's mind with my personal dislike. So I gave my consent to the match.

I was worried about the effect this might have on Alectryon. In recent times he seemed to have paid less and less attention to Myrtilis, but I had occasionally caught him looking at her with eyes narrowed as if with pain. On the day after my conversation with Penthilos I sent for him and suggested that we should walk together on the hills above the city. Winter was coming and dark bands of cloud edged the horizon. I told hm of Myrtilis's betrothal.

He withdrew his eyes slowly from the distance and looked at

me. 'I had expected it.'

I said, 'Poor girl. She deserves a better fate.'

He made a sudden movement, turning his face from me.

I gripped his arm. 'What is it? Are you ill?'

He shook his head quickly, keeping his face averted. I knew then that my suspicions were correct.

'You love her?'

He took a step or two from me, then turned, composed again. 'Yes.'

'But, man, why have you let her go? Why don't you speak to her? She cannot prefer Antilochos to you.'

He looked into my eyes. 'Would you have me do so?'

I stared at him. 'You have not held back for my sake?'

'Should I not have done?'

'Do you think me so selfish?'

He turned away again and heaved a deep sigh. 'Well, I did not hold back. I have spoken to her.'

'And she rejected you?' I was incredulous.

'No.'

'No? Then why …?'

He came back to me. 'She loves me. She has told me so. But she will do nothing other than what her mother orders. And her mother wishes her to marry Antilochos.'

'But this is ridiculous!' I exploded. 'What can her mother hope to gain by marrying her to Antilochos? He has no more wealth or power than you in our present situation. Your breeding is as good, or almost, and for nobility, looks, natural gifts you are as far above him as the sky is above the earth.'

He gave me a small, wistful smile. 'Thank you. I'm flattered. But it's quite useless. Erigone is a woman of extraordinary powers. Her hold over Myrtilis is amazing. I believe the poor child is terrified of her. And Erigone, for some reason, has chosen Antilochos.'

'Well,' I said obstinately, 'what she decides may not be the last word. I shall forbid the match. As my liege man Antilochos cannot marry without my consent.' I smiled at him and put my hand round the back of his neck. 'Be comforted, my dear. You shall have your Myrtilis.'

He gripped my wrist. 'No, Alkmaion. I beg you, don't do it!'

'Why?' I cried in amazement.

'For many reasons. First, even if you should forbid the marriage to Antilochos, Myrtilis will not marry me. I have told you, she is terrified of displeasing her mother. Secondly, it would be an open slight to Antilochos, which he would not be able to tolerate. He would undoubtedly try to stir up feeling against you – and he has his own friends in Mycenae who are not yours. Thirdly, I am afraid to think what revenge Erigone might contrive against you, against me, and worst of all against Myrtilis.'

I stared at him helplessly. 'Then there is nothing I can do to help you?'

'Nothing.' He withdrew my hand from his neck and pressed his lips into the palm and I felt a sudden wrench of anguish, but whether for him or for myself I could not be sure.

I made him sit down with me on a rock and tell me the whole story of his love. For once I forgot the duties which might have called me back to the city and did all I could to cheer him, but I knew that there was a part of his heart which I could no longer reach.

That night, for the first time, I took Andria to my bed.

Chapter 14.

The months of winter passed. The city was loud with the noise of building. Apart from the construction of the Grand Staircase and the repairs to the fire-damaged section of the palace, Penthilos had been given permission to carry out his projects. The first priority was given to the extension of the wall in the northeast so that the whole hilltop was encircled, and the construction of a secret tunnel to reach the spring of Perseus. I was fascinated by the whole process and spent much time accompanying Penthilos and his architect around the sites. In this way I learned much that was to be useful to me in later years.

For the most part I tried to keep my mind away from the Dorians and the coming struggle, but one evening I could not conceal my fears any longer and asked Penthilos what he thought the chances were of our mustering an army large enough to drive them out.

He shook his head uneasily. 'Who can say? Conditions are not the same as they were when Agamemnon summoned the Achaeans to sail against Troy. Then men thought their cities secure. When they returned after ten long years they found in many cases that their security was an illusion. The Achaeans won the war, but they paid a high price for victory. Too many of the real leaders died. Too many women lost sons and husbands. Too many kings returned to find treason and rebellion at home. Most people are not anxious for a repetition of that. With unrest all around they have a good excuse for holding back. But I may be mistaken. Perhaps they will come.'

'And if not?' I asked.

'If not,' he responded heavily, 'I think it will not be long before the Dorians have us all cooped up in our walled cities. They will not be able to get in and we shall not be able to drive them away.'

I looked at him. 'That is a grim prospect. What is the answer?'

He shook his head again. 'I don't know —except for this. There are many lands and islands between here and Asia, or towards the west. I would prefer to take ship with a company of followers and found a colony somewhere we could take root in peace. But of course I cannot leave while I am still needed here.'

Mid-winter came, and we performed the rites appropriate to the season. I had ordered to be constructed a shrine where we could make offerings to the Lady of Pylos and here I carried out as best I could the sacred duties of a king. It was here that I felt most keenly the separation which kingship made between me and my friends. As the earthly consort of the Goddess I was set apart from ordinary men and must keep myself free from all defilement. There were times when the daily ritual hung heavily upon me. I began to understand the air of separateness which had enveloped my father and kept everyone, even myself, at a distance. Alectryon might still have found a way of speaking to the man without encroaching on the dignity of the king, but he was silent and withdrawn these days. Neritos now called me 'My lord' and lowered his eyes before my gaze and my Companions asked my permission before speaking.

The day came for the marriage of Antilochos and Myrtilis. On the evening before I resolved to make a last attempt to save her for Alectryon. I sent for her, and using my royal prerogative, dismissed everyone else so that we were alone. She sat before me, eyes downcast, visibly trembling.

I said, 'Myrtilis, tomorrow you are going to marry Antilochos.' She nodded, almost imperceptibly. 'Do you love him?'

For a moment she made no answer. Then, without looking up, her voice faint and husky, she said, 'It is not for me to chose. He is to be my husband.'

'But you would prefer another. Is that not so?'

Her eyes flew up to my face, wide with terror. 'Why do you say so?'

'Because he told me. Come, Myrtilis, Alectryon is my friend. I long to see him happy. Trust me! You love him, do you not?'

She bent her head and would not answer. I leaned towards her.

'Myrtilis! If you wish it I could even now forbid this match. Some pretext could be found – an evil omen, a bad dream. Once the wedding is put off there would be time for you to change your mind. Marry Alectryon and you will have my blessing, and my protection.'

She raised her eyes again and for a moment gazed into mine. I could see how she longed to accept my offer, but she shook her head slowly and her lips framed the one word, 'No.'

'Why not, Myrtilis?' I insisted.

She rose to her feet, her eyes fixed before her. There was something about her that gave me an eerie feeling that she was not acting of her own free will.

'I may not,' she said faintly.

I rose also and caught her hands. 'What do you mean, you may not?'

'I may not choose for myself. I am only an instrument.'

'An instrument? Of what?'

She tried to tug her hands free, gazing around her as if terrified that we might be overheard. Tears came into her eyes. 'My lord, I beg of you! I must not answer. My mother …'

'Why should you fear your mother so? What has she said to you?'

She pulled free with a little sob of panic and backed away from me. 'I cannot tell you anything. Please, my lord, I beg of you. Let me go!'

There was nothing I could do but allow her to leave.

The marriage took place the following day with suitable celebrations. Antilochos looked triumphant, as though he had achieved a princess for his bride, and I pondered the power of love, reflecting that I would have expected him to marry more to his advantage than this obscure girl. All my friends privately agreed, however, that he had better than he deserved in Myrtilis. Neritos remarked dryly that he would have liked to see him matched with Erigone instead, commenting that they would have been well suited.

Alectryon attended, along with all the other Pylians of rank. When the feasting was over I looked for him but he had already slipped away. I sent Neritos to bring him to me, but he returned alone, with the message that the Count was unwell and begged to be excused.

Antilochos and his bride set up home in the house of a Mycenean nobleman named Pamisios, a man of some wealth and influence with whom he had struck up a friendship. From then on I noticed that he rarely joined my circle, except when his duties demanded it. Before long, Pamisios's house became a second meeting place, the centre of a group quite different from my own and one for which I had little liking.

One evening Karpathia sent a message asking me to come to her so that we could talk privately. I found her at her loom, attended by two of her ladies. She sent the women away and offered me a seat. For a few moments we chatted casually, then she said, 'I do not like the company Antilochos is keeping.'

'Nor do I,' I replied, 'but I have never liked him or his friends, so nothing has changed.'

She shot me a quick look. 'Perhaps not. But you do not know what I know about these people.'

'What do you know?'

'You remember what I told you when you first came here? That the descendants of Aegisthos would gladly see Tisamenos driven from the throne.'

'Yes.'

'Well, all the men who frequent Pamisios's house belong to that faction.'

I stared at her. 'Can you be sure of this?'

She nodded. 'The King has chosen to forget that there was ever a feud. But Penthilos knows the troublemakers. They have tried to make strife between him and the King often enough.'

'And now they are all gathered around Antilochos.'

'And around Antilochos's wife – the granddaughter of Aegisthos.'

I was greatly disturbed by Karpathia's revelation, but unsure of the best way to deal with the situation. I had no proof that Antilochos and his friends intended anything against the King and without that I knew it would be worse than useless to accuse him. I resolved instead to have a close watch kept on everything that happened in Pamisios's house.

My only confidante in those days was Andria. Since the night when I first made her my mistress I had found in her the perfect refuge from my loneliness. She was discreet and never presumed upon my affection and, more importantly, I knew that no power on earth would draw my secrets from her. That night I asked her to listen for any rumours of unusual happenings, particularly concerning the Lady

Erigone, for I knew that very little goes on around a palace that does not very quickly become known in the quarters of the women servants.

One night, not long after, she said, 'Is my lord aware that the Lady Erigone often creeps from the palace after dark and does not return until dawn?'

'How should I be aware of that?' I asked. 'Do you know where she goes?'

Andria shook her head. 'No one knows.'

'An affair, do you think? At her age it seems unlikely.'

'The other women say it is not that. They believe she has magical powers and goes to perform some secret rites. They are all afraid of her.'

I told her to keep careful watch and see what more she could discover. A few nights later she told me, 'Erigone is not the only one who goes out at night. My lord Antilochos's wife does also.'

'Myrtilis? Are you sure?'

'I have it from her waiting-woman.'

'Then Antilochos must know of it.'

'I think not.'

'How can he not know?'

'The waiting woman told me that she has seen the Lady Myrtilis put something in her husband's wine cup. On those nights he sleeps till morning without stirring, and that is when Myrtilis goes out.'

I instructed Andria to speak to her informant and offer her a good reward if she would come at once and tell her the next time Antilochos went to bed drugged. Nothing happened for some days and then one night, just as I was about to fall asleep, Andria slipped into my room and roused me.

'My lord, Antilochos has drunk the potion again tonight.'

I sat up, alert at once. 'Has Erigone left the palace?'

'Not yet, my lord.'

I rose and reached for my clothes. 'Wake Neritos and send him to me. Then go and keep watch and summon me at once if Erigone leaves.'

She caught my hand. 'You will not follow her, my lord? She is a dangerous woman, with evil powers. Send someone else, my lord, I beseech you!'

I caressed her hair. 'I cannot, Andria. If there is evil here it concerns my cousin and perhaps the King. I cannot send someone else to spy on such matters. Now, do as I tell you.'

She went and I dressed quickly. In a few moments Neritos arrived, tousled from sleep, puzzled, trying to conceal his irritation at being woken. Suddenly I felt like my old self. I grinned at him and slapped him on the shoulder.

'Wake up, Neritos! We're going hunting.'

'My lord?'

I became serious again and rapidly explained what I intended to do. As I finished and hung my sword from my shoulder Andria returned and whispered, 'She has left her room, my lord.'

We crept down to the outer courtyard in time to see Erigone with a single attendant unbarring the gate. When she had slipped through the attendant re-fastened the gate and went back inside. I hurried to the gate, Neritos close behind me, but by the time we had opened it there was no sign of Erigone. We made our way along the street that lead into the town, hoping to get a glimpse of her, but she seemed to have melted into the shadows. Then I heard a sound and pulled Neritos into the shelter of a heap of rocks left by the builders. Ahead of us the figure of a man slipped out of an alleyway and began to walk swiftly away from us along the road. I glanced at Neritos and he lifted his shoulders in reply. There was no way of knowing if this man was heading for a meeting with Erigone but it was our only chance. We followed softly.

The man led us to the postern gate and I saw him speak to one of the sentries. The gate was opened and he slipped through. Again I caught Neritos's eye. If there was treason afoot, it had spread to the army. I drew Neritos away from the gate and spoke softly in his ear.

'If we go to the gate they will know they are discovered, but how else can we follow them?'

He thought for a moment. 'The northeast wall? Where the extension is being built there are still loose blocks of stone. It would be quite easy to climb.'

He was right, and before long we stood on the level ground

beyond the wall. Below us ran the path that led away from the postern towards the spring and on to the valley beyond. Presently another figure, a woman this time but not Erigone, passed through the postern and made her way along the path. Once again we followed.

She led us towards a grove of trees that grew in a hollow at the head of the valley. I had walked along the path many times but the grove itself was sacred and no one went there except for the devotees of some obscure cult. I felt Neritos cast me an anxious glance as we struck off the path towards it.

As we neared the place I heard a low murmur of voices, which became recognisable after a moment as a chant. Neritos stopped in his tracks.

I turned to him and whispered, 'There is treason here, Neritos, and danger to Tisamenos who has befriended us. The Gods will not hold us blameworthy if we seek it out.'

He nodded and we went on, but I could hear his teeth chattering. As we neared the grove I dropped to the ground, signalling him to do likewise, and we covered the rest of the distance on our bellies. Once among the trees we could see that there was a clearing in the centre of the hollow. In the middle a fire burned and around it moved a band of men and women, twelve of each, rapt in the rhythms of a sacred dance. In the centre, before the sacred fire, stood Erigone, still and upright.

We watched until the dance came to an end and the dancers proceeded to the next part of the ritual. I will not name the rites that they performed. Neritos buried his face in his arms in order not to watch what is forbidden but I gazed on, unable to tear my eyes away; for which sin the Mistress of all Mysteries has made me pay, as for all my sins towards Her.

As soon as the rites were over Erigone gathered the worshippers about her and spoke, her strong, hard voice carrying easily to where we lay.

'The omens are favourable. The Goddess has chosen the moment when Her true worshippers shall seize power again in Mycenae. She is the ancient Mistress of this place and in the days when Her worship was pure it was in Her priestess that power resided. It is the high priestess who should be queen and rule in Her land. It is in her the power of life and death is vested. Clytemnestra was both queen and high priestess, and she called my father, Aegisthos, to her aid. He understood the power of the Goddess and yielded himself Her willing servant. Between them they killed the tyrant Agamemnon. It was not murder, as some have termed it, but ritual sacrifice. He was killed as he stepped from his bath, taking the first mouthful of the feast laid out before him, his limbs entangled in a sacred net, so that he was neither in water nor on dry land, neither feasting nor fasting, neither clothed nor unclothed. It was thus in times gone by that the Consort of the Goddess was yearly sacrificed. For a while, then, the true worshippers of the Goddess ruled in this land, but Orestes came, Orestes the accursed, and my father died at his hands. Even the queen, his own mother, the earthly representative of the Goddess, was not spared. And then, as if he had not done enough, he took me and robbed me of my virginity and stole away the son I bore him, so that he grew up to hate me. But now the moment of our revenge has come! With the Pylian Antilochos married to my daughter we have a man of royal blood whom the people will accept as king. He has brought us more men and our plans are prepared. A swift blow, struck at night, and we shall rule in Mycenae. Antilochos, in his pride, thinks to be supreme High King. Well, let him think it for a while. Once he has given my daughter a child we shall have no further need of him. After that, the queen will again rule in Mycenae and the true adherents of the Mistress will be set at her right hand.'

She paused and a rapt murmur rose from those around her. Then she went on, 'Come now and once more bind yourselves with solemn oaths to serve the Goddess.'

She bound them with the most terrible oaths, so that I understood why Myrtilis had been so terrified to speak. Then she said, 'Tomorrow night is the appointed time. We meet at Pamisios's house at moonrise.'

Neritos and I lay flattened on the ground until they had all returned, singly as they had arrived, to the city. Then we made our way back by the way we had come.

I spent a sleepless night. I knew that it was my duty to inform

Tisamenos of the plot, indeed I could not afford to do otherwise, but at the same time I feared the consequences. I had no idea whether Antilochos had drawn other Pylians into the conspiracy, or how its discovery might change Tisamenos's attitude towards all of us. My first instinct, as always, was to summon Alectryon and discuss the whole problem with him, but as soon as the thought came to me I knew that this was one occasion on which I could not turn to him for advice.

As soon as morning came I sent Neritos to ask the King to give me a private audience. Somewhat to my annoyance I found Cometes seated beside his father. Over the winter our relations had grown less and less cordial and I should have much preferred to speak to Tisamenos alone. I told my story as concisely as possible and waited for the reaction.

At first Tisamenos was incredulous. Then he began to question me about the identities of the conspirators, repeatedly shaking his head in confusion and disbelief. I could see that he was utterly at a loss to deal with the situation. In a pause Cometes said, 'It seems to me that there was none of this trouble before you and your Pylians came here.'

I replied, with as much restraint as I could muster, 'I think you are mistaken, Prince Cometes. My sister has told me that there has always been a discontented party in the city. Penthilos knew of it well.'

'Penthilos?' Tisamenos said.

I saw the blunder I had made and strove to smooth it over. 'He kept a careful watch on these people, lest they should become a danger to you.'

'He would have done better to tell me of it,' Tisamenos said.

'Erigone is his mother,' Cometes remarked. 'And his wife is your sister, my lord Alkmaion – as Antilochos is your cousin.'

I sprang to my feet. 'Do you believe, my lord, that I am implicated in this conspiracy? That is what Cometes is implying, and I resent it. If you can believe me capable of such a base action, can you also believe that I would come to you and reveal the plot?'

Tisamenos hastened to assure me that he had no such suspicions and I went on to maintain vigorously the innocence of Penthilos and Karpathia. Eventually, we got down to making plans. It was agreed that Pamisios's house should be surrounded and the attack made as soon as all the conspirators were inside.

Cometes said, 'Penthilos will have to take charge of this. The army is under his command.'

'No!' I objected quickly. 'Erigone is his mother, vile as she is. He cannot be involved in this. Besides, my lord, I have reason to believe that some of the army may have defected to the conspirators. The sentries on duty at the postern gate last night must have been party to the plot.'

Tisamenos stared at me for a moment, wild-eyed, and I saw that his bland confidence had been based on a refusal to believe in the possibility of treason. Now that I had forced him to look into the pit I was afraid of the consequences. I said, 'Are you sure of the loyalty of your personal bodyguard, my lord?'

He nodded quickly. 'Yes, they are all members of the Companionhood. I trust them absolutely.'

'Then they should be enough for a surprise attack. If we can arrest the leaders the others will not move without them. But I should advise you to replace the sentries on duty tonight with your own men, just in case.'

Tisamenos sighed deeply. 'I will do as you suggest, but I find it hard to believe that Penthilos knows nothing of this.'

'I assure you that he does not, my lord. No more than any of us would, if I had not been alerted by idle gossip from the women's quarters.'

Cometes put in silkily, 'I understand why you wish to leave him in ignorance about tonight's proceedings, my lord Alkmaion, but I hope you will not refuse to lend us your sword to put down this treachery.'

I saw the trap that had been laid for me. In order to prove my loyalty I must take up arms against my cousin.

At nightfall we met in the palace courtyard, our armour muffled in dark cloaks in case it caught the reflection of the moonlight. I had brought Neritos with me, but had told no one else among my followers what was intended. It quickly became clear that Cometes had been given command of the operation, and also that he intended to keep a very close eye on me.

The men slipped away in small groups to take up their appointed stations. I was with Cometes in the shelter of a gateway opposite the main entrance to Pamisios's house. As the moon rose we saw the conspirators arriving one by one. We waited until the street was deserted again and then Cometes whispered, 'They should all be safely inside by now.'

Suddenly, in the darkness beyond the house there came a shout, followed by a clash of arms. Cometes hissed, 'We are discovered! Charge the gate!'

As he spoke the main gate crashed open and a body of armed men rushed out. I flung off my cloak and drew my sword and we charged forwards, meeting the opposing force with a great clash of metal. The impact was violent but our impetus was such that it carried us through the first ranks of the defenders and into the courtyard of the house. I guessed that Erigone and Antilochos and the other leaders would be waiting in one of the inner rooms and if possible I wanted to get to them before anyone else did. Inside the courtyard there were more armed men and the fighting became a confused mêlée in which it was hard to tell friends from enemies, while an archer in an upper window seemed to be firing indiscriminately on both.

I saw that a staircase led to an upper floor and that the base of it was guarded by a small knot of men. I guessed that it led to the rooms where Erigone and the others had taken refuge. I battled my way towards it, yelling to Neritos and some of Cometes's men to follow. We closed with the guards and met bitter resistance. I succeeded in disposing of my opponent and rushed for the stairs, leaving the others to deal with the rest.

At the top of the staircase a single warrior awaited me. Our swords clashed and I knew at once that this would be a hard man to defeat. Then, suddenly, he lowered his guard and I thrust hard towards his armpit, where the bronze corselet ended. Even as I thrust I recognised Alectryon.

It was too late to prevent my sword from reaching its target. I could only lessen the force of the blow. He fell back on the top step, his weapon clattering to the ground as he clasped his right arm across his body. Then he lifted his chin and offered me his unprotected throat.

Below I could hear the fight continuing. In a moment my friends might come storming up the stairs, or my enemies leap on me from behind. I dropped my sword and shield, sprang up the last few steps and stooped over Alectryon.

'Come!'

He was gasping with pain. I half lifted, half dragged him along the gallery until we came to an open doorway. The room within was in darkness. I dragged Alectryon into it and then went back to the doorway to see how the battle was going. As I stepped onto the gallery I felt a violent blow in the thigh that knocked my leg from under me. The pain came a heartbeat later. The archer in the window opposite had improved his aim and I saw, with a wave of nausea, that the shaft of an arrow stood out from my leg.

I dragged myself back into the room and over to Alectryon. He was lying silent now, gripping his right arm with his left hand to clamp it closer to his chest. I leaned over him and with clumsy and trembling fingers worked at the straps that held his corselet in place until I was able to ease it off him. His chest was wet with the blood that welled up inexorably from his armpit. I tore my tunic and made a pad to go over the wound, then took my belt and strapped his arm tightly to his side to hold it in place. In the faint light from the open door I could not see to do more.

Feet thudded past on the gallery, I could not tell whose. I could feel my own blood running warm and sticky down my leg. Perhaps it was because of this that the sounds of fighting seemed to be receding. I lifted Alectryon and propped him against me.

He whispered hoarsely, 'You are wounded too?'

'An arrow in the leg. It's nothing.'

He said no more and I thought he had lost consciousness. Then he muttered, 'Leave me. Why are you here?'

'Why are *you* here?' I returned. 'You were not fighting for Antilochos.'

Again there was a long pause and when he spoke his voice was fainter. 'No. For Myrtilis. She sent ... a message. Begged for my protection ...'

'Protection from whom?' I asked, but there was no reply.

My own head was swimming. I laid my cheek against his hair. He had bound it up on top of his head, as he always did before a battle. With numb fingers I began to undo the braids until it fell in heavy ringlets across my supporting arm.

Chapter 15.

They found us at first light, lying in a pool of drying blood, but it was the next day before I was fully aware of what was going on around me. I was unconscious most of the time while the surgeon cut the arrow out, so I was spared that suffering, but for some time I could not tell which of the images that crowded my brain were real and which delusions.

At length I woke from a deep sleep and as my brain cleared memory flooded back. I opened my eyes. Neritos was sitting on a stool near my bed, his chin on his hands, his eyes far away. I spoke his name and he started, then came to me and lifted my head and held a cup of water to my lips.

I drank and then said, 'What is happening, Neritos?'

He murmured soothingly, 'Rest, my lord. Everything is all right. You were wounded, but the surgeon says the wound is not dangerous.'

I said impatiently, 'That's not what I mean. What has happened to Antilochos? Is Tisamenos still safe? How did the battle end?'

He saw that I was back in the real world and answered quickly, 'With victory for us, my lord. Penthilos heard the fighting and called out his men. After that it was all over very quickly, but for some time we could not find you. Praise be to the Lord Poseidon who preserved you alive!'

I drew a breath and felt my skin prickle with the sweat of fear. 'And Alectryon?'

'He is alive too – but only just. The doctors say he should recover. But how did he come to be there? You gave me orders that he was not to be told what was happening.'

To gain time I closed my eyes and feigned drowsiness. Behind my closed lids my mind was racing. At length I said, 'He was there on my orders. I wanted someone inside the house to make sure Antilochos did not escape. He was keeping guard over the room where Antilochos was hiding. I went to join him, but we were both wounded. I dragged him out of the way of the fighting. Then I must have lost consciousness.'

I watched Neritos's face as I spoke. There was no flicker of doubt in it. I prayed inwardly that Alectryon would have the sense to say nothing until I had a chance to speak to him.

I went on, 'What has happened to Antilochos?'

'He was there, with the others. The King has him under guard, but he is protesting his innocence. He says he knew nothing of the plot and brings the story of the drugged wine as evidence.'

I bit my lip. 'He is clever. It will be hard to prove otherwise – but perhaps that may be best for us. And the others?'

'Erigone is a prisoner, and all those who survived the fighting.'

'And Myrtilis?'

He lowered his eyes. 'Myrtilis hanged herself, sometime during the battle it seems.'

'Hanged!' I stared at him. 'That poor child!' Then, urgently, 'Does Alectryon know?'

He looked puzzled. 'I do not know, my lord. I think not, probably. He has been unconscious, like you.'

'He must not be told. You understand me? As soon as I have finished with you I want you to go and find Thaleus and tell him it is my order. No one is to mention Myrtilis's death to him. When he is stronger I will tell him myself.'

Neritos frowned at me, wondering perhaps if I was as clear-headed as I seemed. Then I saw the light of understanding dawn in his face, but he was wise enough to say simply, 'Very good, my lord.'

I went on, 'Now, tell me what the situation is now. How do we Pylians stand with the King?'

He bit his lip. 'All sorts of rumours are about. I have heard it said that this was a Pylian plot to regain what we lost when the Dorians took Messenia.'

'And does the King believe that?'

He looked at me unhappily. 'I am hardly in a position to know, my lord.'

'How can he think me treacherous when I revealed the plot to him?' I was talking to myself rather than him.

'I have heard it said also ...' he began, then stopped, shaking his head.

'What?'

'That you were a party to the plot, but revealed it to the King because the Myceneans planned to make Antilochos king instead of you. And also that you warned the conspirators about the coming attack, as the price of their transferring their support from Antilochos to you.'

'It is not possible!' I breathed, but added after a moment's thought, 'They have some grounds to suspect a betrayal, though. It seems the attack was expected. Tell me, were any other Pylians of note involved? What about Perimedes?'

Neritos shook his head. 'He spent the evening at the house of a friend, a loyal supporter of the King. He is no more suspected than the rest of us.'

'Was anyone taken with Antilochos?'

'Only a handful of his personal followers. No one of rank.'

'The Gods be thanked for that at least,' I murmured. 'But it is cruel, is it not Neritos, that for the sake of so few we should all be under suspicion?'

He touched my arm with his fingertips. 'Please, my lord, do not disturb yourself. You must lie quiet and rest.'

I closed my eyes and must have fallen asleep again for when I woke next the evening light was fading and Andria was kneeling by the bed with a dish of broth. Her eyes were red from weeping and I pulled her to me and kissed her, murmuring, 'Don't cry, silly girl. I'm safe, aren't I?'

'I praise the Gods for it,' she whispered in return. 'But you have been close to death, my lord.'

I looked at the dish. 'That smells good. Are you going to give me some before it goes cold?'

She smiled then, and fed me the broth spoonful by spoonful. I had just finished it when Neritos came in to ask if I was well enough to talk to Penthilos. I told him to send him in at once and Andria set a chair for him by the bed and then withdrew.

I began by trying to apologise for putting him in a difficult position but he brushed it aside. 'I have always had enemies in Mycenae. My mother's plot was exactly what they needed to bring me down.'

I said, 'But you brought the army to the King's aid. He cannot suspect your loyalty now.'

He shrugged wryly. 'Tisamenos is afraid. He had convinced himself that the people of Mycenae were united in their devotion to him. He wants to be convinced of that again, but he cannot be while he has any doubts about those who hold positions of power. I do not think he will trust me again.'

'Then he's a fool!' I commented bitterly. 'What will he do now, do you think?'

'For the present he will do nothing. He is waiting until you are well enough to speak with him. The truth is, he cannot decide what to do for the best, or who to believe. He is glad of any excuse for delay.'

He left me to brood gloomily on the future. Spring was coming and soon it would be time for the great army of the Achaean federation to gather. But would Mycenae fight for Messenia now?

I passed a miserable night, plagued both by my dismal forebodings and by the pain from the wound in my leg. I had just finished a breakfast of milk and dried figs when I heard voices outside my door, involved in some kind of argument. One belonged to Neritos, but the other I could not immediately recognise.

I called, 'Neritos!' He came in looking flustered, and closed the door behind him. 'Who is that out there?'

He hesitated. 'Thaleus. I think he has gone now. He …'

I cut him short. 'Thaleus? Bring him in at once.'

I could see that he would have liked to disobey me, but he went to the door and called Thaleus in. The boy's face was white and there were deep shadows under his eyes from lack of sleep.

I said, 'Thaleus, how is Alectryon?'

He knelt by the bed and I saw that his eyes were full of tears.

'My lord, I fear he will die if you do not come to him.'

'Die!' I exclaimed. 'I was told his wound was not life threatening.'

'But he will not eat, my lord. Since we found him with you he has neither eaten nor spoken. He will take a sip of water from time to time but that is all.'

'Where is he?'

'At the temple of Aesculapius, my lord. The priests there are expert physicians. He has the best of care.'

I sat up. 'Neritos, send for a litter. Then help me to dress. And you, Thaleus, go back to the temple and have the kitchen prepare a posset of milk and eggs sweetened with honey. I shall be there by the time it is ready.'

Neritos took a step towards me. 'My lord, you cannot mean to get up!'

I gritted my teeth. 'Do as I tell you.'

He obeyed, but as Thaleus left I heard him say under his breath, 'Now, see what you have done!'

Weakness made my head swim and I could not stand without help but I managed to dress somehow. They carried me to the temple, where a grave faced priest conducted us to the door of a small room. I limped in leaning on Neritos's shoulder and lowered myself into a chair by the bed. Alectryon was as pale as wax and as soon as I came through the door his eyes closed, but I was quite sure that he had seen me. Thaleus stood by with a steaming cup and a spoon.

I said, 'They tell me you will not eat.'

There was no response.

I went on, 'You will eat now, because I shall not leave here until you do.'

Perhaps he heard the pain in my voice, for his eyes flickered open and rested for a moment on my face. Then, still without speaking, he turned his head towards Thaleus. The boy knelt and held the spoon to his mouth. With his eyes on me, Alectryon opened his lips, sipped, swallowed. Three or four spoonfuls disappeared in the same fashion and then he closed his eyes and turned his head away again.

I spoke through gritted teeth. 'Finish it!'

There was a moment's hesitation and then he obeyed. I sat for a moment with my own eyes closed. There was so much than needed to be said, but I knew that neither of us was equal to the strain at that moment.

I said, 'Rest now. I shall return this evening to make sure that you eat again.' Then I gestured to Neritos to help me up. In the doorway I turned. 'Alectryon, you made me a promise once. I expect you to keep it.'

I passed a restless day, dozing and waking, my mind full of anxious thoughts. Towards evening Thaleus came again.

'How is he?' I asked.

'He is more peaceful, my lord. And he sent me with this message. He has eaten, and he begs you not to disturb yourself to come to him.'

'Has he eaten? Properly?'

'Yes, my lord. A bowl of broth with some bread soaked in it.'

'Very well. Wish him goodnight for me. And tell him not to worry. We will speak as soon as he is strong enough.'

Next morning when the King's physician called to examine my wound I asked him if he had attended Alectryon.

'I did, my lord. The wound is serious, but it will heal with time. My main concern is that he has lost a great deal of blood – as have you. What you both need is rest and good food.'

That evening, to Neritos's great displeasure, I had myself carried to Alectryon's room again. Thaleus was feeding him with spoonfuls of broth when I hobbled in and I saw that his eyes were brighter and his cheeks, under the three-day growth of beard, a little less hollow.

He looked at me. 'You don't trust me. Well, you have reason.'

'On the contrary,' I returned, 'I trust you absolutely. I know you would never break faith with me.'

His eyes lingered on mine, full of a pain that I knew was not entirely physical. I waited until the bowl was empty and then said, 'Thaleus, leave us alone for a little. Wait outside with Neritos.'

When he had gone Alectryon said faintly, 'Why do you insist on keeping me alive? I raised my sword against you. There is only one penalty for that. Death.'

'You are mistaken,' I replied. 'You lowered your guard. Otherwise I could never have wounded you. I am so desperately sorry that I did not recognise you until it was too late.'

He said hoarsely, 'Believe me, I am no traitor.'

'I know it. I only curse the unhappy fate that brought us face to face. What were you doing there, Alectryon? You said something about a message from Myrtilis.'

'She sent her waiting woman to me, at sunset that evening. She

266

believed that her life was threatened and begged my protection.'

'Did she tell you about the plot?'

'She told me when I got there. She said it had been discovered and she was afraid of what might happen to her if the King's men took her prisoner.'

'She knew the plot had been discovered? It's true, they seemed to be expecting the attack. But how?'

He frowned, searching his memory. 'One of the king's men, I think. I don't know who.'

'What did Myrtilis expect you to do?'

'She wanted me to help her escape but it was too late. The attack started before we had time to get away. All I could do was try to prevent anyone from getting to her until we had a chance to speak to Tisamenos. She was innocent, Alkmaion, her mother's victim more than anyone else.'

'I know,' I told him gently.

'But I had no idea you were involved.' His voice was weakening. 'Why didn't you tell me?'

'I discovered what was going on and told the King,' I said. 'But how could I ask you to take part in an attack against Myrtilis and her mother? It would have been cruel to put you in that position.' I paused and rubbed my hand over my face. I had drunk poppy juice before setting out, to dull the pain in my leg, and now my brain was clouded and my eyes heavy. 'I would have saved her for you, you know,' I told him. 'That's why I was trying to fight my way up those stairs.'

He looked at me and a faint shadow of his old wry grin touched his lips. 'You mean, we were both fighting on the same side?'

'As always,' I said groggily. I made a great effort to focus my thoughts. There was something else that must be said. 'Listen. If anyone asks, you were there on my orders. I sent you secretly to keep watch on Antilochos. When the battle started you fought your way to my side and then we were both wounded. That's what I shall tell people and you must say the same. You understand?'

He was silent for a moment and I was afraid he had drifted back into sleep. Then I saw that his eyelashes were wet. He made a faint movement of his head and whispered, 'I understand.'

I leaned my head back against the back of the chair. I felt dizzy, but at least the pain in my leg was less and I had said what I came to say. His voice recalled me from the edge of sleep.

'You should be in bed.'

'I know,' I mumbled. 'But that bed's too narrow. There isn't room for both of us.'

I heard a sharp expulsion of breath that could have been the beginning of a laugh, or of a sob, but I was too tired to open my eyes. I was dimly aware of Neritos and Thaleus half carrying me out to the waiting litter, and then nothing more until the following morning.

I woke feeling stronger, though my wound still throbbed abominably. When Neritos came with my breakfast he said, 'My lord, I have been thinking.'

'I thought you looked tired,' I commented.

He grinned at me. 'You're feeling better.'

I grinned back and reflected that there was some compensation for my helpless state. The barrier that my royal position had placed between us had been removed, at least temporarily. It is very difficult to maintain the dignity of sacred kingship when you need help with even the most basic of bodily functions.

'What were you thinking?' I prompted.

'Would it not be possible to bring the count here to the palace? He could be cared for just as well and it would save you having to be jounced about in a litter in order to visit him.'

'That's an excellent idea,' I agreed. 'But I can see two difficulties. Firstly, is there a room for him? I'm loathe to ask any favours of Tisamenos at the moment.'

'That's not a problem,' he said. 'He can have my bed. I don't mind sleeping on the floor.'

'That's generous of you,' I said with a smile, 'but the second point is more important. Can he be moved without coming to harm?'

'We could ask the physician when he comes to see you.'

I put the question to the King's physician while he was examining my wound. He shot me a look from under heavy eyebrows.

'If it will stop you from trying to walk on this leg, my lord, I think it would be an excellent idea. The wound has started to open up again. It will not heal unless you rest it completely. I will consult with the doctors attending the count and see if he can be moved.'

The physician had just left when Neritos came in to say that Peisistratos was outside and asking if he might wait on me.

'I could tell him to come back tomorrow,' he suggested protectively.

'No, send him in. I want to know what's going on.'

Peisistratos came and knelt by the side of the bed and kissed my hand.

I said, 'What news, Peisistratos? What is happening in the city?'

He lifted his shoulders. 'There are all sorts of rumours, my lord, but no one has any definite information. The King keeps Antilochos confined in the palace. He is not a prisoner, exactly, but he is closely watched. No one knows the fate of the other conspirators.'

'And what is the feeling towards the rest of us? Do people think we were all involved?'

He looked sombre. 'It is true, my lord, that we are no longer as welcome as we once were. It is not surprising, I suppose. When we first came here the Myceneans were sorry for us. They expected to be able to defeat the Dorians and send us back to Pylos as their ever-grateful friends. Now they find it is not so easy. They blame us for the Dorian attack last summer, though I think that would have happened whether we were here or not. The Dorians can never feel secure as long as Mycenae stands. But the Myceneans have lost men and property and they don't want to be embroiled in another campaign. Meanwhile here we are, living in their houses, eating their food and making love to their women. And then one of us – at least – is embroiled in an attempt to overthrow the king. No wonder they want to be rid of us.'

'That fool Antilochos!' I exclaimed bitterly.

'Let us hope,' said Peisistratos, ' that King Tisamenos is persuaded by his protestations of innocence. Or at the very least that he is convinced that none of the rest of us were involved.'

After Peisistratos had left I was suddenly aware of movements and voices in the room next door and I realised that Alectryon had been brought from the temple. I waited until the noises ceased and then called Neritos to help me up.

'But you have to rest your leg!' he exclaimed, exasperation overcoming the habit of deference. 'You heard what the doctor said.'

'It's only a few steps,' I protested.

'Then Thaleus and I will carry you, if you insist,' he said firmly. He called Thaleus from the next room and they made a chair for me of their crossed hands and in this rather undignified manner I was transported to Alectryon's bedside. Neritos settled me with my leg supported on a stool and then withdrew. Alectryon's skin looked almost transparent and there were dark shadows under his eyes but when he greeted me his voice sounded stronger than the day before.

I said, 'You are improving. I am thankful to see it.'

'Slowly,' he answered. 'But I heard what Neritos said. Your wound will not heal unless you rest.'

'Well, I am resting.' I indicated my extended leg. 'See?'

There was a pause. I would gladly have avoided the next few minutes but I knew that I had to speak before someone else let slip what I had to tell him.

I said, 'Yesterday we spoke of how we were both trying to save Myrtilis. The Gods have not willed it so. She is dead, my dear.'

He asked, far more calmly than I had expected, 'By her own hand?'

'Yes.'

He nodded slowly. 'I had assumed so. She told me that she was bound by such terrible oaths that only death could release her. I persuaded her that if we could escape we might find some shrine where she could be released from them, but when I failed to return to her she would have had no other way out.'

I said slowly, thinking out the implications for the first time, 'If you had managed to escape, you would have left Mycenae – secretly?'

His eyes dwelt on my face. 'Yes. Now you see to what extent I have broken faith with you.'

We were silent for a long time. Then I said, 'That is all past now. Our future here is uncertain, thanks to Antilochos. I shall need your help and advice more than ever.'

He moistened dry lips with his tongue and said, 'What service I can perform is yours – as long as you need me.'

I reached for his right hand, which lay across his chest, but it did not respond to my touch. Then he took my hand awkwardly with his left. I felt a sudden lurch of dread in my stomach.

'Your arm?'

He said gently, as if trying to break the blow for my sake, 'The doctors say I may regain some use of it when the wound is healed.'

I bent my head and closed my eyes against the tears. After a long time I whispered, 'Truly, I bear the anger of the Goddess like a blight wherever I go, and I destroy all those who befriend me.' He began to protest but I cut him short, raising my burning eyes to his. 'It is so, Alectryon! Even when I have thought myself fortunate it has been a mockery. It was I who brought Cresphontes to Pylos, so he could see how rich and easy a prey it was. My father died because the Goddess forsook us in the hour of battle. Now I have brought rebellion and misfortune on Mycenae, upon Tisamenos who befriended me and upon Penthilos. And lastly, with my own hand, I have robbed you of the use of your right arm. I am accursed!'

He reached up weakly to my shoulder. 'No, no. You must not think that. What has happened to me I have brought upon myself. The rest is all part of a general disaster that has fallen upon all of us. You are not responsible.'

I held his hand against my cheek and said wearily, 'You used to laugh at me for living in the world the bards tell of. Now I see that the world of the heroes is gone forever and the Gods turn their faces from us lesser mortals.'

'I do not believe that,' he murmured. 'We are not different from our forefathers. The Goddess promised you forgiveness. She would not lie to you. Take courage. We may yet see Pylos again and if not – well, wherever our fate leads us, we shall follow the road together.'

The days that followed brought a strange sense of peace. My wound began to heal and Alectryon grew stronger. As his wound mended also, I persuaded him to try to use his arm. At first he could do no more than flex his fingers and I think he would have given up the effort if I had not insisted, but little by little the movement increased. I spent long periods massaging his arm and encouraging him to exercise the muscles and once he began to see that there was hope he worked at

271

it until the sweat stood out on his brow.

Each morning Peisistratos and my remaining Companions waited on me with what news or gossip they had been able to glean, which was precious little. Apart from that Alectryon and I entertained each other through the tedious hours. Most of the time we talked idly, not of the present situation or of our prospects for the future, but mostly of past events in Pylos or during our travels. I had to work hard to win the first smile from him but as the days passed his spirits began to revive. I cannot recall which of us made the first joke, but I remember the delight of that first moment of shared laughter. In later times I was to look back on those days with gratitude.

At length a message came from Tisamenos. If I was strong enough, he desired my attendance in his private apartments.

I was forced to send for a litter, for I still could not stand for more than a short time, but I insisted on being set down outside the door of the audience chamber and limped into Tisamenos's presence supported only by a stout stick which Neritos had found for me. I was prepared for a cold reception, but he greeted me with kindness and was solicitous for my well-being. However, Cometes stood beside him and his expression was less encouraging.

When I was seated Tisamenos began in tones of gentle regret, 'My dear Alkmaion, I cannot tell you how it grieves me that this shadow should have come between us. I regret even more that you should have suffered a wound fighting on my behalf. I trust you are making a good recovery?'

I told him I was well enough. I was on edge and his smooth courtesy did not reassure me. He went on, 'This whole affair is most unfortunate, and the worst part of it is that we cannot be sure exactly who was implicated or to what extent. We do not know how far the rot has spread in the army, for one thing. And the woman Erigone's close connection with – people close to me – has to be taken into consideration.'

'My lord, you will never find a more loyal supporter than Penthilos,' I said firmly.

He smiled faintly. 'Penthilos is your sister's husband. You are bound, of course, to defend him.'

'He is also your brother,' I remarked.

'Half brother,' Cometes put in quickly.

'Whatever his family history,' I returned, 'I am convinced of his loyal support for the King. Did he not come to your aid in the fight against Erigone's forces?'

'When he knew that the plot was discovered he had nothing to gain and everything to lose by holding back,' Cometes commented.

'He could have thrown in his forces on the opposite side,' I pointed out.

'The army would never have obeyed such an order,' Tisamenos said quickly. I saw that he was determined to retain his conviction that the rebellion was the work of a few isolated conspirators. To prove that Penthilos was not one of them would be almost impossible.

Tisamenos went on, 'There is also the question of exactly how far your cousin, Antilochos, was involved. He maintains that he knew nothing of the plot. What is your opinion?'

I hesitated. In my own mind I was certain that Antilochos had been a willing party to the conspiracy, although unaware of Erigone's real intentions. But there was nothing to be gained from admitting that. I said, 'I have not had the opportunity to speak to him since the discovery, as you know, my lord. I cannot give an opinion.'

Tisamenos went on, 'It will be difficult to prove his guilt, or his innocence. Also, I have no desire to cause a breach between the Houses of Atreus and Neleus. If I were to be convinced of his guilt I should have no choice but to sentence him to death and that, though you might admit the justice of my action, would be bound to cause ill-feeling between us.'

I said, 'If you will put him in my custody, my lord, I will see to it that he never has the opportunity to cause trouble again.'

'I feel sure that I can rely on your promise for that,' Tisamenos said. Then he sighed, 'But I fear the solution to the problem is not as simple as that. I am forced to consider the fact that there is a strong feeling among my people that the Pylians have brought us bad luck. Therefore I determined to enquire of the Goddess what is Her will in the matter. I have sent messengers to the Pythia at Delphi and have been awaiting their return. They arrived back yesterday with the Goddess's decree.'

'Which is?'

'I am instructed to shed no blood other than Mycenean blood, but the oracle confirms my fears. The coming of the Pylians has brought the anger of the Goddess upon us. Therefore you must leave Mycenae and seek refuge elsewhere.'

I gazed at him in silence. In all my worst imaginings I had not expected this.

'And the expedition against the Dorians?'

'In the present situation I dare not risk sending my best forces away from the city to embark on a costly and probably lengthy campaign.'

In the silence that followed I caught a smirk of triumph on Cometes's lips. I said heavily, 'And where do you suggest we go?'

Tisamenos looked relieved. I think he had expected an angry outburst. 'That of course is entirely for you to decide. Naturally I will give you any assistance in my power and I shall not require you to leave until your wound is fully healed and you have found some other friendly city willing to take you and your followers in.'

I rose painfully to my feet.

'If that is your decision, my lord, then of course I must abide by it. I thank you for your – temporary – hospitality. I hope that my efforts on your behalf in revealing the plot, and in the fight in which I got this wound, will in some measure repay my debt to you. Have I your permission to retire?'

Tisamenos gave his consent with as much cordiality as if I had been paying a normal courtesy visit. He even ordered Cometes to accompany me to my litter. As I was about to leave I remembered a final point.

'You will place Antilochos under my jurisdiction?'

'Naturally. I will have him sent to you at once.'

Back in my room Alectryon was sitting by the window in the first pale rays of spring sunshine. Neritos helped me to a seat opposite him and they both looked at me enquiringly.

'Bad news,' Alectryon commented.

I told them what Tisamenos had said. Neritos voiced all our feelings with a few choice oaths, some of which called into question the honour of the King's mother.

I said wearily, 'He is not a bad man, Neritos, but he is weak. In spite of the great power of Mycenae, he is afraid.'

'It is a poor thing when a man in his position cannot distinguish between friends and enemies,' Alectryon commented. 'But we are in no position to argue.'

I put my head in my hands. This, on top of days of pain and weakness, was almost too much to bear. 'Where can we go, Alectryon? Who will have us now?'

'We shall find friends somewhere,' he said consolingly. 'Melanthos is already in Athens. Perhaps he can speak for us to the king. Or there is Crete.'

'But how can I go to any friendly city if I carry the curse of the Goddess?' I cried.

He leaned forward. 'Listen to me. We all know that oracles can be interpreted to suit the wish of the worshipper – if he is powerful or wealthy enough. Tisamenos must know of your earlier misfortune. This gives him the perfect excuse to be rid of us.'

I stared at him. 'You are suggesting that the Pythia lies?'

'I am suggesting that the Pythia's words may have been open to interpretation – and the priests at the shrine know where their best advantage lies. Do not give too much credence to what they say.'

A servant appeared at the door to say that Antilochos was outside. I sent word for him to wait and let him kick his heels until Neritos had tidied the room and settled me with my back to the window. I was glad that I had dressed formally for my audience with Tisamenos but I made Neritos bring out the gold circlet which my father had given me and set in on my head. Alectryon withdrew to the next room and I told Neritos to send Antilochos in and then fetch my Companions Aikotas and Hoplomenos.

He had lost weight during his confinement and the old affectation of easy charm had disappeared, leaving only a bitter pride. I kept him standing in front of me. Once I would have savoured this moment, but not any more. I looked at him for a long moment and at the end of it all I could find to say, with a terrible weariness, was, 'You fool, Antilochos!'

His head jerked up and he said, 'My lord is pleased to abuse me. I have done nothing to warrant it.'

I sighed. 'Do not try to convince me of your innocence, Antilochos. I know you too well. Besides, I heard with my own ears Erigone declare that you had married her daughter because you hoped to rule in Mycenae. Do you know what they intended to do with you if the plot succeeded?'

I saw his eyes narrow. 'Do with me? What could they do against the king?'

'You were to be king only as consort to Myrtilis. The power was to be vested in the queen, and you must know that the queen would have been utterly ruled by her mother.'

I saw his nostrils flare as he absorbed this shock, but he gave a short, dismissive laugh.

'Just supposing that I had any part in this – which I deny – if I had been made king do you imagine I would have been ruled by my mother-in-law?'

'It would not have been left long in your hands. They wanted you only to reconcile the people to a change of rule. After that you had one function only – to give Myrtilis a child. Then you were to be disposed of.'

He glared at me. 'Who has told you all this?'

'I heard it spoken by Erigone herself on the night I discovered the plot. You have to thank me for your life, Antilochos. If I had not had you watched and informed Tisamenos of what was going on you would have shared the same fate as a rogue bull, allowed to perform your natural function – and then butchered. And if you doubt it, consider this. How many times were you drugged into unconsciousness without suspecting anything? Any of those cups could have contained a deadly poison.'

He averted his gaze from me and said nothing.

After a moment I went on, 'You are fortunate that Tisamenos is afraid to open a breach between our houses. Therefore he will not insist upon your death. But as a result of your blind folly we shall get no more help against the Dorians. So you have lost not only the crown of Mycenae but your ancestral lands as well – and the position that might have been yours as Lawagetas, had I regained the throne.'

He gave me a bitter look and said slowly, 'What is going to happen now?'

'We are all banished from Mycenae. I do not know yet where we shall go. You will accompany us, of course. But I warn you, Antilochos. From now on my eyes will be on you constantly. If I have reason to believe that you are engaging in anything that might bring the House of Neleus into disrepute, I shall have no mercy. If Tisamenos had wanted to take your life I should have fought it. You are my liegeman and your life is in my hands. But if you betray me again I shall order your death myself.'

For a moment he glowered into my eyes, but he knew there could be no argument. At length he dropped his gaze. Neritos looked in at the door.

'The Counts Aikotas and Hoplomenos are attending you outside, my lord.'

'Send them in.'

The two men came in and made an obeisance.

I said, 'Gentlemen, I entrust my cousin Antilochos to your keeping. He is to lodge with you and be under your surveillance at all times. You understand me?' I knew that they were fully aware of the situation and would give Antilochos no opportunity for further mischief making. I turned to him. 'You may go now. I shall expect you to wait upon me every day from now on – and remember, every step you take will be reported to me.'

I extended my hand and he was forced to kneel and kiss it.

After he had left I sent for Perimedes, who had held aloof since the conspiracy was discovered. I assured him that I had no doubts about his loyalty and reminded him that we had once promised each other than Antilochos's misdeeds should never come between us. He greeted my assurances with relief and reaffirmed his unswerving devotion.

Later that day Penthilos came to visit me. I was surprised to see that he looked remarkably cheerful.

'I have heard what Tisamenos has decreed,' he said, 'and we will speak more of it in a moment, but first I have some news to cheer you. Karpathia was delivered of a son this morning.'

I gasped. I had been so absorbed with my own troubles that I had forgotten that my sister was near her time.

'A son! That's wonderful! My congratulations, Penthilos. Are they both well?'

'Very well, my lord. Karpathia sends her love and begs you to visit her as soon as your wound is sufficiently healed.'

'It is healed enough for that now,' I exclaimed. 'May I come tomorrow?'

'Of course,' he replied, smiling. 'And I think you will approve of the name we have chosen. He is to be called Sillos.'

'After my father. He would be delighted – and so am I.' I drew a breath and felt the momentary surge of optimism die. 'But what is his future, Penthilos? How do you stand with Tisamenos now?'

'That is my second object in coming to speak to you,' Penthilos said. 'I told you some while ago that the king will not feel safe until he is rid of us all. Do you remember that I once spoke to you of founding a colony somewhere away from all the unrest that surrounds us here?'

'I remember,' I agreed.

He went on, 'I would never have left Mycenae while I had the king's trust but now things are different. Today I asked his permission to lead a colony to Lesbos. Reports from our merchant captains say that it is a fair island with good land and very few inhabitants. Tisamenos will give us ships and seed corn and everything else that is necessary and there are enough men who will follow me to provide a good beginning for a new city.'

'It's a brave venture,' I said doubtfully, 'but will you not miss all this? To have been Lawagetas to the High King of Mycenae – the greatest city in the world ...'

'I would rather be master of my own fate and live at peace,' he said quietly, 'even in a place no one has ever heard of. And that brings me to my next point. Come with us, Alkmaion, and bring the men of Pylos with you. Forget your old home and find a new one with us.'

I hesitated. I was weary of the struggle to keep up the spirits of my followers, of the constant raising and then dashing of my hopes, and the idea of settling in a tranquil place far from the depredations of my enemies was appealing. Yet I could not bring myself to abandon all hope of going back to Pylos.

'It's a generous offer, Penthilos,' I said, 'and very tempting in many ways. Certainly I have to find somewhere to take my people. May I take some time to think about it?'

He agreed readily and we spoke of the preparations he was making and of his vision of how the new colony would develop. They planned to leave as soon as Karpathia was strong enough.

The time of the Spring Festival came round and it was celebrated in Mycenae exactly as it had been in Pylos. I felt my anomalous position more acutely than ever at this time. At home I should have assumed my father's role, which would have seemed strange enough, but here Tisamenos was King and I was reduced to the role of an ordinary participant. Yet I could not shake off the feeling that I was failing once again to pay the Goddess my proper dues. As soon as the main rites were over I went alone to the sanctuary of the lady of Pylos and made sacrifice to her of all those things that please her best, but I could not tell from the omens whether or not She received them. Then I went to the spring that marked the sanctuary of Poseidon, God of underground waters, and made sacrifice and supplication to him also.

'Great Lord of earth and water,' I prayed, 'divine ancestor of my house, Father Poseidon, hear my prayer. I have ever honoured you and never failed to pay you due sacrifice. Even my colt Pedasos, the fairest animal that any man ever owned in Pylos, I gave you when you demanded it. Hear me now, and turn away the anger of the Goddess from me. I go once again to strangers. Let me bring no curse upon them. Grant me refuge from my enemies, and if I may not drive them from the land where you were once worshipped by my ancestors, bring me to some other place where I may honour you and the Great Queen herself in peace.'

Here the omens gave fair answer and I returned with a quieter mind to the city. As I reached the palace a servant met me with the words, 'My lord, there is a messenger from Athens waiting for you in your apartments.'

I hurried to my rooms, my mind tortured with contrary hopes and fears. The messenger was none other than Melanthos's own charioteer, Eumedes. At first sight of him I feared the news must be bad, for I knew he never left Melanthos's side. But his face belied my fears.

'Eumedes, what news?' I demanded as he knelt to kiss my hand. 'How is my lord Melanthos?'

He rose with an air of barely restrained delight. 'King Melanthos, ruler of Athens, greets you, my lord.'

I gasped and sat down hastily. My leg was still weak and the effect of his news was almost over-powering.

'King! Praise be to the Gods! Tell me all of it, Eumedes.'

It was a long tale. All through the winter the conspirators had manoeuvred to win support among the leaders of the Athenians. Melanthos's prudence and tact had done him good service here and many men had come to recognise in him one far more suited to rule than Thymoetes's dissolute sons. Nevertheless, the princes were powerful and it was impossible to raise a force large enough to be certain of defeating them.

As soon as the winter was past the Boetians had put an army into the field. The result had been near panic in Athens and for some days confusion had reigned as the rival princes struggled for the right to lead the army. Melanthos's supporters had seized their opportunity. They had proposed a coalition under Melanthos and many who had previously been hesitating gave their support. Melanthos had proved a brilliant commander, and had met and killed in single combat the Boetian champion Xanthos, at which defeat the Boetians broke and fled from Attica.

After this Melanthos had all Athens on his side. There had been a short but bloody battle with the personal supporters of the Theseids, after which Thymoetes agreed to hand over the throne. Melanthos was married at once to the King's daughter, Idomeneia, and the rest of the Theseids with their supporters had gone into exile.

All this was scarcely over before Melanthos had despatched his squire to bring me the news.

The question of where we were to go now presented no

problem. I knew that Melanthos would receive us gladly. I determined to send Eumedes back as soon as he was rested with an account of events in Mycenae and a request for his hospitality. Then I called all my Pylians together and broke the news to them that there would be no great army of the Achaean federation to sweep us back to victory in Pylos. They were not surprised, for rumour had been rife since Antilochos's rebellion was discovered. Nor were they unduly sorry to leave Mycenae, for they were well aware that our welcome there was wearing thin. I cheered them with the thought that Melanthos was one of us and had promised me an Athenian army. It might not happen this summer, I warned them, but by next year everything could be different.

As soon as Eumedes had left for Athens we began to make preparations to follow him. Tisamenos was all too ready to help us in any way. In fact, I noticed a subtle change in his demeanour. He did not want us in Mycenae, but he did not want our enmity either, particularly now that the House of Neleus suddenly had unexpected influence again. Even Cometes became more friendly and I noticed him making overtures to Amphidora again. She, poor girl, torn between her hopes and her loyalty to her family, spurned him proudly, but she had lost her old vitality and coquettishness.

As the day approached I made the rounds of my friends, of whom there were still many in spite of the popular feeling against us, and said goodbye. On the last evening I went to see Karpathia. She had fully recovered from the birth of her child and the bloom of health was on her cheeks. I remembered the tense, stone-carved figure of the priestess and the shrunken wraith she had become after her rejection and rejoiced in the transformation.

We both wept as we said farewell, not knowing if we should ever meet again. She said, 'I know we are doing the will of the Goddess in this. Do you remember? When we consulted the oracle about my marriage to Penthilos the answer was that I should marry him and carry the worship of the Mistress to my new home. It seemed a strange answer at the time, since She is already worshipped in Mycenae, but now I see her purpose. We are to establish Her worship in Lesbos. Now I know that you were right. She has not rejected me. In our new city, at the shrine that we shall establish, I shall be Her priestess again.'

I kissed her and wished her good fortune, begging her to sacrifice regularly to the Goddess for me, that I might regain Her favour.

That night Alectryon and I dined quietly in my rooms as usual. Below the terrace that gave on to my apartments was a small garden looking out over the valley. It was the first warm day of the year and when we had eaten we strolled down to it to enjoy the cool evening air. From somewhere beyond the walls the breeze brought the scent of pine trees and a faint hint of salt from the distant sea. It suddenly occurred to me that I could not remember the last time he and I had made love.

I felt his eyes upon me and turned to meet them. We looked at each other in silence for a long moment and then I said, 'It's finished, isn't it? Between us?'

'Not finished,' he said softly. 'Just changed. We always knew that had to happen one day.'

I drew a deep breath. 'I wish I could remember the last time. I mean, I wish I had known it was the last, so that I could keep it in my memory.'

He shook his head. 'No, that would have been too painful – for both of us.' He put up his hand in the old, familiar gesture to push the hair back from my face and added, 'You know my promise still stands, don't you. We shall never be less than devoted friends.'

'I know,' I said. 'I have never doubted that.'

He kissed me then, but it was a valediction and I did not attempt to prolong the embrace. Then he whispered 'Goodnight' and went back into the house. I stayed where I was, breathing in the scent of the pines and remembering a sandy knoll and moonlight through the branches of a pine tree, and the gentle susurration of summer waves. Then I caught a movement out of the corner of my eye and turned. Andria was standing by the foot of the steps, waiting for me. I went to her and took her in my arms.

For the last time my chariot rolled out under the mighty Lion Gate and down the long valley towards Argos, where the ships Tisamenos had lent us were waiting. He had insisted on accompanying me, keeping up to the last the semblance of friendship. When the ships had been loaded and we were ready to embark we assembled on the shore to made sacrifice to Poseidon. This done, and the omens proving favourable, I embraced Penthilos, took my leave of the King and gave the order for the sailors to cast off.

Chapter 16.

So we came to Athens, the city to which my mind returns now like a child to its mother, or perhaps I should say to a kindly foster-mother. As we sailed into the Bay of Phaleron I stood on the after deck and gazed at the view before me. I saw a wide plain, enclosed on three sides by mountains and on the fourth by the sea. In the centre of the plain, indistinct in the summer haze, a great crag rose abruptly from the surrounding countryside, its sides sheer and rocky. This was the citadel of Athens, the place the bards sing of as 'the strong house of Erectheus'.

Alectryon was reclining nearby on a pile of fleeces. He was much stronger now but still not completely himself, and the journey had tired him. I turned to him.

'Get up and look, Alectryon. Athens is all the bards say it is.'

He got to his feet obediently and gazed ahead. I could tell that the sight stirred him also. He nodded approvingly. 'It will take a formidable enemy to capture that fortress.'

As we sailed closer I saw chariots on the road that led from the city and by the time the ships' keels grated on the shore a crowd had assembled. As we prepared to disembark I realised suddenly that some of the faces were familiar. Not only Melanthos, whom I had identified early in the centre of the crowd surrounded by his attendants, but others whom I had long believed dead. As I reached the shore a cheer went up and voices greeted me as Royal Alkmaion, King of Pylos.

Melanthos came forward to welcome me. He embraced me warmly, managing to blend an easy equality with the formal respect he had once shown me as his king. When we had exchanged greetings others crowded round, kneeling to kiss my hand. There was Dikonaros, one of my father's Companions; two or three of the important land-holders who had had estates around the city; and, incredibly, some of my own band of young warriors whom I had led in that first chariot charge, most of them sons of Companions who had now inherited their fathers' titles. Behind them pressed others of lesser rank, all anxious to pay their respects. My own band of followers had disembarked behind me and there was a scene of mingled joy and tears as old friends embraced and memories of that terrible battle were relived. There was no time then to learn their individual stories but one theme was repeated again and again. They had all believed that I had perished with my father, until Melanthos's arrival in Athens. Their ecstatic greetings reawakened in me a joy and hope I had not felt since we left Pylos, and the obvious respect and affection that Melanthos evoked from his new subjects cheered me further.

On closer inspection the fortress of Erectheus was even more impressive than I had guessed. The sheer sides of the crag on which it stood were topped by walls that rendered it almost impregnable. Within them lay the palace, while the houses of the nobility clustered around the foot of the cliff. I could not help being a little disappointed in the palace itself, however. Impressive though its setting was, the building and its fittings were poor compared with the wealth of Mycenae or the beauty and taste of my own home. This first impression was to be confirmed later. Though life in Athens had all the graces of civilisation neither the king nor his nobles could boast such treasure as the great men of Pylos or Mycenae. I did not understand then how grateful we were to be for that fact.

Within the palace we were presented for the first time to Melanthos's bride, Idomeneia. She was a slender, soft-spoken girl with light blue eyes, who did not strike me at first as a great beauty, but then she smiled and I understood what had won Melanthos's heart. For the remarkable fact was that, in spite of the manner of their marriage, they seemed genuinely fond of each other.

Melanthos had arranged a great feast of welcome, to which all the Messenian exiles had been invited. Before we sat down to eat, each of the nobles knelt to take the oath of fealty to me and then, while the feast was in progress, I moved from place to place, hearing from each in turn the story of how he had survived and come to Athens. Some, I learned, had waited until night fell and then crept down to the shore where they discovered one of our ships, abandoned but still sea-worthy, and had slipped away under cover of darkness. Others had sheltered in caves in the hills or in remote shepherds' huts until it became clear that all resistance was at an end. A few had managed to bring their families to safety with them, but most had no idea what had become of parents, wives and children. Some had already taken Athenian wives and begun to settle down.

I went to bed that night with a sense of well being that amounted almost to elation but I was to learn that such euphoria is always followed by disillusion. I woke early the following morning, before it was light, and lay thinking over my position. Slowly I became aware on what slight foundations I had been building my hopes. Melanthos was King of Athens and my ally. But Athens was inferior in wealth and power to Mycenae or even Pylos. What could they do against the Dorians, when the might of the High King's army had not been able to defeat them? What, then, was I but still a king without a kingdom, a suppliant at the court of a fellow ruler?

When day came I opened the small chest in which I kept those valuables which I had salvaged from Pylos, together with some gifts from Tisamenos and friends in Mycenae. It was hard to select from my poor store a suitable gift for Melanthos but I settled finally on the dagger left me by old Peisistratos. Bearing this, I sought an audience with the King.

I found him alone and as soon as the door had closed behind me I knelt and saluted him by his royal titles. He leapt from his chair and raised me saying, 'My dear Alkmaion, why do you kneel to me? We are both equal now.'

I looked him in the eyes and said, 'Do not mock me, Melanthos. Of what am I a king? All that is past, indeed it never really existed, except in forms and ceremonies. I am only a suppliant, to whom you out of kindness give food and shelter.'

He gripped my shoulders and said fiercely, 'It is not so! You are still King of the Messenians, and shall rule again in Pylos. Have I not promised you the army of Athens?'

I shook my head. 'Let us not delude ourselves, cousin. The army of Athens, together with those Messenians gathered here, has not half the strength of the forces of Mycenae. Without further aid we should be mad to attack the Dorians.'

I saw that he knew this. 'It is true. So we must look for such aid. Mycenae is not the only Achaean city – and there are others, not of our race, who also fear the Dorians. We will see what can be done. I have not forgotten our old friendship, nor the fact that you once saved my life. Whatever help I can give is yours. Meanwhile, there is much you can do for me.'

'What can I do?' I asked.

'I need your counsel,' he said. 'Sit here beside me and let us talk.' I sat and he went on, 'You were trained to kingship, Alkmaion, and there is not one of your followers who would not agree that if Pylos had been left in peace you would have made a good ruler. Now I am ignorant of the whole craft of government so, I beg you, be my counsellor. I need your advice about so many things.'

For a moment I could not speak but at length I mastered myself enough to say, 'You flatter me, cousin, but whatever knowledge I have is at your disposal.'

I presented him with the dagger and I could see that the gift moved him, knowing from what a small stock it came. His answer was to present me, on the following day, with a fine mare in foal to one of the best stallions in Attica.

So, for the time being at least, I had occupation and a purpose in life. Melanthos's first concern was to improve the defences of the city. He saw, wisely, that although the Dorians had ignored Athens up to now in favour of richer prizes, they might descend on us at any moment now that the summer was come again. Already we heard reports of raids on the territory of Sparta and Corinth. Here, I felt I was genuinely able to make a contribution, having worked so closely with Penthilos and his architect. A new wall was built at a weak point where there had hitherto been a postern gate and a cistern was constructed in a cave deep below the palace to provide a water supply in case of siege.

I did not neglect my duty to my own followers. Now that I was once again in full health and able to perform my royal functions the burdensome ceremonial of kingship descended upon me again with all its rituals. Apart from this, I called regular assemblies of all the Messenians to hear disputes and dispense justice, and I organised regular military training for all the warriors. Once again my Companions and I mounted our chariots and practised charging and wheeling as a disciplined formation. I still had my pair of chestnuts, which had been shipped over with me, and Neritos had lost none of his skill. It was exhilarating to feel the wind in my hair and hear the thunder of hooves. We practised on foot, too, with swords and spears, and each of us worked at our skills with a grim determination we had not felt in those careless days in Pylos, for we had all good cause to know that we owed our lives to them, and might well do so again.

It worried me that Alectryon had never regained the full use of his right arm. He could manage most things without too much difficulty but the strength was lacking for combat. Typically, he refused to admit defeat and taught himself to fight left-handed, working harder than any of us. I insisted that he retain his position on my right hand, not so much now so that he could guard my unshielded side but because in this way I could protect his.

Towards the middle of summer we had an unexpected visitor. A fleet of ships arrived from Mycenae bearing no less a personage than Cometes. He saluted Melanthos with due respect and greeted me as if no ripple of dissent had ever disturbed our friendship. He had come, he said, now that the appointed time had elapsed, to request his formal betrothal to Amphidora. I caught Melanthos's eye and knew that the same thought was in his mind. Tisamenos had decided that he needed all the allies he could get and that Athens under her new ruler was too powerful to neglect.

We were in no position to refuse the alliance either, and Amphidora proved more than willing to swallow her wounded pride, so they were betrothed and the wedding was planned for later in the summer.

When Cometes returned home he carried a message from Melanthos formally requesting that Tisamenos re-open the negotiations to bring together a united army to oppose the Dorians. Once again ambassadors went out to all the Achaean cities, but this time from Athens. Once again, the answers were equivocal or even less encouraging than before. Then came Tisamenos's answer. He could not at this time undertake such a campaign. Perhaps next spring …

I called the Messenians together and told them that they must be patient for another year. I sensed that they were already beginning to lose their sense of unity, in spite of my efforts. They had made new lives for themselves in Athens and were starting to forget Pylos.

I had been anxious that the Athenian nobles might come to resent our presence as those in Mycenae had. However, when they saw that I longed only to return to my own land and had no desire to interfere with theirs, they accepted me and extended a warm hospitality that did much to cheer me as the summer slid past. Several of them presented their daughters to me and I guessed that more than one would have been happy to turn my thoughts towards marriage, but I could not envisage any future other than one of death in battle or constant exile. In the circumstances, marriage was out of the question.

One house in which I felt particularly at ease belonged to a man named Philaos. He was held in great respect in the city and, although he was considerably older than I was, we had a mutual interest in the breeding of fine horses that brought us together. He led a quiet life, devoting himself to the cultivation of his estate, which was one of the largest in Attica. The farm reminded me of Alectryon's estate and I spent some of my most peaceful hours there.

Philaos's wife had died some years before, leaving him with an only daughter named Philona. She was little more than a girl, poised awkwardly between childhood and womanhood, slight and rather gawky, with a great mass of golden hair framing a pointed face and eyes that still had the mischievous gaiety of a child. Whenever I visited she was always most solicitous for my welfare, profoundly conscious of her position as lady of the house. It amused me to see her making her first attempts at the sophisticated airs of a court lady.

As the summer drew to a close Cometes returned for his wedding to Amphidora. The resources of the palace were stretched to the limit to provide a suitable celebration, but Cometes seemed well pleased with his bargain and Amphidora was radiant. However, in private conversation we learned that Tisamenos was worried. The Dorians were raiding the borders of the Argolid and causing considerable losses to the Mycenean economy. Also, it was proving difficult to replace Penthilos. I hoped Tisamenos was regretting his unwarranted suspicions.

Shortly after Cometes had left we had our first visit from the Dorians. It was only a raiding party and they took to their ships when we sallied out against them, Melanthos at the head of the Athenian army and myself in the vanguard with my battle hardened Pylians. Nevertheless, they carried off with them recently harvested crops, livestock and captives. Melanthos remarked grimly that we could expect more such incursions in the future.

Summer ended, and with the shortening days I fell prey once again to the melancholy that often afflicted me at this time of year, but this time it was of a different sort, a black pall of despair which no entertainment or good counsel could lift. I had ceased to believe that we should ever assemble a sufficient force to defeat our enemies and with the worsening weather there seemed little point in keeping my Companions in training. A future of endless exile stretched before me. I was eighteen years old, and my life seemed to be over.

It was clear that my fellow countrymen were also losing hope, and Melanthos's well-meaning attempts to make us feel at home in Athens only served to reconcile them further to their fate. Although he had wisely divided most of the land left vacant by the heirs of Thymoetes among his supporters, some still remained in his gift. One fair estate he presented to Peisistratos and soon after we discovered that it was as well that he had a new home, since his wife Kerameia was pregnant again. This was a great joy to both of them, since they had lost their only son, Aretos, in the battle for Pylos. In due course she gave birth to another boy, who was named Andropompous in memory of Melanthos's father.

I knew that any land in Melanthos's gift would have been mine for the asking but he tactfully refrained from a gesture that would have implied that all hopes of my return to my own kingdom had been abandoned. He was always meticulous in treating me as a visiting monarch and still sought my advice, but as I had guessed many years ago, he had little to learn about kingship, and as his need of me lessened I began to withdraw gratefully from state affairs.

Perimedes rapidly made friends and began to court the daughter of one of Melanthos's chief supporters. Only Antilochos remained aloof, silent and bitter. Once or twice I had reason to suspect that he was associating with discontented elements in the city, of which there were inevitably a few, but Melanthos's power was firmly based and it needed only a word from me to draw his attention to these budding conspiracies for them to collapse before they could present any danger. There was never enough evidence to warrant my taking action against Antilochos, but I let him know that he was constantly watched. Frustration at his own impotence ate into his soul and he became like a wolf prowling the outskirts of a settled community.

Little by little I abandoned all those pursuits that had once given me pleasure. I still performed the ceremonial duties of the king but once they were over I sought solitude and turned away my Companions' offers of company. Neritos, of course, remained always at hand, but his spirits were incapable of being permanently weighed down by misfortune. He, too, found a wife and made new friends, but the deeper I sank into depression the more his cheerful manner grated on me. I became short-tempered with him and often found him gazing at me with sad incomprehension.

As always, only Alectryon and Andria understood my mood. At first Alectryon was the only person whose company I could tolerate, but he had never recovered the vivacity of temperament that had once made him such a delightful companion and we passed much of our time in silence, each immersed in his own gloomy thoughts. In time I found his despondency as trying as Neritos's cheerfulness and began to avoid his company as well. Andria was my one comfort, but as the winter advanced and my depression deepened I stopped taking her into my bed and ignored her pale face and her reproachful, wounded eyes.

As the days lengthened into another spring I found myself strangely eager for one thing. The Athenians celebrate the New Year festival at Eleusis, which I knew was one of the most sacred of the Goddess's shrines, and the priestesses there were reputed to be among the wisest of Her acolytes. I remembered the comfort I had received from the wise old woman in the sanctuary on the Holy Island and began to hope that perhaps at Eleusis I might be released from the crippling sense of the Goddess's anger.

I went to the sanctuary with the other worshippers filled with a mixture of hope and dread. I could not banish the memory of that terrible first experience at Pylos and at the same time it filled me with bitterness to see Melanthos, this time, as the central figure in the rites. I did not grudge him his position, but it brought home to me that my kingship had never been confirmed by this mystical union with the Goddess.

At what point during the ritual my fear and self-disgust departed and were replaced by a sense of awe and wonder I cannot now recall. I knew, as soon as we stood within the sacred precinct, that this was a place beloved by the Goddess and at once I was aware of Her presence. At first She seemed, as She had always seemed to me, terrible and cruel and I felt myself crushed and obliterated by Her power. But little by little I began to perceive Her as the gentle Mother of all things and myself as Her joyful and submissive child. When the festival was over I remained in Eleusis and sought an audience with the High Priestess. She received me courteously and without apparent surprise. I told her the story of that first, disastrous festival and its consequences and explained that I was convinced that, in spite of my purification in the Holy Island, I still lay under the displeasure of the Goddess.

She listened gravely and said finally, 'I cannot tell why the Goddess is still angry with you. But remain here in the sanctuary and undertake a second purification. Perhaps in the course of that we shall come to understand what the Mistress requires.'

I passed some days within the sanctuary during which, as well as the ritual observances and the fasts prescribed by the priestess, I had several long discussions with her on matters relating to the worship of the Great Queen.

Finally she sent for me and said, 'I believe now I have learned what it is that brings the disfavour of the Goddess upon you. Is it not true that you have never fully given yourself to Her? She will not tolerate a half-hearted worshipper. Has not your mind always held back and refused its full devotion?'

I struggled to reach down to feelings I had buried deep within me and to explain them – the terror and revulsion, the angry rebellion I had tried to conceal even from myself. Having told her all this I added a description of how my feelings had changed during the Festival.

She nodded approvingly. 'It is as I thought. The Goddess now offers you the opportunity to reinstate yourself. But we have yet to discover exactly what act of yours first angered Her. Think back now.

Before that false priestess led you to the sacred couch had you in any way, by word or deed, rebelled against Her?'

Suddenly I recalled early sunlight on my shivering body and my own voice saying, 'The Kings of Pylos draw their descent from Poseidon Himself … and yet the King must submit to the Goddess even unto death!' and Alectryon's shocked reply, 'It is a fearful thing to rebel against Her on her own Holy Mountain and on such a day as this.'

I related the incident to the priestess and she nodded again. 'My suspicions were correct. Now, tell me, at the festival the next year, after you had made your voyage of penance, were you utterly at one with Her, without thought of rebellion?'

I had to admit that I had not been, at least at first. The brutal rites of the night of the New Wine still horrified me.

'And last year?'

'Last year in Mycenae I was bitter because Tisamenos was the consort of the Goddess and not me.'

'There, then, lies the source of all your misfortune. But be comforted. It is clear to me that you are now truly repentant and have come to understand the power of the Goddess. There is now one more aspect of Her will that you must learn to accept.'

'What is that?' I asked. 'Tell me and I will bend myself to it.'

'I think your mind is already in part reconciled to it,' she replied. 'The Goddess has allowed you to be driven from your kingdom. That is your punishment. Accept it. Do not strive to return, for She has decreed it otherwise.'

I bowed my head. This, then, was the end of all my hopes. 'What must I do?'

'Remain in Athens until She wills it otherwise. Be content to live quietly among your friends and submit yourself to whatever She decrees.'

Slowly I looked up. The eyes of the priestess were wise and compassionate. For the first time I began to feel the burden lifting from my shoulders.

'Very well. I will submit myself to Her will.'

She smiled. 'It is good. Do not be downcast. The Goddess is kind to those who truly love Her. Return now to Athens and good fortune will meet you at the gate.'

I did as she told me and as I approached the city gate a group of girls came towards me. Among them was Philona. In the past months my eyes had been too much turned in upon myself to notice how she had grown out of her childish awkwardness and become a lovely girl. As I met them she came up and greeted me and hoped, with eyes of warm compassion, that I was in better health than when we last met.

The following day I summoned the Messenians to an assembly and told them of the Goddess's decree. Pylos was forbidden to us, so I bade them find new lives for themselves wherever their destinies might lead them. For my own part, I abrogated all rights and duties of a king and proposed to live from here on as a private citizen. Some of them, I think, were disappointed but most were relieved to hear that there would be no new campaign.

When I dismissed them my Companions remained behind and requested an audience. Alectryon acted as their spokesman.

'You have told us the Goddess's decree and we must accept that. And you have said that you relinquish your position as King. We understand your desire to retire from public life, and respect it, but we wish you to know that to us you will always be our Royal Lord and you may command our loyalty in whatever way will do you service. There is only one thing we would beg of you,' he hesitated and glanced at the others for confirmation, 'do not withdraw yourself completely from us. We lacked your company too much last winter.'

I looked from face to face, each one bringing back memories of my boyhood, and saw the honest affection in their eyes. Through a throat constricted with emotion I answered, 'You have your wish. I am to blame for neglecting you all. I thank you for your loyalty and for my own part I promise that whatever I can do for any of you I will do. But there is one thing I ask in return. Let me be a man among men, a friend among friends. I have known too much of the isolation of kingship and I do not wish to be alone again.'

They crowded round me and I embraced each one in turn. When I came to Alectryon I saw his eyes were wet. I said, 'And you, too, have been too sad for too long. We must find ways of being happy again.'

Later that day I had Neritos harness the chestnuts and drove out to Philaos's estate.

I was betrothed to Philona a few days later and the promise the High Priestess had made me was abundantly fulfilled. Like a seed that has lain silent and apparently dead all winter, my heart awoke to new life. My friends rejoiced to see me take to all my old pursuits. I became again an athlete and a daring charioteer and was always at the forefront of the hunt, but I no longer sought to use my prowess as a means to command the loyalties of men. I had my friends and needed no other adherents. Freed from the burdensome ceremonial of kingship I recaptured the carefree joy of my years as Prince of Pylos. I married Philona at midsummer and no bridegroom ever went more eagerly to his wedding, or found for his bride a creature so lovely, so happy and so serene.

Philaos was glad to have a younger man to help in the running of his estate and I soon found an unexpected delight in ordering its affairs. When I was not so occupied I would drive into the city to discuss affairs of state with Melanthos or to see friends, and never a day passed without a visit from one or more of my Companions. In the evening we would sit around the hearth and pass the lyre from hand to hand and keep alive the old tales of the heroic past.

We were not allowed, however, to pass the summer in uninterrupted peace. Several times the Dorians raided us, the last in such force that we had to fight a pitched battle before driving them back to their ships. At such times I resumed my position as commander of the Pylian force and we soon became known in Athens as the best troops in the army. Other states, we heard, were faring worse than ourselves and new areas were coming under Dorian control. Only the walled cities could withstand them.

Alectryon was still my closest friend and he had recovered both physically and to a large extent spiritually from his wound and the death of Myrtilis. At the same time, I knew he had not found anything in Athens to truly occupy his mind. He had not, like so many of us, found a wife and had refused the offer of an estate from Melanthos. He was restless and moody.

One evening in autumn he came to visit me and we dined together quietly as we had done so many times before. He seemed more than usually preoccupied and at length, before Philona joined us, he said, 'My prince,' (I had never persuaded him to abandon the title and in truth it seemed to me now more like an endearment) 'I wish to ask your leave for an enterprise which has been in my mind for some time.'

'What enterprise?' I asked.

He hesitated a moment, then went on, 'You know that there is little to keep me in Athens except yourself. Now that you have married and reconciled yourself so happily to your new life you have little need of me. Therefore I wish to attempt to find a new life for myself also.'

'Where?' I asked, although I had a foreboding that I already knew his intention.

'We have had many reports from merchants and other travellers of the fertile land on the coasts of Asia. There is one place I have heard praised particularly, a little settlement of our people at a place called Colophon. Recently I spoke to a man who had not long returned from there and he told me that very few Achaeans remain and they are in danger of being driven out by the native Lydians. It occurred to me that there are many in Athens, Messenians and others, who would gladly undertake an expedition to found a new colony there. I should like to lead such a colony.'

I was silent for a moment. The thought of losing him was like a blow at the heart, but I recognised that his need outweighed mine.

He said quietly, 'You are thinking that I put little value on our friendship since I wish to leave you.'

I sighed and shook my head. 'No, my dear, I am thinking that I should be a poor friend if I tried to keep you idle in Athens. It is not true that I have little need of you. No one else can ever replace what we have had together and I shall miss you sorely. But I could not bear to watch you eating your heart out for want of occupation.'

So the decision was taken and he began to make preparations to sail the following spring. Melanthos provided ships and seed corn and everything else that was necessary and there was no shortage of volunteers. All through the summer refuges had poured into Athens from areas overrun by the Dorians and the city was crowded. By the coming of Plowistos a very well equipped expedition was ready to set out.

On the night before he left Alectryon dined with me again. We were both heavy hearted and could find little to say but at the same time I felt closer to him than I had for a long time. To cheer him I said, 'You remember how we spoke once of finding a bride each on our travels? Well, I have found an Athenian lady. Perhaps for you there is a foreign princess.'

He smiled briefly. 'Perhaps. A new colony must be peopled, certainly.'

As we parted on the shore the following morning the last threads of my life as Prince of Pylos seemed to be torn away from me. I turned back to my new home, and the new life within it, for Philona had just informed me that she was with child.

We learned in due course that the expedition had reached its destination and, after overcoming some initial opposition from the native inhabitants, had settled at Colophon.

One further story must be told of those early years in Athens, although it pains me to recall it. Not very long after my marriage Antilochos found himself a bride also, the heiress to a large estate. She was a plain girl and he never made much pretence of caring for her but I hoped that now he had land of his own he would settle down.

Soon after Philona told me she was pregnant I heard that Antilochos's wife was also with child. Now it happened that during her pregnancy my sweet natured Philona grew jealous of Andria, who still served as my handmaiden. I had not had the heart to send her away and if she resented the fact that I was in love with another woman she never showed it. I never gave my wife any reason to doubt my absolute fidelity and until her pregnancy was well advanced she accepted Andria with great kindness. But the time came when she could not bear to have her in the same house and begged me to get rid of her.

I spoke to Melanthos and he agreed to find her a place at the palace until such time as Philona was delivered and might be persuaded to have her back. The poor girl wept bitterly when I told her my decision but I comforted her with the thought that the arrangement was only temporary.

About a month later I received a message from Melanthos

requesting my immediate attendance. I found him alone and grave faced.

'I have serious news, Alkmaion,' he said. 'It concerns Antilochos – and Andria.'

'Antilochos and Andria?' I repeated, bewildered.

He nodded. 'It is a terrible story and will be a great shock to you, so I will tell it as briefly as possible. You know that Antilochos's wife is with child. The other day he came to me and told me that his wife had heard that Andria knew many spells from her own country which have power to ensure an easy birth, and that nothing would satisfy her now but to have Andria in the house to care for her.' He paused and sighed. 'I should have remembered what I know of him and realised that he does nothing without a double motive but at the time I could see none. I questioned Andria and she agreed that she did indeed know certain spells that might be helpful, so I sent her to him. It seems that once he had her under his roof he tried to force himself upon her …'

I got to my feet. 'That is enough! I have lost my patience with him. This time he shall be punished.'

He said quietly, 'He is dead already.'

'Dead?'

'Apparently, rather than submit to him, Andria snatched his dagger from its sheath and stabbed him. Then, seeing what she had done, she stabbed herself with the same weapon.'

I sank back into my chair. 'So they are both dead.'

'Both.' He paused and then added, 'I cannot understand Antilochos. Andria had been with you for years. Had he ever shown any interest in her before?'

I said heavily, 'I understand it, only too well. When we were children if ever I was given something of beauty or value he would always try to take it from me. If he could not have it, or get something better for himself, he would do his best to spoil it. I remember once I had a young hunting dog, a lovely animal and only a puppy. I found it one day with its tail cut off. I could never prove it was Antilochos, but I knew it was. I suppose when I first brought Andria back he was more concerned with trying to take my kingdom from me. Then he hoped to rule in Mycenae. Since I foiled that plot he has been looking for some way of taking his revenge. He hoped for something on a grand scale, but between us we have thwarted him. Finally he saw Andria and his mind seized upon this petty cruelty. Poor girl! She deserved far better than to be the victim of our hatred. I wish we had never raided that village, Melanthos. She should have been left with her father.'

'It was not you who kidnapped her, if I remember rightly,' Melanthos said gently. 'At least you saved her from life with Cresphontes – and she loved you. She was happy with you.'

'I am still responsible for her death – even if indirectly.'

'Not so. It is Antilochos who is to blame for that. Well, he has come to a fitting end, dying ignominiously at a woman's hand.'

'What will happen to his wife?' I asked.

'Perimedes will take her under his care – and the child, when it is born.'

Andria had performed her last service for me, and with Antilochos's death I was at last relieved of an enmity that had dogged me all my life.

Chapter 17.

In the course of the next three years Philona bore me two children, a daughter Electra and a son, Philon. I was amazed to discover what intense delight I took in them. I had never had much to do with small children, but now I was fascinated by watching their first steps, or listening to their first babbled attempts at words. I had no memory of my mother and I could not recall my father ever coming to the nursery to lift me in his arms or play games with me. But then, he had been a king, with more important matters to attend to.

They were happy years. Philaos was beginning to feel some of the infirmities of age, so I took on more and more of the running of the estate. I bought a fine stallion, a little like Pedasos, and bred promising foals from mares Philaos had collected. My land prospered, as did the whole of Athens under Melanthos's rule. Even the Dorians left us in peace and we began to think that our troubles were over. Nonetheless, we did not let down our guard completely. Both Melanthos and I kept our troops in training, bringing along new young recruits and polishing the skills of the veterans; and we maintained watchers along the coast to give early warning of another attack.

It was in the spring of the year when Electra was approaching her fourth birthday when the guards on the city ramparts shouted that the warning beacons had been lighted at the harbour. By luck I was in the city and not out at the estate and within minutes I had summoned my Companions, the horses had been harnessed and the chariots rolled out through the city gate, following Melanthos and his men. We assumed that this would be like earlier attacks, a small force aiming to land, grab what they could and run back to their ships as soon as we appeared; but when we came within sight of the sea we saw that this was something very different. The ocean, from horizon to horizon, seemed to be covered in ships, like black beetles crawling on a field of dung.

Perimedes, as always, had taken station on my right hand. I looked across at him and he caught my eye with a grim nod. I knew what he was thinking. This reminded us both of the battle for Pylos. There was no chance of beating off an attack in such numbers, but we could not stand by and let the enemy land unimpeded. As the first craft beached I gave the order to charge and we made the early arrivals regret their impetuosity. But more and more came on behind them and men swarmed from them, splashing through the shallows to throw themselves into the battle. Little by little we were forced back by sheer weight of numbers. As so many times before I cut and thrust until my sword felt too heavy to lift and my shield arm ached and throbbed from parrying blows. In the brief breathing space between striking down one opponent and turning to face the next I looked around me and saw that on each side of us a column of Dorian troops was pressing inland. Very soon they would be able to circle round to our rear and cut off our retreat and if that happened there would be nothing left for us to do but sell our lives as dearly as possible.

I turned to look for my chariot and found Neritos close on my heels, as always. I leapt up and scanned the field. A short distance away Melanthos was hard pressed by five or six men.

'Over there, to Melanthos!' I shouted and Neritos lashed the horses into a gallop. Men jumped aside or fell beneath the hooves and I stabbed down at any that stood firm and as we reached Melanthos some of those attacking him turned to meet the new threat.

'Get back!' I screamed at him. 'We must retreat and close the city gates. Back to the city while we still can!'

He saw the danger and ran to regain his own chariot. I waved my sword to the rest of my Companions. 'Back! Back to the city!' Neritos wheeled the horses and for the first time in my life I fled the field of battle, with my Companions streaming behind me.

It was as well that we moved when we did. As it was we were hard pressed to escape the net that was closing around us, but once we were clear of the battlefield the Dorians did not attempt to pursue us. They had no horses and saw that they could prevent us from reaching the city. Besides, they had other plans.

From the ramparts we watched them as they spread out over the surrounding plain.

Perimedes said, 'Do you notice something? They are not destroying the crops or burning the houses. You know what that means.'

'They intend to stay,' Melanthos replied. 'They want the crops to

301

sustain themselves. Praise be to the Goddess, the city granaries are full and we have plentiful water, thanks to your foresight, Alkmaion, in suggesting the creation of the reservoir. It will be a long summer, but we shall not starve. And come winter, they will be the ones who find themselves short of food.'

'They are not given to the arts of agriculture,' Perimedes said. 'I'm willing to wager that they will not replant what they harvest.'

'So,' Melanthos concluded, 'before winter makes sailing impossible, they will head for home.'

'Let us pray that you are right,' I murmured, but, looking at their faces I knew that we were all remembering that our ancestors had camped for ten years outside Troy.

Melanthos was right in one respect. We should not go short of food. In addition to the wheat in the granaries, at the first sign of attack local shepherds had driven their flocks of sheep and goats into the city. For the time being, at least, we should have meat and milk as well as bread. But this soon proved a curse as well as a blessing. With the shepherds had come their families and workers from surrounding farms with their families, so that the city was packed with people. As the long, hot days of summer progressed quarrels broke out among the tight pressed crowds and the stench of excrement, both animal and human, became almost overpowering.

The Dorians stole horses and chariots from the surrounding estates and every few days their warriors would drive round and round the crag on which the city was built and taunt us to come out and fight. As the days drew into months some of the fighting men in the city lost patience and began demanding the chance to 'teach the barbarians a lesson'. Melanthos and I had to exercise all our authority to prevent a mutiny. We knew that our only chance was to sit it out and wait for Dorians to get bored and go home.

As autumn winds began to blow we watched in expectation that any day we should see our enemies packing up and heading for their ships. Instead, we saw that they were cutting wood and building themselves shelters. With drooping spirits, we realised that they had no intention of lifting the seige. A bitter winter followed. With no access to the surrounding forests we had little firewood and were reduced to chopping up our furniture to burn. Food supplies, which had seemed so plentiful for the duration of the summer, now had to be strictly rationed. Nights were filled with the sound of children crying with cold and hunger.

I passed my days going from house to house, trying to lift spirits and maintain order, and I suppose that distracted my attention from my own household until the woman we employed as nursemaid came up to me and spoke quietly.

'Lord, have you not noticed how pale and drawn your lady is? She gives her food to the children and denies herself. You must speak to her.'

For the first time I saw how thin Philona had grown and how dark the circles under her eyes were. I sat down beside her and took her hand.

'Nerissa tells me you have been giving your food to the children. Is it true?'

She looked up at me and the weariness in her eyes stabbed at my heart. 'I cannot let them go hungry. Their needs are greater than mine.'

'But what about my needs? I need you! I need you to be strong. What would the children and I do without you? Your duty to us is to take care of yourself. Now, promise me you will eat your own ration. I will see to it that the children do not suffer.'

From that day on I made sure that I was present for the evening meal and I watched Philona swallow every morsel of the food put before her. The extra for the children came out of my own ration and neither of them ever went to bed crying.

The Dorians, too, suffered from the cold, but not as much as we did. They had cut down and burnt most of the trees close to their camp. Now they destroyed the houses on the outlying estates and used the timber for their fires. From the ramparts I watched the house I had come to think of as home go up in flames.

Winter came to an end at last but by now our needs were desperate. We had to confiscate the last few ewes and nanny goats to prevent them being slaughtered for meat, so that there would still be some milk for the children. The bread ration was cut yet again. The old and the weak began to die and we were forced to cremate them in the main square before the palace. Out in the fields there was no new growth of wheat. As Perimedes had predicted, the Dorians had not bothered to plant afresh. With the lengthening days and the growing heat came the first case of plague. In the crowded conditions, among people weakened by hunger it spread with terrifying speed. One of the first to succumb was Philaos, my father-in-law. I ordered Philona to remain in the house and to refuse entry to anyone except myself in the hope that this might save her and the children from the contagion.

One evening I returned from guard duty on the ramparts to find my door locked and barred. When I knocked the porter shouted from behind it that I must not enter.

'Fool!' I bellowed. 'Do you not recognise my voice? It is I, your master. Let me in.'

'Sir, forgive me!' came the reply. 'It is by the order of the mistress. Your son is sick and my lady is afraid that you may catch it from him. She begs you to go to the house of a friend and remain there until the danger is past.'

I hammered on the door, demanding to be let in. The thought of my beloved little boy suffering and perhaps near to death was unbearable. Worse still was the knowledge that in nursing him Philona was putting herself at risk. At length, she came herself and spoke to me through the closed door.

'My dearest, I beg you to be patient. The sickness may not be serious. Perhaps it it no more than a summer chill. But you must not risk yourself. You told me once that I had a duty to look after myself for you. Now I tell you that you too have a duty, to your people. You are their leader. They need you to remain strong. I have sent Electra to my cousin's house. Her children are still well. By the blessing of the Goddess they may remain so and she will be safe. Now go, my love. Sacrifice to the Goddess and pray for her protection. Come back in the morning to see how we are.'

I refused to listen to her. I thumped the door and threatened retribution on all those who did not obey me and when that was of no avail I collapsed, sobbing, on the threshold. It was there that Perimedes and Neritos, alerted by our neighbours, found me and almost dragged me back with them to Perimedes's house.

With the dawn came the message. Both my son and my adored wife were dead. I had wept for them all night, knowing how quickly and mercilessly the disease progressed. I had no more tears to shed. Now I was possessed by an icy fury. I rose to my feet and looked at my two friends.

'It is enough! Now Cresphontes will pay. I have suffered enough at his hands.'

Neritos sprang up. 'What do you mean? You cannot intend to go out against him.'

'I will not stay here, like a rat in a trap, waiting for the same death to claim me as has taken my wife and child. Better by far to die fighting, as long as I can first kill him. Do not try to stop me. I do not ask anyone to come with me. I will go alone, if need be. But I will go!'

Perimedes came to my side. 'Where you go, I go. That has always been the way. Let us make one last glorious stand and die as heroes, rather than perishing from this foul contagion.'

'And I will come with you, too,' Neritos said. 'How could I let you go without a charioteer?'

'And the men on Pylos will be behind you,' Perimedes assured me. 'They have been too long cooped up here, listening to the taunts of the enemy. They are desperate for a fight.'

'Then I will go to Melanthos and tell him what we have decided,' I said. 'I will not ask him to risk himself, but we must warn him of what we intend to do. You and Neritos rouse the others. Tell them that no man is obliged to follow me. I give no orders. They must choose for themselves.'

'Any man who chooses to stay behind will live dishonoured, even if he survives the plague,' Perimedes said. 'They will come.'

I made my way to the palace and found Melanthos in the throne room. As soon as I entered he jumped to his feet and came to me.

'Alkmaion! I've just heard. I am so sorry ...'

I cut across his words without ceremony and told him what I intended. He caught hold of my hand and gazed at me with anguished eyes.

'Every fibre of my being is urging me to say I will come with you and we will fight side by side as we have so often in the past. But you know I must not. If I lead my men out to die a hero's death the city will be left unprotected and the Dorians will be free to lay it waste as they did Pylos. I cannot let that happen.'

I gripped his hand tightly. 'I know that. I do not ask you to sacrifice yourself. Athens may be the last flickering candle in a dark world. That light must not be put out. Only pray to the Mistress to strengthen my arm so that I may revenge myself on the man who has brought this misery to us. That is all I ask.'

'I will pray and make sacrifice to Her, and beg her to bring you safely home,' he responded.

I shook my head. 'That is something I do not hope for. I have nothing to come back for now.' Suddenly it came to me that all my hopes were not lost. In the misery of the death of my wife and son I had forgotten my daughter. 'There is one more thing I would ask of you. My daughter, Electra, still lives – or did yesterday. She is with Philona's cousin. Will you take her into your care, if she survives?'

'She shall be as my own child,' Melanthos promised. 'And when she grows old enough to understand I shall make sure that she knows her royal heritage.'

'Let her live peacefully as a private citizen. She will be happier that way.' I gripped both his hands. 'Farewell, my friend. May the favour of the Mistress go with you.'

We embraced with tears in our eyes and then I turned hastily away before I betrayed my manhood. In the courtyard outside my Companions were waiting for me. Not one of them had refused to heed the call. I mounted my chariot, the guards opened the great gate in the walls and we thundered through, Perimedes close behind me and all the others following. Once on the open plain we spread out into battle formation, myself and Neritos in the centre and slightly in advance, Perimedes on my right, the others stretching out to either side. As we approached the Dorian camp it was clear that we had taken them by surprise. We could see men scurrying from their tents, strapping on their armour as they went; but by the time we reached them they had formed their battle lines, a dense mass of shields many men deep.

It is our usual way, as I have said, to fight on foot with our chariots close at hand to carry us out of danger if the need arises, and as we reached the enemy lines my Companions halted and leaped down to face their opponents. But I yelled to Neritos to drive on and we galloped straight into the midst of them. Taken by surprise some of them jumped back to escape the flying hooves but then they rallied and men tried to seize the horses' bridles. Neritos held them off by slashing at them with his whip and I stabbed and thrust at all who came close enough to reach. All the time I was screaming the one word, 'Cresphontes! Cresphontes!'

Suddenly we were through the massed lines of men and into a clear space and there he stood, hands on hips, a mocking smile on his face. Neritos hauled the horses to a standstill and I leaped down and faced him.

'Cresphontes! This has always been a matter between the two of us. Let us now settle it once and for all in single combat. I will make a pact with you. If you kill me, my Pylians will withdraw back to the city and you will give them safe conduct. If I kill you, your army will pack up its tents and take ship for home and leave Athens in peace. Is it agreed?'

He laughed. 'Little prince! Why should I agreed to such terms? Your men are surrounded and Athens is starving. Victory is ours in matter of days. Why should I fight you?'

'Because,' I said, 'if you refuse you will stand exposed as a coward before your men and all will see that you put the safety of your own skin before your honour.'

It was the one challenge he could not refuse and I saw his eyes narrow as he understood. He drew his sword.

'Very well, since you wish to put an end to your life, let us begin. But I make no promises. This is a matter, as you say, entirely between ourselves. The rest must fend for themselves as best they can.'

All round us, as if at a signal, the fighting had stopped and men who had been hacking at each other a moment ago now stood shoulder to shoulder to watch. He came at me, whirling his sword about his head so that the blade, catching the sun, seemed to draw circles of light on the air. I stood still, keeping my muscles loose and watching, not his sword but his eyes, so that when he made a sudden lunge my own blade came up in the same breath to turn his aside. For an instant I saw surprise in his eyes and knew that my tactics were the right ones. He came at me again, more fiercely. I gave ground, making no attempt to strike him, but parrying every thrust, letting him tire himself. I saw his anger and frustration grow and he ground out, 'Fight, coward! Is this the best you can do?'

I let him go on, his blows becoming wilder, until on one stroke he over-reached himself and left his head exposed. My blade flashed in and opened a long cut along his cheek, between the protecting flaps of his helmet. If victory had been to him who drew first blood, as in our fight all those years ago, it would have been over; but we both knew that nothing but the death of one of us would end this struggle. He growled in fury and came at me, battering my shield with violent blows that sent jolts of pain along my arm. I twisted away and flicked my sword point across his thigh, in the small gap between the bottom of his mailed tunic and the top of the greaves that protected his legs. The wound was not disabling, but the flow of blood was enough to weaken him if the fight was prolonged. He knew it and attacked with greater fury then ever. We closed and unexpectedly he changed his tactics and rammed his shield into my right shoulder with a force that sent me to my knees and made my sword arm go numb. With a cry of triumph he seized my helmet by the crest and dragged it off, pulling my head back and leaving my throat exposed. I saw his sword upraised for the final blow but at that moment the Goddess must have intervened. My arm regained its strength. I forced myself up from my knees, driving the sword upwards with all the strength of my body. The point went in beneath his chin and penetrated deep into his skull. For a moment his eyes goggled at me, as if he was unable to believe that I had snatched his victory from him, then he collapsed backwards and I dragged my blade free. Blood spurted from the wound, but it was obvious that Cresphontes was already dead.

I stooped and wiped my sword on the hem of his tunic, hearing the cheers of my Companions behind me.

I turned to them. 'It is finished. Let us return to the city.'

We remounted out chariots and no one attempted to prevent us. Cresphontes's men stood silent, seemingly unable to believe that their leader was dead. I gave Neritos the command to drive on and we led our small force back across the plain. As we went I became aware that there was blood on the rail of the chariot, and looking down saw that there was more pooling on the floor. I looked at my arms and legs and found no sign of a wound, and I felt no pain. The chariot jolted and Neritos slumped against me.

'Look where you are going!' I exclaimed. Then I saw that his eyes were closed and his face was deadly pale. I grabbed the reins and pulled the horses to a halt and half lifted, half dragged him from the chariot and laid him on the ground.

'Where are you hurt? What has happened?'

He shook his head, wordlessly. I struggled to loosen the straps of his armour and peeled away the breastplate. Then I saw that a sword point had penetrated from beneath the corselet and pierced his side. It must have happened during our reckless charge, but he had given no sign. His whole flank was covered in blood but as I watched the flow lessened. I ripped at the hem of my tunic, trying to make a bandage to staunch it but even as I did so I knew it was useless.

A chariot drew up beside me. Perimedes had seen that I had stopped and come back to discover the reason. He knelt by Neritos and I pointed to the wound. He shook his head.

'There is nothing we can do. It is too deep and he has lost too much blood.'

I cradled Neritos's head on my arm and stroked his face. 'My dear faithful friend. No triumph was worth your loss. Forgive me!'

He opened his eyes. 'I saw Cresphontes dead and you victorious. I can die happily. Take care of my boys.'

'With my life! They shall be as my own children.'

He smiled. 'We had some good races.'

'Yes, we did. And you were the best charioteer in the whole of Pylos. Greet my father for me and all our friends who have passed before us. Dexeus will be glad of your company.'

'And I his ....' The last words were so faint I hardly heard them. His eyelids quivered and closed and his body shuddered and was still. I kissed him in farewell and held him until I was sure that his spirit wandered on the shores of Acheron.

Perimedes's hand gripping my shoulder roused me. 'We must take his body back to the city and we have no time to waste. The

Dorians are stunned for the moment but at any time now they will come to themselves and want revenge. Come, while we still have the chance.'

I saw the strength of his argument and we lifted Neritos's body into my chariot. I took the reins and drove the horses at the gallop back to the city gates. We were cheered from the ramparts as we approached and the streets of the city were crowded with people waving and calling their congratulations, but I felt no sense of triumph. My old enemy was dead, but I had not expected to return alive and now I had one more loss to mourn. Melanthos greeted us as we drew up outside the palace and embraced me with tears of joy, and my own men gathered round to clasp my hands and add their praises but as soon as I could I begged to be excused. There was only one place that offered any hope or consolation.

Electra greeted me with squeals of delight when I entered the courtyard of the house and ran to clasp her chubby arms about my knees. I picked her up and buried my face in her hair, breathing in the smell of her till she struggled and protested at being held so tightly. Then I put her down and examined her for any sign of the telltale harbingers of infection.

At my side, Chriseis, Philona's cousin, said quietly, 'She is well, Alkmaion. I have watched her closely and there is no sign of the disease. By the mercy of the Goddess it seems she may escape.'

I let her lead me away then and hand me over to her servants to be bathed and have my few slight wounds dressed. After that, I spent the rest of the day sitting in the courtyard in a kind of stupor, watching my daughter at play. That night I slept as deeply as if I had drunk poppy juice and woke at dawn to the sound of excited voices in the street beyond my window. I was still pulling on my clothes when Perimedes came to the door.

'Alkaion, come! There is something you must see. Quickly!'

He refused to explain what had happened but led me rapidly up onto the ramparts overlooking the Dorian camp. The walls were lined with men, all staring seawards, and below us the camp lay deserted, save for heaps of debris where the dogs were already scavenging. Far off, we could see the last stragglers trudging towards their ships.

'They have given up!' I murmured in amazement. 'But there was no pact, no agreement.'

'Perhaps there is some honour amongst them after all.' Melanthos had joined us.

Perimedes grunted. 'I doubt it. My guess is that they were glad to have an excuse to head for home. No doubt most of them were as fed up with the siege as we were. They must have been short of food by now. Probably only Cresphontes's authority kept them from heading for home long ago. Now he's gone ...'

'Whatever the reason,' Melanthos said, 'the siege is ended and we are saved. And it is thanks to you, Alkmaion. There should be a great feast in your honour, but that will have to wait until we have secured fresh supplies. Tomorrow we will go in procession to Eleusis and give thanks to the Goddess for our deliverance.'

CHAPTER EIGHTEEN

The procession took place as Melanthos had decreed and even before that men had been sent out to scour the region for food and firewood. There was little to be had. Like locusts, the Dorians had consumed everything that grew and left devastation behind them. The men had to go high into the hills to find trees for wood to burn and, equally as important, to rebuild our shattered homes. No new crops had been planted, but with the departure of the Dorians shepherds who had hidden themselves and their flocks in the remote valleys appeared, driving their beasts towards what they knew would be a good market. Messengers were sent northwards to Thebes and west to Corinth and ships set off for the islands off the coast. Some had already been pillaged by the invaders but from others came supplies of wheat and oil. Sooner than I had imagined possible Melanthos was able to hold the feast he had promised.

How I should have relished an occasion like that once! Everyone pressed around me, repeating their praise and hailing me as the saviour of the city and Melanthos's bard had already written a song re-telling the story of my fight with Cresphontes – a song which I knew would be carried by other bards into the courts of other rulers; those that still remained free, at least. I tried to enter into the spirit of the feast but there was a hollowness inside me that could not be filled.

As the days passed the people of Athens resumed the ways of their old lives. The streets of the city were cleansed, the land was ploughed and planted, houses were rebuilt. The plague lost its grip and the courtyards rang with the voices of children at play. I tried to join in the general relief but I could not banish the sorrow for what I had lost. One day I drove out to the estate that had once belonged to Philaos and was now mine. The house had been reduced to a blackened ruin and I wandered through the empty shell of it, remembering my first meeting with Philona, the shy girl trying so hard to fill the role of the lady of the house; remembering our marriage and the promise of new life that had come with it. Was I fated, I asked myself, never to have a settled home and a loving family?

I knew I should make plans for the ruins to be razed and a new house built in place of the old, but I could not bring myself to give the orders. I went back to my chariot and returned to my house in the city. As I entered the vestibule the porter met me.

'Sir, there is a visitor for you. He is waiting in the courtyard.'

'Who is it?'

'A stranger, sir. He said he has a message for you.'

In the courtyard a figure rose to greet me. It was a young man, perhaps seventeen or eighteen years old, and I felt I should recognise him but I could not call a name to mind. To my surprise he fell on his knees in front of me and greeted me with the royal titles I had once born as King of Pylos.

I bent and raised him. 'There is no need to kneel. I have not been a king for many years now.'

He looked at me. 'You do not remember me? I am Amyntas, the son of Chryses.'

His words turned the key which unlocked my memory. 'Of course! Forgive me, but you were a boy of – what, ten years? - last time I saw you. Your father, Chryses, was one of my father's most loyal Companions. I heard that he was killed trying to protect my escape when the Dorians over-ran Pylos. My commiserations. He was a brave man.'

The boy's eyes were shining. 'Brave, indeed, my lord. But he was not killed. He sends you greetings by me.'

'Not killed! Praise be to the Mistress! But how did he escape? And where is he now?'

Amyntas hesitated and I saw that he was at a loss as to where to start answering. I remembered my manners then and sent a servant for wine and honey cakes. When we were seated in the shade of the porch I asked again, 'How did your father escape? I was told all those who remained behind were killed.'

'He was left for dead, sir. When he regained consciousness the palace was on fire and the enemy had left it to burn. Somehow he managed to find a way out before the building collapsed and staggered to the house of a man he knew, a merchant he had had dealings with and had found honest. The man had hidden his goods in a deep cellar and he put my father in there too and heaped stones at the entrance so that the Dorians would not find their way in. The ruse worked. The Dorians ransacked the house but did not find the cellar and the merchant plied them with wine, so they let him live. When they were all drunk and sleeping he let my father out and tended his wounds and then lent him a donkey. When the first ships were sighted, my father had sent me and my mother and my two young brothers to our uncle on our country estate. He managed to reach us there and as soon as he arrived, with his tale of the destruction being wreaked on the city, it was decided that we must abandon everything and try to find refuge somewhere else. At first, we intended to try to rejoin you, my lord. We heard from other refugees that you had been seen on the road to Mycenae. But by then the Dorians had swept inland and the roads were too dangerous to travel. We made our way down the coast and by good luck we came upon a Cretan ship about to set sail. My uncle had money, and they agreed to give us passage to Knossos. There we were kindly received, but after a year there it was clear that there was no chance of getting land where we could build a new life for ourselves. One day a traveller came to the city and from him we heard that other refugees, not only from Pylos but from other Achaean cities the Dorians had invaded, had founded a settlement on the shores of Lydia. He told us that the land was good and the people friendly. So we set out and found it just as the traveller had said. We call the new city Colophon and we have lived there now for nearly seven years.'

'Colophon!' I almost spilt my wine at the name. 'Then you must have seen Alectryon, my dearest friend.'

He smiled, with the delight of one who has withheld the best news till last. 'It is Alectryon who sent me here, sir. He greets you by me and prays that you are in good health.'

'And he? Is he in good health? And does he prosper?'

'He is, my lord. He leads the council that rules the city, and I was to tell you ….'He hesitated, shyly.

'Go on, tell me what?'

'He said to remind you that once in jest he suggested to you that one day you would both go travelling to find a foreign princess to marry. I am to tell you that he has found his.'

'He is married?'

'To a Lydian princess. It was part of a pact that brought us peace with the local people. But I believe it was a happy choice.'

'And are there children?'

'A son and a daughter.'

For a moment the memory of my own son rose up and choked my throat, but I pushed the thought aside. 'I rejoice for him.'

His smile faded. 'Forgive me. I spoke thoughtlessly. I know that recently you suffered a terrible loss.'

I sighed. 'Indeed so. Two years ago, before the Dorians attacked again, I would have told you I had everything a man could hope for in this life. Sadly I now find myself almost as bereft as I was when I left Pylos.' I forced my thoughts back to the present. 'But what brings you to Athens at this time?'

'Not long ago a ship arrived, bringing news of the siege you had endured here, and also of your heroic battle which finally ended it. It was from those men that we also heard of the death of your wife and son. That was why Alectryon sent me.'

I nodded. 'It is like him, to seek to send me comfort.'

The boy hesitated, his young face suddenly serious. 'It is more than that, sir. I have not yet told you the most important part of my message. He and the elders of Colophon have charged me to say this. Colophon prospers. The land is rich and fair and the women beautiful. The new city grows, month by month. Now it needs a ruler. Many of the leaders of the community are Messenians. Until now the government of it has been in the hands of a few men, once Companions to King Sillos, under the leadership of Alectryon. Now Colophon requires a king. I am charged to invite, nay to beg you, to come to us so that the descendants of great King Nestor may rule over us as before.'

My mind whirled. I was being offered a new life, a new beginning. And I would see Alectryon again. But was this really the right path for me? Should I leave Melanthos and the Companions who had travelled with me so faithfully? But I knew that he had his kingdom and his family, and most of the others were well settled and had no real need of me. Was it my destiny to be a king once more? Did I owe it to my great ancestors to restore their line? An answer came to me.

'I must seek the will of the Goddess. Tomorrow we will go to Eleusis and consult her priestess. She is a wise woman and if anyone can understand the will of the Mistress of All Things it is she. I will give you my answer after She has spoken.'

At the holy shrine of Eleusis the same High Priestess who had set my feet upon the path of happiness years before took the omens for me and told me that the Goddess had so ordained my life that I should now be Her Royal Consort in Colophon. Melanthos gave me reluctant leave and I set about making my preparations. The ship that had brought Amyntas to Athens was still in port, awaiting my decision. I packed a chest with those possessions that were most precious to me and made the round of my friends to say farewell. Melanthos gave a parting feast for me and the following morning we drove in procession to the harbour, followed by a carriage bearing my daughter Electra, with her nursemaid, and Neritos's two young sons.

As the sacrificial fires were lit I was suddenly powerfully reminded of the day eight years earlier when I had set out with Alectryon on that momentous voyage that had first brought us into contact with the Dorians. I had been filled with such hope then, and now I found the same excitement stirring in my heart. Just when I had begin to think that the best years of my life were over, I was embarking on a new adventure. I embraced my friends for the last time and gave the order to cast off.

As the ship approached the shore I could see a great crowd of people assembled to greet me. I scanned the faces, searching for one fire-bright head, and found him just as I was about to disembark. The fire had dimmed to glowing embers, but those amazing sea-blue eyes were as vivid and expressive as ever. We approached each other slowly, striving to maintain a dignified restraint. His control broke before mine, but only just. We covered the remaining distance at a run and threw ourselves into each others' arms.

When we had embraced he dropped to his knees and saluted me as King and as he did so the whole crowd behind him knelt and did likewise. As I raised him to his feet I looked around me at the eager faces, some strange, others wonderfully familiar; at the city behind them and the fertile land beyond; all offered to me to rule and care for. I realized suddenly that I was only twenty-five years old. If I were to live as long as my great ancestor Nestor I could look forward to another forty or fifty years of life.

I have lived almost that length of time now, here in this quiet place, in peace and prosperity. Alectryon found me a new wife, a dark haired Lydian beauty, with laughing eyes, high spirited as a thoroughbred horse. Different enough in looks and temperament from my beloved Philona not to invite comparisons but soon as dear to me as she had been. She has born me further sons, who I hope will succeed me here. Also, to our great joy, Alectryon's son married my daughter Electra, so grandchildren of my blood and his are around me at this day.

Alectryon has been dead for some time now, but we shared many years of happy companionship together. Together we watched our city grow. We are far from the great centres here and to a large extent the movements of hostile peoples, which still continue, have passed us by: but we have had to fight more than once for our land, and shall have to do so again. Nevertheless, we have managed to preserve here something of the life we knew in Pylos. I cannot tell how much will remain after I am dead.

Each year has brought news of further destruction in our homeland. Melanthos died from the plague a few years after my departure, and his son Kodros has succeeded him. The walls of Athens still stand, but each year the Dorians come in greater force. Soon the great battle must be fought. Mycenae is also free of the invaders, but only her great walls keep them out. I expect daily the news that the sons of Heracles sit upon the throne of Atreus. When that happens our world, the world of the heroes who were our ancestors, will be gone. I pray the Goddess daily that Athens may survive, to keep alive the fame that they have passed down to us.

AUTHOR'S NOTE

The Mycenean Empire really existed. Excavations at Troy and Mycenae and later at Pylos have revealed a highly sophisticated civilization, where there were palaces decorated with beautiful frescoes. The dead were buried with rich grave goods and masks of beaten gold were placed over their faces. The city of Mycenae was surrounded by massive walls. Archaeologists have found evidence of a fire which destroyed part of it, followed by a rebuilding programme which was clearly intended to strengthen the defences. Yet not long afterwards the city was razed to the ground. All that was left visible was the Lion Gate, which once gave entrance through the walls. Mycenae, the city of Agamemnon, was consigned to the realm of myth for three thousand years.

How did this happen? The first clues were found during the excavation of Pylos on the west coast of the Peloponnese, the city of the legendary King Nestor, who plays a large role in the Iliad. Among the ruins of the palace were hundreds of clay tablets inscribed in a script no one was able to decipher. In fact there were two different scripts, which were given the names Linear A and Linear B. It was not until Michael Ventris and John Chadwick succeeded in decoding Linear B that it was understood that it was an early form of Greek. Most of the tablets were simple records kept by the palaces scribes of taxes received and items given out; but in the highest and therefore most recent layer of the dig the tablets tell a different story. There are orders for chariots to be assembled and repaired in necessary; ships to be stationed at points along the coast; men to be despatched to the northern borders of the country; even for the bronze votive vessels from the temples to be requisitioned and melted down for weapons. It is quite clear that Pylos was preparing for an invasion. The layer above these tablets shows evidence of a devastating fire after which the city was abandoned. Clearly these preparations were not enough.

So who were the invaders, and how were they able to overcome such a powerful empire? That is the question I have endeavoured to answer in this book.